Between the Lines

Pauletta Otis and Steven H. Kaplan, Editors

Between the Lines

International Short Stories of War

University Press of Colorado

© 1994 by the University Press of Colorado
Published by the University Press of Colorado
P.O. Box 849
Niwot, Colorado 80544

The University Press of Colorado is a cooperative publishing enterprise supported, in part, by Adams State College, Colorado State University, Fort Lewis College, Mesa State College, Metropolitan State College of Denver, University of Colorado, University of Northern Colorado, University of Southern Colorado, and Western State College of Colorado.

Library of Congress Cataloging-in-Publication Data

Otis, Pauletta, 1942–
Kaplan, Steven, 1953–
    Between the lines: international short stories of war / Pauletta Otis and Steven Kaplan, editors.
    p.   cm.
    Includes biographical references.
    ISBN 0-87081-328-5 (cloth) — ISBN 0-87081-329-3 (paper)
    1. Short stories. 2. War—Fiction.
    PN6120.95.W35B48   1994
    808.83'9358—dc20

                                    94-650
                                    CIP

The paper used in this publication meets the minimum requirements of the American National Standard for Information Sciences—Permanence of Paper for Printed Library Materials. ANSI Z39.48–1984

10 9 8 7 6 5 4 3 2 1

This book is dedicated to all who have experienced war . . .
and have not been able to tell their story.

Contents

Preface

Michael Herr writes in the introduction to his Vietnam book, *Dispatches*: "War stories aren't really anything more than stories about people anyway." The stories in this volume reveal the validity of that statement. A story is a war story when it depicts the impact of war on all human beings not just on men in combat. The following collection of international war stories should serve as a catalyst for re-examining war fiction on an international scale.

Short stories about war and its effects on human beings have been written and read in virtually every country of the world, and most of them share a similar theme: the clash between the value of individual lives and the demands of the societies in which those individuals live. *Between the Lines* is a collection of contemporary war stories from nearly thirty different nations and conflict situations. Each was selected on the basis of one criterion — its appeal to the reader's sense of humanity. Each seems to have an eloquence beyond that of normal language, an almost primal cry of pain and suffering.

The mass media has made the general public across our planet aware of the constancy with which lives are disrupted and destroyed by war. As Doris Lessing demonstrates in the novel *Shikasta*, war affects not only the people who are directly exposed to it; war also plays a critical role in the way we all understand ourselves and our world — which is one reason for reading war fiction.

There is a large body of fiction by important authors from around the world that depicts the human experience of war, but most of this fiction has remained unknown in the English-speaking world. Primarily, this is because many literary critics have insisted on maintaining an outdated and far-too-restrictive definition of what constitutes a war story. In most studies of war fiction in English, a "war story" must be about men fighting on the front. Stories about civilian casualties and suffering, or about women and children fighting in wars, have been systematically excluded from the genre, because they do not fit the stereotype perpetuated by most critics that war stories must be about male bravery, camaraderie, and "grace under fire."

Numerous studies of Western war fiction have been published in English during this century, but an almost equal number of stories from around the globe about the impact of war on women, children, and families have received little or no critical attention. It is time that literary critics begin to pay closer attention to war fiction from all countries and to redefine their conception of this genre so that it includes the human experience of war for all people.

Most studies of war fiction in English are not only chauvinistic but also ethnocentric. Paul Fussell, for example, has written important books on the literature of the first and second world wars, but his books share the major shortcoming of most other books on modern war fiction in English: in general, critics have focussed on fiction about white males fighting in Europe. Fussell himself admits in his preface to *The Great War and Modern Memory* that he disregarded fiction about fighting in Mesopotamia, Turkey, and Africa. Like other critics of war fiction, Fussell is guilty of perpetuating what Wilfred Owen called "the old lie": *"Dulce et decorum est pro patriae mori."* (It is sweet and becoming to die for one's country.) Fussell's books, as critical of war as they might be at times, contain such clichés as: "We must rely on the young, for only they have the two things fighting requires: physical stamina and innocence about their own mortality" (*Wartime* 52). This statement was published after the close of the Vietnam War, a war in which tens of thousands of women, children, and elderly people fought.

Jeffrey Walsh, in his study of U.S. war literature from 1914 to Vietnam, promotes another old myth about war and war fiction when he writes: "And yet out of such holocaustal visions come stirrings of redemption: if war can destroy a man, it can also remake him in a better mould; he may for example discover a more permanent group identity in the army, and arrive at a lasting solidarity with his fellow men" (4). Time and again, critics of war fiction reinforce the old cliché that "war makes men out of boys."

Most critics select the fiction that they analyze on the basis of what it says about men in battle. The literature of the home front seems for them to be only an extension of battlefield literature. For example, Holger Klein allows for the discussion of fiction depicting life on the home front in his collection of essays on modern European war fiction, but only because some of the works portray "the interaction, for the soldiers, of experiences in the trenches and experiences in the hinterlands" (*The First World War in Fiction* 8).

In the past few years, some critics have begun to expand the definition of war fiction by including works that portray the war experiences of women and children. Lynne Hanley's book, *Writing War: Fiction, Gender, and Memory*, for example, is a critique of the notion that the "locale of war literature is the front, the battlefield. The author of war literature has to have been there" (20). Clearly, books such as Mary Cadogan and Patricia Craig's *Women and Children First: The Fiction of Two World Wars* are a step in the direction of an expanded definition of war literature. However, most of the war fiction that they examine has a Western bias: it is written mainly by Western authors and concerns battlefield experiences of men during the major wars of the twentieth century: World War I, World War II, Korea, and Vietnam. This focus reveals the tendency of Western critics to treat war as a Western experience rather than as a universal human experience. Works by authors from non-Western countries, concerning non-Western conflicts, are virtually unknown in the United States and Europe.

The definition of war fiction underlying this collection attempts to be more broadly inclusive than those previously mentioned. The authors of these stories and the people they portray are young and old, male and female, rural and urban, "victims" and "victimizers."

We found it interesting, and revealing, to discover that, in many instances, a country's major writer(s) produced one single wrenching piece of war fiction. With notable exceptions, few seem to have had the emotional or intellectual energy to write war stories in great number. Some of the authors will be familiar to the reader because of their other works, some of them are Noble Prize recipients, and some are virtually unknown in the English-speaking world.

We kept the definition of a short story simple. In order to be considered for this collection, a text had to be a complete work of fiction, which could be read within an hour. This excluded excerpts from novels and personal narratives. The definition of war was kept equally simple: violent conflict between political groups. This obviated the necessity of counting bodies in order to have "enough" for a war, quibble about the difference between internal and international conflict, and debate about how long or recognized a conflict must be to qualify as a war. When individuals suffer for a political cause, the intensity, severity, and duration of the violence become moot.

This collection of stories is divided into four sections: "Men and War," "Women and War," "Children and War," and "Death." Each of these sections is introduced by a short discussion in which plot, structure, and various literary devices used in the stories are analyzed. Furthermore, each story is prefaced by a brief biographical note about the author and a short discussion of the story's setting.

Some of these stories portray men in battle, but the emphasis is always on the totality of the war experience. All of them show in unique ways how individuals and families in war-torn societies are affected by the fighting going on around them. Unlike most conventional war fiction, these stories do not typecast the enemy as evil or as dispensable. The enemy is war itself. These stories lack the moral bellicosity epitomized in Admiral William F. Halsey's victory message to his fleet when the Japanese surrendered: "The forces of righteousness and decency have triumphed" (*Wartime* 129). These are not propaganda pieces.

When we did the preliminary reading for this collection of international war stories, we were amazed to find that the hundreds of stories that we examined from around the world all made similar statements, both directly and indirectly, about the human experience of war. When we have taught the stories from this collection in various English and political science classes, the students — regardless of age, ethnicity, religion, or gender — responded with interest and compassion to each one.

Most interdisciplinary works bear the marks of compromise between the authors and their respective academic specialties. There are initial problems of jargon, perspective, emphasis, and analysis — turf battles. This book has been edited by two published authors from different disciplines who also differ in age, religion, sex, background, education, and personality. Surprisingly, although we both read and ranked hundreds of stories, we agreed on every single story's inclusion or exclusion. It is our hope that the stories we selected will stimulate readers to develop a comprehensive, global understanding of the "war story."

Finally, this book is not a representation of war cries but a cry for peace.

PAULETTA OTIS

STEVEN KAPLAN

Works Cited

Cadogan, Mary, and Patricia Craig, *Women and Children First: The Fiction of Two World Wars.* London: Gillancz, 1978.

Fussell, Paul. *The Norton Book of Modern War.* New York: W. W. Norton, 1991.

Fussell, Paul. *Wartime: Understanding and Behavior in the Second World War.* New York: Oxford UP, 1989.

Hanley, Lynne. *Writing War: Fiction, Gender, and Memory*. Amherst: U of Mass P, 1991.

Klein, Holger, ed. *The First World War in Fiction*. London: Macmillan, 1978.

Walsh, Jeffrey. *American War Literature: 1914 to Vietnam, New York: St. Martin's Press, 1992*.

★ ★ ★

Acknowledgments

We would like to acknowledge our indebtedness to friends and family who have endured our enthusiasm. We also wish to thank faculty colleagues and the administration at the University of Southern Colorado for encouragement and support. Sharon Pruett, Micki Markowski, and Annette Aragon have been cheerful as well as competent in preparing the manuscript for publication. Thanks to our children: Aljoscha, Silia, Noemi, Janina, Radhika, Devika, Daniel, and Marcus. We hope that this book in some way contributes to a global understanding of the human costs of war.

Between the Lines

International Short Stories of War

Part I

Men and War

Since Homer and the ancient Greeks, courage has consistently emerged as the dominant theme in literature that portrays war. Rarely, however, are readers of this genre introduced to the reverse side of courage: fear.

The theme of how the arbitrary cruelty and inhumanity of war can instill a deep-rooted fear in an individual appears in Yihar Smilansky's grotesquely humorous story, "The Prisoner," which describes the ludicrous arrest of a Palestinian shepherd and his flock by an Israeli officer and his troops. Smilansky's fiction often portrays the loneliness of the individual within society, and this story is no exception. It shows in explicit terms the brutal fear and isolation that the Palestinian prisoner feels as he is interrogated and beaten by his Israeli captors. The story revolves around the contrast between the shepherd's humility and humanity and the soldiers' arrogance and capricious violence. The conflict culminates when the story's narrator realizes that he is incapable of demonstrating his humanity by setting the prisoner free in a gesture that would enable him to "be a human being at last the way [he wants] to be." The story opens and closes with nature imagery, which suggests the timeless beauty and innocence of the land that the two opposing groups inhabit.

"The Sonofabitch and the Dog," by Native American author Ralph Salisbury, depicts racism in the military. It is the story of a seventeen-year-old Indian's confrontation with the chauvinism and bigotry of U.S. military personnel during the Korean War. A young Native American youth, who has "never had to fight," learns how to take the violent gestures that he has been taught by the military and turn them against his fellow countrymen when they treat him like a foe. Like the dog referred to in the story's title — which learns to behave like a beer-drinking, cigar-smoking, foul-mouthed, rough and tough soldier — the protagonist of this story discovers how to function like a "man" in a man's world: he kills another human being who has mocked him.

Learning to kill, suspending mercy and remorse, is also the main theme of "My First Goose," by Russian war correspondent Isaac Babel, and "FTP," by French journalist Edith Thomas. In "My First Goose" a young Jewish-Russian intellectual with an ideological commitment to the peasantry is confronted with a group of generally uncouth, ideologically indifferent cossacks. In an attempt to overcome the disdain and mockery of these "seasoned" soldiers, the young man kills his first victim. The victim, a stupid, babbling, but innocent goose, falls prey to his hunger for food and respect. After the kill, he dreams that his heart, "stained with the blood of the killing, creaked and bled." This first act of violence somehow prepares him for the systematic "annihilation" of war that his commander speaks of in the story's opening paragraphs. This story does more than portray the rite of passage of conventional war fiction; it also illustrates one type of war: war fought for a "good" idea. The author ideally expected the creation of a common identity for intellectuals and peasants — the new Soviet citizen — through the common shedding of blood. His story also speaks of age-old rituals related to "blood passage": the sacrifice of the old giving birth to the new.

In "FTP," Edith Thomas illustrates how otherwise caring individuals can be reduced in war to performing callous and ruthless deeds. Throughout this story we hear repeatedly of the "train full of Germans," which a small group of French Resistance fighters plans to ambush. The Germans are a faceless group of enemies, foreigners lacking lives or humanity. In contrast, the members of the Resistance are carefully characterized and made human through the narrator's description of their family lives and childhoods — until the last sentence of the story, where we find them slaughtering a group of Germans fleeing the wrecked train: "And calmly the six men started shooting. With no more hatred than a surgeon."

"Maple Leaves" is a sensitive tale by Ho Ku-Yen of friendship between two Chinese soldiers during the Korean War. The story ends by portraying the grief of one man when his companion is killed during a night bombing raid. This story renders loss in poignant terms. Its central symbol, the maple leaf, represents the destruction of innocence and beauty by modern technological warfare. As individual maple trees are cut down in the process of "winning" the industrialization of China, so, too, the individual soldier is cut down in the process of "winning" a war. As Hu Wenfa watches his friend die, the latter's face takes on "the colour of earth," an image of desolation.

The theme of friendship and brotherhood can also be found in "Cranes," "The Last Salute," and "The Sniper." Like Thomas Hardy's poem "The Man He Killed," these stories emphasize how war can arbitrarily separate those who normally belong together and can create enemies out of those toward whom we feel no natural enmity. In Hwang Sunwon's "Cranes," for example, the purity and freedom of the childhood friendship between a security officer from South Korea and his North Korean prisoner is starkly contrasted with the confusion and alienation that emerge during the aftermath of war. In Hassan Manto Saadat's "The Last Salute" we find men who recently had fought to save each other's lives in one war tormenting and killing one another in a new war. Finally, in "The Sniper," by Liam O'Flaherty, we are thrust into the midst of sniper fire between two men fighting on opposite sides in Ireland's civil war. This story powerfully describes the thoughts and fears of the sniper who ultimately kills his invisible adversary. The enemy soldier turns out to be his brother. In all these stories of friendship, the camaraderie depicted in conventional war fiction is subordinated to the theme that war can lead to the corruption and destruction of human relations.

Augusto Roa Bastos's "Encounter With the Traitor" depicts the inner conflicts of two individuals who have fought on opposite sides, but in this story the opposite sides are those of an alleged traitor and a man whom he supposedly betrayed. This story, set thirty years after the Chaco War in Paraguay, vividly portrays the unquenchable pain of suffering and betrayal. The "old cause" referred to in the story is not so much the sources of the war as the "cause" of seeking revenge for betrayal in war. In its use of dramatic irony and in its structure, this story strongly resembles "The Sniper." Both serve as stark reminders that war, which is generally characterized by grand strategies and careful calculations, can be unpredictable.

One other story in this section deals with the complex human relationships between men who fight together. "Why Do They Go Back?", by the Iranian author Nadir Ibrahimi, tells of a rebel guerrilla fighter's disillusionment. The story unfolds through a verbal exchange between the rebel Sha'ir Khan and his lifelong servant, friend, and fellow outlaw, Sha'il. After being an outlaw for twenty years, Sha'ir Khan recognizes the changing conditions in his country and realizes that the original causes for his rebellion have vanished. The result of the men's conversation is a realization that their rebellion has become senseless and futile. Sha'il suddenly understands that killing for a revolutionary cause falls into a now "extinct" tradition of "outlaws" going back three hundred years.

The next story is "Whelps of War," wherein Blair Fuller depicts with deep irony how the crew members of a supply boat in the Pacific experience frustration that the war is over. They have not had an opportunity to confront and kill any enemy soldiers. Their immense disappointment at not having engaged the enemy expresses itself in their attempts to physically injure the surrendered Japanese sailors to whom they are providing life sustenance — food. When the U.S. sailors fail to provoke a fight with the Japanese, they turn on one another. Fuller's last sentence is full of irony: "At last we had our war." The eagerness for battle that the sailors in this story have provides a subtle, but appropriate, contrast to the effects of war on individual soldiers that are shown in the earlier stories.

The final selection in "Men and War" is Sakaguchi Ango's "The Idiot." The story takes place in Japan during the firebombing of World War II. The story opens on a Japanese neighborhood in which each of the neighbors symbolizes a systemic dysfunction of Japanese society. The most noticeable of these individuals is a madman's wife who is deemed to be an "idiot" incapable of comprehension and communication. The idiot symbolizes all of Japanese history and tradition with its concomitant inability to function in a modern world. The fire destroys, but in destroying, it gives life. The storyteller and the idiot flee the fire, and the idiot awakens to life. The story reflects a philosophy that is common around the world: that destruction may be a prerequisite to the regeneration of life.

★

★ ★ ★ ★

AUTHOR: *Yihar Smilansky (S. Yizhar, 1916-) is a man of many talents. A teacher by profession, he has been a member of the Knesset for nineteen years and has received the Israel Prize, the highest literary award bestowed by that country. Although he is well known for his many short stories and editorials, he is best known for the novel* Days of Ziklag.

SETTING: *When Israel became a state in 1947, as many as eight hundred thousand Arabs fled to neighboring countries. Those who remained, approximately 1.5 million, have been second-class citizens with little legal protection. Strangers in their own land, continually under suspicion as potential traitors, they complain of censorship, curfews, mass roundups, and even torture. The government of Israel has been accused of being complicitous in demolishing Arab houses and towns, in destroying four hundred mosques, in exploiting Arab labor, and even in forbidding Arabs to drill for water. Although this story was written in the 1960s, fear, hostility, and suspicion continue unabated between the Jewish and Arab populations while many of the complaints remain unanswered and the issues unresolved.*

The Prisoner

Yihar Smilansky

Flocks and shepherds were scattered over the rock hillsides, under the terebinths, in barren places where the mountain rose flourishes and even in winding little valleys where lights gleamed and sparkled amid the rustling, glittering durrah plants; greeny-yellow summer motes under which dust gathered in little piles that were rounded like nuts ground down to grey flour when the foot touches them, and retaining the sense of ripe, good earth. Little groups of sheep were wandering over the slopes and valleys as they grazed, while the hilltops were shaded by olive trees on either side. It was clearly impossible to penetrate any deeper without attracting attention; and that would promptly rob our patrol of its purpose.

So we sat down on the stones to rest awhile and allow our running sweat to cool off in the sunlight. Summer was buzzing all around like a

Translated by I. M. Lask. "The Prisoner" is reprinted from *The New Israeli Writers: Short Stories of the First Generation*, edited by Dalia Rabikovitz (New York: Sabra Brooks, Funk and Wagnalls, 1969). Copyright by the author, ACUM, ISRAEL.

golden beehive. The medley of golden mountain fields, of green durrah turning gold, of green hills, dark green olive leaves and their greyish-umber trunks, the blazing sky and the vast, almighty silence were simply dazzling. From time to time they bemused the heart so that one longed for some happy word.

Distant shepherds somewhere beyond were leading their flocks tranquilly across the unchanged fields and quiet hills, with the casual stride of those good times when trouble had not yet come. It nipped at one in a fashion that presaged something very different. Nearby there were flocks grazing, flocks belonging to the days of Abraham, Isaac and Jacob. Somewhere in the vicinity the distant village slumbered, with its frieze of olives, a kind of dull copper. In the hollow hillsides the ewes were thronging together. There were mountains in the distance.

Our C.O. stared for a long time through his field glasses, puffing his cigarette and preparing his plans. Number one, there was no point going further. Number two, going back empty-handed was simply unthinkable. One of the shepherds, or one of the boys, or maybe several of them, would have to be caught or else something would have to be done. Alternatively something would have to be burnt, and then they could return with results, with real and undeniable facts.

This commander of ours was a middle-sized chap with deep-set eyes and eyebrows joining together. He was baldish in front and wore his cap in such a way that his forehead and what little hair he had left were open to the breeze. We watched him as he made his survey. He saw whatever it was that he saw. As for us, we could see a world of hills, all woolly with greenstuff and stony ground and olives in the distance, a world criss crossed and bedappled with little golden hollows and dips of durrah. So entirely was it such a world that it infused a silence in one, together with a longing for good fruitful soil that warms like a flame. It enticed one and made one wish for the toil that is accompanied by bending and stretching, it made one wish for greyish sandy dust, for all that is required at the height of the harvesting; for anything rather than being a member of the rank and file while the commander was working out how he would fling us across this chuck of afternoon silence.

What was more, he was well-nigh ready and prepared. In the shadow of a youthfully green tree we had already discovered a shepherd with his sheep before him, at rest among the growing durrah. A sudden circle drew tight within the universe. Everything both beyond and within that circle was concentrated on a single person, who had to be taken alive. The huntsmen were already on the way. Most of us were to take cover in the undergrowth and amid the flattish rocks on the right, while to the left and moving downwards the C.O. would set off with two or three others in order to encircle the quarry, make a sudden onslaught and drive him into the arms of those lying in ambush above.

We stole into the heart of the gentle durrah. Our heels trod on the chewed shoots and stubble that had been gnawed by those selfsame flocks. Our hobnailed soles kissed the dust, both brown and greyish. We took full advantage of the area at our disposal, the topography, the natural vegetation and the shelter to be gained from blind spots. Then we came bursting at a gallop down on the fellow seated on a stone in the tree's shadow. Panic-stricken he jumped to his feet, flung away his staff and ran like a fleeing hind, vanishing to the other side of the slope right into the arms of the huntsmen.

That was a joke, that was! Funny wasn't the word for it! But our C.O. was always on the job. He was already full of a bright new idea, and that was really tricky and clever. We would finish the job properly collecting the sheep as well. He clapped his hands and then rubbed his palms together in genial self-satisfaction, as much as to say: "That's the ticket!"

Someone swallowed his spit and remarked: "There'll be goulash for us, I can tell you!" We all set to work cheerfully with the satisfaction of victors, and the prospects of a reward for all our labors. Now he became genuinely enthusiastic: "Get on with it, quick!"

But the trouble was, all this excitement had frightened the sheep. Some of them had raised their heads, some were preparing to run away, and some wanted to know just what those who were preparing to do something were actually preparing to do. Besides, how does one handle sheep? We proved to be a mockery and a derision.

Our C.O. made that quite clear, insisting that a pack of schoolteachers like us and idiots like us were good for nothing except to mess up anything that was fine and good. Then he began with a *brrrr* and a *grrrr* and a *te-e-e-, te-e-e*, and all the other noises that have been the basis of communication between shepherd and flock since time began. What was more, nothing would satisfy him except to have one of us go ahead as a wether, *baa*ing all the way along, while two more on either side flourished their rifles as though they were shepherds' staffs and burst into song as though they were shepherds keeping their flocks amused. Behind them another three or so were to walk in exactly the same way, in order that our energy and wide laughter might help us control our hesitant and somewhat confused stupidity, so that we would end up better and finer, in brief, as soldiers.

Amid all this confusion we simply forgot that on the other side of a rock down on the slope there sat, in between two rifle butts and two pairs of hobnailed shoes, a prisoner who was trembling like a rabbit. A man of forty or so he was, with a drift of mustache around his mouth, a stupid nose and somewhat open lips and eyes; except that the latter had been blindfolded with his own *keffieh* in order that he should see nothing. Though I don't know what the nothing was that he was not supposed to see.

"Stand up!" they ordered when the C.O. came over to inspect the spoils of war at close quarters and look him up and down. What they said to the C.O. was: "Did you really think we wouldn't catch him? Of course we did! And how! There's no nonsense with us. Not a single bullet, but he understood he'd better put his hands up. That's certain sure!"

"You're good and iron!" the C.O. approved of them. "Sheep and shepherd together, just imagine! What will they say when we get back! Perfectly lovely!" He took a look at the prisoner and found him to be a little sort of fellow in a faded yellow robe, shivering as he breathed through the kerchief bound over his eyes. His sandals were trodden down, all of a piece, he had a hooflike leg, and alas-this-is-the-very-end was inscribed all over his hunched shoulders.

"Uncover his eyes and tie his hands together. He'll lead the flock ahead of us!" Our C.O. had had another of those flashes of genius which the intoxication of battle engendered in him so plentifully.

At that a spark of delight flashed from one to the other of us. Good. They took off his black *agal*, which is the rope of horsehair worn around the *keffieh*, otherwise known as the headcloth. They wrapped the *agal* around his hands, pulled it and bound and knotted it tight for a second and a third time. Then they took the blindfold off the frightened fellow's eyes and nose and addressed him thus: *"Nabi el anam kudmana!"* Meaning, lead the flock ahead of us.

I don't know what the prisoner thought to himself when his eyes saw the light, nor what was going on in his heart nor what his blood said or roared or what was going on frustratedly inside him. All I know is — he began gnashing and puffing at his flock as though nothing had ever gone wrong. Down he went from rock to rock through the undergrowth, the way shepherds always go down from rock to rock through the undergrowth. The astonished and frightened sheep followed him, while behind them and around them came our hoarse voices, our kicking legs and the buffeting of our rifles as we went down into the valley, carelessly guffawing.

So busy were we with all this that we paid no attention to several other shepherds who suddenly started up and vanished over the line of the hilltops, crowded as those were with golden silence and speechless melancholy. They gathered silently, driving off their flocks while managing to keep an eye on us from the distance. Nor had we noticed the sun which all this noisy while was going gradually lower, gradually growing more golden until suddenly, as we came around the mountain spur, we were smitten by a huge and dazzling wave of brilliance, glazed, dusty, glowing and flaming, so that it seemed to be a kind of silent remote rebuke, and a great outcry even more.

Naturally we had no time to spare for all that. We had to worry about the sheep and the prisoner. The former were bleating and scattering, while the latter was cringing and turning dumb. A kind of dull stupidity had fallen upon him, a sort of stupefaction in which everything was lost in face of which all was beyond despair. He merely strode along, silent and unhappy, growing more and more bemused and stupefied.

It would take too long to describe how we moved through the valleys amid the hills with all their crowded golden silence, through all the summer tranquility; how the frightened sheep were hurried along in a fashion to which they were not accustomed; and how our prisoner continued to be as dumbly silent as an uprooted plant. Indeed, he was growing miserable to the point of mockery, alarmed and starting and quivering and tumbling over with the kerchief which was, of course, tied round his forehead, whenever he was given a sudden tug. He grew steadily more alarmed and startled, not to say ridiculous after a fashion, though virtually untouchable. And meanwhile the durrah went on yellowing, the sun added its silent pride, the dusty paths between the ends of the fields and the flank of the mountain absorbed our fit and proper paces as though they were silently bearing some additional burden. In brief, we were returning to base.

All the marks of a strongpoint began to emerge. There was an emptiness, a fine dust, a desolation. Echoes ceased abruptly. A forsaken ant-hill, the rags and tatters of human life. The mustiness of don't-give-a-damn. A stinking, flea-bitten, lice-infested existence. The poverty and doltishness of miserable villages. All of a sudden their outskirts, their homes, their courtyards, their inmost sanctums had been laid bare. All of a sudden their clothes had been flung over their faces, their shameful nakedness displayed, and here they were, poverty-stricken, withered and stinking. A sudden emptiness, an apoplectic death. Strange, rancorous orphanhood. In the heat of the day the place seemed to be squinting through a haze of dust, uncertain whether it was mournfully lamenting or simply bored or whether it mattered either way.

Over above, to be sure, they wandered about in the grey plumpish trenches, those citizens whose food was not food, whose water was not water, whose day was not day and whose night was not night, and may the devil take whatever they might do or whatever might happen, devil take what used to be decent and pleasant and customary, in short devil take everything. So let us stink good and proper and grow beards and talk smut and muck. Let sweaty clothes stick to unwashed bodies with all their sores and pimples. And let us shoot the stray dogs so that they also begin to stink. And let us sit down in the sticky dust with the smell of the burnt tires all around, and sleep in the muck and case-harden our hearts, all because nothing mattered.

The identifying marks of the outpost became clearer. We marched more pridefully. What magnificent spoils of war we were bringing with us! Rhythm entered into our feet. The sheep were bleating and flowing along in confusion. The prisoner, over whose nose and eyes the kerchief had been replaced for security reasons, was dragging his sandals and shambling helplessly along in his semi-blindness, generous and hearty curses accompanying him. Apart from all of which our satisfaction was growing and swelling, our genuine pleasure at this achievement, this real enterprise. We were sweating and dusty, so soldierly, such he-men. What words we could use to describe our C.O.! And it is easy to imagine the way we were received and how everybody roared with laughter and cheerful self-satisfaction, just like barrels with burst hoops.

Someone busting with laughter, the sweat running all over him, came up to our C.O., pointed to the blindfolded prisoner and asked casually:

"Is that him? Settling him? Give me!" And our C.O., still grinning as he gulped some water down, wiped off his own sweat and answered glisteningly:

"Just you sit down quietly over there, it isn't yours."

The gang all around burst out laughing to hear it all. Who gave a damn for strong point, for trouble, for the whole set up, for the whole snafu, for freedom and anything of the kind as long as we had all this? Oh, we were old horses. The harness did not gall us any longer. On the contrary. It covered any number of healed and unhealed sores and fitted well over the hollows of the spine which was no longer straight after the hard times we had gone through.

Then someone came along and photographed the whole kaboodle. When he went on leave he would develop the films and make photos of

without any possible alternative, that very specific truth out of all others would be revealed.

"What's your name?"

The tall fellow started his investigation very suddenly. The prisoner, still confused by his entry, paid no attention to the question. The chap leaning against the wall ran a wrinkle of certainty down to his lips as though he had expected that as well beforehand.

"What's your name?" the tall fellow now repeated, hissing the words.

"Who? Me?" the shepherd jumped and lifted a hesitant hand to the kerchief over his eyes. He pulled it away again halfway, as though he had been scorched.

"Your name?" the bristly-haired fellow repeated once more, very clearly and with full accentuation.

"Hassan," croaked the other, moving his head in an effort to enhance his attention, in order to make up for his novel absence of sight.

"Hassan what?"

"Hassan Ahmad," he said more rapidly as though being shunted onto rails; and he nodded his head in confirmation.

"How old?"

"Can't say," he shrugged his shoulders, rubbing the palms of his hands together, wishing to be helpful.

"How old?"

"I simply don't know, *ya sidi*," he croaked through his fleshy lips, half-smiling for some reason so that his drift of mustache danced gently. "Twenty, or maybe thirty-two," he gladly contributed to the joint session.

"Well, and what's going on in your village?" the tall fellow went on with the same accented tranquility, a tranquility which was stressed and presaged the rage that would follow. It was a tranquility of petty and highly original cunning towards what comes, circling around and around from a distance, and suddenly striking straight at the main artery in the very middle of the breast.

"They are working in the village, *ya sidi*," the prisoner sketched a picture of village life as he sensed some impending evil.

"Working, eh! Just as usual?" The questioner took a tiny step along the spider's web. One of the numerous threads began vibrating and announcing the prey.

"Yes, *ya sidi*," the fly insisted on invading the entangling threads. It was absolutely obvious that he would begin to lie now. At this point he would undoubtedly lie. It was his duty to lie and we would catch him at it, the contemptible cur; and we would show him. Yet just as it was clear that we would get nothing out of him this way, that he would say nothing, so it was clear that, this time, us, those of us who were present, he would not mislead, oh no, not us; and he would have plenty to say.

"And who is there in the village?" the hawk retracted its wings directly above its quarry.

"Ah — eh?" the prisoner did not grasp the question, and licked his lips as an animal might.

"Jews? Englishmen? Frenchmen?" The questioner went on like a teacher setting a trap for a pupil; just to catch him, just to find out and that's all.

"No, *ya sidi*, there are no Jews, only Arabs," he answered gravely, not in the least as though he were trying to dodge the issue. Once more he forgetfully raised his hand to the kerchief covering his eyes, as though the danger had already passed. The questioner glanced around at his comrades in the room, as much as to say: "You see! Now it's going to begin. That's how it is when you know how to get the facts."

"Are you married?" he began again from another flank. "And have you any children? And where is your father? And how many brothers have you? And where do people get their water in the village?" He went on spinning his fine net of investigation, this tall fellow. The one being investigated labored and toiled to give satisfaction. He moved his hands in exaggerated, meaningless fashion, shifting his head about, stammering and stuttering and giving tiny details which annoyed the investigators and confused him himself. He had a story to tell about two daughters and a son, but the son had gone away and his sisters were not entirely to blame for it, and had become sick and died and departed this world. In the middle of it all he thrust his thumb against his back ribs, and scratched there, up and down. He pressed all four fingers against the thumb in his endeavors, while stammering for the one word he wanted. Simply disgusting it was, for those listening to him.

There was a pause. The sentry at the door shifted from foot to foot.

The grimace on the face of the fellow leaning against the wall, and the way our bald C.O. stood beside the table, suddenly made it clear that it was not correct for the prisoner to have nothing to add. Nothing would help, blows were necessary.

"Listen, Hassan," the questioner now said. "In that village of yours, are there any Egyptians?"

Now he'll be talking. Now it will begin. Now he'll start lying.

"There are," answered the prisoner with disappointing frankness.

"There are . . ." echoed the questioner with a measure of dubiousness that contained a certain dissatisfaction, as if somebody had given him something too early. He lit a cigarette as he began to meditate whether he should now move his castle or his knight.

Our own C.O. began striding up and down the room. He moved the kicked-away chair back into place, fixed his tunic within his trousers, turned his back on us and stared out of the window with obvious dissatisfaction. The chap by the wall also ran his hand over his face and gently pinched his nose. Breathing deep and presenting a shrewd countenance as much as to say: "You have to know how to take things in hand!"

"How many are there?"

"Can't say exactly, not many."

(Ah, now the lying begins. This must be a lie. There'll have to be some slapping about.)

"How many are there?"

"Ten or fifteen maybe, about that."

"Listen, Hassan, you'd better tell the truth."

"The truth, *ya sidi*, it is all the truth."

"And don't lie."

"Aye, *ya sidi*." The prisoner did not know what to do with his hands which had remained spread out ahead of him. He let them drop.

"And there's no monkey business with us!" the tall fellow boiled over and added since it had to be added: "How many soldiers are there in your village?"

"Fifteen."

"A lie!"

Our bald C.O., who had been looking out of the window, now turned his head. His eyes were smiling. He was beginning to feel the pleasure a man knows when he is due to enjoy something in another moment, and meanwhile there is satisfaction in restraining that pleasure for the additional sweet moment that will exist later. He thrust a cigarette in the smiling corner of his compressed lips and lit it. The five with open eyes in the room all exchanged the same secret, satisfied gaze. The sentry at the door shifted from one foot to the other once again.

"By my life, *ya sidi*, fifteen!"

"No more?"

"*Abadan*, no more."

"How do you know there are no more?" That was how the questioner dextrously proved there was no fooling him. Maybe he showed a trifle too much shrewdness.

"There are no more."

"What if there are more?" (What can anyone answer to that?)

"There are no more."

There is no saying where the kick suddenly came from. Flashing from its self-restraint and finally liberating itself slantwise, uncomfortably, for lack of the necessary distance for a real good kick, shaking up the prisoner who was quite unprepared with his covered eyes. He suddenly cried out with astonishment rather than with pain, and stumbled against the table. It all seemed so much more like an unfair game than a means of getting at the facts. It was something unexpected and unnatural, something that was not what was needed, not that at all.

"Talk up now, and see you tell the truth!"

"*Ya sidi,* by my eyes, by Allah, fifteen!"

The chap by the wall was clearly apprehensive that someone might believe the blatant lie. In his hands he held a long stick which he ran between his fingers with the gracious motion of a nobleman drawing his sword. Silently he placed it on the table.

Questions went on piling up. Swiftly presented questions. Without an interval. From time to time they were besprinkled, and more and more easily and naturally, first with one kick and then with another. Cold kicks, kicked without anger, steadily more skillful. From time to time they seemed not to be added at the right point. But from time to time it became even clearer that they were absolutely necessary.

For if you are out for the truth, then you have to hit. If the man lies, then hit. If he does tell the truth, don't believe it but hit him so that he shouldn't lie later on. Hit just in case there may be some other truth. Hit because it is a habit. Just as shaking the tree brings down the ripe fruit, so beating the prisoner gives rise to the maximum possible truth. Obviously that's how it is. If anyone thinks different, don't argue with him. He's a defeatist, and that kind of fellow shouldn't make war. Don't have pity, hit. No one has any pity on you either. And apart from that, these fellows are accustomed to being hit.

By this time they were asking about the sub-machine guns in the village. An urgent issue that, and it had to be thrashed out. It was impossible to take as much as a single step forward in this connection without using force all the way. Anything else might lead to the shedding of Jewish blood, the blood of our lads; so the business had to be cleared thoroughly. They chewed it up, over and over, again and again. They went back and chewed it from the other side until it began to stink, and they had no choice except to believe that he must be lying. Then followed the business of fortifications. They ordered him to describe the village defenses.

Here the prisoner became absolutely confused. He found them hard to describe. He could not go into abstractions or talk geometry or mathematics. He wigwagged his hands, he capered about on his legs, he hopped this way and that, he did his best to convince with waving arm. The kerchief over his eyes dimmed everything, made it all meaningless and confused. But in the room it was absolutely clear that none of this could be anything but sheer deliberate falsehood.

"You're a liar," insisted the examiner despairingly. "I can see by your eyes that you're a liar!" And he menaced the blindfold with his fist.

They were making no progress. The whole business was boring, and by now they were thoroughly sick of it. They had entangled themselves in a cold and clumsy cross-examination. Nobody was enthusiastic. There was not even any satisfaction in hitting him. So it became even more astonishing when the sound of a whistling stick was heard, coming down from somewhere or other on the prisoner's back in an alien, discordant thud; something being done as a thoroughly unpleasant duty.

All good and fine. Now came the artillery. The prisoner insisted that the barrels of their cannon were no longer than his arm, starting from the shoulder and finishing at the palm. He demonstrated the size with chopper-like blows of his left hand aimed at the very root of his right shoulder, and then exactly halfway down the right hand; as much as to say, from here to here, saying it devotedly and sacramentally, hitting again and again until he eliminated all doubt; without knowing whether that was enough or whether he would have to go on and on. And meanwhile a blind grimace entwined itself on his lips and around his mustache.

The questioning petered out miserably. The sentry at the door shifting from one foot to another at his post had been peeping out of the doorway from time to time. Maybe he was seeking something in the bright sky that differed from the sheer mess of this dirty room. Now he began to feel apprehensive. Something dreadful was about to happen and there was no other choice. For what could be left, after all, except to have them tell him to take the carcass along and finish him?

"Well, that's the way it is." The examiner stretched back against his chair, wanting to take a breather after all this nonsense. He crushed his cigarette impatiently, dropped it on the floor and crushed it.

"I'll finish him off," suggested bald-head as he flicked his cigarette through the doorway.

"An absolute dumbbell," decided one officer.

"Just pretending to be a dumbbell," said the other.

"What you have to know is how to talk to him," said the chap leaning against the wall, twisting his lips in recognition of a truth which they had presumably doubted and denied.

The prisoner had already sensed that there was an interval. He licked his thick lips, stuck out his thick hand and said:

"*Fi sigara, ya sidi?*" (Got a cigarette, mister?)

Of course no one paid any attention to the idiot. He waited a few moments, then drew his outstretched hand back, thought the matter over and stood still again, an absolute donkey for you. And only to himself alone did he moan: "*ahhh, ya rab.*" Meaning: Oh, Lord God.

Well, what next? Where to now? To the quarry slopes in the villages? Or maybe to some torture of the kind that opens mouths and restores truth instead of falsehood? Or was there any other way? How were they to get rid of him? Or maybe . . . Suppose they were to give him a cigarette and send the dolt back home? Get the hell out of here and we don't ever want to see you again!

Finally they phoned somewhere or other and spoke to the Assistant Boss himself; and it was decided to send him on to another camp (at least three of the fellows in the room disgustedly turned their noses up at this shamefaced, civilian, namby-pamby trick); a camp where prisoners were questioned and handled the way they deserved. With this end in view the sentry at the door, the same one who had felt uneasy all the time without knowing why, would go off and fetch the dusty jeep and the growling duty driver who was annoyed at being called out of turn, which was so easily proved by so many facts and also by objurgations. Apart from which, as far as he himself was concerned he did not have the least objection to going off to some place where he could see human beings, but this was a matter of principle, sheer principle. And then another soldier also came and sat down beside the driver, since there was some job which could not be done until now in the absence of transport. He was not given this additional objective of accompanying the prisoner. And that was the way they would pass through the town, Spandau in front and prisoner behind. Burdened with these two functions in order to make sure that never under any circumstances would this trip be deducted from his leave (that being a separate account), he sat and loaded the machine-gun.

As for the prisoner, after he had been pushed and began groping around and banged against the side of the car and was helped in, the only place left for him was on the floor where he half-lay, half-kneeled and crouched entirely. Two were in front and the former sentry behind him, his pocket bulging with the proper papers and travel orders and chits and all the rest of it. That afternoon, which had begun some time or other between the hills and the trees and the flocks, was now due to finish in a way nobody could forecast.

They were already out of the smelly village and crossing from the wadi to the fields, then on through the fields. The jeep dashed along bouncing on all fours, and stretches of the not-so-distant future began to be transformed into reality. It was nice to sit facing the fields as they bathed in an increasingly reddish light that comprehended everything in a sweep of tiny bright golden clouds, a light rising higher than anything; than all those things which concern you and me so much, even though they did not in the least matter to the driver or his comrade with the mustache beside him. They smoked, whistled and sang, "In the Negev plains a man defending fell", and, "Your eyes are bright with a green green light", one after the other. There was someone else on the floor of the jeep, but it wasn't easy to know what could be going on inside him since he was blindfolded, beastlike and silent.

A fuzz of dust rose behind them, a smoke wake which wavered and grew pink at the edges. Irrelevant ditches and unimportant potholes in the road made the jeep jump, while fields spread their arms out to infinity and gave themselves up to a twilight that was fuddled with forgetfulness and gentleness — and something so far away, so far away, so dreamlike — until all of a sudden and unexpectedly a strange thought jumped into his head and would not budge. "The woman, she's undoubtedly lost." For up to now it was astonishing where they could have come from, you understand; as though you were thunderstruck to think that here, right here beside you, something was happening; the same thing which in other circumstances is called by other names, and which is also known as Fate.

You'd better take a jump at once, one, two, and get right out from under this bad business. Sing as a second voice to the two in front, set out for distant regions in the twilight through which the sun was burning with a reddish-citron color; only you would at once see again what had so suddenly emerged through the astounding breach.

The fellow here at your feet, his life, his well-being, his home, three souls, the whole thread of his existence with all that was involved, were in your grip somehow or other as though you were some lesser demigod here

in the jeep. The man carried along, the collective flock of sheep and
several souls in the mountain village, these variegated threads of life were
twined together to be cut or grow inextricably involved, all because you
were suddenly their master. If you liked you could just stop the jeep and let
him go free, and everything would cut up differently. But . . . just a
moment. The fellow on the back seat of the little jeep suddenly felt the
spirit darting aloft within him. Just a moment: Let the fellow go?

Here we could stop the jeep, here by the wadi. We could let the fellow
down, uncover his eyes, face him towards the mountains, point straight
ahead and tell him: Go home, man, go straight along. Take care about that
hill, there are Jews on it. Take care and don't fall into our hands again.
And then he would take his feet over and dash home. He would go back
home. Precisely that. And listen, what a story! The dreadful, tense waiting,
the fate of a woman and her children (an Arab woman!). Forebodings at
the heart that wrestled with the decree of Fate, wondering will he, won't he
come back, guessing what might happen next; and then everything solved
satisfactorily so that she could breathe easily, he's condemned to life. Hi
lad, come and let's let the fellow go!

And why not? What was to stop it? Simple, decent and human. so just
get up and tell the driver to stop. No more fine phrases about humanity
any longer. This time it's up to you yourself. This time it's not someone
else's malice, this time it's your own conscience you're facing. Let him off
and you've saved him. Today that alternative, that ominous, tremendous
alternative we always used to talk about so nervously, is firmly in your own
two hands. There's no dodging it now, not with Soldier, not with Orders,
and not with Suppose they caught you, not even with What will the boys
say. You're standing naked, facing your duty. And the choice is all your
own, nobody else's.

Then stop the jeep. Stop the driver. Let the poor devil go. You don't
have to give any reasons. It's his right and your duty. If there's any
meaning or sense in this war, now's the time for it to be seen. Men, men,
there was a man and they sent him home. Snap your fingers at all this
customary cruelty and send the fellow away. Just release him. Hallelujah!
That peasant, that shepherd would go home to his wife.

There could be no alternative. Otherwise years would pass and then in
some remarkable way he would go free and return to the mountains to
look for his wife and his home. And meanwhile they would be starving
refugees going from bad to worse, sick with typhoid, so much human dust.
And who would say what that meanwhile would be or where it would be
and even that it would be, provided only that meanwhile some fellow

somewhere or other doesn't simply knock him off and send him to heaven by sheer chance, or maybe not just by sheer chance.

Why don't you stop the jeep then? It's your duty. You can't dodge it. That has become so clear, it's hard to wait until you decide to do it. This is where you stand up, this is where you do it. Say a word to the driver, tell him and the other fellow it's the order, spin them a yarn, tell them anything — and you don't need to do even that. You don't need to explain, you don't need to tell them anything. No matter what may happen. There was once a man. Just look at the way things are. Let him go. (How can I? He isn't mine. He isn't in my hands. That's not correct, I'm not his master, I'm an agent and nothing more. What have I done wrong? Since when am I responsible for the hardheartedness of others?)

Stop it! That's shameful evasion. That's how every scamp dodges a decision and hides himself behind a "no alternative" that has gone shabby with use. Where's your sense of honor? Where's that far-famed independence of thought? Where's the freedom, three cheers for freedom, the love of liberty? Let him go! By all means, and then be prepared to give an account of what you've done. It's an honor. All your words, all your complaints, all your dissatisfaction about trifles and oppression, all your thoughts about ways of forcing yourself to move towards truth and freedom — where are they all? Today the account has been presented, it's payday. So pay up my lad, pay up, it's all yours now. (I can't. I'm only an agent. Besides it's wartime and this fellow comes from the other side which is fighting us. Maybe he is a futile victim. Yet as for me I mustn't free him and I haven't the power to do it. Here's a fresh idea for you. Everybody begins releasing and where are we? Or maybe he really does know something important and merely pretends to be a fool?)

Is that the case? Then is the fellow a soldier? Have you caught him with a weapon in hand? Where have you fetched him from? He isn't a fighter. He's a stinking, miserable civilian. All that prisoner-of-war business is a lie, and don't you forget it. It's a crime, it is. Have you questioned him? Then set him free now. More than he has already told they certainly won't get out of him. And the cost of one extra item of information is not worth the suppression of truth in his release.

(Hard for me to decide. I don't dare. Many unpleasant things simply have to be done. Talk to the driver, explain it to the other fellow, face the investigations afterwards, get into a hell of a fix because of some miserable Hassan; quite apart from which it's not at all clear that he must be released here and now, before he has been properly questioned and put through the mill.)

Nonsense! If anybody else knew only a quarter of what you know and the conclusions you've reached about truth and freedom, he would stop the jeep here and now and send the fellow packing. Then go on and forget this business, plain and simple, short and sweet, in the most practical fashion and without patting yourself on the shoulder. But when it comes to you, with all the thousand facts you know and argue about and demonstrate and dream of, you're clearly thinking you won't do it. You have a nice sweet soul, you'll think it over, you'll get all excited, you'll feel sorry, you'll think it over again, and after all that you'll go diving into a sea of deep thought wondering why didn't I do it? And you'll put the blame for missing this opportunity, for never rounding off your existence, on the whole wide world. It's a crude and ugly world, you'll say. So do something instead. Do something, just this once. Stand up to it. Get out and fight. Of course! (I do feel sorry for him. It's a pity they chose me for this job. I'd do it if I weren't afraid of I don't know what. If at least we were alone here. The business is already thrilling and throbbing in me like an unsatisfied appetite, yet still I can't. I can't begin. It's simply beyond me. When I remember that it will be necessary to explain things; to come to people and argue, to prove myself, to begin to justify myself — no, I simply can't.)

Now listen lad, do you weigh all these miserable trills and tremolos against a human life? How would you like it if you were crouching on the floor of a jeep, if your wife was waiting at home and everything was destroyed, flying about like chaff, lost and done for, waiting and waiting while the heart burns away and you're not at home; waiting with tears, waiting with your fist, with humility, with prayer and protest . . .

He has already said all he has to say. He told us all he has to tell. And now what next? Even if he did lie, even if it was untrue seven times over, still who and what is he more than a miserable nonentity, a withering submissive creature, a face wrapped around with a kerchief, all squeezed up and twisted, worthless, an empty frightened bag, fading away to nothing, abnegating himself, expecting to be kicked and regarding kicks as natural. (Take a kick at an Arab, it doesn't mean anything to him.)

And you, his guard, you simply have to let him go even if he himself laughs at you, even if he or somebody else regards it as sheer incapacity, even if your companions mock you, even if they ask you to prevent his liberation, even if they send you to the Chief Prosecutor because of it, or to a score of prosecutors. It still remains your duty and you had better set about it and escape from this swinish routine. Then there'll have been somebody who was prepared even if he paid for it to get out for once; to get away from the pigsties which rose so high and spread so far and wide while we were good citizens, and which have now officially and solemnly and by general agreement become the way of the world, the practice of everybody who wants to be worthy of the magnificent name of soldier.

We don't get any leave, we can't go home, it's hot here, filthy here, miserable here, dangerous here — so what? Let's take it out on the enemy. Let's do something. Let's knock off some miserable Arab. (Who asked him to start this damned war anyway?) Let's permit ourselves to do everything we were once forbidden to do.

Ah well, here's a certain Hassan Ahmad. His wife is either Halima or Fatma and he has two daughters and his flock has been stolen and he has been taken away somewhere or other on a bright and sunny afternoon. And who are you and what's your life good for? All a fellow like you is worth is for having all the black bile inside us emptied out on you, and the hell with it.

Of course, you're not going to let him go. That's perfectly plain. It's just fine thoughts. It's not even cowardice, it's something worse. You're a partner in the business, that's what you are. Hiding behind that stinking "what's to be done, it's an order", just this time when you have the choice and it's all in your own power, in your very own hands.

The choice is yours. A great day it is. A day of revolt. A day when you have the choice in your own hands at last, and the power to turn it into a decision, to give life back to a misused man. Think it over. To act as your heart desires. In full accordance with your own love and your own truth, in accordance with the greatest of all things — the liberation of a man.

Let him go.

Be a man.

Let him go!

Well, it's quite clear nothing will happen. Fly away, good idea. You'll dodge, that's plain. You'll look the other way. Of course it's all lost. I'm sorry for you, prisoner. He simply doesn't have the strength to do it.

Yet maybe, in spite of everything? Right away, here and now. It would just take this moment. Pull up, driver. Get off, Hassan. Go home. Do something. Talk. Stop the jeep. Say something now, this moment. After all your aching and bellyaching all these long and empty days, be a human being at last the way you want to be.

The fields were one vast shallow pinkish-gold expanse, all the tens of thousands of dunams made up one single enchanted plain without valleys, without hills, without acclivities or declivities, without villages or trees. Everything had been beaten down to one single gold foil, one leveled expanse above which were scattered quivering restless golden dust-blobs around a vast land of gold that stretched on to infinity; even if it were possible that on the other side (where nobody watches) amid the evening mists making their way down from the hills, even if there is some other sadness over there maybe, some misery, some misery of who knows what, some misery of shameful inaction, some waiting woman, some who-can-know-what decree of life, who knows what very very private individual, who knows what else that may be even more universal, which the setting sun is going to leave here, among us, never brought to an end?

★

$\star \quad \star \quad \star \quad \star$

AUTHOR: *Ralph Salisbury (1926-) has made enormous contributions to American literature, particularly with his short stories and poetry. After serving in the U.S. Army Air Force (1944-1946), he pursued a career in academia and is currently at the University of Oregon. He continues to write and is especially appreciated for his support of community participation in the arts. Some of his better-known works are:* Pointing at the Rainbow: Poems of a Cherokee Heritage, Going to the Water: Poems of a Cherokee Heritage, *and* A White Rainbow: Poems of a Cherokee Heritage.

SETTING: *At the end of World War II, the Allies, as part of their attempt to disarm the Japanese occupiers, established the 38th Parallel between communist North Korea and democratic South Korea. Efforts to reunite the country failed. On June 25, 1950, North Korea invaded South Korea. The United States, as part of an international force commanded by General Douglas MacArthur, sent a significant military contingent to Korea. The U.S. Army, like the U.S. population, was composed of many national, racial, and ethnic groups. This story, told from the perspective of a Native American, depicts intentional and unintentional misunderstandings between individual soldiers whose cultural backgrounds differ significantly.*

The Sonofabitch and the Dog

Ralph Salisbury

"This sonofabitch remembers everything."

I had never killed anyone before, but I knew how to do it the instant I had to.

Fist slammed against jaw bone. Throat twisted like a giant snake between hands.

His friends pulled at me. Hit me.

Instead of the firing-squad, they sent me to be a Behind-the-Enemy-Lines Soldier.

Too late. That mouth would never twist air again.

"The Sonofabitch and the Dog" originally appeared in *Earth Power Coming*, edited by Simon Ortiz) Tsaile, Ariz.: Navajo Community College). Reprinted by permission of the author.

"This man remembers everything," the assignments officer said, remembering what he had been told. "And he's a bare-hands killer."

They explained that it was all right for all of us to call each other sonsofbitches, it didn't really mean our mothers, they said. They said we wouldn't let the enemy call us anything, we would kill them, but if we insulted each other we were only practicing like we did with our weapons.

We practiced before the sun and after the sun.

I learned knives, pistols, rifles, machine-guns, mortars, rocket-launchers, land-mines — compass, maps, radio — to fly a helicopter in case the pick-up pilot was killed. I learned the White people's language better than before. I learned the enemy's language.

"This sonofabitch remembers everything," the training sergeants said. They'd all heard my story, and they liked practicing.

"You sonsofbitches are good teachers," I said.

"He's never had a fight," my mother had told the soldiers who came for me. "He's never been with a woman. His father was killed the first year of the war. He's only seventeen."

"No problem," the corporal told my mother. "He'll be eighteen next year. If he lives that long. And this'll save our coming back for him."

I felt pretty good about all the things I learned.

"If they all caught on as fast as this sonofabitch catches on, we'd win the fucking war before the fucking year was over," my unit sergeant told the Inspecting Officer.

"Good man," the officer said. His decorations shined like bullets. He had white hair and a white mustache. There were little shining eagles on his shoulders. I guessed he was one of their important ones, very wise. "They tell me you're not only smart, they tell me you're also one mean, tough little sonofabitch," the old officer smiled.

I smiled back. "They tell me you are one super duper chickenshit sonofabitch, sir," I told him.

The sergeant made a little sound even though he was supposed to be at attention. I never knew a sergeant could make a mistake.

"The Inspecting Officer didn't utter a sound for a long time. It was like it is before a big storm, the silence is big, as big as the wind is going to be. It was like that before I hit the city soldier and choked him to death.

Then the Inspecting Officer hit the sergeant in the stomach, but it was just a practice hit.

"You leave off instructing this man and send him on a mission," the officer said. "He knows too fucking much already."

Once I was assigned to a mission, they let me visit the city at night.

At first I felt nervous. It was because I remembered all the streets from the train station that the city soldier had said I remembered everything.

But now it was all right because my buddies went with me. We gave some of our money to women, and the women never asked who our family was or anything. It was very easy. No problem. I liked all this very well.

One night one of my Oriental buddies said something not very friendly to a white woman and later she called me a "sonofabitch Indian."

"Don't you call him any Indian. He's a soldier. And you're a whore," one of my Black buddies told her. He wasn't practicing. And she hadn't been practicing either. I didn't like it so well after that.

I finally learned that "bitch" meant female dog in the White language. Some soldiers had brought a mongrel pup onto the base one night when they were drunk and after everybody was sober the next day they thought they'd use the pup for target practice, but it kept offering to shake hands and standing on its hind legs and rolling over and covering its eyes with its little paws and finally they realized somebody, probably some little kid, had taught the pup these tricks and so they fed the pup and taught it to lap beer out of a mug and take a few puffs on a cigar and after it got big they even got it to take a mortar shell between its teeth and drop it down the tube; then they said the dog was a commando, and they named it "Commando."

When it thought some soldier was playing "fetch" and brought back the grenade he'd thrown, the sergeant — who'd just managed to throw the grenade a second time far enough — ordered an end to Commando's military training. The dog accepted this like a veteran soldier. He'd been almost close enough to fetch the grenade a second time, and after that he'd slink off whenever some innocent new soldier offered to throw a stick for him.

Commando still drank beer, but a smoking cigar would send him squirming out of his buddy's arms and off to the far end of the base. They taught Commando to go to town and taught him where to catch the bus to return to base after his night out.

"Poor old Commando is shell-shocked. He got that there combat-fatigue. He just ain't motivated no more. But he's still big on booze and bitches."

That was when I learned that "bitch" wasn't just a White insult word.

I came into training shortly before the grenade-fetching incident, but I wasn't on the grenade range and only heard about that, just as I'd only heard about Commando's puppy days.

"He ended his training about the same time you started," a buddy laughed. "Maybe we should all be as smart as this dog and freak out like he did — before some enemy wastes us."

We weren't supposed to talk like that, but sometimes when soldiers were drunk they did talk like that. I decided it was only practice talk.

We weren't supposed to fight when we went to town, and other soldiers from ordinary units were supposed to recognize a Behind-the-Lines-Soldier's uniform and leave him strictly alone, but one night when I was about to get on the bus back to base, a White soldier said to me, "Stand aside there, Indian, and let this gentleman on the bus ahead of you all." He meant wait for Commando, who was just about to follow me onto the bus.

My Black buddies grabbed the joking soldier, kicked him in the balls and left him writhing on the sidewalk.

"This man isn't an Indian, you sonofabitch, he's a commando, and don't you ever forget it."

Hearing "Commando," Commando ran up to the Black soldier and sat at attention as he'd been trained to do.

"At ease, Commando. Dismissed," the Black soldier laughed, and Commando strolled over, raised his hind leg in a jaunty salute and pissed on the head of the ordinary soldier, who was still writhing on the sidewalk.

Feeling the warm liquid, the soldier took one hand away from his crotch and hooked it over his head like a schoolkid expecting a hard cuff.

I felt kind of sorry for him, but I knew he hadn't been practicing when he called me "Indian" just as I knew the soldier I'd killed had not been practicing really but had really been saying something he'd been used to saying ever since he was small.

I knew, too, that the Black soldier wasn't right. I was a commando, yes, but I was still an Indian. But by now I had learned that words meant different things to different people at different times.

"Enemy."

I was only two days back from my first behind-the-lines mission. I'd killed seven people, six with my rifle, one with my knife. I'd been given a medal. And freedom to go to town every night for a week. All three of my buddies had been blown up by the same land mine.

"You get drunk for them. You get laid for them. Live it up," the Base Psychiatrist said. "It's the only way."

"Enemy."

Only Commando and I had been waiting at the bus stop, but it was dark there, as all streets were, blacked out to prevent attracting enemy bombing planes. I looked around to see who had joined us, but I saw only Commando's grinning teeth.

"That smart aleck soldier I pissed on was right," Commando said. "You're an Indian. You understand the earth. You understand nature. You understand animals. You understand what I'm saying, and you understand that I'm not just bullshitting you."

I was pretty sober in the chill night, and I thought Commando was correct in what he was saying, but I'd never heard a dog talk White language before. I'd been hearing my dead buddies' voices. And I wasn't sure in just what way I was hearing the dog. And it didn't seem right to answer back in an ordinary way.

"How old are you?" Commando asked.

"Seventeen."

"Do you want to be eighteen?"

"Hell, yes," I looked around, but I wasn't in any doubt about who I was answering. I just wanted to be sure no one had come up to hear me talking to a dog.

"Everybody keeps telling everybody how smart I am to learn where and when to catch a bus," Commando said. "And they keep telling how fast you learn," Commando told me. "What's two Blacks plus one Oriental plus one seventeen year old Indian?"

I knew the silence was really his answer, but when Commando continued, "The cadre selected for one of the most dangerous missions on the list," I didn't argue.

"So what do you want to be, proud and stupid and dead, or humble and freaked-out and alive?"

When the bus pulled up, Commando trotted on first and went straight to the furthest back seat. I went back there, too, but there was no more talking.

Next day, instead of reporting for further combat-interrogation, I went to the only piece of earth that wasn't covered with concrete or grass cut short like a military-haircut — the firing range.

Spreadeagle in the sacred way, I gazed at shaggy white buffalo clouds and prayed while stones under me softened.

"Leave him alone," they said at first, "he's had a hard mission. He's just doing some Indian stuff. He'll get it back together."

But when target practice time came, and somebody said they should drag me off, the Range Sergeant said something else.

For hours, bullets twanged air over me, and I thought of the bullets that had driven my buddies to run into the mine-field, and I remembered Commando's first word: "Enemy."

After target practice, there was less reason to move me.

For seven days I fasted. For seven days I prayed.

When they marched me in, the Base Psychiatrist gave me a shrewd, knowing grin, and after the tests, he grinned again, pulled a card from a box and said that from now on I'd be the Chaplain's Assistant.

"Are you a Christian?" the Chaplain asked.

"No."

"No problem," he said. "Just do what you're told."

I do what I'm told. I remember every detail. And by now I'm eighteen.

★

★ ★ ★ ★

AUTHOR: *Isaac Babel (1894-1941) was a prominent Jewish intellectual in Russia during the Civil War of 1918 to 1920. Between 1917 and 1920 he held positions in both the military and civilian sectors, including a short stint in the Cheka (secret police). He is best known for the Red Cavalry stories, which are set during the Russian Civil War. These are neither stories of glorious heroes nor documentary reporting but are generally plotless and anecdotal stories, narrated in the first person by a Jewish intellectual named Lyutov.*

SETTING: *The Bolshevik Revolution (1917) led by Vladimir I. Lenin set the stage for the bloody Russian Civil War (1918-1920). In that war, the Red Army under Leon Trotsky ultimately defeated the three armies of the Whites in the Caucasus, Baltic, and Siberian regions. Some of the heaviest fighting was in the Ukraine, where this story takes place.*

My First Goose

Isaac Babel

Savitsky, commander of the sixth division, stood up when he saw me, and I was surprised by the beauty of his gigantic body. He stood up and the purple of his breeches, the crimson of his hat, tilted to one side, the medals pinned to his chest, cleaved the hut in half as a standard cleaves the sky. He smelled of scent and the cloying, fresh smell of soap. His long legs were like girls sheathed to their shoulders in polished riding boots.

He smiled at me, struck the table with his whip and drew toward him the order that had just been dictated by the staff commander. It was an order for Ivan Chesnokov to advance with the regiment under his command in the direction of Chugunov-Dobryvodka and, after making contact with the enemy, to annihilate the same . . .

"For which annihilation," the commander began to write and smeared the whole sheet, "I am making entirely responsible the same Chesnokov, whom I will strike down on the spot, of which you, Comrade Chesnokov, who have been working with me at the front for some months,

Translated by Ronald Meyer. Reprinted by permission of S. G. Phillips, Inc., from: *The Collected Stories of Isaac Babel*, copyright 1955 by S. G. Phillips, Inc.

31

can have no doubt."

The commander of the sixth division signed the order with a flourish, tossed it to the orderlies and turned on me his gray eyes, dancing with gaiety; I gave him the paper that ordered my appointment to the division staff.

"Register the order!" said the commander. "Register the order and sign him up for any amusement except the front. Can you read and write?"

"Yes," I answered, envying the iron and flower of this youth. "I have a law degree from Petersburg University . . ."

"So you're one of those scholar-kids," he shouted, smiling, "and glasses on your nose too. What a mangy specimen! . . . They send you without asking, but here you could get killed for those glasses. Going to make it with us?"

"I'll make it," I answered and left for the village with the quartermaster to find lodgings for the night.

The quartermaster carried my trunk on his shoulders, the village street extended before us, the dying sun, round and yellow as a pumpkin, breathed its last rosy ray on the sky.

We approached a hut decorated with painted wreaths; the quartermaster stopped and said suddenly with a guilty smile:

"It's a bad business here with glasses, and nobody can put a stop to it. No place here for a distinguished fellow. But you go and bed down some lady, a nice upright lady, then the boys'll be good to you . . ."

He hesitated with my trunk on his shoulders, came up close to me, then jumped back in despair and ran to the nearest yard. Cossacks were sitting there on hay and were shaving each other.

"Here, soldiers," the quartermaster said and put my trunk down on the ground. "According to Comrade Savitsky's orders you have to take this fellow in and without any fooling around, because this fellow's got a lot of learning."

The quartermaster turned purple in the face and left without turning back. I raised my hand and tipped my hat to the Cossacks. A young fellow with long, flaxen hair and a handsome Ryazan face went up to my trunk and threw it over the gate. Then he turned his back to me and with surprising skill he began to emit shameful noises.

"Weapon No. Zero-Zero," shouted an older Cossack to him and then began to laugh. "Rapid fire . . ."

The fellow exhausted his unsubtle talents and walked away. Then, crawling on the ground, I started to collect the manuscripts and my old clothes, full of holes, that had fallen out of the trunk. I collected and carried them to the other end of the yard. By the hut, on a stove made of bricks, was a pot of cooking pork; it smoked as my far-away home in the country smoked, and hunger became confused with my unparalleled loneliness. I covered my trunk with hay, made a pillow of it and lay down on the ground to read Lenin's speech at the Second Congress of the Comintern in *Pravda*. The sun fell upon me from behind the jagged hillocks, the Cossacks stepped on my feet, the same young fellow did not tire of making fun at my expense, the beloved lines were approaching me along the thorny path but were unable to reach me. I then put the newspaper aside and went to see the landlady who was spinning on the porch.

"Landlady," I said, "I need to eat . . ."

The old woman raised the spreading whites of her half-blind eyes and again lowered them.

"Comrade," she said after her silence, "all of this makes me want to go and hang myself."

"By God I'll strangle you, woman," I muttered irritably and shoved the old woman with my fist to her chest. "I'm supposed to explain it to you . . ."

And, when I turned around I saw somebody's sword lying around not far away. A tyrannical goose was waddling around the yard and was serenely preening its feathers. I caught up with it and pushed it down to the ground, the goose's head cracked under my boot, snapped, and blood began to flow. The white neck lay in the dung and the wings began to flap over the dead body.

"By God, I'll strangle you, woman!" I said, rooting in the goose with my sword. "Landlady, cook it for me."

The old woman, sparkling with her blindness and glasses, picked the bird up, wrapped it in her apron and carried it to the kitchen.

In the yard the Cossacks were already sitting around their pot. They were sitting motionlessly, erect, like priests, and didn't look at the goose.

"The fellow's okay," one of them said about me, winked and ladled the cabbage soup.

The Cossacks began eating with the restrained elegance of peasants who respect each other, and I cleaned the sword with sand, walked out through the gate and came back again, weary. The moon hung over the yard like a cheap earring.

"Hey," Surovkov, the eldest of the Cossacks, said to me suddenly, "come and have some grub with us until your goose is done."

He pulled an extra spoon out of his boot and gave it to me. We guzzled down the homemade cabbage soup and ate the pork.

"Anything in the newspaper?" the fellow with the flaxen hair asked and he made room for me.

"Lenin writes in the newspaper," I said, pulling out *Pravda*, "Lenin writes that there's shortages of everything . . ."

And loudly, like an exultant blind man, I read Lenin's speech to the Cossacks.

Evening wrapped me in the intoxicating liquor of its twilight sheets, evening put its maternal palms to my enflamed forehead.

I read and rejoiced and was on the watch, while rejoicing, for the secret curve in Lenin's straight line.

"Truth tickles everybody's nose," Surovkov said when I had finished, "but the problem is picking it out of the heap, but he hits on it right away, like a chicken with a piece of grain."

That's what Surovkov, the platoon commander of the staff squadron, said about Lenin, and then we went to bed in the hayloft. The six of us slept there, sharing our warmth with each other, our legs entangled, under the roof, full of holes, which let the stars in.

I dreamed and saw women in my dreams, and only my heart, stained with the blood of the killing, creaked and bled.

★

★ ★ ★ ★

AUTHOR: *Edith Thomas (d'Auxois, 1909–), the French journalist and author, was a member of the subversive Francs-Tireurs Partisans (FTP), a French Resistance group organized during World War II to engage in subversive activities against the Germans and the Vichy government. Thomas helped to reorganize the* Comité National des Écrivains *after the execution of its founder, the communist deputy Jacques Decour. She has contributed to* Lettres Françaises, *the* Éternelle Revue, *and has published a collection of short stories,* Conte, *under the pseudonym "d'Auxois."*

SETTING: *In 1941 the southern part of France agreed to an armistice with Germany when the Vichy government, headed by the elderly World War I hero, Marshal Philippe Pétain, compromised with nazism and fascism. Rather than live under the Vichy regime, many French citizens took exile in England and formed the Free French Government under Charles de Gaulle. Those French who had not escaped and who disagreed with the pogroms of fascism formed various resistance organizations and were a constant menace to the Germans and to French collaborators. This story takes place in unoccupied France, the Vichy-held regions. It is an example of some of the fine literature inspired by the French Resistance.*

FTP

Edith Thomas

He was told: "A train full of Germans will be passing tonight at eleven thirty-four."

It was hardly five minutes from the station to the forest. So the Germans would pass at eleven thirty-nine. But he went to the *bistrot* near the station where René usually had lunch. René was eating with the stationmaster in a corner of the room. They greeted each other nonchalantly and talked about the weather.

René said: "Aren't you eating here? There's some rabbit and potatoes. It's fabulous." He replied: "No, my wife's expecting me. She'll be livid if I'm late." So René got up and said: "I'll go a little way with you. I'll be back for my coffee in a minute," he shouted to the stationmaster.

Translated by Alastair Hamilton. Reprinted from *Defeat and Beyond: An Anthology of French Wartime Writing, 1940–1945,* edited by Germaine Brée and George Bernauer (New York: Random House, 1970) by permission of the publishers.

They went out as nonchalantly as ever and lit a cigarette on the doorstep.

After a few steps they turned down a side street. Grass was growing between the cobbles. From time to time an old woman raised a curtain and dropped it again. Familiar faces — they were part of the street. It's René who works at the station, and Paul, the bank clerk, they've always been pals. They did their military service together and they were in prison together during the "phony war." But they managed to escape before being sent to Germany. And I know Paul's mother: we went to school together. He married a schoolteacher, a little brunette from Paris, rather proud, but better than one thinks. René's still a bachelor. It's too bad he doesn't marry: he could make a girl happy. Paul's going home: he lives at the end of the road, nearly in the fields, a house with one story, and a flower garden in front, but he's planted some potatoes and spinach in it.

They dropped the curtains: nothing ever happens in this street worth looking at. It's not as if I were living in the Grande Place with all the movement of the market and the *Kommandantur* in the town hall; or even the Rue de la République, which is now called the Rue du Maréchal Pétain.

Paul's going home and René's with him because they're two old pals, that's all.

Paul asked: "Is it true that a train full of Germans is passing at eleven thirty-four this evening? Have you checked?"

"Yes," said René, "I've checked."

"What time is the last train before it?" asked Paul.

"It's a freight train. It passes at ten and doesn't stop."

"Five minutes from the station to the forest," calculated Paul. "That's five past ten. You need ten good minutes to go from Pierre Levée to the railroad. So you must be at Pierre Levée at five to ten. You'd better come directly to make sure the freight train has been passed. Tell Louis and Alain. I'll tell Big Paul" (because he was bigger than Paul and Robert).

They stopped to light a cigarette — "I smoke a mixture of tobacco and cornsilk" — someone passed them. The road inspector. They greeted him.

"All right," said René.

"All right," said Paul.

And Paul pushed open the garden gate, making the bell tinkle in the empty lane. His steps creaked on the gravel path.

Paul went home for lunch while René went back to the station. "That boy should get himself a wife, Madame Gentillon, I'm telling you."

And now he told Alice.

"This afternoon you must warn Big Paul and Robert: tonight, five to ten, at Pierre Levée."

She paled slightly: her skin turned gray. She didn't ask anything. She waited.

"Tell them not to forget their notebooks."

She knew what "their notebooks" meant. But the blood returned to her cheeks. She didn't say anything. She waited. He added:

"It's for a train."

She threw her coat over her shoulders and went off to school.

She was training her class for the school certificate,[1] and she was sure that at least fifteen of her pupils would pass. She made sure no one could detect her anxiety. Then she went to get a book from the school library. It was the *Song of Roland.*[2] She slipped a note into it. At four o'clock she kept back her best pupil, Marie-Catherine, for a few seconds. She said: "Here, Marie-Catherine, give your father this book. He asked me for it. Don't forget, Marie-Catherine."

But she knew that Marie-Catherine never forgot anything.

On her way back she stopped at the cobbler's. There were some people in the shop. She asked:

"When can I bring you my clogs to repair? The sole has broken again."

"That's all junk," said Big Paul.

"And please, would you remove a nail from this shoe immediately. It hurts."

She was sitting on a low chair and had started to take off her shoe. In the meantime the other customers had left. She said very quickly:

"This evening, at five to ten, at Pierre Levée. You won't forget your notebook."

Then she put on her shoe again.

He smiled with all the wrinkles in his face which lined his mouth and eyes. He was about fifty, well built, but lined.

"So when can I bring my clogs?"

"Not before next week," he replied. "I've got too much work."

They had dinner. They listened to the radio. He pretended to be calm. But she sensed his anxiety. No, it wasn't anxiety, it was interest, great interest in everything. But for her it was anxiety. She watched him as she dried the dishes and said to herself: "If this were the last time I were to see him." And she felt her heart. She wasn't made to be a hero's wife. She wasn't made to hand a shield to her husband or her son, and say, "Come back on top of it, or beneath it." She was made for everyday life and peace, reading and writing lessons, dictation, domestic problems, coming home to clean the house and cook at night. She was made to have a child and cradle it, to have a husband she loved and love him to the end.

What was missing for them to be happy? But she knew that happiness was impossible, that you had to forget the rest and that every moment reminds you there is no happiness, even the simplest, even the humblest, *now,* without lies or selfishness. So much the worse: happiness will be for tomorrow and maybe for others. But not for us, for tomorrow.

He must go if he wants to be on time. And he mustn't be late. But Paul never knows the time.

"It's nearly a quarter to ten," she said.

He kissed her vaguely. And what if it were the last time, she wondered. She heard his steps on the gravel path. But the bell didn't tinkle. She unhooked it at night so that nobody could hear who was coming or going. She put it back early in the morning.

*   *   *

She took her knitting, and her hands worked fast. Then her hands fell onto her knees again and there was nothing but waiting and the anguish of waiting.

There was no moon, but there were stars. A warm night which forecast summer nights. A fine night, and who were you under it?

First he had to leave the town. That's easy: at this time of night one doesn't meet anybody. And even if he did meet someone he could say he was going to smoke a cigarette on this fine night before going to bed. And his papers were in order: he was a conscientious employee who did his job and was well known in town. What's so strange about smoking a cigarette on such a fine night?

He took a lane which passed behind the wall of the gasworks. After the fences came the fields and his feet sank into the soft earth.

Pierre Levée was where the paths crossed: there was a large beech tree and no stones. Long ago there may have been a standing stone, a menhir,[3] or something like that, as Alice would say, who knew all the old stories and old names. He thought of Alice, of what he'd acquired since she had been his wife. And if she hadn't been his wife he might not have had the courage and faith to be here tonight: a man.

A shadow, two shadows, were glued to the trees. He went up to them: there was Big Paul, there was Alain. There was Louis, then Robert.

"René's expecting us over there. Have you got the machine guns? Have you got the sleeper screws?"

They said "Yes, yes," one after the other.

Why were they here tonight, all six of them, instead of being asleep in the dismal slumber of the little town?

There was Big Paul, walking ahead. He had once believed in the peaceful transformation of the earth, the disappearance of injustice, abundance, peace, joy; that you only had to stretch out your hand and talk of justice; that the rich would renounce their riches and share them. And then he gradually discovered that you only earn by toil. And that was why he was with those who knew what they wanted and wanted the means of what they wanted.

There was Paul. His wife Alice had taught him that man created history by his will and that his will of liberation continued, today as it had yesterday, through the history of every day, and that history isn't something you submit to; it's something you accomplish.

And there was Robert who was here because he wouldn't admit that his country could be conquered and do nothing to gain its independence. And that was why he sided with those who no longer expected help from elsewhere, and fought for the liberation of his country.

And there was Louis, the tanner. He was here to be together with the workers and peasants of the U.S.S.R., who had accomplished their liberation and knew what they were defending and why they died.

And there was Alain who wasn't seventeen yet, because he liked to be near the fighters, because he liked blows — giving them and if need be receiving them — because he liked courage, without even knowing its name.

And there was René walking in the distance, alone, along the track to meet them. René who was from the Public Assistance[4] and had never known his parents. He knew how hard the world was if you had no parents, and that working in a station was a success for him. "You see that anybody can do anything in our society." But he knew it was a lie and that there was a terrible handicap at the start which settled the future, and that this future should at last be settled justly.

And so these six men walked in silence on the empty earth under the naked sky, and because these six men were there together in an act of will and liberty, something had been changed in the history of men, something in the Europe bruised by the blows of jackboots, in the bleeding Europe without a face or a voice.

And because these six men were there, and others like them in France and other European countries, men who wouldn't yield, who refused to be dupes, who committed themselves entirely, something was changed, a step had been made which moved man from the abyss and put him closer to that other Man, the Man he would be tomorrow.

They got to the main road which cut the forest. They stopped a moment, listening to the noises — frogs croaked. Then the wind blew and the still, leafless branches waved. That squeak was one pine grating against another.

Above the noise of the sky and the forest they tried to hear the sound of men: the steps of a patrol, the imperceptible tinkle of a bicycle, the distant roar of a car. But there was nothing.

Then, rapidly, they crossed the road and assembled under the trees on the other side. A few yards on and there was the railroad. A kneeling shadow was already working on it. They went onto the ballast. And now, crouching or bent over the rails, they looked like odd gnomes curiously lit by electric lights.

Paul looked at his watch.

"Is it done?" he asked.

They replied in a whisper: "Yes, it's done."

Then they met again under the trees with their machine guns.

They heard the train in the distance. It had gathered speed since the station, and in a few more minutes it would be there.

They saw the engine heel over and the tender follow it in a crash of iron. The other cars stayed on the track. They saw frightened Germans get out of the cars.

And calmly the six men started shooting. With no more hatred than a surgeon.

With no more hatred.

★

Notes

1. *School certificate:* a primary school diploma.

2. *Chanson de Roland:* twelfth-century French epic of Charlemagne, his valient nephew Roland, and their battle against the Saracens in Spain.

3. *Menhir:* large upright stone of a type that can be seen in Brittany today and which was perhaps linked to a Druid cult.

4. *Public Assistance:* governmental department for the assistance of the needy.

★ ★ ★ ★

AUTHOR: *Ho Ku-Yen (He Guyan) is the Chinese author of this story set in 1955 during the Korean War. Because of the relationship between the Chinese governmen.. and intellectuals, little information is available concerning the author and his other writings.*

SETTING: *The Chinese supported the Koreans in the Korean War (1950–1953) against United Nations forces led by General Douglas MacArthur. China could not afford to let Korea fight on its own against the imperialist aggressors, lest the aggressors attack China next. China, impoverished after World War II and its own civil war, could ill-afford a war on its periphery either in terms of men or money. Only by massive sacrifice was it able to confront the major powers with some success. One of China's amazing accomplishments was the development and maintenance of supply arteries, which provided food and munitions to troops at the front, in spite of constant bombardment from U.S. aircraft.*

Some of the Chinese literature inspired by this feat was undoubtedly used as propaganda. That fact does not detract from the quality and universal nature of this particular story. Ostensibly, it is a tale about the heroism and sacrifice of two Chinese soldier-heroes, but it is also a universal war story of lasting friendship between men doing their duty in a conflict neither of their understanding nor of their making.

Maple Leaves

Ho Ku-Yen

One autumn evening, as the sun was reddening the western sky, Hu Wenfa walked briskly out of the gully in which he was billeted. He was a driver in the Second Transport Company. He stuffed his last steamed bread roll into his mouth and brushed the dirt and crumbs off his uniform with his greasy hands as he walked to the shelters where the trucks were kept.

The shelters were in a wood to his right. Of the dozen or so that had been dug along the foot of a hill all were now empty except the one in which Hu Wenfa's new GAZ truck squatted like a great dark green beast

Translated by W.J.F. Jenner and Gladys Yang. Copyright Oxford University Press 1970. Reprinted from *Modern Chinese Stories* edited by W.J.F. Jenner (1970) by permission of Oxford University Press.

with its shoulders hunched. Outside the shelter Hu Wenfa's assistant Wang Zhixiu was stretched out snoring happily on his greatcoat, which was by now dirt-brown right through to the fleece lining.

Hu Wenfa smiled at the sight, kicked him gently on the leg, and said, "Wake up, we're going."

Wang Zhixiu scrambled to his feet, looking blearily at Hu Wenfa. Then without a word he took the bucket that was beside him and went down to the river to fetch some water. Hu Wenfa opened the bonnet, inspected the engine closely, and oiled it. It was only when they were both sitting in the cab that Wang Zhixiu asked, as if he had only just been woken up, "What's it this time?"

"Taking ammo from divisional stores to the strongpoint on Height Four One Two."

"But haven't three trucks gone already?"

"Yes. Three went, but planes got two of them on the way. I don't know how the hell it happened. How could two grown men let their trucks be hit by a ruddy plane? They're still waiting for the ammunition on Height Four One Two. We've got a tough one today, young Wang. We've got to cross some air-strafed interdiction zones and another that's under artillery fire. If a plane gets us tonight our record of thirty-five thousand kilometres of safe driving will be snatched from under our noses."

"We won't let it happen."

"I hope not. Let's get one thing clear from the word go — no sleep for you this evening."

Young Wang yawned as if to suggest that Hu Wenfa was wasting his breath saying anything so obvious and replied, "Start her up."

The motor roared into life. Long after the truck had bumped its way up to the military road Hu Wenfa kept looking round to see if Wang Zhixiu had gone to sleep.

Wang Zhixiu was an odd sort of bloke. Although he was only just twenty there were already two deep furrows in his brown forehead. He was quiet, unflappable, and always seemed to have the hint of a smile on his face. His eyesight was good and he worked with a will. The only thing wrong with him was that he was such a glutton for sleep. It made no difference where he was: whenever he had a moment to spare he would spread his greatcoat out on the ground and lie down on it. Within two minutes he would be right out, and neither wind nor rain could wake him.

There were two things that could shake him out of this habit. One was when something had gone wrong with the truck. This would fill him with so much energy that even the company commander or the political instructor would be wasting their breath telling him to go to sleep. His soft, warm greatcoat might have turned into a bed of nails as he climbed over the truck or lay underneath to repair it. If it was a minor fault he might take a nap when he had put it right; but if there was something seriously wrong he would work at it all day through till the truck had to be moving again at night. He could not be bothered to eat properly on the job. He would ask someone to fetch him a couple of steamed rolls, and if there were none of those to be had, he would wash a biscuit down with a mug of hot water. He never let Hu Wenfa have anything to do with day-time repairs because he felt that the driver needed sleep more than his mate did. He only asked Hu Wenfa's advice when the problem was one he could not cope with himself.

The other thing that could stop him from sleeping was an urgent assignment like today's. Hu Wenfa need not have worried on that score. When they came across enemy aircraft at night they drove without lights under a blanket of darkness. Wang Zhixiu would rock to and fro breathing lightly as he sat beside Hu Wenfa as if he were asleep, but at any moment he might suddenly shout, "Stop! Bomb crater!" then jump down from the truck to see how deep it was and whether it was possible to go round it. If it was not possible he would take his shovel from the truck without a word. Within ten minutes the hole would have been skillfully filled.

Hu Wenfa's character was the opposite of Wang Zhixiu's. He was an alert and active man of inexhaustible energy who wanted to get on with any job he was doing as quickly as possible, and was never happy when driving at less than sixty kilometres an hour. This often made Wang argue with him. Once when they had been crossing a zone under artillery fire Hu had wanted to go flat out, but Wang had been dead set against it. Instead of going into all the details he just said slowly, "However fast you drive you aren't going to be able to race the shells."

"What do you suggest then?" Hu had asked him.

"I'm all in favour of going fast along decent roads, but the ground in front of us here is honeycombed with craters. If you drive like a madman a crash will be enough to write off the lorry even if we dodge the shells."

On Wang's advice Hu had taken it quietly. All that happened to them was that shrapnel tore some holes in the truck's canopy.

Another time they had to cross a river in winter when the water, covered in a thin sheet of ice, was higher than the surface of the bridge.[1] The wooden bridge itself, about a kilometre long, was invisible; all that could be seen of it were a few wooden posts. Hu Wenfa's idea was to go straight along the line of the posts, reckoning that as the rivers were never flooded in winter the bridge was bound to be there under the ice. Wang Zhixiu would have nothing of it. After an argument he jumped down from the truck. "A truck costs a fortune," he said, "and we can't fool about with it. I'm going to make sure." He took off his cotton-padded trousers, socks, and boots, then leapt into the river. Although lumps of ice kept bumping noisily into him he said nothing as he felt his way across along the posts and confirmed that the bridge really could be crossed. His teeth were still chattering audibly when he came back and climbed into the cab. When Hu Wenfa advised him to put his greatcoat back on at once he replied in a matter-of-fact way, "It's nothing to what our mates have to put up with at the front."

Wang Zhixiu was a meticulous but slow worker. Hu Wenfa was always pulling his leg about the way he took his time, to which Wang would coolly reply that by taking their time the Chinese People's Volunteers would wear the Americans out.

The difference between the driver and his mate was like that between a straight and hard *Cunninghamia* tree and a tough, flexible mountain creeper. Hu Wenfa had not liked working with Wang Zhixiu at all to begin with, but by now he felt he would never find a better Number Two.

Wang's life was very simple, and seemed to consist of nothing other than driving, going to classes, eating, and sleeping. He was not interested in singing, dancing, or playing cards, and as far as Hu Wenfa could see there were only two things of which he was really fond. One was a coloured picture of Chairman Mao he had bought at a stationer's when he went back to Andong (on the Chinese side of the Korean frontier) three months earlier. As Hu liked it too he let him paste it up in the right-hand corner of the cab. The other thing Wang liked was the maple leaf of the Korean autumn. Before every journey he would break off a spray of the red leaves to put in the cab by the picture of Chairman Mao, and when they withered he would replace them with fresh ones. Hu Wenfa, with the veteran truck-driver's passion for tidiness, liked to keep his cab as neat as a bridal chamber. Once he removed the leaves and threw them out when Wang was not around, but a new spray was there when they set out the next day. "What do you want those mucky leaves in the truck for?" he asked. "They get in the way." "No they don't," replied Wang. "I didn't put them in your steering wheel."

"You're going cissy with all your leaves and flowers."

"Don't you like them then?" asked Wang with a grin.

"No."

"You will soon enough."

"Never. They smell bad and they look worse."

Putting the leaves to his nose Wang replied. "I suppose you've never been to my province, Jehol?"

"No."

"Our maple forests cover mountains and plains. You should see them in autumn. Whole mountains turn red — from light red to purple and crimson. The most beautiful flowers in the world aren't a patch on them. When I joined the army the head of our engineering team took me to the top of a hill and showed me where the construction site had been measured out below. 'When you come back from Korea after victory,' he said to me, 'a big factory will have been built there. By then you won't be able to recognize your own front door.' I heard that they'd started work on it soon after I joined up. It's a great thing to have a factory built, but I wish I'd remembered to tell him not to cut the maples down."

"We're industrializing now," interrupted Hu Wenfa, "so of course trees must be cut down when necessary."

"The fewer the better. If they're really in the way they can be moved and replanted. It would be very good to have a line of maples round the outside of the factory."

When the first star began to shimmer in the sky a lorry loaded with ammunition was roaring south. It was too dark for its number-plate to be readable, but a spray of red maple leaves danced like a flame behind the ammunition lorry's windscreen when another truck coming towards it flashed its headlights.

Wang was feeling sleepy again. "We haven't had a single plane so far," he said with a gigantic yawn. "I hope it's all going to be as peaceful as the last few miles."

"Not a chance. The Yanks won't be that obliging. Where are we coming to now?"

"We're almost at Jiuhuali."

"We'll have to be careful. This is where it begins."

"Stop and let me climb on top. I can see a lot farther from up there."

At just the moment when the truck stopped one, two and then a dozen flares lit up in an S-shaped pattern in front of them, turning the sky a lurid white. The truck's shadow was picked out clearly in the road. "Damn," said Hu furiously. "Talk of the devil. You're too bloody clever."

"Let's go then."

"O.K."

Hu slammed the cab door shut and shouted, "Hold tight, Wang." The truck shot forward like a hurricane. Knowing that the enemy aircraft was circling above him Hu could not leave his lights on all the time. But there was the danger of driving into a bomb crater. He used all his skill as he shot forward, flashing his lights on obstacles for about as long as it takes to blink. They were out again before the pilot had time to mark his position. Hu Wenfa had played blind-man's bluff with enemy aircraft more often than he could remember, and he had always won.

Young Wang was clinging to the top of the truck and probing into the night with his eyes as if they were searchlights. One or two kilometres later, when they were almost through the area lit by flares, he suddenly heard a grating roar. He turned and saw the black form of an aircraft diving towards them under the flares. Instinctively he banged the top of the cab three times and shouted, "Stop!" As the brakes slammed on, a stream of blue tracer shells exploded and sent sparks dancing on the road two or three yards in front of the truck. The aircraft could not come back straight away, so after this strafing run the lorry raced forward even faster than before. Wang felt his stomach being all but shaken right out of him as he clung to the sides of the truck, his eyes fixed on the sky. The aircraft was soon diving on them again, coming in lower and faster this time. Wang thumped the cab three times again to tell Hu to stop. Instead Hu turned his lights on and drove flat out for several dozen yards. Then the lights went out again as the truck made a fast right-hand turn off the road and into a wood. Wang heard three explosions behind him and saw that thick smoke was blotting out the stars. Blue streaks were bouncing off the road.

Hu Wenfa stopped the truck under a tall tree, jumped down from the cab, blew his nose hard, and said, "Blast! It's like a toad jumping on your foot — it gives you a scare even though it doesn't bite you."

"Is the truck O.K.?" asked Wang, scrambling down from the top.

"Yes."

"When you did that crash turn I thought it was because you couldn't stop."

"If you try the same trick twice you give the game away. The sod would have got me if I'd done it again."

Wang was full of admiration for Hu Wenfa as he remembered where the three rockets had just exploded. "That's another tip I've picked up from you," he said. "You know your stuff all right."

As the aircraft had now lost its target it dropped more flares. The tree just covered the truck. Wang looked at the sky that was a pale yellow in their glare and said, "The bloody plane's still hanging about." Hu pulled his greatcoat over his head, lit a cigarette, took a deep drag, exhaled and replied, "He's welcome to fly round in circles up there. The more of their fuel they burn the better."

Ten minutes or so later the sound of its engine faded away in the sky. The last flare slowly burned itself out and dropped as a glowing red spark. They climbed back into the cab and drove back to the road. Some half a dozen kilometres later a large mountain loomed up in front of them, and on the other side of it were flashes like sheet lightning. Hu stopped the engine and leaned out of the truck to listen. There was an unbroken roar of exploding shells. "We'll have to be careful on the way up that: it's the King of Hell's Nose. The road's narrow, the mountain's high, and it's under permanent shelling. You can't use your headlights or drive fast. Being hit by a shell isn't worth worrying about, but if we go into a ravine that'll be our lot."

"Start the engine. They won't be able to get us." Wang opened the side window of the cab and put his head and arms outside to watch the narrow, winding road that the truck was climbing. Wang's clipped shouts could be heard clearly over the shells and the engine: "Left . . . further left . . . that's it . . . straight ahead . . . slower . . . slower, shell hole . . . right. . . ."

The truck kept stopping for Wang to jump out, grab his shovel, and walk ahead to find which way they could go. After countless stops and bends they were almost at the top. Just when they were going to follow the hairpin bends down the southern side there was a great flash and what sounded like a roll of thunder as a huge volley of shells exploded on the slope. Stones and branches showered on the truck. They were choked by the shell smoke that swept into the cab. Hu Wenfa cursed furiously and stopped the engine. Wang hesitated for a moment, quietly jumped out, and strode southwards through the smoke. It was two or three minutes before he came back. "What's it like?" Hu Wenfa asked.

"The road surface has been blown to bits. I think we can get across if we take it a bit faster. Whatever you do, don't stop. Let's go."

Wang leant out and shouted as he had before: "Left . . . left . . . that's it . . . careful . . . right . . . straight ahead."

The lorry rocked from side to side in the shellfire like a small boat in a stormy sea. At times the cab was tilted at such an angle that they fell out of their seats, and Hu only righted the truck with a tremendous effort. As Hu clung to the steering wheel his hands ran with sweat, and he clenched his teeth till they hurt. On either side were cliffs and deep ravines, and at any moment a whole cluster of shells might explode beside him. Not that he was worrying about this; the one thought in his mind was to follow Wang's instructions and press on without stopping.

"Left . . . left . . . ," Wang was shouting hoarsely. "Mind the crater . . . slower . . . slower . . . right. . . ."

As soon as the last word was out of his mouth flames leapt up all around the truck with powerful shock-waves that almost lifted it clear off the road. Wang was thrown back into his seat. Hu grabbed his arm with one hand and asked, "Are you all right, Wang?"

"Don't stop. Never mind about me. Keep going." Wang dragged himself up and seized hold of the window. "Faster," he shouted, louder than ever. "Left . . . left . . . that's it . . . carry on . . . right, shell hole. . . ."

The lorry went down the southern slope of the mountain round the hairpin bends. There was a continual explosion of shells on the road and the mountainside that showered the truck with a hail of stones and shrapnel. All Hu could hear was Wang's voice shouting, "Left . . . turn right . . . carry on . . ." until they drove into a deep gully. Hu breathed a sign of relief. "We're through," he said. Then he turned to Wang and added, "But for your sharp eyes we'd have ended up in a ravine tonight."

They drove along the gully for nearly a mile until somebody appeared from behind a boulder, stopped the lorry and asked, "Are you the ammunition truck?"

Hu Wenfa jumped down from the cab and said, "Yes. Are you the Second Detachment of the Zhenjiang unit?"

Before the other man had time to reply a group of men came out of another gully saying softly to each other, "Hurry, the ammo's here." They were all round the lorry in a moment.

"Have you come to help unload the truck?" Hu asked one of them who was wearing a greatcoat.

"No. We've come to collect the ammunition."

"Blimey," interrupted another soldier, "you really had us worried. If you'd been any longer we'd have run right out. Got any grenades?"

"Plenty."

"Do we need them! We've been hard at it ever since sunset. Let's get the stuff unloaded."

Hu Wenfa could hear a continuous rumble of hand-grenades going off almost as fast as machine-guns on the other side of a nearby mountain. "Wang," he shouted in his excitement, "come and help unload."

The others were bustling on and around the lorry. With so many men on the job the load was soon off. Because he had been sweating heavily Hu was very thirsty, so he went into a dug-out with the ammunition detail for a drink of water. Thinking that Wang must be thirsty too after shouting so many instructions on the journey he filled a water-bottle for him. When he was almost back at the truck he called Wang a couple of times but nothing moved. He looked into the cab and saw Wang still slumped against the window with one arm dangling and the other cradling his head. Hu shook him by the shoulder. "Hey, wake up. Time to turn round and go back."

Wang still did not move.

Hu Wenfa put his hand out to feel his head and was horrified. He jumped into the cab, groped for the torch, and saw in its light that Wang's face was the colour of earth. There was no light in his half-closed eyes. One of Wang's hands was clutching the clothes on his chest. Blood was dripping from his wrist down to his trousers and the seat.

Hu Wenfa lifted him up and poured a little warm water into his mouth. He shouted loudly at him a couple of times. It was a very long time before he heard the familiar voice murmuring, "Hu. . . . We got through. . . . I won't be going back with you. . . . Be very careful . . . in the interdiction zones. . . . Watch the road. . . . Whatever you do . . . don't stop in the interdiction zones. . . ."

Wang was growing heavier and heavier. Hu lifted up his head and looked through the windscreen at the lightning-like flashes from the other side of the black mountain in the distance and the red fireballs climbing into the sky. "Open your eyes again and look, Wang," he was thinking. "Our boys are going to wipe them out." As he brushed against Wang's icy cold hand his heart contracted and something warm welled up in his throat. He buried his head in Wang's chest and wept.

After Wang's death Hu Wenfa became rather quiet. He rarely rocked his head and whistled as he had before, and he was often seen lost in thought in front of the lorry. The political instructor and his comrades all felt sympathy and concern for him. They too were all saddened by Wang's sacrifice. Some of them even said anxiously when Hu Wenfa was not in earshot that they doubted whether he would finish his 35,000 kilometres of safe driving now that he had lost so good a mate.

In the tense days of that autumn Hu Wenfa's truck drove as usual along roads knee-deep in mud. He beat 42,000 kilometres before 7 November. The whole company held a meeting to celebrate and they expected that this would certainly cheer him up. He was as gloomy as ever. Even he could not have explained what was on his mind. As the truck drove through the Korean mountains pock-marked with craters, maple woods would flash past the windows. Every time he saw the rows of maples on some mountain pass he would think of his dead friend. Wang had been like a single maple tree on the plains of China. Compared to the vast forests it was next to nothing, but it was just such trees that made up the forests. Although maples did not have the scent of flowers they were more beautiful than any flower on earth, particularly when the cold winds of autumn bit through to the bone after the heavy frosts had begun.

His new mate had not been in the company long before he discovered that his teacher, Hu Wenfa, had the strange habit of putting a spray of maple leaves beside the picture of Chairman Mao in the corner of the cab. Once the truck started, the pink, crimson, and purple leaves would rustle and dance. In the light of an oncoming headlight they were like flames.

★

Note

1. Bridges were often built below the surface of rivers during the Korean War to hide them from U.S. aircraft.

★ ★ ★ ★

AUTHOR: *Hwang Sunwon (1915-), a professor at Kyonghui University in Seoul, received his early training at Waseda University in Japan. Although his first publication in 1934 was of verse, his subsequent writing has been short stories and novels. A master of the modern short story, he captures the human spirit with his use of natural imagery and the delicate rhythm of his prose. He has been a member of the Korean Academy of Arts since 1957.*

SETTING: *After the Korean War (1950–1953), the Koreans faced the problem of sorting out the "good guys" (those loyal to the South Korean government) and the "bad guys" (those who had supported the North Koreans: Communists and their sympathizers). Communities, families, and friends were torn apart; everyone was suspicious of everyone else – especially those who lived in villages close to the 38th Parallel.*

Cranes

Hwang Sunwon

The northern village lay snug beneath the high, bright autumn sky, near the border at the Thirty-eighth Parallel. White gourds lay one against the other on the dirt floor of an empty farmhouse. Any village elders who passed by extinguished their bamboo pipes first, and the children, too, turned back some distance off. Their faces were marked with fear.

As a whole, the village showed little damage from the war, but it still did not seem like the same village Songsam had known as a boy.

At the foot of a chestnut grove on the hill behind the village he stopped and climbed a chestnut tree. Somewhere far back in his mind he heard the old man with a wen shout, "You bad boy, climbing up my chestnut tree again!"

The old man must have passed away, for he was not among the few village elders Songsam had met. Holding onto the trunk of the tree, Songsam gazed up at the blue sky for a time. Some chestnuts fell to the

Translated by Peter H. Lee. "Cranes" originally appeared in *Modern Korean Literature: An Anthology*, compiled and edited by Peter H. Lee (Honolulu, Hawaii: Univ. of Hawaii Press, 1990). Reprinted by permission of the publisher.

ground as the dry clusters opened of their own accord.

A young man stood, his hands bound, before a farmhouse that had been converted into a Public Peace Police office. He seemed to be a stranger, so Songsam went up for a closer look. He was stunned: this young man was none other than his boyhood playmate, Tokchae.

Songsam asked the police officer who had come with him from Ch'ont'ae for an explanation. The prisoner was the vice-chairman of the Farmers' Communist League and had just been flushed out of hiding in his own house, Songsam learned.

Songsam sat down on the dirt floor and lit a cigarette.

Tokchae was to be escorted to Ch'ongdan by one of the peace police.

After a time, Songsam lit a new cigarette from the first and stood up.

"I'll take him with me."

Tokchae averted his face and refused to look at Songsam. The two left the village.

Songsam went on smoking, but the tobacco had no flavor. He just kept drawing the smoke in and blowing it out. Then suddenly he thought that Tokchae, too, must want a puff. He thought of the days when they had shared dried gourd leaves behind sheltering walls, hidden from the adults' view. But today, how could he offer a cigarette to a fellow like this?

Once, when they were small, he went with Tokchae to steal some chestnuts from the old man with the wen. It was Songsam's turn to climb the tree. Suddenly the old man began shouting. Songsam slipped and fell to the ground. He got chestnut burrs all over his bottom, but he kept on running. Only when the two had reached a safe place where the old man could not overtake them did Songsam turn his bottom to Tokchae. The burrs hurt so much as they were plucked out that Songsam could not keep tears from welling up in his eyes. Tokchae produced a fistful of chestnuts from his pocket and thrust them into Songsam's. . . . Songsam threw away the cigarette he had just lit, and then made up his mind not to light another while he was escorting Tokchae.

They reached the pass at the hill where he and Tokchae had cut fodder for the cows until Songsam had to move to a spot near Ch'ont'ae, south of the Thirty-eighth Parallel, two years before the liberation.

Songsam felt a sudden surge of anger in spite of himself and shouted, "So how many have you killed?"

For the first time, Tokchae cast a quick glance at him and then looked away.

"You! How many have you killed?" he asked again.

Tokchae looked at him again and glared. The glare grew intense, and his mouth twitched.

"So you managed to kill quite a few, eh?" Songsam felt his mind clearing itself, as if some obstruction had been removed. "If you were vice-chairman of the Communist League, why didn't you run? You must have been lying low with a secret mission."

Tokchae did not reply.

"Speak up. What was your mission?"

Tokchae kept walking. Tokchae was hiding something, Songsam thought. He wanted to take a good look at him, but Tokchae kept his face averted.

Fingering the revolver at his side, Songsam went on: "There's no need to make excuses. You're going to be shot anyway. Why don't you tell the truth here and now?"

"I'm not going to make any excuses. They made me vice-chairman of the League because I was a hardworking farmer, and one of the poorest. If that's a capital offense, so be it. I'm still what I used to be — the only thing I'm good at is tilling the soil." After a short pause, he added, "My old man is bedridden at home. He's been ill almost half a year." Tokchae's father was a widower, a poor, hardworking farmer who lived only for his son. Seven years ago his back had given out, and he had contracted a skin disease.

"Are you married?"

"Yes," Tokchae replied after a time.

"To whom?"

"Shorty."

"To Shorty?" How interesting! A woman so small and plump that she knew the earth's vastness, but not the sky's height. Such a cold fish! He and Tokchae had teased her and made her cry. And Tokchae had married her!

"How many kids?"

"The first is arriving this fall, she says."

Songsam had difficulty swallowing a laugh that he was about to let burst forth in spite of himself. Although he had asked how many children Tokchae had, he could not help wanting to break out laughing at the thought of the wife sitting there with her huge stomach, one span around. But he realized that this was no time for joking.

"Anyway, it's strange you didn't run away."

"I tried to escape. They said that once the South invaded, not a man would be spared. So all of us between seventeen and forty were taken to the North. I thought of evacuating, even if I had to carry my father on my back. But Father said no. How could we farmers leave the land behind when the crops were ready for harvesting? He grew old on that farm depending on me as the prop and mainstay of the family. I wanted to be with him in his last moments so I could close his eyes with my own hand. Besides, where can farmers like us go, when all we know how to do is live on the land?"

Songsam had had to flee the previous June. At night he had broken the news privately to his father. But his father had said the same thing: Where could a farmer go, leaving all the chores behind? So Songsam had left alone. Roaming about the strange streets and villages in the South, Songsam had been haunted by thoughts of his old parents and the young children, who had been left with all the chores. Fortunately, his family had been safe then, as it was now.

They had crossed over a hill. This time Songsam walked with his face averted. The autumn sun was hot on his forehead. This was an ideal day for the harvest, he thought.

When they reached the foot of the hill, Songsam gradually came to a halt. In the middle of a field he spied a group of cranes that resembled men in white, all bent over. This had been the demilitarized zone along the Thirty-eighth Parallel. The cranes were still living here, as before, though all the people were gone.

Once, when Songsam and Tokchae were about twelve, they had set a trap here, without anybody else knowing, and caught a crane, a Tanjong crane. They had tied the crane up, even binding its wings, and paid it daily visits, patting its neck and riding on its back. Then one day they overheard the neighbors whispering: someone had come from Seoul with a permit from the governor-general's office to catch cranes as some kind of specimens. Then and there the two boys had dashed off to the field. That they would be found out and punished had no longer mattered; all they cared about was the fate of their crane. Without a moment's delay, still out of breath from running, they untied the crane's feet and wings, but the bird could hardly walk. It must have been weak from having been bound.

The two held the crane up. Then, suddenly, they heard a gunshot. The crane fluttered its wings once or twice and then sank back to the ground.

The boys thought their crane had been shot. But the next moment, as another crane from a nearby bush fluttered its wings, the boys' crane stretched its long neck, gave out a whoop, and disappeared into the sky. For a long while the two boys could not tear their eyes away from the blue sky into which their crane had soared.

"Hey, why don't we stop here for a crane hunt?" Songsam said suddenly.

Tokchae was dumbfounded.

"I'll make a trap with this rope; you flush a crane over here."

Songsam had untied Tokchae's hands and was already crawling through the weeds.

Tokchae's face whitened. "You're sure to be shot anyway" — these words flashed through his mind. Any instant a bullet would come flying from Songsam's direction, Tokchae thought.

Some paces away, Songsam quickly turned toward him.

"Hey, how come you're standing there like a dummy? Go flush a crane!"

Only then did Tokchae understand. He began crawling through the weeds.

A pair of Tanjong cranes soared high into the clear blue autumn sky, flapping their huge wings.

★

★ ★ ★ ★

AUTHOR: *Hassan Manto Saadat is a Muslim writer from Pakistan who writes with sensitivity and insight about the Kashmiri War between India and Pakistan.*

SETTING: *The Indian Civil War of 1947-1948 and the conflict over Kashmir resulted in more than one million deaths and five and a half million refugees. Many of the men on the front lines had fought together as soldiers under the British in the British Indian Army. They had been particularly effective fighting Germany and Italy during World War II. They returned to India to face the turmoil of newly acquired independence, hatred between Hindu and Muslim, and the subsequent partition of India and Pakistan. After partition, conflict between India and Pakistan was renewed — ostensibly over which country claimed Kashmir. Men who had once fought side by side against the Germans now were on opposite sides.*

The Last Salute

Hassan Manto Saadat

This Kashmir war was a very odd affair. Subedar Rab Nawaz often felt as if his brain had turned into a rifle with a faulty safety catch.

He had fought with distinction on many major fronts in the Second World War. He was respected by both his seniors and juniors because of his intelligence and valour. He was always given the most difficult and dangerous assignments and he had never failed the trust placed in him.

But he had never been in a war like this one. He had come to it full of enthusiasm and with the itch to fight and liquidate the enemy. However, the first encounter had shown that the men arrayed against them on the other side were mostly old friends and comrades with whom he had fought in the old British Indian army against the Germans and the Italians. The friends of yesterday had been transformed into the enemies of today.

At times, the whole thing felt like a dream to Subedar Rab Nawaz. He could remember the day the Second World War was declared. He had

Translated by Khalid Hasan. "The Last Salute" originally appeared in *Kingdom's End and Other Stories*, edited by Khalis Hasan (New York: Verso Schocken Books, 1987). Reprinted by permission of the publisher.

enlisted immediately. They had been given some basic training and then packed off to the front. He had been moved from one theatre of war to another and, one day, the war had ended. Then had come Pakistan and the new war he was now fighting. So much had happened in these last few years at such breakneck speed. Often it made no sense at all. Those who had planned and executed these great events had perhaps deliberately maintained a dizzying pace so that the participants should get no time to think. How else could one explain one revolution followed by another and then another?

One thing Subedar Rab Nawaz could understand. They were fighting this war to win Kashmir. Why did they want to win Kashmir? Because it was crucial to Pakistan's security and survival. However, sometimes when he sat behind a gun emplacement and caught sight of a familiar face on the other side, for a moment he forgot why they were fighting. He forgot why he was carrying a gun and killing people. At such times, he would remind himself that he was not fighting to win medals or earn a salary, but to secure the survival of his country.

This was his country before the establishment of Pakistan and it was his country now. This was his land. But now he was fighting against men who were his countrymen until only the other day. Men who had grown up in the same village, whose families had been known to his family for generations. These men had now been turned into citizens of a country to which they were complete strangers. They had been told: we are placing a gun in your hands so that you can go and fight for a country which you have yet to know, where you do not even have a roof over your head, where even the air and water are strange to you. Go and fight for it against Pakistan, the land where you were born and grew up.

Rab Nawaz would think of those Muslim soldiers who had moved to Pakistan, leaving their ancestral homes behind, and come to this new country with empty hands. They had been given nothing, except the guns that had been put in their hands. The same guns they had always used, the same make, the same bore, guns to fight their new enemy with.

Before the partition of the country, they used to fight one common enemy who was not really their enemy perhaps but whom they had accepted as their enemy for the sake of employment and rewards and medals. Formerly, all of them were Indian soldiers, but now some were Indian and others were Pakistani soldiers. Rab Nawaz could not unravel this puzzle. And when he thought about Kashmir, he became even more confused. Were the Pakistani soldiers fighting for Kashmir or for the Muslims of Kashmir? If they were being asked to fight in defence of the

Muslims of Kashmir, why had they not been asked to fight for the Muslims of the princely states of Junagarh and Hyderabad? And if this was an Islamic war, then why were other Muslim countries of the world not fighting shoulder to shoulder with them?

Rab Nawaz had finally come to the conclusion that such intricate and subtle matters were beyond the comprehension of a simple soldier. A soldier should be thick in the head. Only the thick-headed made good soldiers, but despite this resolution, he couldn't help wondering sometimes about the war he was now in.

The fighting in what was called the Titwal sector was spread across the Kishan Ganga river and along the road which led from Muzaffarabad to Kiran. It was a strange war. Often at night, instead of gunfire, one heard abuse being exchanged in loud voices.

One late evening, while Subedar Rab Nawaz was preparing his platoon for a foray into enemy territory, he heard loud voices from across the hill the enemy was supposed to be on. He could not believe his ears. There was loud laughter followed by abuse. "Pig's trotters," he murmured, "what on earth is going on?"

One of his men returned the abuse in as loud a voice as he could muster, then complained to him, "Subedar sahib, they are abusing us again, the motherfuckers."

Rab Nawaz's first instinct was to join the slanging match, but he thought better of it. The men fell silent also, following his example. However, after a while, the torrent of abuse from the other side became so intolerable that his men lost control and began to match abuse with abuse. He ordered them a couple of times to keep quiet, but did not insist because, frankly, it was difficult for a human being not to react violently.

They couldn't, of course, see the enemy at night, and hardly did so during the day because of the hilly country which provided perfect cover. All they heard was abuse which echoed across the hills and valleys and then evaporated in the air.

Some of the hills were barren, while others were covered with tall pine trees. It was very difficult terrain. Subedar Rab Nawaz's platoon was on a bare, treeless hill which provided no cover. His men were itching to go into attack to avenge the abuse which had been hurled at them without respite for several weeks. An attack was planned and executed with success, though they lost two men and suffered four injuries. The enemy lost three and abandoned the position, leaving behind food and provisions.

Subedar Rab Nawaz and his men were sorry they had not been able to capture an enemy soldier. They could then have avenged the abuse face to face. However, they had captured an important and difficult feature. Rab Nawaz relayed the news of the victory to his commander, Major Aslam, and was commended for gallantry.

On top of most of the hills, one found ponds. There was a large one on the hill they had captured. The water was clear and sweet, and although it was cold, they took off their clothes and jumped in. Suddenly, they heard firing. They jumped out of the pond and hit the ground — naked. Subedar Rab Nawaz crawled towards his binoculars, picked them up and surveyed the area carefully. He could see no one. There was more firing. This time he was able to determine its origin. It was coming from a small hill, lying a few hundred feet below their perch. He ordered his men to open up.

The enemy troops did not have very good cover and Rab Nawaz was confident they could not stay there much longer. The moment they decided to move, they would come in direct range of their guns. Sporadic firing kept getting exchanged. Finally, Rab Nawaz ordered that no more ammunition should be wasted. They should just wait for the enemy to break cover. Then he looked at his still naked body and murmured, "Pig's trotters. Man does look silly without clothes."

For two whole days, this game continued. Occasional fire was exchanged, but the enemy had obviously decided to lie low. Then suddenly the temperature dropped several degrees. To keep his men warm, Subedar Rab Nawaz ordered that the tea-kettle should be kept on the boil all the time. It was like an unending tea party.

On the third day — it was unbearably cold — the soldier on the lookout reported that some movement could be detected around the enemy position. Subedar Rab Nawaz looked through his binoculars. Yes, something was going on. Rab Nawaz raised his rifle and fired. Someone called his name, or so he thought. It echoed through the valley. "Pig's trotters," Rab Nawaz shouted, "what do you want?"

The distance that separated their two positions was not great. The voice came back. "Don't hurl abuse, brother."

Rab Nawaz looked at his men. The word brother seemed to hang in the air. He raised his hands to his mouth and shouted, "Brother! There are no brothers here, only your mother's lovers."

"Rab Nawaz," the voice shouted.

He trembled. The words reverberated around the hills and then faded into the atmosphere.

"Pig's trotters," he whispered, "who was that?"

He knew that the troops in the Titwal sector were mostly from the old 6/9 Jat Regiment, his own regiment. But who was this joker shouting his name? He had many friends in the Regiment, and some enemies too. But who was this man who had called him brother?

Rab Nawaz looked through his binoculars again, but could see nothing. He shouted, "Who was that? This is Rab Nawaz. Rab Nawaz. Rab Nawaz."

"It is me . . . Ram Singh," the same voice answered.

Rab Nawaz nearly jumped. "Ram Singh, oh Ram Singha, Ram Singha, you pig's trotters."

"Shut your trap, you potter's ass," came the reply.

Rab Nawaz looked at his men, who appeared startled at this strange exchange in the middle of battle. "He's talking rot, pig's trotters." Then he shouted, "You slaughtered swine, watch your tongue."

Ram Singh began to laugh. Rab Nawaz could not contain himself either. His men watched him in silence.

"Look, my friend, we want to drink tea," Ram Singh said.

"Go ahead then. Have a good time," Rab Nawaz replied.

"We can't. The tea things are lying elsewhere."

"Where's elsewhere?"

"Let me put it this way. If we tried to get them, you could blow us to bits. We'd have to break cover."

"So what do you want, pig's trotters?" Rab Nawaz laughed.

"That you hold your fire until we get our things."

"Go ahead," Rab Nawaz said.

"You will blow us up, you potter's ass," Ram Singh shouted.

"Shut your mouth, you crawly Sikh tortoise," Rab Nawaz said.

"Take an oath on something that you won't open fire."

"On what?"

"Anything you like."

Rab Nawaz laughed, "You have my word. Now go get your things."

Nothing happened for a few minutes. One of the men was watching the small hill through his binoculars. He pointed at his gun and asked Rab Nawaz in gestures if he should open fire. "No, no, no shooting," Rab Nawaz said.

Suddenly, a man darted forward, running low towards some bushes. A few minutes later he ran back, carrying an armful of things. Then he disappeared. Rab Nawaz picked up his rifle and fired. "Thank you," Ram Singh's voice came.

"No mention," Rab Nawaz answered. "OK, boys, let's give the buggers one round."

More by way of entertainment than war, this exchange of fire continued for some time. Rab Nawaz could see smoke going up in a thin blue spiral where the enemy was. "Is your tea ready, Ram Singha?" he shouted.

"Not yet, you potter's ass."

Rab Nawaz was a potter by caste and any reference to his origins always enraged him. Ram Singh was the one person who could get away with calling him a potter's ass. They had grown up together in the same village in the Punjab. They were the same age, had gone to the same primary school, and their fathers had been childhood friends. They had joined the army the same day. In the last war, they had fought together on the same fronts.

"Pig's trotters," Rab Nawaz said to his men, "he never gives up, that one. Shut up, lice-infested donkey Ram Singha," he shouted.

He saw a man stand up. Rab Nawaz raised his rifle and fired in his direction. He heard a scream. He looked through his binoculars. It was Ram Singh. He was doubled up, holding his stomach. Then he fell to the ground.

Rab Nawaz shouted, "Ram Singh" and stood up. There was rapid gunfire from the other side. One bullet brushed past his left arm. He fell to the ground. Some enemy soldiers, taking advantage of this confusion, began to run across open ground to securer positions. Rab Nawaz ordered his platoon to attack the hill. Three were killed, but the others managed to capture the position with Rab Nawaz in the lead.

He found Ram Singh lying on the bare ground. He had been shot in the stomach. His eyes lit up when he saw Rab Nawaz. "You potter's ass, whatever did you do that for?" he asked.

Rab Nawaz felt as if it was he who had been shot. But he smiled, bent over Ram Singh and began to undo his belt. "Pig's trotters, who told you to stand up?"

"I was only trying to show myself to you, but you shot me," Ram Singh said with difficulty. Rab Nawaz unfastened his belt. It was a very bad wound and bleeding profusely.

Rab Nawaz's voice choked, "I swear upon God, I only fired out of fun. How could I know it was you? You were always an ass, Ram Singha."

Ram Singh was rapidly losing blood. Rab Nawaz was surprised he was still alive. He did not want to move him. He spoke to his platoon commander Major Aslam on the wireless, requesting urgent medical help.

He was sure it would take a long time to arrive. He had a feeling Ram Singh wouldn't last that long. But he laughed. "Don't you worry. The doctor is on his way."

Ram Singh said in a weak voice, "I am not worried, but tell me, how many of my men did you kill?"

"Just one," Rab Nawaz said.

"And how many did you lose?"

"Six," Rab Nawaz lied.

"Six," Ram Singh said. "When I fell, they were disheartened, but I told them to fight on, give it everything they'd got. Six, yes." Then his mind began to wander.

He began to talk of their village, their childhood, stories from school, the 6/9 Jat Regiment, its commanding officers, affairs with strange women in strange cities. He was in excruciating pain, but he carried on. "Do you remember that madam, you pig?"

"Which one?" Rab Nawaz asked.

"That one in Italy. You remember what we used to call her? Man-eater."

Rab Nawaz remembered her. "Yes, yes. She was called Madam Minitafanto or some such thing. And she used to say: no money, no action. But she had a soft spot for you, that daughter of Mussolini."

Ram Singh laughed loudly, causing blood to gush out of his wound. Rab Nawaz dressed it with a makeshift bandage. "Now keep quiet," he admonished him gently.

Ram Singh's body was burning. He did not have the strength to speak, but he was talking nineteen to the dozen. At times, he would stop, as if to see how much petrol was still left in his tank.

After some time, he went into a sort of delirium. Briefly, he would come out of it, only to sink again. During one brief moment of clarity, he said to Rab Nawaz, "Tell me truthfully, do you people really want Kashmir?"

"Yes, Ram Singha," Ram Nawaz said passionately.

"I don't believe that. You have been misled," Ram Singh said.

"No, you have been misled, I swear by the Holy Prophet and his family," Rab Nawaz said.

"Don't take that oath . . . you must be right." But there was a strange look on his face, as if he didn't really believe Rab Nawaz.

A little before sunset, Major Aslam arrived with some soldiers. There was no doctor. Ram Singh was hovering between consciousness and delirium. He was muttering, but his voice was so weak that it was difficult to follow him.

Major Aslam was an old 6/9 Jat Regiment officer. Ram Singh had served under him for years. He bent over the dying soldier and called his name, "Ram Singh, Ram Singh."

Ram Singh opened his eyes and stiffened his body as if he was coming to attention. With one great effort, he raised his arm and saluted. A strange look of incomprehension suddenly suffused his face. His arm fell limply to his side and he murmured, "Ram Singha, you ass, you forgot this was a war, a war . . ." He could not complete the sentence. With half-opened eyes, he looked at Rab Nawaz, took one last breath and died.

★

★   ★   ★   ★

AUTHOR: *Liam O'Flaherty (1896–1984) was undoubtedly one of Ireland's most outstanding writers. His stories are simple and direct, reflecting his feelings about the people of Ireland. This story is typical of his writing: it has energy, sanity, and passion.*

SETTING: *The conflict in Ireland has long fascinated the rest of the world. The antagonists have been educated, literate, European, Christian peoples, and yet the situation seems resistant to all attempts at management or resolution. The conflict is long-standing: in the 1600s the British government settled a number of Protestants from Scotland in northern Ireland in an attempt to colonize, pacify, or subdue the Irish. This produced bitter antagonism between the Protestant Scots (the Orange) and the Catholic Irish (the Republicans). Although fighting has occurred regularly, the total number of individuals killed in comparison to other world conflicts is relatively small (perhaps three thousand in the past ten years). However, the numbers give little indication of the antagonists' anger and intransigence. Given the nature and duration of the conflict, some might expect that pain and despair would have become commonplace, boring — that the people would "get used to it." However, as this story reflects, each death renews the agony.*

The Sniper

Liam O'Flaherty

The long June twilight faded into night. Dublin lay enveloped in darkness, but for the dim light of the moon, that shone through fleecy clouds, casting a pale light as of approaching dawn over the streets and the dark waters of the Liffey. Around the beleaguered Four Courts the heavy guns roared. Here and there through the city machine guns and rifles broke the silence of the night, spasmodically, like dogs barking on lone farms. Republicans and Free Staters were waging civil war.

On a roof-top near O'Connell Bridge, a Republican sniper lay watching. Beside him lay his rifle and over his shoulders were slung a pair of field-glasses. His face was the face of a student — thin and ascetic, but his eyes had the cold gleam of a fanatic. They were deep and thoughtful,

"The Sniper" originally appeared in *The Short Stories of Liam O'Flaherty* (London: Jonathan Cape Limited, 1937). Reprinted by permission of the Estate of the author and Jonathan Cape.

the eyes of a man who is used to looking at death.

He was eating a sandwich hungrily. He had eaten nothing since morning. He had been too excited to eat. He finished the sandwich, and taking a flask of whiskey from his pocket, he took a short draught. Then he returned the flask to his pocket. He paused for a moment, considering whether he should risk a smoke. It was dangerous. The flash might be seen in the darkness and there were enemies watching. He decided to take the risk. Placing a cigarette between his lips, he struck a match, inhaled the smoke hurriedly and put out the light. Almost immediately a bullet flattened itself against the parapet of the roof. The sniper took another whiff and put out the cigarette. Then he swore softly and crawled away to the left.

Cautiously he raised himself and peered over the parapet. There was a flash and a bullet whizzed over his head. He dropped immediately. He had seen the flash. It came from the opposite side of the street.

He rolled over the roof to a chimney stack in the rear, and slowly drew himself up behind it, until his eyes were level with the top of the parapet. There was nothing to be seen — just the dim outline of the opposite housetop against the blue sky. His enemy was under cover.

Just then an armoured car came across the bridge and advanced slowly up the street. It stopped on the opposite side of the street fifty yards ahead. The sniper could hear the dull panting of the motor. His heart beat faster. It was an enemy car. He wanted to fire, but he knew it was useless. His bullets would never pierce the steel that covered the grey monster.

Then round the corner of a side street came an old woman, her head covered by a tattered shawl. She began to talk to the man in the turret of the car. She was pointing to the roof where the sniper lay. An informer.

The turret opened. A man's head and shoulders appeared, looking towards the sniper. The sniper raised his rifle and fired. The head fell heavily on the turret wall. The woman darted toward the side street. The sniper fired again. The woman whirled round and fell with a shriek into the gutter.

Suddenly from the opposite roof a shot rang out and the sniper dropped his rifle with a curse. The rifle clattered to the roof. The sniper thought the noise would wake the dead. He stopped to pick the rifle up. He couldn't lift it. His forearm was dead. "Christ," he muttered, "I'm hit."

Dropping flat on to the roof, he crawled back to the parapet. With his left hand he felt the injured right forearm. The blood was oozing through the sleeve of his coat. There was no pain — just a deadened sensation, as if the arm had been cut off.

Quickly he drew his knife from his pocket, opened it on the breastwork of the parapet and ripped open the sleeve. There was a small hole where the bullet had entered. On the other side there was no hole. The bullet had lodged in the bone. It must have fractured it. He bent the arm below the wound. The arm bent back easily. He ground his teeth to overcome the pain.

Then, taking out his field dressing, he ripped open the packet with his knife. He broke the neck of the iodine bottle and let the bitter fluid drip into the wound. A paroxysm of pain swept through him. He placed the cotton wadding over the wound and wrapped the dressing over it. He tied the end with his teeth.

Then he lay still against the parapet, and closing his eyes, he made an effort of will to overcome the pain.

In the street beneath all was still. The armoured car had retired speedily over the bridge, with the machine gunner's head hanging lifeless over the turret. The woman's corpse lay still in the gutter.

The sniper lay for a long time nursing his wounded arm and planning escape. Morning must not find him wounded on the roof. The enemy on the opposite roof covered his escape. He must kill that enemy and he could not use his rifle. He had only a revolver to do it. Then he thought of a plan.

Taking off his cap, he placed it over the muzzle of his rifle. Then he pushed the rifle slowly upwards over the parapet, until the cap was visible from the opposite side of the street. Almost immediately there was a report, and a bullet pierced the centre of the cap. The sniper slanted the rifle forward. The cap slipped down into the street. Then, catching the rifle in the middle, the sniper dropped his left hand over the roof and let it hang, lifelessly. After a few moments he let the rifle drop to the street. Then he sank to the roof, dragging his hand with him.

Crawling quickly to the left, he peered up at the corner of the roof. His ruse had succeeded. The other sniper, seeing the cap and rifle fall, thought that he had killed his man. He was now standing before a row of chimney pots, looking across, with his head clearly silhouetted against the western sky.

The Republican sniper smiled and lifted his revolver above the edge of the parapet. The distance was about fifty yards — a hard shot in the dim light, and his right arm was paining him like a thousand devils. He took a steady aim. His hand trembled with eagerness. Pressing his lips together, he took a deep breath through his nostrils and fired. He was almost deafened with the report and his arm shook with the recoil.

Then, when the smoke cleared, he peered across and uttered a cry of joy. His enemy had been hit. He was reeling over the parapet in his death agony. He struggled to keep his feet, but he was slowly falling forward, as if in a dream. The rifle fell from his grasp, hit the parapet, fell over, bounded off the pole of a barber's shop beneath and then clattered on to the pavement.

Then the dying man on the roof crumpled up and fell forward. The body turned over and over in space and hit the ground with a dull thud. Then it lay still.

The sniper looked at his enemy falling and he shuddered. The lust of battle died in him. He became bitten by remorse. The sweat stood out in beads on his forehead. Weakened by his wound and the long summer day of fasting and watching on the roof, he revolted from the sight of the shattered mass of his dead enemy. His teeth chattered. He began to gibber to himself, cursing the war, cursing himself, cursing everybody.

He looked at the smoking revolver in his hand and with an oath he hurled it to the roof at his feet. The revolver went off with the concussion, and the bullet whizzed past the sniper's head. He was frightened back to his senses by the shock. His nerves steadied. The cloud of fear scattered from his mind and he laughed.

Taking the whiskey flask from his pocket, he emptied it at a draught. He felt reckless under the influence of the spirits. He decided to leave the roof and look for his company commander to report. Everywhere around was quiet. There was not much danger in going through the streets. He picked up his revolver and put it in his pocket. Then he crawled down through the sky-light to the house underneath.

When the sniper reached the laneway on the street level, he felt a sudden curiosity as to the identity of the enemy sniper whom he had killed. He decided that he was a good shot whoever he was. He wondered if he knew him. Perhaps he had been in his own company before the split in the army. He decided to risk going over to have a look at him. He peered round the corner into O'Connell Street. In the upper part of the street there was heavy firing, but around here all was quiet.

The sniper darted across the street. A machine gun tore up the ground around him with a hail of bullets, but he escaped. He threw himself downwards beside the corpse. The machine gun stopped.

Then the sniper turned over the dead body and looked into his brother's face.

★

★ ★ ★ ★

AUTHOR: *Augusto Roa Bastos (1917-) is one of Paraguay's most noted writers. He served in the army during the Chaco War and subsequently wrote about that war. Partly as a result of the hostile political climate in Paraguay, he has worked as a journalist, teacher, scriptwriter, novelist, and short story writer in Buenos Aires, Argentina. He is known for his novel about the Chaco war,* Son of Man, *as well as for short story collections, including* El trueno entre las hojas.

SETTING: *The Chaco War was a border dispute between Paraguay and Bolivia. The Chaco, a wasteland one hundred thousand square miles west of the Paraguay River and north of the Rio Pilcomayo, was believed to have oil deposits. Furthermore, Bolivia, which had lost its seacoast to Chile, saw the Chaco as a shipping route to the Atlantic via the Paraguay and Parana rivers. A Pan-American Conference attempted to settle the dispute through arbitration but failed. In 1928 the two nations attacked each other. Between 1928 and 1935, more than two hundred thousand lives were lost. The Treaty of Buenos Aires gave Paraguay most of the Chaco region; Bolivia was given access to the Atlantic via the Paraguay and Parana rivers. The war was particularly bloody. It also set up political conditions that would later support a military dictatorship in Paraguay.*

Encounter With the Traitor

Augusto Roa Bastos

The news vendor was holding out the change, but he did not reach for it or even remember to reach for it. His attention was suddenly fixed on a man walking past along the sidewalk, swinging a thin walking stick. He started after him. "It's him," he told himself. "It has to be him." A long span of time, crammed with events both large and small, struggled to fit into the flash of a second. In this vivid second, he had recognized the man from behind. For there are certain men with many faces — faces on all sides of them, front and back, faces of an unalterable identity down to the slightest expression — who, for all they may do to pass unnoticed, are unmistakable. This was how, in a single glimpse, he had instantly recognized the man

Translated by Norman Thomas di Giovanni. "Encounter With the Traitor" is reprinted from *The Eye of the Heart: Short Stories from Latin America*, edited by Barbara Howes (Indianapolis, Ind.: Bobbs-Merrill, 1973) by permission of the translator.

with the stick among the anonymous rush of passersby — even though the man already had his back to him.

But the other man had recognized him at first glance, too, in that instant when his delicate stick wavered in his hands (it was a barely noticeable change of rhythm), not out of fear, nor stupor, nor even surprise, but more in adjustment to a new center of gravity brought on by a sudden shift in time, a rapid change in thoughts. It was like stepping unexpectedly on those slippery tiles that also lurk in the mind. He had seen the first man take the newspaper from the vendor and fold it neatly in three. He had glimpsed the movement of the hand as it tightened around the paper. "It's him," the man with the stick had also told himself. "He's put on weight, but it's him." What convinced him was the way the first man had handed his money to the news vendor. "He still has his pride," he said to himself, not seeing now that the other man had refused his change. The man with the stick did not turn around. He either feigned ignorance or recovered his indifference. It was a custom of his. But his self-possession was not feigned. Were there a trace of simulation in his attitude, one would have said that he took pleasure in it. The lacquered cane, with its amber reflection, also regained its rhythmic motion.

The man who followed hurried his pace. The old cause, long stored away but far from over, came alive again in his mind without the loss of a single detail. Now he hung back in his haste to overtake the figure up ahead. The other man walked slowly, barely resting the point of his stick on the pavement or else twisting it in his fingers, not like an aging show-off dandy but out of old habit. "Scarecrow!" muttered the man who was following. "The same as ever!" Then, in control of his mounting anger, he studied the man ahead of him. He was solid and straight, his neck was boyish under his gray hair, and, though his left shoulder drooped slightly and his long legs had lost their youthful spring, there was still — even if faded and out of training — a martial air about him. Or the somewhat cynical mimicry of a martial air. The man with the newspaper noted the other's worn but neat suit and fancied that, with its close-fitting military jacket, it was even cut in the style of those days. Of himself, however, it was obvious that growing obesity had forced him into looser and looser clothing. He passed the back of his hand over his dripping face. Sweat also dampened his rolled newspaper.

"He's right behind me," the man with the stick said to himself. "I wonder if he'll go into all that now. Of course, I haven't given them satisfaction enough. Thirty years we've been dead, but one of them can rise up all at once and pursue me."

The two men were returning to life on a city street, in another country, in a chance encounter which neither of them, perhaps, had ever again expected. But the man with the walking stick suddenly realized that the other man had been in pursuit of him the whole time, and that in the space of a few yards the persecution of all these years was being recapitulated, was coming clear, in all its subtleties. The man was tracking him not from a newsstand, where he had stopped by coincidence, but from much farther back — from that uprising sent to its doom by the report of an informer, from the ensuing court-martial, and from their prison camp out in an arid, desolate land where the coconut palms were like bars and the surrounding waste was a parody of freedom. It was that same savage land of the Chaco which several months later would begin swallowing the flesh and blood of a hundred thousand soldiers. The two men had survived that war for a reason as fortuitous and no more valid than the one that had chosen the victims of the slaughter. And now one of them again found himself pitted against the other, as if nothing had intervened, as if nothing had been enough to atone for the unfounded insult, the hatred, the thirst for vengeance, which only seemed lulled into resentful indifference, while not so much the body but the spirit gradually fattened and aged.

"Stop the fight!" the doctor had shouted at them. "Don't you see this man cannot go on?"

But go on he did, stubbornly, though lacking courage, lacking conviction, with no other will than that of a man who must carry a thing through to the end, or the blind obstinacy of drunkards who invent their own heroism. With his left hand he clutched one side of his bloody face, and the blurred damaged eye looked out from between his fingers into a space that was out of focus — the fadeout of a burning, drenched darkness — under the almost spasmodic sally of the last attack. Sabers glistened in the drizzly dawn that smudged the blackish trees and muffled the clash of weapons until they came to a stop, dripping, the blade of one redder than the other, while neither of the duelers expected or hoped for a reconciliation they knew to be impossible.

"He's still after me," said the tall, gray-haired man to himself. "I can't very well turn and wait for him. What would I say? Can I possibly tell him the truth now — after so many years? He wouldn't believe it. Truth also ages, sometimes faster than men. Besides, truth is not for the weak. And he's fat and sad. All he has is his pride. Even his hatred is no more than a feeling of viciousness now. If only I could be sorry for him, the poor guy! Hatred has to feed on something present to be a faith. My guilt isn't even a memory any longer, because it doesn't exist. It simply does not exist; it never existed — at least not the way other things existed. If I were to turn around, what could I say to him?"

"Traitor! Miserable informer!" one of the accused had shouted, raising his fist at the silent witness. He addressed the man who had presumably bought his freedom with betrayal and who now stood there, testifying with his silence — for at no time did he speak — against his fellow-insurrectionists. The insult came again, more plangent and more furious. The judge gaveled the table, making the papers jump, then leaned back in his chair. His face was livid with anger, as much at the stubborn silence of the one as at the outburst of the other. The rest of the accused stirred uncomfortably on the benches — one of them in particular, the brother of the man who had been insulted. His head was bowed. He seemed weighed down by an insupportable burden, as if only he were suffering the shame just inflicted on his brother. But every other face was craned toward the insulted man, who seemed not to have heard the words spoken against him. Impassive, he stared out the window at the branches rocking in the wind against the barracks wall.

"More than one of them has been after me since then," the man with the walking stick thought to himself, unwittingly slowing his pace. "The war wasn't enough. A hundred thousand killed in the Chaco — dead for nothing. And the absurd duel, barely a day after the Victory Parade, between two specters scorched by the Chaco's metallic sun. And again the round of revolutions, conspiracies, and uprisings — each with its new heroes and traitors in an endless chain. Yesterday's executioners, today's victims; today's victims, tomorrow's executioners." He remembered the colonel who had presided over the court-martial. After one of the barracks coups following the war, he too was thrown into prison, where he was beaten every morning with pieces of wire by the barefoot guards who were steeped in hatred. The colonel finally went mad and took to wandering about crooning unintelligibly, covered with thick welts, with new sores, and always with a halo of flies.

The walking stick jerked quickly now, but the pace grew slower with each step, as if the man with the boyish neck might have to snap around at any moment and stand face to face with the person following him.

"More than one of them has been after me since then," the man with the walking stick told himself. "My comrades — my ex-comrades, that is — do not forget me. Some watch me go by and shrug their shoulders, unable to make up their minds about a confrontation. A lot of time has passed, they figure, and my guilt vegetates under a statute of limitations. In a way, that duel, the very fact of that challenge, partly sealed my rehabilitation.

Because who is going to fight with a damned man? Of course, I would never have been able to fight with each of my thirty-seven ex-comrades. But this one has not been placated. He was the most offended, the most excitable. Now he has nothing left but his old pride, the knowledge that his life has amounted to even less than the deaths of the others. He blindly believed, and goes on believing, that I —"

The man had pressed ahead of him, cutting him off, and now stood facing him. He was excitedly waving his newspaper, which was crumpled at one end. The pursued man stopped too. He turned a little, put the walking stick behind him, and leaned on it, both hands at his back.

"Do you know who I am?" he mumbled.

"Naturally."

They glared at each other, the pursuer with eyes that were hard, colored by the old bitterness that made them bulge and that turned the blood vessels bright red; the pursued man with one eye more alive than the other, but tolerant, almost compassionate, though he appeared to be trying not to show the latter sentiment.

"Traitor! Miserable informer!"

The words, worn hollow with time, were now barely an echo of the old courtroom insult, and again they merely struck impassiveness. But then the rolled newspaper cracked like a whip, reaching its destination after a trajectory of thirty years. The eye dropped out and fell to the sidewalk, where it rolled a few inches and came to rest in a crack. The aggressor's hand remained suspended in the air, torn from its initial fury, which the gaping eye socket seemed suddenly to have sucked away. His face, too, was quickly draining itself of anger and bitterness. Its new expression seemed to emanate from within, under an impulse perhaps of mockery and perhaps akin to compassion. It was as if greatness of soul could not be engendered except by a matching wretchedness.

It was hard for the first man to stop staring at the eye he had knocked loose with a flick of his crumpled newspaper. When he turned to his adversary, it was with the helpless surprise of someone who confuses one person with another, whom he nevertheless recognizes.

How, after thirty years, was the second man going to explain that the informer had not been he but his brother, who had died in the Chaco as a hero? He, meanwhile, had gone on living as a dishonored man. With a secret like his, the difference was not so great. How could he ever explain that he liked his role, that he had actually come to enjoy it?

The first man stammered something, an apology perhaps, while he stooped to pick up the dusty eye.

"Don't bother," the man with the stick said. "I have others. That one was already a bit dull."

A few curious onlookers had formed a circle around them. The two pushed through the spectators and went their separate ways.

★

★ ★ ★ ★

AUTHOR: *The short stories of Nadir Ibrahimi, like those of many other Persian authors, do not concentrate on plot. Instead, they are short vignettes or sketches. This story was originally written in Farsi in 1967 and published in Tehran. It represents the continuing tradition of Persian war literature.*

SETTING: *Iran, the ancient country of Persia and its environs, has had a long history of civil and ethnic conflict. The southern area of Iran, rich in resources, has been the center of Persian life and culture. The northern area is mountainous and remote. Traditionally, revolutionaries, or outlaws, have gone to the north to escape persecution — thereby presenting a constant nuisance for the government in power. Outlaws would often be separated from social and political events in the south for long periods of time, during which the original causes for their brigandage may have disappeared.*

Why Do They Go Back?

Nadir Ibrahimi

"Sha'ir Khan, are you really going back?"

"Stop bothering me, old man. Why do you keep asking? I've told you a hundred times, I'm going back. You can see for yourself the direction we're riding."

"No, Khan, you're kidding your servant. No one would believe that Sha'ir would go back — go back and surrender."

"Sha'il, who would believe that Sha'ir Khan would deliver Akbar Mirza and not go back? Who would believe that?"

"No one, Khan. No one."

"Then shut up, old man. There's nothing else to be done."

The night was like the description of night in stories about outlaws. The two horsemen rode oblivious of darkness, or of the small, mist-covered lantern of the moon at night's end.

"Sha'ir Khan, I have a right to know, don't I? For sixty years I've fought for you and for your father. For sixty years. Now you tell me you're going back. Don't I have a right to know why? Has everything been

Translated by Minoo S. Southgate. "Why Do They Go Back?" reprinted from *Modern Persian Short Stories* (Washington, D.C.: Three Continents Press, 1980) by permission of the publisher.

straightened out? Is there no more reason to carry a gun?"

"Old man, you don't understand."

"That's what I'm saying, Khan. But I must understand. I mustn't be kept in the dark. If something has changed, if something has been straightened out, tell your servant . . ."

"Sha'il, it has changed. Lots of things have changed."

"Too bad . . . too bad."

Sha'ir Khan turned and looked back at the mountains that moved almost imperceptibly farther away from them. The mountains were his clothing and his shelter; in the plain he was naked.

The wounded moon, in the eyes of the old man, was like a lantern about to die out.

"Khan, tell your servant why you're going back. Have you heard something I don't know?"

Sha'ir Khan was fingering his mustache, teaching it to stay up as he rode down the slope. The wind spread the bitter scent of poppies.

"Old man, the smell of opium. Don't you like it?"

"No, Khan. I only like the smell of gunpowder."

Sha'ir Khan laughed. "You old outlaw . . . it's all finished. That sort of talk belongs to the good old days. Once we wash and hang up our guns, you'll forget the smell of gunpowder."

"No Khan . . . you don't mean it."

"Tomorrow, at sunrise . . ."

"If you've surrendered by then . . ."

"Mashhadi Sha'il will also surrender himself."

The old man made no answer. He struggled against doubt, disbelief, anger — but his age and his faith in the Khan would not let him rebel. "Does it really mean we're going back to surrender?" he wondered. "What will they do to us? Will they reward the Khan and give him a medal for surrendering his gun? Will they give him his land back and praise him for having come round? But, no . . . they're sure to hang him."

"Sha'ir Khan, they're sure to hang you," he said.

"What? What did you say?"

"I said they're sure to hang you. They'll hang you up like an old gun, they'll print your picture in the paper with your head bent to one side and your tongue sticking out."

"And what's wrong with that? How long do we have to roam around like this? How long can we fight without knowing what we're fighting for? Do you remember when I came back from England? I was my own man, full of ideals, full of plans. But my father . . ."

"God bless his soul."

"Yes . . . my father convinced me that we had to fight. Maybe what he said was right — thirty years ago. Thirty years. Do you remember it all? Homeless, our guns on our shoulders . . . now we'll go back. We'll rest, smoke opium to our hearts' content, then stand against the wall and tell them to finish us. That's all."

"You don't make the rules, Khan. They'll hang you."

The Khan rubbed his mustache and laughed. "No, old man, they'll listen to me. I'll beg them to shoot me."

"Sha'ir Khan, you will beg?"

"Yes, what's wrong with that?"

"No. No . . . Khan."

"Sha'il you think like the outlaws three centuries ago. Can't you see we're becoming extinct? One by one. Some get killed, some give up. . . . Today or tomorrow, what difference does it make?"

"Too bad. Too bad I'm not like the outlaws three centuries ago. If I were, I'd stand here until you'd moved a hundred steps from me . . . and then I'd shoot you."

Sha'ir Khan laughed aloud and patted the old man on the back.

"Old man, I wish I were twenty again. But we're men without a cause. That's the trouble with us . . . men without a cause."

Mashhadi Sha'il tried to understand. He thought about past years and past days. "What does it mean? For all those years the Khan had held his life in his hands and had never once talked like this. Why? Had he always silently regretted that he'd come from England with those ideals and had ended up a wanderer with a gun on his back? He had sacrificed Akbar Mirza, and had not gone back. Why now? Why did he want to beg them not to hang him . . . ?"

"Do you think they'll kill me?" asked the Khan suddenly.

"Yes, certainly."

"No. There's no reason why they should. If I go back and tell them, 'I'm here and I've come on my own,' they won't kill me. Once more we'll all be together. I'll plant wheat. All with machines. Not like the old days. I'll plant every inch of the land."

"What land, Khan? You no longer have any land."

Sha'ir smiled as he replied, but he feigned anger. "What? I don't have any land? All that land is mine. I can grow wheat whenever I want. Abdollah has protected my land like a watchdog."

Mashhadi Sha'il stared at him. "Abdollah? You're talking nonsense. Sha'ir Khan! Abdollah is working for himself, on his own land."

"His own land? Where's his own land?"

"Sha'ir Khan, you know what I'm talking about. You're making fun of me. I can tell from your smile. You sound like an outlaw who hasn't even heard the radio. No one is working for you anymore. Everybody is working on his own land. They're even given the grain they sow. If you go back you'll disgrace yourself. The only way you can save your honor is by remaining an outlaw, far away; by refusing to go back. Why won't you admit it?"

"Are you saying that even my wife doesn't want me? Is she planting on her own land too?"

"I didn't say that, Khan. No. I know Sa'ideh Khanom loves you. Those days, every time you went to see the children she was so happy to see you . . ."

"So? Do I get a piece of the land or don't I?"

"No, Khan. Outlaws don't get anything."

"And what about the sheep? Those are my own."

"Right, the sheep. You're going to become a shepherd in your old age, Khan?"

"My old age? Shut up, old man. Sha'ir Khan will never get old."

"When you go back, you'll be old. So old you won't have the strength to carry a gun and walk."

"Nonsense. I still can carry the cannon on my back. But why should I? Why should I go on killing for no reason? I'll go back. If they don't give me land, I'll raise milk cows."

The old man was on the verge of tears. He wanted suddenly to say something that would hurt the Khan, that would burn his heart.

"They'll mock you in verse, Sha'ir Khan," he said. "They'll mock you in verse all over the South."

Sha'ir Khan laughed again. "What kind?" he asked. "Wait . . . let me make one myself, and you can give it to them to recite . . ."

He smiled, humming the words under his breath, searching for rhymes.

"Sha'ir Khan is going back, disgraced and old,
Sha'ir Khan is going back, back to the fold.
Sha'ir Khan fought aimlessly many years,
Sha'ir Khan, Oh, Sha'ir Khan, Oh Sha'ir Khan . . ."

"No, old man, I can't do it. You'd better find someone and give him a couple of sheep to write some decent lines."

The old man gave no answer. The farther they went, the sadder he became. From the corner of his eyes he watched the Khan, who kept running his fingers over his mustache, and smiling. He remembered the year the Khan swore that he would never go back unless he'd won the war. Now he was going back, and he was smiling.

"Khan, if you had planned to go back and surrender, why did you kill those two people by the road? Couldn't you have surrendered to them?"

"No, Sha'il, no. I needed a little time. If I'd surrendered to them they would claim they'd fought with me and caught me. They should've stayed out of my way. It was their own fault."

When they reached the Zobeir, the old man broke the darkness with the sad color of his voice. "Do you remember this spot, Sha'ir Khan?" he asked softly.

"So?"

"Do you remember?"

"Hosein was killed here."

"Not Hosein alone. They killed Hasan and Fatemeh here too. Your children, Khan."

For a moment the weight of sorrow tightened the eyelids of the Khan, his sharp glance cut through the night. He swallowed a sigh.

"Well, they had to kill them. The soldiers were shooting from up there, weren't they?"

"Yes, Khan. From up there."

"Were they good shots?"

"No, it took them many shots . . ."

"Don't belittle them like that, old man. I've seen some of them. They're good shots."

"They shot one after the other . . ."

"What's the difference? What's the difference, old man? Why shouldn't an outlaw get killed? Weren't my children outlaws? Weren't they?"

"Yes, they were. But they fought for Sha'ir Khan, their father, and they were killed for Sha'ir Khan, their father — the same man who is now going back to raise and milk cows. Who is breaking his vow . . ."

"Sha'il, remember what I'm saying: no one should fight for the sake of his father. To fight for your father's sake is to fight for something old and worn out. He should know himself what he's doing, what he wants, what he's getting killed for. If they fought only for my sake, then they deserved to die in their youth."

The old man looked at a rock. "Hosein was shot here, behind this rock," he said.

"Bravo, Hosein! Bravo! So he was behind the rock and he still got shot?"

"Khan, it doesn't suit you to talk like this."

"Look, Sha'il, didn't you say I sounded like outlaws who haven't even heard the radio? Well, hadn't my children heard the radio? Hadn't they? Didn't the newspaper reach them? Didn't they know that they would get killed if they didn't surrender?"

"What about Akbar Mirza? He surrendered."

"No, they caught him. I didn't want to go back for someone who had been taken captive."

"Sha'ir Khan, we are at Zobeir. We don't have very far to go. Think it over. You're making a mistake, Khan."

Sha'ir Khan hummed under his breath:

"Sha'ir Khan is going back disgraced and old,

Sha'ir Khan is going back, back to the fold.

Sha'ir Khan and his servant, Mashhadi Sha'il.

Sha'ir Khan, Oh Sha'ir Khan, Oh Sha'ir Khan . . ."

"How many children did I have, old man?"

"Seven."

"And were they all killed?"

"No. One died — Abedin Khan."

"No, none of my children had a right to die," Sha'ir Khan shouted. "None! Not peacefully, in a bed!"

"But Abedin Khan died. He died, with sores all over his body."

"Yes . . . now I remember. But they put a curse on him, he died of their curse. That in a way was like getting killed."

"Yes, Khan. They put a curse on him."

"I remember. He gave everybody a hard time . . . everybody. By the way, how old was my wife when we hit the mountains?"

"Thirty or so."

"Yes. She was thirty."

Later:

"You're tired, Sha'il. You're very tired."

"No, Khan. I'm not tired."

"Then why are you dozing?"

"I'm not dozing, just thinking."

"About what, old man? Still asking yourself why I'm going back? Listen, Sha'il, I'm going to talk to you. You must learn to accept that everything has changed. This time they're not joking. They've done a lot of things. Things you and I can't judge. They've built schools and towns for you. You told me this yourself, you can't deny it. Abdollah is working on his own land. What am I supposed to fight against? What? They didn't take my land for themselves, they didn't take my sheep for themselves. They divided them among the people. Not only didn't they take anything, they even gave something of their own. They fought those who opposed them. They had a right to. And many of their own people were killed. People who fought in their own country against their own kind — against you and me and my children. Who is going to tell me what all the fighting will come to? Who's going to help Sha'ir Khan? Why fight? To please a handful of people who sit in their cozy rooms in cities and like to hear about outlaws? Or to impress a bunch of weakling city kids who think of us as wild animals who starve in the mountains, yet somehow survive? When they hear we've broken a siege they applaud us in the safety of their rooms. 'What strange animals!' they think. Is this enough, old man? Is it? Not once in all these years did you ask me what we're fighting for, who we're fighting for. But for over a month now all day long you ask why we're going back. Be patient, old man. I've thought it over. It's because I have thought it over that we're going back. You're like an outlaw who has lingered on from the time of Nader Shah. An outlaw who thinks he can win Shiraz by battle, take Isfahan and Tehran, and become sole ruler. An outlaw who doesn't know which way the wind is blowing; who is a great shot, but doesn't know why he's shooting; who can tumble on the horse and spread-eagle himself, clinging to its belly, but doesn't know why he's doing these things."

Tears were rolling from the old man's eyes. Sha'ir Khan was shouting now. "Maybe you know what you're fighting for. All right. Then tell me. Tell your master so he'll follow you wherever you want to go. But don't tell me we're fighting against injustice and that sort of thing. We're nowhere near fighting injustice, Sha'il, nowhere near that."

The Khan lowered his voice and spoke more kindly. "Being an outlaw has become a tradition with us. A tradition that must remain — but for how long, it's not clear. You think I have become tired? You think I've become reconciled? You think I'm scared? Sha'ir Khan scared? No. It's like I told you, what's wrong with us is that we don't have a cause. We don't know. Abdollah doesn't know. My children didn't know."

Sha'ir Khan rubbed his mustache as he talked, and the mustache was like a white bird he'd caught in his mouth, a white bird with its wings stretched out. He was smiling, as if he'd heard his own speech and liked it.

"Sha'ir Khan is going back, back to the fold.
Sha'ir Khan is going back, disgraced and old.
Sha'ir Khan with his servant . . ."

"All right, Khan," the old man said sadly. "I've no objection. No objection at all. You should have said this before."

"I haven't said anything yet. I only asked you to think and be patient, old man."

"All right. But you said you wished you were twenty. Why did you say that? You claim you'll never grow old, so why did you say that?"

"You caught me in a contradiction, old man. I said that because I thought if I were twenty I would understand why one should fight."

"Khan, here's the river. Finish with what you are saying."

"No, old man. There's no more. I hope they won't trap us here. Let's camp until morning."

On the other side of the river, the plain, with its lonely dim lights looked like the resting place of glow-worms.

"Get up, old man!"

"Where are we, Khan? Where are we?"

"Get up, Sha'il. Hurry up! Get your gun, let's go."

"It's still night, Khan. We didn't get any sleep . . . where are we going?"

"Anywhere. Get up."

The old man tied his cartridge belt, shouldered his gun. They mounted their horses.

"Goodbye, Sha'il."

"Goodbye."

"Goodbye, old man."

"Sha'ir Khan, have you changed your mind?"

"No, old man. I hold to what I said. We aren't fit to be outlaws. I'm sorry I killed those two . . ."

At daybreak the two outlaws crossed the Zobeir.

"How old did you say my wife was when we hit the mountains?"

"Thirty, Khan, thirty."

They heard a shot from the mountain top, and then more shots.

The Khan and Sha'il jumped off their horses and took shelter behind two rocks.

"I told you it was useless to kill them, didn't I."

"Yes, Khan, you did."

"They've trapped us."

"You're right, Khan. They've trapped us."

Another shot echoed. The Khan's horse knelt, then rolled to the ground. The Khan watched the horse sadly. "Old man," he cried. "Do you think my wife could still have children?"

"Certainly, Sha'ir Khan. 'Til fifty, maybe even more."

"Good. She's not over fifty, is she?"

"No, Khan, she's not."

"Where are they shooting from?"

"Facing us, from up there."

Sha'ir Khan took his gun and looked.

"Why aren't you shooting, Sha'il?"

"I don't see anything. They're too far away."

"You too have stopped being an outlaw, old man."

More shots. The bullets whistled over the rock that sheltered the Khan. Sha'ir Khan answered the volley aimlessly. The old man was glad.

"Look, Sha'il. They mean business — one of them made a hole in my back."

The old man stretched his neck to look at Sha'ir Khan's back. It was soaked with blood.

"They hit you, Sha'ir Khan."

"They shoot well."

"But it takes them too many shots."

"Oh, come, Sha'il. Leave off. You keep belittling them. They're like us. I like them. I like them . . . a . . . lot."

The Khan's voice was a broken boat, sinking.

"They see better than you . . . Better than you . . . And they have a cause. They're fighting the outlaws."

"Sha'ir Khan!" the old man shouted.

And Sha'ir Khan's head was on the ground. More shots snapped through the valley; blood leapt everywhere from his body. Still he hummed in the silence of his head . . .

"Sha'ir Kahn is going back, back to the fold,
Sha'ir Khan and his servant, Mashhadi Sha'il . . ."

★

★ ★ ★ ★

AUTHOR: *Blair Fuller (1927–) has been a professor of English and creative writing and has published three major books:* A Far Place, Three, *and* A Butterfly Net and a Kingdom. *He has edited the* Paris Review *since 1955 and has served as the director of the progressive Squaw Valley Community of Writers. He served in the U.S. Navy from 1944 to 1946 and writes with great sensitivity and insight about the Pacific arena.*

SETTING: *The Pacific arena of World War II pitted Japan against the United States in a particularly difficult conflict. U.S. soldiers, sailors, and airmen faced enormous distances (six thousand miles from east to west and five thousand miles from north to south), hurricanes, malaria, yellow fever, dysentery, and inhospitable lands and peoples. The enormous language and cultural differences added culture shock to the shock of war itself. On September 2, 1945, on the battleship* Missouri *in Tokyo Bay, the war, which had begun for the United States with the bombing of Pearl Harbor, was concluded. The U.S. military, according to the requirements of the Geneva Conventions, was then required to keep alive – to feed – the Japanese whom they so recently had been ordered to kill. The enormous incongruity of the situation led to confusion, hostility, and insubordination.*

Whelps of War

Blair Fuller

We had been mustered over the PA system, eight of us for a work party, and we waited together on the fantail until the chunky Greek coxswain, Krikorian, shouted attention and told us we were to take one of the landing boats in to General Stores, Manila, load it with rations, and provision every captured Japanese ship in the bay!

"Admiral" Nelson, a gunner's mate from Georgia said, "You mean we're gonna sweat our ass for *them?*"

"You read me, 'Admiral,'" Krikorian said. "Prisoners of war, they got a right to eat. Geneva 'ventions." Krikorian was bucking to go regular Navy and you could see that in the way he about-faced and saluted the gangway officer and then checked us off on a clipboard as we went over the side.

There was silence in the boat. Nelson was up forward by himself and others sat on the engine housing amidships with their backs to one another. I leaned on the outboard combing, looking at the bows and bridges of the sunken ships which jutted at strange angles out of the shallow water. All of them had been freighters, some ours sunk by the Japanese taking the Philippines, some Japanese sunk by us returning. Rust had flaked the ships' names off the hulls so that they could have been either nationality. At night, alone on the bridge on signal watch, I made up stories about them, working out itineraries and involvements in battles from the history of the war, in which neither I nor our ship, the USS Walter B. Cobb, APD 106, had fired or heard a shot after training. I had scarcely heard one at all, since I had enlisted at seventeen and had come aboard as a replacement only two months before in San Diego, a week before the Japanese surrendered.

General Stores was up a canal in downtown Manila which was a dusty, smelly mess of broken streets and walls in which thousands of slender brown people were constantly moving, tote-yokes over their shoulders, trading, putting together makeshift places to live in the bombed out shells. We passed the liberty landing and were called to by the busiest people of all — the crowd of ragtag pimps around the gate.

Nelson yelled at them, "Fuck y'own sisters, fuckin' gooks."

"You think they do that, Admiral?"

He was furious. "Fuckin' gook do any fuckin' thing."

We tied up and filed into the warehouse behind swaggering Krikorian. There were handcarts and dollies for our use, and they saved labor, but the heat inside was cruel. We panted, loading, and rushed out to the boat, dogging it in the outside air for as long as we could. When we had the consignment aboard, Krikorian gave us a break and we flopped down on the dock. He was worrying over the location of the Japanese ships and whether anyone aboard them could speak English.

"I'd as leave deep six the stuff," a deckhand said.

"I got my orders," Krikorian said, turning on him. "Orders is orders." He got the chart out of the boat and went to find someone who'd confirm the ships lay where he thought they did.

"He can stuff it."

When Krikorian came back he said, "OK, men, got the course laid out now. Let's get to her. Inna boat now." As we clambered aboard over the cases and sacks he said, "All right, assholes, move it. You think I'm liking this any better than you?"

Which made me realize that a part of me was liking it — I was curious about the Japanese. On our voyage out we'd put in at Guam and had been given an afternoon's liberty in a navy beer garden. The area was kept clean by a detail of Japanese prisoners guarded by SPs with shotguns, and watching them I'd found it hard to believe such men could have attacked us. They were so small, frail-looking, it seemed their hands could hardly get around the broom handles. Often when a sailor had finished a can of beer he would throw it at one of them and if it hit, on the head or anywhere, the Japanese would pick it up without a trace of anger, without a glance, and put it in one of the garbage cans. How had they managed to hurt us?

When we had cleared the canal I scrambled over some crates — condensed milk, for example, what would they do with condensed milk? — to the wheel. Krikorian was happy to show me the chart. "Figure this'n be that DE, or like our DE, there." Her bow and stack were a bit more sharply swept than our destroyer escorts; her color was a little lighter. She flew no flags — an astonishing thing for a ship, bare as something newborn — but, closer, there was nothing fresh about her. She needed paint, needed to be chipped and sanded, zinc oxidized, and then painted, and before a crewman's face was distinct you could see their uniforms were in tatters. All kinds of clothes they had — T-shirts of odd sizes, trousers and chopped off trousers, caps and hats, and the damndest variety of shoes! Basketball shoes with rubber disks on the ankles, brown work boots up to midcalf, black slippers, and some of them were barefoot. Coming alongside, several in our crew spat over the side, and the Japanese, whose feet were at about eye level, did the same, not at, but towards us. Krikorian idled the engine and yelled, "Spikka de English?"

An officer — gold bars on a shirt half bleached out, like camouflage cloth — stepped to the head of their ladder and said, oddly, "English here."

"Bloody limey," someone said.

"Gotta provisions," Krikorian shouted, making spooning motions.

"Very well," said the officer. "Please to throw lines." He singsonged some orders and several Japanese stepped to the rail but none of us picked up the lines until Krikorian barked. I threw the bowline and it hit a man in the ribs and he and his partner yammered at me. Both were squat, big knots in their legs and thick necks, and their jaws seemed to work in an odd way, not really closing on their words. How would they have liked the line thrown? Goddamnit, there was only one way to throw a line!

I shouted, "Shut your stupid mouths!" and they all began to chatter, maybe twenty men milling around, not threatening us exactly, but still, there were more of them than us and they were above us. Krikorian drew his sidearm automatic and now he waved it over his head. They mainly stopped moving and their voices dropped.

We got braced against the DE's ladder and the two crews formed irregular chains to pass the cases along. "OK," said Krikorian, and handed me the list of provisions. I read it off: dehydrated potatoes, powdered scrambled eggs, a case of baked beans. They weren't turning anything down. Their man at the head of the ladder was plucking the cases out of our man's hands so quickly he was always ready for the next one. Someone said, "Hurry it up, mates, we're falling behind."

At the end of the list I said, "That's all for these birds, Krik."

"Finish!" he yelled at the officer. "Cast off the lines!" They were confused, perhaps they thought the entire boatload was for them, and they didn't move to the cleats. "Lines!" Krikorian yelled. "Lines!" Still they didn't move and I had an instant nightmare: they were going to fall on us. I jumped to the bowline wanting to cast it off from our side, and then they understood. A couple of them smiled, perhaps at my fear, chucking the lines down into the boat.

We headed for a second DE in about the same condition as the first. And the same routine: confusion, Krikorian waving his automatic around, the lines going over the side. This crew was comparatively well dressed, lots of tan baseball caps with insignia on the brow. I started reading off the same menu, "Four cases dehydrated spuds," and heard a thump and a noise that was something like a shriek. The Japanese were all looking at the end man in our chain — Nelson, he'd moved. He was taking a second case from the man behind him and when he had it at shoulder height he launched it like a shotput at the nearest Japanese legs — and hit them. The man crumpled forward, mouth open, eyeglasses flying off, then fell backward to the deck, and scuttled away on hands and knees.

"Ho!" went Krikorian.

"Yeah, Admiral!"

Others laughed, including me. He threw the third case from his waist, more like the hammer throw, and it sailed higher than the shotput, but it hit nothing, landing on, and collapsing, one of its corners.

The Japanese had scattered back from the ladder. "Gimme somethin' lighter," Nelson said to me.

"Two powdered eggs."

When he had them he yelled at the Japanese, "Misuble chickens!" They didn't move and his two throws were harmless, landing beyond the potatoes.

There was some Japanese talk and a man darted in to drag away a case of eggs. Nelson picked up a third case of eggs and waited, but they were watching him. Krikorian said, "They're on to you, Admiral. Hold up till the next ship." Nelson threw what remained as hard as he could anyway, and a case of condensed milk broke open and the cans ran around, the Japs chasing them.

They threw down our lines — Krikorian was waving his automatic again — and we pulled away. Krikorian said to me, "Tell the Admiral just two PCs left. Ought to have lower decks."

I took the message to him but he was very red, drenched with sweat, and didn't pay much attention. The PC's deck was certainly lower, and apparently they had seen us at the DEs for they were ready to tie us up. They did that sloppily enough, discipline appeared to be lax, but they wouldn't come near the gangway to take the cases from Nelson. He waited, but they wouldn't budge from an arc outside his range. He said, "Don't give 'em the rations, Krik. I'll bust your ass, you do."

"You want to go on report, Admiral?" To me, Krikorian said, "Read the list."

I did and others shoved the provisions aboard while Nelson swore. The Japanese watched him, shuffling their feet and crossing their arms.

The final PC was anchored quite separately from the other three ships. The man on watch looked stupefied as we approached. "Ain't seen us," Nelson said. "Ain't, by God, seen us."

Krikorian's shout made the watchman jump through a hatch, and some seconds later he came back with an officer. Krikorian went through his pantomime again, and as he spooned, more Japanese came out on the fantail. These were in the poorest condition of all, a lot of them with ulcerated skins and patchy heads of hair.

I said, "Everything that's left's for them, Admiral."

"Put it all right here," he said, pointing at the engine housing. "Gonna get it off like automatic fire."

We stacked the cases, Nelson spitting on his hands, and, yes, the Japanese were making a chain from the gangway to a cargo hatch and there was a man with a shaved head, wearing bib overalls, at the head of the ladder waiting for Nelson to hand him something. Nelson hefted a case of beans, the heaviest kind of case, up to his shoulder and jounced it there, securing his grip. Overalls didn't move. Nelson's back foot was braced, his arm came back and he shot the case forward — *missed!* He had slipped and was draped over the combing, his head in the boat's well, and the case had gone off to the right of the Japanese and was bumping harmlessly over their deck.

Nelson came up cursing and there was no question the Japanese had understood his intention for they quickly got back from the ladder, pointing and jabbering.

Nelson tapped the next biggest man in our crew, and they climbed up on the engine housing and picked up a case between them. One, two, three! It sailed maybe fifteen feet in the air and came down in the middle of their fantail and broke apart, cans of beans rolling everywhere. One, two, three! And cans of milk were added. Then the powdered eggs, at least one sack of which punctured, for there was a spray of egg yellow, and the potatoes, until everything had been delivered and lay in a crazy heap.

"Lines!" Krikorian yelled, "Lines!"

I shook the bowline and a couple of them came gingerly to the side and cast us off, and once the lines were in the boat and there was a little water between us and the PC there was a strange sound, Japanese laughter. They were looking at us and at the pile of stuff and laughing! Nelson leaped up on the gunwhale to jump for their ladder but two men, then more, grabbed him and wrestled him back to the deck. Krikorian gunned the engine and we pulled away and the further we got, the louder, somehow, was the Japanese laughter.

Nelson stopped fighting and they let him up. The back of his head had been cut and blood was running down and around his neck.

"I didn't hit but one of them," he said. "I didn't hit but one."

He shook his head, saying it over and over again, and then began to sob. "Couldn't hit . . . but one of them!" His great shoulders heaved as he leaned on the forward combing. "Just . . . a goddamn one of 'em!"

Krikorian tapped me to take the wheel, went to Nelson, and patted his back.

"Just only a goddamn one of 'em!" Nelson said furiously and let out a bellow of a sob.

"You done real good, Admiral," Krikorian said. "Real good. Ain't anyone coulda done better."

Nelson shook Krikorian's hand away and wiped his cheekbones.

Krikorian said again, "You done good, Admiral."

Nelson's knuckles were white as he gripped the combing.

"Couldn't even . . . break me a leg," he said. "Not even."

Krikorian began, "Ain't anyone — " Nelson turned and decked him, hit him one hard punch with his right hand and Krikorian was flat on his back, blinking, trying to raise his head. A couple of men jumped to him.

Nelson thought they were coming to retaliate and dropped into a crouch. So did they. Krikorian sat up and spat out part of a tooth, a gleaming white dot on the bilge boards. The two men helped him to his feet. He made a gargling sound, spat over the side and said hoarsely, "You're on report, Admiral."

"If'n you do that . . ."

Someone shouted, and I turned to see we were about to ram a U.S. destroyer under its bows. I yanked the wheel over and the boat careened, and I could hear the others grabbing for holds and falling, lots of cursing.

We cleared the destroyer and I was lost for a minute. The gray water and sky had no dividing line, and the Cobb, when I located her, seemed to be floating in the air, and the bridge to be floating above the hull.

Krikorian yelled at me, "On course! On course!"

"Take the wheel yourself," I said, and left it.

The back of Nelson's hand had been jaggedly ripped from the first knuckle to his wrist. He was squeezing his hand white with his left hand, lots of blood running down his forearm. "Fucking sharp Greek teeth," Nelson said.

I looked at Krikorian at the wheel, and the men who had gathered near him, "regular" types, guys who sucked up to him.

Krikorian said something to them, nodded his head at Nelson and the rest of us, and spat over the side.

At last, we had our war.

★

★ ★ ★ ★

AUTHOR: *Sakaguchi Ango (1906–1955) looked for a utopia amid the chaos of the world. His works reflect a personal disdain for tradition, conventionality, and accepted moral or social values. An existentialist, he focused attention on the emptiness and corruption of the individual and wartime Japan. The titles of his works give some indication of his eccentricity:* Overcoat and Blue Sky; Wind, Light, and I at Twenty; A Woman Who Washes the Loincloth of a Blue Ogre; *and* Tale of Nippon — A History Begins With Sukiyaki.

SETTING: *The night bombing of Japan's cities may have been even more devastating than the final atomic blasts at Hiroshima and Nagasaki. The fires that resulted sent people into the streets in mass hysteria.*

The Idiot

Sakaguchi Ango

Various species lived in the house: human beings, a pig, a dog, a hen, a duck. But actually there was hardly any difference in their style of lodging or in the food they ate. It was a crooked building like a storehouse. The owner and his wife lived on the groundfloor, while a mother and her daughter rented the attic. The daughter was pregnant, but no one knew who was responsible.

The room that Izawa rented was in a hut detached from the main house. It had formerly been occupied by the family's consumptive son, who had died. Even if it had been assigned to a consumptive pig, the hut could hardly have been considered extravagant. Nevertheless, it had drawers, shelves, and a lavatory.

The owner and his wife were tailors. They also gave sewing lessons to the neighbors, and this was the reason that the son had been placed in a separate hut. The owner was an official of the neighborhood association, in which the girl who lived in the attic had originally worked. It appeared that while she was living in the association's office, she had enjoyed sexual relations indiscriminately with all the officials of the association except the president and the tailor. She had

Translated by George Saito. "The Idiot" by Sakaguchi Ango is reprinted from *Modern Japanese Stories*, ed. Ivan Morris (Tokyo: Charles E. Tuttle, 1962) by permission of the publisher.

had more than ten lovers and now she was with child by one of them. When this unfortunate fact became known, the officials collected a fund to take care of the child when it was born. In this world nothing goes to waste: among the officials was a bean-curd dealer who continued to visit the girl even after she had become pregnant and had taken refuge in the attic. In the end, the girl was virtually established as this man's mistress. When the other officials learned of the situation, they immediately withdrew their contributions and asserted that the bean-curd dealer ought to bear her living expenses. There were seven or eight of them who refused to pay, including the greengrocer, the watchmaker, and the landlord. Since they had been giving five yen each, the loss was considerable and there was no end to the girl's resentment.

She had a big mouth and two large eyes, yet she was fearfully thin. She disliked the duck and tried to give all the leftovers to the hen, but since the duck invariably butted in and snatched the food, she would chase it furiously round the room. The way she ran in a strangely erect posture, with her huge belly and her buttocks jutting out to the front and the rear, bore a striking resemblance to the duck's waddle.

At the entrance to the alley was a tobacconist, a thickly powdered woman of fifty-five. She had just got rid of her seventh or eighth lover, and rumor had it that she was now having trouble making up her mind about whether to choose in his stead a middle-aged Buddhist priest or a certain shopkeeper, also middle-aged. She was known to sell a couple of cigarettes (at the black-market price) to any young man who went to the back door of her shop. "Why don't you try buying some, sir?" the tailor had suggested to Izawa. Izawa, however, had no need to call on the old woman since he received a special ration at his office.

Behind the rice-supply office diagonally opposite the tobacconist's lived a widow who had accumulated some savings. She had two children: a son, who was a factory hand, and a younger daughter. Though really brother and sister, these two had lived as man and wife. The widow had connived at this, feeling that it would be cheaper in the long run. In the meantime, however, the son had acquired a mistress on the side. The need had therefore arisen to marry off the daughter, and it had been decided that she should become the bride of a man of fifty or sixty who was vaguely related. Thereupon the daughter had taken rat poison. After swallowing the poison, she had come to the tailor's (where Izawa lodged) for her sewing lesson. There she had begun to suffer the most atrocious agonies, and had finally died. The local doctor certified that she had died from a heart attack and this had been the end of the matter. "Eh?" Izawa had asked the tailor in surprise. "Where do you find doctors who'll issue such convenient certificates?" The tailor had been even more surprised. "D'you mean to say they don't do that sort of thing everywhere?" he said.

It was a neighborhood where tenements were clustered together. A considerable proportion of the rooms was occupied by kept women or prostitutes. Since these women had no children and since they were all inclined to keep their rooms neat, the caretakers of the buildings liked having them as tenants and did not mind about the disorderliness and immorality of their private lives. More than half of the apartments had become dormitories used by munition factories and were occupied by groups of women volunteer-workers. Among the tenants were pregnant volunteers who continued receiving their salaries even though they never went to work; the girl friend of Mr. So-and-So in such-and-such a section of the government; the "wartime wife" of the section chief (which meant that the real wife had been evacuated from Tokyo); the official mistress of a company director.

One of the women was reported to be a five-hundred-yen mistress and was the object of general envy. Next door to the soldier of fortune from Manchuria, who proudly boasted that his profession used to be murder (his younger sister studied sewing with the tailor), lived a manual therapist; next to him lived a man who, it was rumored, belonged to one of the traditional schools that practiced the fine art of picking pockets. Behind him lived a naval sub-lieutenant who ate fish, drank coffee, feasted on tinned food, and had saké every day. Because of the subterranean water which one found on digging a foot or so below the surface, it was almost impossible to construct air-raid shelters in this neighborhood; the sub-lieutenant, however, had somehow contrived to build a concrete shelter which was even finer than his actual apartment.

The department store, a wooden, two-story building on the route that Izawa took on his way to work, was closed because of the wartime lack of commodities; but on the upper floor gambling was being carried on every day. The boss of the gambling gang also controlled a number of "people's bars." He got dead drunk every day of the week and used to glare fiercely at the people who stood in queues waiting to enter his bars.

On graduating from the university, Izawa had become a newspaper reporter; subsequently he had started working on educational films. This was his present job, but he was still an apprentice and had not yet directed anything independently. He was twenty-seven, an age at which one is likely to know something about the seamy side of society; and in fact he had managed to pick up a good deal of inside information about politicians, army officers, businessmen, geisha, and entertainers. Yet he had never imagined that life in a suburban shopping district surrounded by small factories and apartment buildings could be anything like this. It occurred to him that it might be due to the roughening effect of the war on people's characters, but when he asked the tailor about it one day, the man replied in a quiet, philosophical way: "No, to tell the truth, things have always been like this in our neighborhood."

But the outstanding character of them all was the man next door. This neighbor was mad. He was quite well off and one way in which his madness revealed itself was in an excessive fear of intrusion by burglars or other undesirable people. This had led him to choose for his house a place at the very end of the alley and to construct the entrance in such a way that one could not find it even if one went up to the house and past the gate. There was nothing to be seen from the front but a latticed window. The real entrance was at the opposite end of the house from the gate and one had to go around the entire building to reach it. The owner's plan was that an intruder would either give up and beat a hasty retreat, or else would be discovered as he roamed about the house looking for the elusive entrance. Izawa's mad neighbor had little liking for the common people of this floating world. His house was a two-story building with quite a large number of rooms, but even the well-informed tailor knew hardly anything about the interior design.

The madman was about thirty; he had a wife of about twenty-five, and a mother. People said that at least the mother should be classed as sane. She had an extremely hysterical nature, however, and was without doubt the most mettlesome woman in the neighborhood, so much so that when she was dissatisfied with her rationed allocations she would rush out of the house barefoot to complain instantly to the town block-association.

The man's wife was an idiot. One lucky year he had undergone a religious awakening, clad himself in white, and set out on a pilgrimage to Shikoku. In the course of the trip he had become friendly with a feeble-minded woman somewhere in Shikoku: he had brought her back as a sort of souvenir of his pilgrimage and had married her.

The madman was a handsome fellow. His feeble-minded wife had an elegance becoming a daughter of a good family; her narrow-eyed, oval face had the prettiness of an old-fashioned doll or of a Noh mask. Outwardly the two were not only good-looking but appeared to be a well-matched couple of considerable breeding. The madman was extremely shortsighted and wore strong spectacles. As a rule he had a pensive air, as though tired from reading innumerable books.

One day when an air-raid drill was being held in the alley and the housewives were all bustling about efficiently, the madman had stood there in his everyday kimono, giggling inanely as he observed the scene. Then he had suddenly left and reappeared wearing an air-raid uniform. Grabbing a bucket from someone, he had started to draw water and to throw it about the place, uttering various curious exclamations all the while. After that he placed a ladder against the wall, climbed to the top, and began shouting orders from the roof, ending in a stirring admonitory speech. This was the first time that Izawa had actually realized that the man was mad. He had, it is true, already noticed certain eccentricities in his neighbor. For instance, the man would occasionally break through the fence into the tailor's garden and empty a bucket of leftovers into the pigpen; after this he would suddenly throw a stone at the duck or, with an air of perfect nonchalance, start feeding the hen and then abruptly give her a kick. But on the whole Izawa had taken the man to be compos mentis and he used to exchange silent greetings with him when they happened to meet.

What was the real difference, he wondered, between the madman and normal people? The difference, if any, was that the madman was essentially more discreet. To be sure, he giggled when he wanted to, gave a speech when he felt like it, threw stones at the duck, and would spend a couple of hours poking a pig's head and rear if the spirit so moved him. Nevertheless, he was essentially far more apprehensive of public opinion than normal people and he took special care in trying to isolate the main part of his private life from others. This was another reason that he had placed the entrance to his house on exactly the opposite side from the gate. On the whole the madman's private life was devoid of noise, he did not go in for useless chatting, and he lived in a meditative way. On the opposite side of the alley was an apartment from which the sound of running water and of vulgar female voices constantly encroached upon Izawa's hut. The apartment was occupied by two sisters who were prostitutes. On nights when the elder sister had a customer, the younger one would pace the corridor; when the younger sister had a customer, the elder one would walk up and down deep into the night. And people considered the madman to be of a different race, thought Izawa, merely because he was in the habit of giggling.

The madman's feeble-minded wife was a remarkably quiet and gentle woman. Her speech consisted of a timid mumble; even when one could make out the words, her meaning was usually obscure. She did not know how to prepare a meal or boil rice. She might have been able to cook if she had had to, but as soon as she made a mistake and was scolded, she became so nervous that she began to spill and drop everything. Even when she went to get rations she could do nothing herself; she merely stood there and let the neighbors manage for her. People said that since she was the wife of a madman it was quite appropriate that she should be an idiot and that the man's family could hardly expect anything better. The mother, however, was greatly dissatisfied and was constantly complaining about the misfortune of having a daughter-in-law who could not even boil rice. As a rule she was a modest and refined old woman, but owing to her hysteria she could become even fiercer than her mad son once she had been aroused. Among the three unbalanced occupants of the house it was the old mother who uttered the loudest screams. The idiot wife was so intimidated by this that she was in a perpetual state of nerves, even on peaceful days when nothing had gone wrong. The mere sound of footsteps would fill her with alarm. When Izawa greeted her on the street, she would stand there petrified, with a vacant look on her face.

The wife, too, occasionally came to the tailor's pigpen. Whereas the husband broke in openly, as if the house belonged to him, and threw stones at the duck or poked the pig's jowls, the feeble-minded woman slipped in silently like a shadow and hid behind the pigpen. In a way this had become her sanctuary. After she had been there for a while, the old woman's croaking voice would usually come from the next door, shouting "Osayo, Osayo!" and the idiot's body would react to each call by crouching further in the corner or by bending over. Before reluctantly emerging from her hiding place, the wife would time after time repeat her impotent, worm-like movements of resistance.

Izawa's occupations of newspaper reporter and educational-film director were the meanest of the mean. The only thing such people seemed to understand was the current fashion, and their lives consisted of a constant effort not to be left behind by the times. In this world there was no room for personality, or the pursuit of the ego, or originality. Like office workers, civil servants, or school teachers, their daily conversation abounded with such words as ego, mankind, personality, originality. But all this was mere verbiage. What they meant by "human suffering" was some such nonsense as the discomfort of a hangover after a drunken night during which one has spent all one's money trying to seduce a woman. They absorbed themselves in making films or writing fanciful pieces of colored prose which had neither spiritual value nor any element of real feeling but made ample use of such clichés as "ah, how inspiring the sight of the Rising Sun flag!"; "all our thanks to you, brave soldiers!"; "despite oneself the hot tears well up"; "the thud-thud of bombs"; "frantically one hurls oneself to the ground"; "the chattering of machine-gun fire"; and they firmly believed that with this kind of drivel they were actually portraying war.

Some said they could not write because of military censorship, but the fact was that, war or no war, they had not the slightest idea how to write honestly on any subject. Truth or real feeling in writing has nothing to do with censorship. In whatever period these gentry had happened to live, their personalities would surely have displayed the same emptiness. They changed in accordance with the prevailing fashion, and took for their models expressions culled from popular novels of the day.

To be sure, the period itself was both crude and senseless. What relationship could there be between human honesty and the cataclysm of war and defeat in which Japan's two thousand-year-old history was being submerged? The entire fate of the nation was being decided by the will of those men who had the feeblest power of introspection, and by the blind action of the ignorant mob that followed them. If you spoke about personality and originality in front of the city editor or the president, he would turn away as if to say that you were a fool. After all, a newspaper reporter was merely a machine whose function it was to spout forth "all our thanks to you, brave soldiers!"; "ah, how inspiring the sight of the Rising Sun flag!"; "despite oneself the hot tears well up." And so, indeed, was the entire period — it was all a mere machine. If you asked whether it was really necessary to give a full report of the speech by the divisional commander to his men, or whether you had to record every word of the weird Shinto prayer that the factory workers were obliged to recite each morning, the city editor would look away and click his tongue with annoyance; then he would suddenly turn round, crush his precious cigarette in the ash tray, and, glaring at you, shout: "Look here, what does beauty mean at a time like this? Art is powerless! Only news is real."

The directors, the members of the planning department, and the other groups had banded together to constitute their own private cabals, rather like the professional gambling societies of the Tokugawa period. Everything was based on group comradeship, and the individual talents of the members were used on a rotational basis with special emphasis on the traditional precepts of "duty" and "human feeling." The entire organization became more bureaucratic than the bureaucracy itself. Thus they managed to protect their respective mediocrities and to form a sort of mutual-aid relief organization founded on a hopeless dearth of talent. Any attempt to work one's way up by means of artistic individuality was regarded as a wicked violation of union rules. Internally the groups were relief organizations for the dearth of talent, but in their relations to the outside world they were alcohol-acquiring gangs whose members occupied the "people's bars" and argued drunkenly about art as they swilled their bottles of beer. Their berets, their long hair, their ties, and their blouses were those of artists; but in their souls they were more bureaucratic than the bureaucrats. Since Izawa believed in artistic creativeness and individuality, he found it hard to breathe in the atmosphere of these cabals; their mediocrity, their vulgar and sordid spirit, were sheer anathema. He became an outcast: no one returned his greetings and some people in the office even glared at him when he made his appearance.

One day he strode resolutely into the president's office and asked whether there was any inevitable, logical link between the war and the current poverty of artistic output. Or was this poverty, he asked, the deliberate aim of the military, who insisted that all one needed to portray reality was a camera and a couple of fingers? Surely, said Izawa, the special duty of us artists is to decide on the particular angle from which we should portray reality so as to produce a work of art. While Izawa was still talking, the president turned aside and puffed at his cigarette with a look of disgust. Then he smiled sardonically as if to say "Why don't you leave our company if you don't like it here? Is it because you're afraid of being drafted for hard labor?" Gradually his expression changed to one of annoyance. "Why can't you fit in with our way of working?" he seemed to say. "Just do your daily stint like the other men and you'll collect your salary all the same! And stop thinking about what doesn't concern you. Damned impertinence!" Without a single word in reply to Izawa's questions, the president motioned for him to leave the room.

How could this job of his be anything but the meanest of the mean? Sometimes he felt that it would be best to be done with it all and to be called into the army. If only he could escape from the anguish of thinking, even bullets and starvation might seem a blessing.

While Izawa's company was working on films like "Don't Let Rabaul Fall to the Enemy!" and "More Planes for Rabaul!" the American forces had already passed Rabaul and landed on Saipan. Saipan fell before they had finished "The All-Out Fight for Saipan"; and soon American planes based on Saipan were flying overhead in Japan. Strange was the enthusiasm with which Izawa's colleagues planned their films. "How to Extinguish Incendiary Bombs"; "Bodies That Crash in Midair"; "How to Grow Potatoes"; "Let Not a Single Enemy Plane Survive!"; "Power Saving and Airplanes" — one after another they turned out their infinitely boring lengths of celluloid.

Soon they began to run out of film stock, and usable cameras also grew scarce. The artists' enthusiasm reached new heights, as though they were possessed by some lyrical frenzy. Their films now bore such titles as "The Kamikazé Suicide Pilots"; "The Decisive Battle for the Mainland"; "The Cherry Blossoms Have Fallen." Infinitely boring films, films like pieces of pale paper. And Tokyo was about to turn into ruins.

Izawa's enthusiasm was dead. When he woke up in the morning and realized that he had to go to work again, he immediately became sleepy. Just as he was dozing off, the air-raid warning sounded. He got up and put on his leggings. Then he took out a cigarette and lit it. It occurred to him that if he missed work he would run out of cigarettes.

One night Izawa was late and barely managed to catch the last tram. The private electric line had already closed down and to get home he had to walk a considerable distance through the dark streets. When he turned on the light he was surprised to find that his bedding, which he always left spread out on the floor, had disappeared. This was strange since no one ever came into his room when he was out. He opened the closet. There, next to the heaps of his bedding, crouched the idiot woman from next door.

She glanced uneasily at Izawa and buried her face in the bedding. But when she discovered that he was not going to be angry, her relief gave rise to a great deluge of friendliness. She became remarkably composed. Yet she was still unable to talk coherently. All she could produce was a series of mumblings, and even when Izawa could make out what she was saying, it had no connection with what he was asking her. In a vague, fragmentary manner she voiced the confused scraps of thought in her head. Izawa surmised that she had been thoroughly scolded at home and that when it had become too much for her she had taken refuge in his hut. Since questions only seemed to frighten her, he limited himself to asking when and how she had arrived. After a spate of unintelligible mumblings, the woman rolled up her sleeve and rubbed a bruise on her arm.

"It hurts," she said. "It still hurts . . . it's been hurting for some time now." From her stumbling efforts to point out the time sequence — the distinction between past pain and present pain — Izawa finally gathered that she had climbed into his room through the window after it had become dark. She also mumbled something to the effect that she had been walking about barefoot outside and that she was sorry for having muddied the floor. But since Izawa had to extricate her meaning from among a confusion of mutterings that meandered up one blind alley after another, he was quite unable to tell the direction in which this particular apology was aimed.

It seemed difficult to rouse his neighbor in the dead of night to return this thoroughly frightened woman to her house. At the same time, if he brought her back in the morning, there was no telling what misunderstanding might arise from his having let her stay the night, especially since her husband was a madman.

"I don't care," he thought, suddenly imbued with a peculiar form of courage. "I'll let her stay."

The substance of his courage was simply this: the loss of emotion in his life had provoked in him a certain curiosity; he felt it did not matter what happened and that it was essential for his own way of life that he should regard the present reality as a sort of test. He told himself that there was no need to think about anything other than his duty to protect this feeble-minded woman for a night. He told himself that there was nothing to be ashamed of in the fact that he was so strangely moved by this unexpected turn of events.

Izawa made up two sets of bedding on the floor and told the woman to lie down. Then he switched off the light. A couple of minutes later he heard her crawling out of bed. She went to the corner of the room and crouched down. If it had not been the middle of winter, Izawa would probably have gone to sleep without troubling about her. But it was a bitterly cold night — so cold that he could not stop shivering. Since he had sacrificed one half of his bedding to his guest, the icy air seemed to impinge directly on his skin. He got up and turned on the light. The woman was crouching by the door, holding the front of her dress tightly about her body. Her eyes were those of a creature who has lost its hiding place and is driven to bay.

"What's the matter?" he said. "Go to bed."

The woman nodded — almost too readily — and crawled back into the bed. Izawa turned out the light. A moment later he heard her getting up as before. When he took the woman back to her bed this time, he tried to reassure her. "Don't worry," he said. "I'm not going to touch you." With a startled expression the woman muttered something that sounded vaguely like an excuse. The third time that he turned out the light, she got up without a moment's delay, opened the closet door, stepped inside, and shut herself in.

The woman's persistence had begun to annoy Izawa. He opened the closet roughly. "I don't know what you think you're doing," he said crossly, "but you seem to have got the wrong idea about me. Why on earth do you have to hide in the closet like that when I've told you I don't have the slightest intention of touching you? It's damned insulting. If you can't trust me, why come here in the first place? You've humiliated me, made a fool of me. What right have you to act as if you were being victimized in this place? I've had quite enough of your nonsense for one night."

Then it occurred to him that the woman could not possibly understand a word he was saying. What could be more futile than to remonstrate with a half-wit? Probably the best thing would be to give her a good slap on the cheek and then to go to sleep without bothering any more about her. He noticed that the woman was muttering away with an inscrutable look on her face. Apparently she was stuttering out something to the effect that she wanted to go home and that it would have been better if she had never come.

"But now I have nowhere to go home to," she added.

Izawa could not help being touched. "Then why not spend the night here quietly?" he said. "There's really nothing to worry about, you know. The only reason I got a bit angry just now is that you started setting yourself up in the role of a victim when I didn't have the slightest intention of harming you. Now then, stay out of that closet and get into bed and have a good night's sleep!"

The woman stared at Izawa and launched into some more rapid mumbling.

"What?" he asked.

Then Izawa had the shock of his life. For out of her confused mumblings he clearly caught the words "I see you don't like me."

"Eh?" said Izawa, gazing at her with open-eyed amazement. "What's that you said?"

With a dejected expression, the woman began to explain herself, repeating over and over: "I shouldn't have come"; "You don't really like me"; "I thought you liked me, but you don't." Finally she lapsed into silence and gazed vacantly at a spot in the air.

Now Izawa understood for the first time. The woman had not been afraid of him. The situation was exactly the reverse. The woman had not come just because she had been scolded at home and didn't have anywhere else to hide. She had been counting on Izawa's imagined love for her. But what on earth could have made the woman believe that Izawa loved her? He had only exchanged the briefest possible greetings with her a few times near the pigpen or in the alley or on the road. The situation could hardly have been more absurd. Here he was being coerced by an idiot's will, by an idiot's susceptibility — forces that must be completely different from those of normal people. It was not clear to Izawa whether what had happened to the woman that evening was, in her idiot mind, a truly painful experience. Having lain in bed for a few minutes without Izawa's so much as touching her, the woman had come to the conclusion that she was unloved; this had filled her with shame and she had got out of bed. Finally she had shut herself in the closet. How could one interpret this peculiar action? As an expression of an idiot's shame · and self-abasement? The trouble was that in the language of normal people there did not even exist the proper words in which to phrase a conclusion. In such a situation the only way was to lower oneself to the same level as the idiot's mentality. And after all, thought Izawa, what need was there for normal human wisdom? Would it be all that shameful if he himself adopted the frank simplicity of an idiot's mind? Perhaps that was what he needed more than anything else — the childlike, candid mind of an idiot. He had mislaid it somewhere, and in the meantime he had become bedraggled with thoughts of the workaday people who surrounded him; he had pursued false shadows and had nothing to show for it all but exhaustion.

He tucked the woman in bed and, sitting by the pillow, stroked her forelocks as if he were stroking a little girl — his own child perhaps — and trying to put her to sleep. Her eyes stayed open with a vacant look. There was an innocence about her, exactly like that of a little child's.

"I do not dislike you," Izawa began solemnly. "there are other ways, you know, of expressing love than by simple physical contact. The ultimate abode for us human beings is our birthplace, and in a strange way you seem to be living permanently in such a birthplace."

Of course there was no possibility of her understanding what he said. But what, after all, were words? What real value did they have? And where did reality reside? There was no evidence that it could be found even in human love. Where, if anywhere, could there be anything so real that it warranted a man's devoting his entire passion to it? Everything was merely a false shadow. But as he stroked the woman's hair, he felt like bursting into tears. He was overcome by the heartrending idea that this small, elusive, utterly uncertain love was the very haven of his life, that involuntarily he was stroking the hair of his own fate.

How was the war going to turn out? No doubt Japan would be defeated, the Americans would land on the mainland, and the greater part of the Japanese people would be annihilated. But all this could be conceived only as part of a supernatural destiny — the decree of Heaven, so to speak. What really bothered Izawa was a far more trivial problem — a surprisingly trivial problem, yet one that always flickered exigently before his eyes. It was the question of the two-hundred-yen wage he received every month from his company. How long would he continue to receive his salary? He never knew from one day to another when he would be dismissed and reduced to utter destitution. Each time he went to collect his salary he was terrified that he would also be given his dismissal notice. And when he actually held his pay envelope in his hand he was invariably overcome by intense joy at having survived for another month. He always felt like crying at the thought of how trivial it all was. Here he was — a man who dreamed about the great ideals of art — yet a wage of two hundred yen, which in the presence of art was less than the smallest speck of dust, could become a source of such agony that it penetrated to his marrow and shook the entire foundation of his existence. It was not merely his external life that was circumscribed by the two hundred yen; his very mind and soul were absorbed by it. And the fact that he could gaze calmly, steadily, at this triviality, and retain his sanity made him even more wretched.

The editor's loud, stupid voice, shouting "What does beauty mean at a time like this? Art is powerless!" filled Izawa's mind with a completely different sort of reality and ate into him with a great, biting force. Ah yes, he thought, Japan would lose. His countrymen would fall one after another like so many clay dolls, innumerable legs and heads and arms would fly skyward mixed with the debris of bricks and concrete, and the land would become a flat graveyard devoid of trees, buildings, everything. Where would he seek refuge? Which hole would he be driven into? Where would he be when finally he was blown up, hole and all?

Yet sometimes he dreamed of how things would be if, by some peculiar chance, he survived. What he felt chiefly at such moments was curiosity — curiosity about life in an unpredictable new world, life in rubble-buried fields, curiosity also about the regeneration that would come. It was bound to happen, in six months or perhaps a year; yet he could only imagine it as some remote fancy, like a world of dreams. Meanwhile the decisive force of a mere two hundred yen blocked off everything else and swept away all hope from his life; even in his dreams it choked and haunted him; it bleached every emotion of his youth, so that although he was still only twenty-seven years old, he already found himself wandering aimlessly over a dark moorland.

Izawa wanted a woman; this was what he longed for most of all. Yet life with any woman would ineluctably be limited by the two hundred yen.

His saucepan, his cooking pot, his bean paste, his rice — everything bore this curse. When his child was born, it too would be haunted by the curse, and the woman herself would turn into a demon obsessed by the same curse and would be grumbling from morning until night. His enthusiasm and his art and the light of his hopes were all dead; his very life was being trampled on like horse dung by the wayside; drying up and being blown away by the wind to disappear without a trace, without so much as the slightest nail mark. Such a curse it was that would cling to the woman's back.

His way of living was unbearably trivial and he himself lacked the power to resolve this triviality. War — this vast destructive force in which everyone was being judged with fantastic impartiality, in which all Japan was becoming a rubble-covered wasteland and the people were collapsing like clay dolls — what a heart-rending, what a gigantic love it represented on the part of nothingness! Izawa felt a desire to sleep soundly in the arms of the god of destruction. This resignation to the force of nothingness had the effect of making him rather more active than before, and when the air-raid alarm sounded he would briskly put on his leggings. The only thing that made life worth living each day was to toy with the uneasiness of life. When the all clear sounded, he would be thoroughly dispirited and once more would be overcome by the despair of having lost all emotion.

This feeble-minded woman did not know how to boil rice or to make bean-paste soup. She had trouble in expressing the simplest thought and the most she could do was to stand in line to get the rations. Like a thin sheet of glass, she reacted to the slightest suggestion of joy or anger; between the furrows of her fear and her abstractedness she simply received the will of others and passed it on. Even the evil spirit of the two hundred yen could not haunt such a soul. This woman, thought Izawa, was a forlorn puppet made for him. In his mind's eye he pictured an endless journey in which he would roam over the dark moorland with this woman in his arms and the wind blowing about him.

Yet he felt that there was something rather fantastic and ludicrous about the whole idea. This was probably because his external triviality had by now begun to erode his very heart in such a way that the frank feeling of love that was gushing up within him seemed entirely false. But why should it be false? Was there some intrinsic rule which said that the prostitutes in their apartments and the society ladies in their houses were more human than this feeble-minded woman? Yes, absurdly enough, it looked as if there really was such a rule.

What am I afraid of? It all comes from the evil spirit of those two hundred yen. Yes, now when I am on the point of freeing myself from the evil spirit by means of this woman, I find that I am still bound by its curse. The only thing I am really afraid of is worldly appearances. And what I mean by "world" is merely the collection of women who live here in the apartments — the prostitutes and the kept women and the pregnant volunteer-workers and the housewives who cackle away in their nasal voices like so many geese. I know that there is no other world. Yet, indisputable as this fact is, I am completely unable to *believe* it. For I live in fear of some strange rule.

It was surprisingly short (yet at the same time an endlessly long) night. Dawn broke before he knew it and the chill of daybreak numbed his body into an unfeeling block of stone. All night long he had simply stayed by the woman's pillow, stroking her hair.

*   *   *

From that day a new life began for Izawa.

Yet, aside from the fact that a woman's body had been added to a house, there was nothing peculiar or even different. Unbelievable though it might seem, not a single new bud appeared to sprout forth round him or within him. His reason perceived what an extraordinary event it was; but apart from that, there was not the slightest alteration in his life — not so much as the position of his desk was changed. He went to work each morning, and while he was out a feeble-minded woman stayed in the closet awaiting his return. Once he had stepped outside, he forgot entirely about the woman, as if he thought at all about the event, it seemed like something that had happened in the indefinite past, ten or even twenty years before.

War produced a strangely wholesome kind of amnesia. Its fantastic destructive power caused a century of change to take place in a single day, made last week's events seem as if they had happened several years before and submerged the events of the previous year at the very bottom of one's memory. It was only recently that the buildings surrounding the factories near where Izawa lived had been torn down in a frenzy of "planned evacuation," which had turned the entire neighborhood into a whirling mass of dust; yet, though the debris had still not been cleared away, the demolition had already receded into the past as if it were something that had taken place over a year before. Immense changes that completely transformed the city were taken for granted when one saw them for the second time.

The feeble-minded woman too had become one of the multifarious blurred fragments belonging to this wholesome amnesia. Her face lay among the various other fragments: among the sticks and splinters on the site of the evacuated "people's bar" in front of the railway station where, until a couple of days before, people had been waiting in queues, among the holes in the nearby building that had been wrecked by a bomb, among the fire-ravaged ruins of the city.

Every day the siren rang out. Sometimes it was an air-raid warning. At its sound Izawa would be plunged into deep disquiet. What worried him was that there might be an air raid near where he lived and that even now, while he sat in his office, some unknown change might be taking place at home. If there was an air raid, the feeble-minded woman might well become excited and rush out of the house, thus exposing their secret to the entire neighborhood. Fear about an unknown change concerned Izawa more than anything else and made it impossible for him to return home while it was still light. Many were the times that he vainly struggled against this pitiful condition in which he was dominated by vulgar worries. If nothing else, he would have liked to be able to confide everything to the tailor; but this struck him as a hopelessly mean action, for it would simply have meant getting rid of his worries by the least damaging possible form of confession. So he remained silent and angrily cursed himself for being no better in his true nature than the common run of men whom he despised.

For Izawa the feeble-minded woman had two unforgettable faces. When turning a street corner, when walking up the stairs in his office building, when detaching himself from the crowd of people in front of a tram — at these and other unexpected moments he would suddenly recall the two faces. His thoughts would freeze up and he would be congealed in a momentary frenzy.

One face was that which he had seen when he first touched her body. The occurrence itself had on the very next day receded into the memories of a year before; only the face would come back to him, detached from the surrounding events.

From that day the feeble-minded woman had been no more than a waiting body with no other life, with not so much as a scrap of thought. She was always waiting. Merely from the fact that Izawa's hands had touched a part of her body, the woman's entire consciousness was absorbed by the sexual act; her body, her face, were simply waiting for it.

Even in the middle of the night, if Izawa's hand happened to touch her, the woman's sleep-drugged body would show exactly the same reaction. Her body alone was alive, always waiting. Yes, even while asleep.

When it came to the question of what the woman was thinking about when awake, Izawa realized that her mind was a void. A coma of the mind combined with a vitality of the flesh — that was the sum and total of this woman. Even when she was awake, her mind slept; and even when she was asleep, her body was awake. Nothing existed in her but a sort of unconscious lust. The woman's body was constantly awake and reacted to outer stimuli by a tireless, worm-like wriggling.

But she had another face as well. There happened to be a daytime air-raid on Izawa's day off and for two solid hours the bombers had concentrated on a nearby part of the city. Since Izawa had no air-raid shelter, he hid in the closet with the woman, barricading their bodies with the thick bedding. The center of the bombing was about five hundred yards away, but the houses in Izawa's neighborhood trembled as the earth shook; with each great thud of the bombs Izawa's breath and thoughts stood still.

Although both incendiary and demolition bombs were dropped alike from the planes, they had all the difference in degree of horror that exists between a common grass snake and a viper. Incendiary bombs were equipped with a mechanism that produced a ghastly, rattling sound, but they did not explode on reaching the ground and the noise fizzled out above one's head. "A dragon's head and a serpent's tail,"[1] people used to say. In fact there was no tail at all, serpentine or otherwise, and one was spared the culminating terror. In the case of TNT bombs, however, the sound as they fell was like the subdued swishing of rain, but this ended in a fabulous explosion that seemed to shatter the very axis of the earth. The horror of the rain-like warning, the hopeless terror as the thud of the explosions approached, made one feel more dead than alive. Worse still, since the American planes flew at a high altitude, the sound of their passage overhead was extremely faint, and they gave the impression of being totally unconcerned with what was happening below. Accordingly, when the bombs fell, it was exactly like being struck by a huge axe wielded by a monster who is looking the other way. Because one could have no idea what the enemy planes were going to do, the strange buzzing of their motors in the distance filled one with a peculiar sense of uneasiness; then on top of this would come the swish of the falling bomb. The terror one felt while waiting for the explosion was really enough to stop every word and breath and thought. The only thing in one's mind was the despair that flashed through one, icy like impending madness — despair at the idea that this was assuredly one's final moment on earth.

Izawa's hut was fortunately surrounded on all sides by two-story buildings (apartments, the madman's house, the tailor's house) and it alone escaped without so much as a cracked windowpane, whereas the windows in the neighboring houses were shattered and, in some cases, the roofs badly damaged. The only untoward incident was that a blood-drenched hood, of the type people wore in air raids, fell on the field in front of the pigpen. In the darkness of the closet Izawa's eyes glittered. Then he saw it — he saw the idiot's face and its writhing agony of despair.

Ah yes, he thought, most people have intellect and even at the worst of times they retain control and resistance. How appalling it was to see someone who was entirely bereft of intellect and restraint and resistance! To the woman's face and body, as she gazed into the window of death, nothing adhered but anguish. Her anguish moved, it writhed, it shed a tear. If a dog's eyes were to shed tears, it would probably be infinitely ugly, just as if he were to laugh. Izawa was shocked to see how ugly tears could be when there was no trace of intellect behind them. Strangely enough, children of five or six rarely cry in the middle of a bombing. Their hearts beat like hammers, they become speechless, and they stare ahead with wide-open eyes. Only their eyes are alive; but apparently they are just kept wide open and they fail to show any direct or dramatic fear. The fact is that children calmly subdue their emotions to the extent that they appear more intelligent than under normal circumstances. At the instant of danger, they are the equal of adults. One might even say that they are superior, for adults plainly manifest their fears of death. Yes, children actually appear more intelligent at such times than adults.

But the idiot's anguish did not bear the slightest resemblance to the wide-eyed reaction that children show at times of danger. It was merely an instinctive fear of death, a single ugly movement. Her reaction was not that of a human being or even of an insect. If it could be said to resemble anything, it was like the writhings of a small three-inch caterpillar that has swollen to about six feet — and that has a teardrop in its eye.

There were no words, no screams, no groans; nor was there any expression. She was not even aware of Izawa's existence. If she were human, she would be incapable of such solitude. It was impossible that a man and a woman could be together in a closet with one of them entirely forgetting about the other. People talk of absolute solitude, but absolute solitude can exist only by one's being aware of the existence of others. Absolute solitude could never be such a blind and unconscious thing as what Izawa was now witnessing. This woman's solitude was like a caterpillar's — the ultimate in wretchedness. How unbearable it was — this anguish entirely devoid of any thought!

The bombing ended. Izawa raised the crouching woman in his arms. As a rule she reacted amorously if Izawa's finger so much as brushed against her breast, but now she appeared to have lost even her sense of lust. He was falling through space with a corpse in his arms. Nothing existed but the dark, dark, endless fall.

Immediately after the bombing Izawa took a walk past the houses that had just been mowed down. In the ruins he saw a woman's leg that had been torn from her body, a woman's trunk with the intestines protruding, and a woman's severed head.

Among the ruins of the great air raid of March tenth, Izawa had also wandered aimlessly through the still rising smoke. On all sides people lay dead like so many roast fowl. They lay dead in great clusters. Yes, they were exactly like roast fowl. They were neither gruesome nor dirty. Some of the corpses lay next to the bodies of dogs and were burned in exactly the same manner, as if to emphasize how utterly useless their deaths had been. Yet these bodies lacked even the pathos implied in the expression "a dog's death."[2] It was a case, not of people's having died like dogs, but of dogs lying there in the ruins next to other objects, as though they were all pieces of roast fowl neatly arranged on a platter. Those four-legged things were not really dogs; still less were those two-legged objects human beings.

If the idiot woman should be burned to death, would it not simply mean that a clay doll had returned to the earth whence it came? Izawa imagined the night that might come at any time when incendiary bombs would rain down on his street, and he could not help being conscious of his own form, his face, his eyes, as he lay there strangely calm, sunk in thought. I am calm, he thought. And I am waiting for an air raid. That's all right. He smiled scornfully. It's merely that I dislike ugly things. Is it not natural that a body which has no mind should burn and die? I shan't kill the woman. I am a cowardly and vulgar man. I don't have the courage for that. But the war will probably kill her. All that is necessary is to grasp the first opportunity to direct the unfeeling hand of war toward this woman's head. I shall not really be concerned. It will probably be a matter of having everything automatically settled by some crucial instant. Very calmly, Izawa awaited the next air raid.

*   *   *

It was April fifteenth. Two days before, on the thirteenth, the second great night-bombing had taken place, inflicting immense damage on Ikebukuro, Sugamo, and other residential districts in Tokyo. As a result of that raid, Izawa had managed to obtain a calamity certificate. This enabled him to take a train to Saitama Prefecture and to return with some rice in his rucksack. The air-raid alarm had started the moment he reached home.

By examining the areas of Tokyo that still remained unburned, anyone could surmise that the next raid would be directed at Izawa's neighborhood. Izawa knew that the fatal moment was near; at the earliest it would come on the following day, at the latest within a month. The reason Izawa thought it would not happen before the following day was that the tempo of raids until then indicated that at least another twenty-four hours would be necessary to complete preparations for a night attack. It never occurred to him that this might be the day of doom. That is why he had gone food-hunting. The main purpose of his trip, however, was not to buy food. Since his school days he had had connections with a certain farm in Saitama, and his principal objective in going to the country had been to deposit his belongings, which he had packed in a couple of trunks and a rucksack.

Izawa was tired out. He had made the trip in his air-raid uniform and when he reached his room he lay down as he was, using his rucksack as a pillow. When the crucial moment came, he had actually dozed off. He awoke to the blaring of radios. At that moment the front of the attacking squadron was approaching the southern tip of Izu Peninsula. A moment later, the bombers were over the mainland and the sirens started to shriek out their warning. Instinctively Izawa knew that the final day for his neighborhood had come. He put the feeble-minded woman in the closet and went outside to the well with a towel in his hand and a toothbrush in his mouth. A few days before, Izawa had managed to obtain a tube of Lion toothpaste and he had been enjoying the astringent taste that had been denied him for such a long time. When it dawned on him that the fatal moment had come, he was for some reason inspired to brush his teeth and wash his face. But first it took him a while — it seemed like ages — to find the tube, which had been moved a small distance from where he remembered having put it; then he had trouble finding the soap (it was a perfumed cake of a type that was no longer obtainable in the shops) because it too had been slightly misplaced. "I'm getting rattled," he told himself. "Calm down, Izawa, calm down!" Thereupon he struck his head against the closet and stumbled over the desk.

For a while he tried to gather his wits by suspending all movement and thought; but his entire body was flustered and refused to respond to orderly control.

Finally he found the soap and went to the well. The tailor and his wife were throwing their belongings into the shelter that they had dug in the corner of the field, and the duck-like girl from the attic was bustling about with a suitcase in her hand. Izawa congratulated himself for his persistence in having found the toothpaste and the soap, and wondered what fate really had in store for him that night.

While he was still wiping his face, the anti-aircraft guns started banging away. When he looked up, he saw that a dozen or more searchlights were already crisscrossing overhead. In the very center of their beams an American plane showed up clearly. Then another plane and yet another. When he happened to glance in the direction of the station, he saw that the whole area was a sea of flames.

The time had finally come. Now that the situation was clear, Izawa calmed down. He put on his air-raid hood and covered himself in his bedding. Standing outside his hut, he counted up to twenty-four planes. They all flew overhead, clearly exposed in the beams of the searchlights.

The anti-aircraft guns boomed crazily, but there was still no sound of bombing. When he had counted the twenty-fifth plane, he heard the familiar rattling sound of incendiary bombs, like a freight train crossing a bridge. Apparently the planes were passing over Izawa's head and concentrating their attack on the factory area behind. Since he could not see from where he was standing, he went to the pigpen and looked back. The factory area was bathed in flames, and to his amazement Izawa saw that, apart from the bombers which had just passed overhead, planes were approaching in quick succession from the exact opposite direction and were bombing the entire area to the rear. Then the radios stopped. The whole sky was hidden by a thick, red curtain of smoke, which blotted out the American planes and the beams of the searchlights.

The tailor and his wife were a prudent couple. Some time before, they had made the shelter for their belongings and had even provided mud to seal up the entrance. Now they briskly stored everything in the shelter as planned, sealed it, and covered it with earth from the rice field.

"With a fire like this," said the tailor, "it's absolutely hopeless." He stood there in his old fireman's clothes, with his arms folded, and gazed at the flames. "It's all very well their telling us to put it out," he continued, "but when the fire gets as bad as this there's nothing to be done. I'm going to run for it. What's the use of staying here and being choked to death by the smoke?"

The tailor heaped his remaining belongings onto a bicycle-drawn cart. "Why don't you come along with me, sir?" he said to Izawa.

Izawa was seized with a complex form of terror. His body was on the verge of running away with the tailor, but he was checked by a strong internal resistance. As he stood there immobile, he felt that a splitting shriek was rising in his heart: because of this moment's delay I'm going to be burned to death! His terror almost benumbed his mind, yet somehow he managed to withstand the urgings of his body as it staggered into the motions of flight.

"I'll stay a little longer," he said. "I've got a job to do, you see. After all, I'm an entertainer and when I have an opportunity to study myself in the face of death I've got to carry on to the very end. I'd like to escape, but I can't. I can't miss this opportunity. You'd better run for it now. Hurry, Hurry! In a minute it'll all be too late."

Hurry, hurry! In a minute it'll all be too late. In saying "all," Izawa was, of course, referring to his own life. "Hurry, hurry" was not aimed at urging the tailor to escape, but came from his own desire to get away as soon as possible. For him to get away, it was essential that everyone in the neighborhood should leave ahead of him. If not, people might find out about his feeble-minded woman.

"Very well, then," said the tailor, "but be careful." He started to pull his cart. But he too was thoroughly flustered and as he hurried along the alley he kept bumping into things. That was Izawa's last picture of his neighbors as they fled from their dwellings.

A ghastly rustling continued without pause or modulation. It sounded like the roaring of waves as they beat against the rocks, or like the endless pattering on rooftops of splinters from anti-aircraft guns; but it was the footsteps of a mass of evacuees scurrying along the main road. The sound of the anti-aircraft guns now seemed out of place, and the flow of footsteps had a strange vitality. Who in the world could possibly have imagined that the endless flow of this uncanny sound — this sound without pause or modulation — was produced by human footsteps? The sky and the earth were filled with countless sounds: the whirring of American planes, the anti-aircraft guns, the downpour, the roar of explosions, the sound of feet, the splinters striking the roofs. But the area immediately surrounding Izawa formed a quiet little realm of darkness in the midst of the red sky and earth. The walls of a strange silence, the walls of a maddening solitude, surrounded Izawa on all sides.

"Wait another thirty seconds. . . . Now just ten more." He did not know who was ordering him nor why; nor did he know what made him obey. He felt that he was going insane. He felt that at any moment he would start running along blindly, screaming in agony.

At that moment something started to fall immediately above his head and seemed to churn the insides of his eardrums. Frantically, he threw himself to the ground. The sound abruptly vanished and an incredible quiet once more descended on the surroundings. "Well, that gave me quite a fright," thought Izawa. He arose slowly and brushed the earth from his clothes. When he looked up, he found the madman's house in flames. "Oh, so it's finally been hit." He was strangely calm. Then he realized that the houses on both sides and the apartments opposite were also in flames.

Izawa rushed into his hut. He sent the door of the closet flying (it slipped from its groove and fell with a clatter) and rushed out covered with his bedding and holding the feeble-minded woman in his arms. For the next minute or so he was in a daze and had no idea what he was doing. As he reached the entrance to the alley, he once more heard the falling sound overhead. He threw himself down. When he stood up, he saw that the tobacco shop was burning, and that in the house opposite, violent flames were gushing from the family Buddhist altar. Looking back as he left the alley, he noticed that the tailor's house had also caught fire; no doubt his own hut was already in flames.

The entire neighborhood was burning and sparks of fire were swirling all about. Izawa felt that the situation was hopeless. When he reached the crossroads, he found that all was in utter confusion. Everybody was pressing forward in a single direction — the direction furthest from the flames. It was no longer a road but just a deluge of people, baggage, and screams, a deluge of hustling and jostling, shoving and pushing, stumbling and staggering forward. As people heard the swishing sound of bombs overhead, they would fall to the ground at once and the deluge would come to a complete standstill. A few people would run on, trampling over the others. But the majority had their personal belongings and were accompanied by children, women, and aged people. They were calling out to the members of their party, halting, turning back, bumping into one another.

The flames drew close on both sides of the road. Izawa reached a small intersection. Here, too, the entire deluge was pressing forward in one direction, again because it was farthest from the flames. Izawa, however, knew that in that direction there were neither open spaces nor fields: if the next batch of incendiary bombs from the American planes were to block the way, that particular road would lead to certain death. The houses on both sides of the other road were already burning, but Izawa remembered that some way ahead there was a river, and that a few hundred yards farther upstream one came to a wheat field. Not a single person seemed to have chosen that road, however, and for a moment Izawa hesitated. Then he noticed that about a hundred and fifty yards up the road a man was standing by himself, throwing water on the raging flames. Though he was throwing water on the flames, he certainly did not cut a valiant figure. He was merely a man with a bucket; occasionally he would throw some water about, but most of the time he stood there vacantly or wandered up and down. His movements were curiously sluggish and Izawa wondered whether he was not deranged. At any rate, thought Izawa, a man can stand there without burning to death. I'll try my luck. Luck, one thread of luck and the resolve to try it — that was all that remained.

At the crossroads was a ditch, and Izawa soaked his bedding in the muddy water. Then he pulled the woman close to him and, covering both their bodies with the bedding, left the mass of people with whom they had been walking. But as they approached the road that was lined with raging flames, the woman instinctively stopped and falteringly tried to return toward the human deluge as if she were being sucked back into a whirlpool.

"You fool!" cried Izawa, pulling the woman with all his might. He hugged her shoulders and held her close to his breast. "You'll only die if you go that way," he whispered. "When we die, we'll be together — just like this. Don't be frightened! And don't leave my side whatever you do! Forget about those flames and those bombs! The road of our two lives will always be this road. You just look straight ahead along this road and rely on me! Do you understand?"

The woman nodded. It was a childish nod, but Izawa was overwhelmed with emotion. For this was the first sign of volition, the first answer, that the woman had shown in these long, repeated hours of terror during the day and night bombings. It was so touching that Izawa felt quite dizzy. Now at last he was embracing a human being, and he was filled with immeasurable pride about that human being.

The two of them rushed through the wild flames. When they emerged from under the mass of hot air, both sides of the road were still a sea of flame; but the houses had already collapsed in the fire and as a result the force of the conflagration had decreased and the heat was less intense. Here again there was a ditch full of water. Izawa doused the woman from head to toe, soaked the bedding, and covered her and himself with it once again. Burned belongings and bedding lay strewn on the road, and two dead bodies also lay there. They were a middle-aged man and woman.

Izawa again put his arm around the woman and the two dashed through the flames. At last they reached the stream. The factories on both sides were sending up furious jets of flame. Retreat and advance were equally impossible, nor could they stay where they were. Looking around, Izawa noticed a ladder leading down to the stream. He covered the woman with the bedding and had her walk down, while he himself jumped for it.

People were walking along by the stream in little groups. Now and then the woman dipped herself in the water of her own accord. The situation was such that even a dog would have had to do so, but Izawa was wide-eyed at the sight of the birth of a new and lovable woman, and he watched her figure greedily as she immersed herself.

The stream emerged from beneath the flames and flowed beneath the darkness. It was not really dark because of the glow of the fire that covered the sky; but this semi-darkness, which he could see once again inasmuch as he was still alive, filled Izawa with a sense of vacancy — vacancy that came from a vast, ineffable weariness, from a boundless feeling of nothingness. At the bottom of it all lay a small sense of relief, but that struck him as strangely insignificant and absurd. He felt that everything was absurd.

Upstream they came to the wheat field. It was a large field enclosed on three sides by hills; a highway ran across the middle, cutting through the hills. The houses on the hills were all burning; and the buildings around the field — the Buddhist temple, the factory, the bathhouse — were also burning. The flames of each fire were a different color — white, red, orange, blue. A sudden wind sprang up and filled the air with a great roar, while minute, misty drops of water showered all around.

The crowd was still meandering down the highway. There were only a few hundred people resting in the wheat field — nothing in comparison with the crowds that stretched along the road. Next to the field was a little thicket-covered hill. There were hardly any people in this grove. Izawa and the woman spread their bedding under a tree and lay down. At the side of the field below the hill a farmhouse was burning. A few people could be seen throwing water on the flames. At the rear was a well where a man was working the pump handle and was drinking water. Seeing this, about twenty men and women rushed toward the well from all directions. They took turns in working the pump handle and drinking. Then they crowded about the burning house and stretched their hands toward the flames to warm themselves. As burning fragments fell from the house they sprang back and turned away from the smoke. They then went on talking. Nobody lent a hand to try to put out the fire.

The woman said that she was sleepy. She also muttered that her feet ached, that her eyes smarted; but her main complaint was that she was sleepy.

"All right, then," said Izawa, "sleep for a while." He wrapped her in the bedding and lit a cigarette for himself. When he had smoked a number of cigarettes and was about to light another, the all-clear signal sounded in the distance and several policemen came running through the wheat field to announce that the alarm had been lifted. Their voices were hoarse, not like the voices of human beings at all.

"The raid is over," they shouted. "Everyone living in the area of the Kamata Police Station is to assemble at the Yaguchi Elementary School. The school building is still standing."

The people rose from the ridges in the field and walked down to the highway. But Izawa did not move. A policeman came up to him.

"What's the matter with that woman? Is she hurt?"

"No," said Izawa, "she's tired and sleeping."

"Do you know the Yaguchi Elementary School?"

"Yes. We'll have a rest here for a while and then we'll come along."

"Brace up, man! You mustn't let a little raid get you down."

The policeman's voice trailed off as he disappeared down the hill. Only two people were left in the grove. Two people? But wasn't the woman in fact a mere lump of flesh? Now she lay there sound asleep. Everyone else was walking through the smoke of the fire-ravaged ruins. They had all lost their homes and they were all walking. Certainly none of them was thinking about sleep. The only ones who could sleep now were the dead and this woman. The dead would never wake again, but this woman would eventually wake up. Yet even when she awoke nothing would be added to this sleeping lump of flesh.

She was snoring faintly. It was the first time that he had heard her snore. It sounded like the grunting of a little pig. Yes, thought Izawa, everything about her is porcine. And abruptly a fragmentary memory from his childhood came back to him. A group of about a dozen urchins had been chasing a baby pig at the command of their gang leader. When they cornered the animal, the leader took out his jackknife and sliced a piece of flesh off its thigh. Izawa recalled that the pig's face had showed no sign of pain and that it had not even squealed very loudly. It simply ran away, evidently unaware that some flesh had been sliced off its thigh.

Now Izawa's mind conjured up a picture of himself and the woman as they would run away, stumbling among the clouds of dust, the crumbled buildings, the gaping holes. The American forces would have landed; the heavy artillery shells would be roaring on all sides, huge concrete buildings would be blown sky-high, enemy planes would be diving and spraying them with machine-gun fire. Behind a pile of rubble a woman would be held down by a man; he would overpower her and, while indulging in the sexual act, would be tearing off the flesh from her buttocks and devouring it. The flesh on the woman's buttocks would gradually diminish, but the woman would be so preoccupied with her carnal enjoyment that she would not even notice the depredations from behind.

As dawn approached, it began to grow cold. Izawa was wearing his winter overcoat and also had on a thick jacket, yet the cold was quite unbearable. The field below was still burning in places. Izawa wanted to go and warm himself, but he was unable to move because he was afraid of waking the woman. Somehow the thought of the woman waking up seemed intolerable.

He wanted to go away and leave her as she slept, but even that seemed too much trouble. When a person discards something, even a piece of waste paper, it means that he still possesses the necessary initiative and fastidiousness. But Izawa did not even have enough initiative or fastidiousness left to abandon this woman of his. He did not have the slightest affection for her now, not the slightest lingering attachment; yet neither did he have sufficient incentive to discard her. For he was devoid of any hopes for the future. Even if he were to get rid of the woman without delay, where would there be any hope for him? What was there to lean on in life? He did not even know where he would find a house to live in, a hole to sleep in. The Americans would land, and there would be all kinds of destruction in the heavens and on earth; and the gigantic love extended by the destructiveness of war would pass impartial judgment upon everything. There was no longer any need even to think.

Izawa decided that at daybreak he would wake the woman and that, without even a glance in the direction of the devastated area, they would set out for the most distant possible railway station in search of a roost. He wondered whether the trams and trains would be running. He wondered whether there would be a clear sky and whether the sun would pour down on his back and on the back of the pig that lay beside him. For it was a very cold morning.

★

Notes

1. Proverbial expression, roughly corresponding to "Up like a rocket and down like a stick."

2. To "die like a dog" (*inujini sura*) means to die in vain.

★

Part II

Women and War

In an interview, Tim O'Brien — a novelist whom critics herald as the most important author to write about the Vietnam War — argued that men and women do not differ radically in the ways they respond to war. The stories in this section on women and war give evidence to support his claim.

The first two stories, "Two Faces, One Woman" and "Sati," depict women as eager and violent participants in war. The two faces referred to in the title of Nuha Samara's story symbolize the two sides, mirror images, of the protagonist's character. In the opening paragraph a woman undresses and washes her long, blond hair, which for many years has symbolized her femininity. Her husband, who has fled to Paris to escape the Lebanese Civil War, had compared her to an animal, a palomino — an appropriate comparison in light of the way he had exploited, dominated, and sexually ridden her. When her husband leaves, she feels liberated and exhilarated. She cuts and dyes her hair and enrolls in civil defense training, quickly learning how to shoot and to enjoy the violence. This story contrasts words with action and lust in peace with lust in war.

The transformation is reversed in "Sati," in which Prem Chand shows the conversion of a woman from someone who loves battle and all things masculine to a creature who finds "love" and becomes soft, docile, and submissive — the antithesis of her former self. Her newly wedded husband undergoes his own transformation. He was once a reckless, brave, Rajput hero, but his love for Sati turns him into a quivering coward. At the conclusion of the story, Sati comes to her senses, renounces her husband, and rediscovers her love of valor and military martyrdom. "Sati" is a subtle but powerful political allegory.

"One Last Look at Paradise Road," by the South African novelist Gladys Thomas, is the story of a black woman who is a maid for a wealthy, white South African family. The story recounts her gradual realization of her own personal freedom and her commitment to her children's eventual freedom. Her confusion, pain, and hopelessness are skillfully portrayed, but her metamorphosis is even more compelling. Committed to the eventuality of conflict, to necessary sacrifice in pursuit of a noble end, she gains strength and beauty.

The effect of war on a mother and wife is sensitively examined in Andrei Platonov's "The Homecoming." Although war tears men from the hearthside and causes incalculable suffering, it also has a dimension of excitement, of movement. War is often, therefore, compared to a mistress: dangerous, but exciting. In this story, a Russian soldier, on his way home from war, takes a brief detour with another woman, who is herself returning from war. His wife and children wait until he returns, and when he returns, all the costs of war are revealed. This story is an indictment of the double standard that allows a man to betray his love when he is at war but demands from a woman "constancy . . . patience" and a "faithful and unchanging heart." It reveals the mental and physical suffering of women who are left to fight "on the home front."

The next story in this section puts traditional African oral history in a modern context. "Certain Winds From the South," by one of Ghana's most popular authors, Ama Ata Aidoo, portrays the suffering caused by war from generation to generation. The never-ending cycle of wars is starkly contrasted with the peaceful and seemingly timeless village life, which is symbolized by a reed bowl.

In "Girls at War," internationally acclaimed African novelist Chinua Achebe shows how war often forces individuals into degrading and self-alienating situations. In this instance, a young, politically minded woman becomes co-opted by the men in power. She becomes a sexual object of the men who provide her with luxuries that most other women in war-torn Nigeria are forced to do without. The price she pays is not so much the sacrifice of her body but the reunification of her political and social ideals. She becomes a symbol of many African civil wars, corrupted and co-opted by materialism.

Kay Boyle's "Frankfurt in Our Blood" relates a conversation that takes place on a train from Paris to Frankfurt five years after the Second World War. A middle-aged German-Jewish woman is returning to Germany for the first time in years, returning to the country where her husband died and her two sons were killed by the Nazis. Her interlocutor is a young American woman who is working for the War Department in Occupied Germany, a foreigner with no past or present ties to Germany. In the story's title, "our" refers to the older woman and her two remaining sons, who fled with her to China. Figuratively, it also suggests that the humanism, liberalism, and free thinking embodied in Frankfurt's most renowned citizen, Johann Wolfgang von Goethe, are something that is potentially in every human being's "blood" — even if history seems to belie this. The story opens with lush images of nature: "gently sloping green hills . . . luxuriant fields . . . feathery trees" and the "pastoral stillness of the continent." The narrator also refers to many of the great European centers of civilization: "Paris, Prague, Warsaw and Budapest . . . Vienna, Munich, and Bucharest," recalling the fact that these were shattered by war. The pastoral scenes and formerly grand cities are used as a foil for the bomb-gutted cities. In this story Kay Boyle asserts the basic constancy of humanity even in the wake of destruction and brutality.

Technology makes killing at a distance possible. In Bui Ngoc Tan's "Sao" we are shown the close-up and personal effects of aerial warfare. Each character in this story is sensitively and uniquely portrayed; each is personally affected by aerial warfare. It is in the manipulation of personal perspective that this story is unique. Especially poignant is the changing perspective of a captured French flier. Before his capture, he had looked at his bombing of the Vietnamese countryside in purely aesthetic terms: "A whole village burns like a sea of flames as picturesque as a painting." His personal acquaintance and conversation with the Vietnamese help him overcome the distance between bomber and victims. He gradually discovers that the enemy is personal, the bombing, impersonal.

"Mori" is probably an allusion to a phrase from Horace: *Dulce et decorum est pro patriae mori.* (It is sweet and becoming to die for one's country.) This brief story by Tim O'Brien depicts the various responses of a group of U.S. soldiers to the accidental killing of a Vietnamese woman. The narrator repeatedly refers to the remorse of the "man who shot her," and yet the callousness of some of the other soldiers makes him appear naive. The most interesting aspect of this story is that some of the men are sympathetic only because she is a woman and is pretty. It is apparent that they would not have felt pity if the enemy victim had been a man.

The last story in this section provides a compassionate portrayal of grief. A woman who has never really understood why her husband was executed by the military for desertion retells the story of how she discovered that he was to be put to death. Her naïveté and innocence serve to underline the basic corruptness of forced military service. The driver of the oxcart referred to in the title, himself a deserter, observes in the story's closing sentence that the fog in March "means either a war or famine."

Like so many other stories in this volume, Hsiao Hung's "On the Oxcart"
reminds us of the vicious cycle of wars in human history.

★

★ ★ ★ ★

AUTHOR: *Nuha Samara (1944–) was born in Tulkarem, Palestine. When she was four, her family fled to Beirut, Lebanon. By 1962 she was writing for Beiruti newspapers. She published* Fi Madinat al-Mustanqa (In the Swamp City) *in 1973 and, during the Lebanese Civil War,* Al-Tawilat Ashat Akthar min Amin (The Tables Lived Longer Than Amin). *In 1975 she moved to Qatar. She later lived in London and Paris but returned to the Middle East in 1982.*

SETTING: *Casualties in the Lebanese Civil War of 1975 numbered more than fifty thousand. The confrontation was between the Lebanese Front and the National Movement, backed by the Palestine Liberation Movement (PLO). It ended with the invasion of Syrian troops. The Lebanese Front was composed of the Phalange, the National Liberal party, and Zghorta Liberation Army. The National Movement – a cooperative effort of the Progressive Socialist party, the Syrian National Socialist party, the Independent Nasserites, the Lebanese Communist party, and the Ba'ath parties – was generally Druze and Sunni Muslim. The Amal faction represented the Shiites. Faced with the choice of killing or being killed, men fled; women, who were not expected to kill or be killed, were left to "take care."*

This is the story of one such woman. Her husband has fled to Paris, leaving her to "take care" of herself, her father, and her country.

Two Faces, One Woman

Nuha Samara

Calmly she went to bathe. She had learnt how to hold on to time, how to touch things calmly. She undressed slowly. As she washed her long, blond hair she remembered him and how he had loved and admired her hair: "The hair of a palomino"; "It fills me with desire for you"; "The day it's cut short I'll leave you for another woman."

Ever since the beginning of the war, she had accustomed herself to bathing quickly, fearing that a shell might hit and kill her when she was naked. Her death would become a funny story for the neighbours to repeat!

"Two Faces, One Woman" is reprinted from *The Tables Lived Longer Than Amin,* trans. Miriam Cooke (Durham, N.C.: Duke Univ. Press, 1990) by permission of the publisher.

She felt afraid . . . and decided to finish quickly. Why shouldn't she admit that he had chosen to abandon her with her helpless father!

She dried her hair thoroughly. And then, sitting in front of the mirror, she set up another one behind her and began to cut her hair. She saw the locks fall, but felt no sadness. It's a lie that women make themselves beautiful for men . . . Now that the man had gone she could stop lying. In the mirror her features hardened. Then she had an idea. She took some hair bleach and, mixing it into a paste, she brushed it on to her hair. Then she washed her hair and contemplated it in the mirror. Her features had become more sharply defined; this bleached hair made her look like a Nazi officer. She wanted him to see her now, to rid him of those sweet images. What did he mean by abandoning her in this filthy war, where survival depended on chance alone! He knew perfectly well how the daily chores of wartime existence exhausted her. And her father . . . what an enormous responsibility! How could she take him down to the shelter in his wheel-chair when the shelling got heavy? And what of the neighbours' questioning, infuriating glances: "He left her the responsibility of this helpless old man!"

Earlier her father had lived with her sister and her four children. It was he who had suggested that they should bring him here to lighten her sister's accumulated responsibilities. He had driven there under the bombs and had quickly brought him back, like a conqueror. Exactly a month later his director had given him the choice between staying or transferring to Paris . . . and he had chosen the latter.

He stuttered a lot as he announced his decision. She remained silent, neither encouraging, nor dissuading him. He knew her well, she didn't interfere in anyone's decision. She muttered under her breath: "It's your right to choose to stay alive."

She wondered if he would have chosen to travel had she not aborted the baby a few months ago. Would she have retained her passivity?

Two days after this decision, he told her that he was leaving the next day. Throughout those three days he noticed that she couldn't look him in the eye. She had even lost interest in following the news of the war . . . And when the dining room window shattered after a shell exploded nearby, he had held her tight and said: "Be strong in my absence!"

And that's how she was now . . . Her features were those of a man, her demeanor that of a Nazi in Hitler's army. She went to the wardrobe, and put on a pair of jeans and a khaki shirt. She looked ready to go into battle, all she lacked were weapons. And then she remembered. She opened an old cupboard and took out his pistol. Why hadn't she agreed at his friend

Manah's suggestion to train near the house? She could do that in the early hours of dawn while her father was asleep, when the sounds of shells and death had receded.

She contacts Manah immediately. He responds quickly and tells her that she's made an excellent decision. She tells him of Abdallah's departure. He's surprised, and then he understands, and is quiet. Then she hears him reassure her: "You've made a great decision. Tomorrow morning at six, we'll see you over there."

In the morning . . . Manah was not there. But he had given her name to the drill master. All those present were men. Not one of them looked at her curiously, nor admiringly nor even lustfully as he had . . . Was it the war? Or was it her new face that made her look like a Nazi officer?

The training exercises were not difficult. The sound of the first bullets exploding out of her pistol didn't frighten or disturb her . . . She was amazed by her lust to kill. When the bullets exploded in quick succession, she wished that the dummies that were falling had been people. When it was over, the drill master congratulated her on her courage, and she answered: "I want to complete the training. I want to know all fighting techniques."

At night the shelling increased, but she was no longer afraid as she had been before. She heard the neighbours scream as they rushed down to the shelter. She decided to take her father in his wheel-chair down to the shelter, not forgetting to take some bread and cheese. Probably the toughest thing that day were the neighbours' looks. Ohh! . . . How she hated to be pitied. The only pity she had been able to stand had been his when he returned home and saw her cooking and cleaning. After returning from a day's teaching, he would mutter something she could not understand: "Ah, the beautiful proletariat!"

She never asked him what that meant, but when she dusted his office, she noticed many titles about revolution and change and books stuffed with the word "proletariat." She wasn't at all curious to read any of these books. Maybe she didn't have the time. But then, she'd never seen him read any of them. He preferred to chat with friends, to inhale the aroma of her food and to smoke an ivory *narghile*, of which his friends made fun. At one point Manah had said to him:

"Words! This revolution about which you keep talking doesn't go with this *narghile* of yours!"

Down in the shelter she felt ravenously hungry. She gave her father some bread and cheese. In time with the pounding shells he started to gnaw. She loathed the sound of chewing. All that was left of the people in the war was greedy mouths that did nothing but chew. The shelter was like the Day of Resurrection with all those kids screaming. She touched her stomach where the embryo had been on that day that she had rejoiced to have aborted it. Had she known at the time that her relationship could not stand this?

A neighbour asked her presumptuously: "Where's Abdallah?"

"He's gone."

"Where?"

"Paris."

"Why?"

"They transferred him."

She didn't tell her that his company had given him the choice between staying and leaving, lest the woman pity her even more!

"Has he seen what you've done to your hair?"

"Yes."

She had to lie. Why should everyone know what she'd gone through. The neighbour went on:

"I'm not surprised that Abdallah's gone. I overheard him talking to my husband a while back here in the shelter, and he said that he couldn't stand it. Don't forget, it's been a year and a half! But why didn't he take you with him?"

"How could I leave my father? My sister's already left with her husband and children."

The neighbour shook her head, not quite convinced. Then she said pointing to her father: "May God help you with this responsibility."

She turned to her responsibility. He was gnawing at the bread and cheese as anxiously as someone eating his last meal. All his appetites in life had turned to eating. Every day he'd ask her what there was to eat, and whether they had enough money for it.

He had given her his whole salary before he left, and as usual had left the money on the table. He knew that she hated to take the money from his hand. He noticed that she hadn't hidden the money and he chided her: "Be careful! Everyone's become a thief!"

And when it was time for him to go, he stood there in embarrassment wanting to kiss her, and he said: "Take good care of yourself. If you need anything, go to my brother or uncle. I'll get in touch through my uncle."

Words . . . words!!

Most of the people in the shelter were sleeping, completely exhausted. They had spread out their bedding and had fallen asleep. Even her father was asleep in his wheel-chair. She covered him with a blanket, and then went up to the apartment calmly. The shells persisted outside, lighting up the skies and then going out, shining and then disappearing. Like red and green traffic lights. She remembered peace time, when the traffic lights used to work.

She felt very calm when she found herself alone. From birth, she had never been quite alone. Her family and siblings had always been there. After marriage, either he or his absence had been there. But now she was completely alone with the night. She sat in front of the hall mirror in her apartment hallway, where there were the safest corners. Suddenly she felt like taking off her clothes. She contemplated her body in the mirror, it was still radiant. She started to touch it as though bewitched, as though noticing it for the first time. She felt a desire to possess it, and she touched herself until she climaxed. Then she thought: I have to have a lover!

She thought about the men she knew, most of whom she knew through Abdallah. She had not once thought of any of them as men. They had different voices. She could remember their voices clearly, but she could not remember their features, their heights or sizes. She saw them through him. Whoever he had liked, she had liked. And he had really liked Manah and praised her in front of him! Manah . . . Maybe he was the one to pursue? He had been his best friend, and his was the only face she could clearly recollect. This was the man. He was almost primitive with his bulging muscles, the hair emerging from the open shirt and his black, piercing, captivating eyes . . .

Manah. Why not? She decided to talk to him the next morning.

She was a bit embarrassed when she saw him at the training ground. He approached and shyly asked her how she was. Did she need anything in Abdallah's absence. She didn't hesitate to ask him if he could find a hospital for her father where she could be sure that he would be well cared for. He promised to arrange something as soon as possible.

She went on to tell him about her anxiety for her father during bombardments. Sometimes she couldn't find him a doctor when he had a relapse. He praised her for her rational decision. Then he said before leaving: "I'll be in touch as soon as I've found something suitable."

Manah wasn't long in contacting her. One morning he told her of a suitable, safe place and he promised to get an ambulance to transport him. And then he asked: "How is he?"

She noticed that he avoided mentioning her husband's name. She answered briefly that he had asked his uncle about her and had tentatively asked if there was anything she needed.

When Manah left, she hurried to her father to tell him of her plan. She assured him somewhat harshly and peremptorily that this was ideal during the war, and that his safety and food would be surer there than with her. He looked distracted and sad, and shook his head a lot because he had difficulty in speaking. In the end she assured him that this was just for the duration of the war, and that when it was over he would return to her.

She rushed out so as not to burst into tears. In her room she began to undress. Manah's face leapt out in front of her. Why was her body beginning to awaken to desires of which she had been unaware when she had been with him? Was it Abdallah's absence? Or the repeated reports of death? He had accused her of frigidity, and she had never responded because she hadn't had the right keys to her body.

And when he had insistently made love to her during the war, she had questioned him and he had answered confidently:

"When you keep hearing of death your desires increase. This is particularly true during wars. Europe went through its moral decline after its two wars." And he went on: "In the face of death all values go by the board. All that remains alive are the limits of the body and the pulse of feeling and instinct."

Another time he had said something that was hard to forget: "The most important consequence of this war is that our pursuit of work, social relationships and petty misguided ambitions has slowed down. It has reduced us to life size . . . But if it goes on we may lose ourselves once again, but in another way . . ."

How often had she looked back on her life with him before the war. Her marriage had been a rush between her work as a teacher and a wife. He had been very concerned about his clothes, his food and the cleanliness of the house. He had often exploded in anger, swearing and slamming the door when he hadn't found things exactly right. She was used to this, because her father had been like this. And her response to these explosions had been the same as her mother's . . . silence! She had only felt a refusal grow in her after he had left. The only difference between her and her mother was that she worked outside the home. The only difference between him and her father was that he didn't object to her sitting with his friends when they came over, and he wasn't ashamed to express his feelings for her openly. Whereas she had never heard her father praise her mother in front of others. Her father was a man: not once had he left his family, and he had shouldered his responsibilities until he was paralysed two years after her mother's death.

How embarrassed she had been by his openness in front of his friends. He had exaggerated, as though wanting them to feel dissatisfied with their wives. But when they had left, he would pick up any old newspaper as though he had not said all those passionate things a few seconds ago. At first, she couldn't understand the change, couldn't explain it. She had attributed it to moodiness, because he had often said that he was moody, his temper mercurial.

Manah had been on her mind when she opened the door to him after a wild night of shelling spent in the shelter with her father. He looked a little disturbed:

"Have you prepared all your father's things? The war might last."

"Will it?"

"Probably. Your drill master has given you an 'A.' He says that you shoot with an amazing ability that he doesn't find in men. I wonder if you can hit all your targets?"

"Yes. And particularly now that he's gone!"

He interrupted her: "Where's your father?"

"In the bedroom . . . Here."

Her father's face was tense, as though he were on his way to the gallows. She loved the way that Manah stroked his tired face and held her father's hand saying:

"Listen, uncle. We're doing all this for your good. These inhuman conditions have compelled us to put you in hospital where everyone will take care of you. In the hospital they will protect you against this damned war. You'll get food, drink, shelter, electricity and medicine. I'll always make sure you're O.K. . . . and so will your daughter. If ever you need anything, just let me know . . ."

"And now?"

He carried her father from the bed to the wheel-chair. He indicated that she should bring the case and follow him. Fortunately, the lift was working that day. She rushed after them, and they got into the ambulance.

When they arrived at the hospital after a silent trip, her father's face reflected all the harshness of the war. She followed them into the hospital. She tried not to look through the partially open doors of rooms housing the injured and the maimed of the war. Manah murmured reassuringly:

"He'll be in the geriatrics ward, not here . . ."

She relaxed when she saw how clean the place was and when she realized that he was going to be put into a sunny, private room. She kissed him. Not a single tear. This war was tough. Manah took her hand. She trembled and he must have felt it.

She heard him say: "I left my car at the hospital entrance so we can return together." She followed him as though bewitched.

When she sat next to him she was as calm and relaxed as though she were his wife. He said:

"You had no other choice. Imagine what would have happened if your house had been hit, or if you had needed a doctor during a bombardment. What would you have done?"

Silence. Then she heard him say, "He's in the proper place now."

When they arrived at the house she asked him if he wanted some morning coffee, and he answered, his black eyes laughing: "I'd love to have some of your famous coffee!"

In the elevator, he stared silently at the lights that indicated the first floor, the second . . . the fifth then the seventh . . .

She was very embarrassed when they were alone together without his shadow or the shadow of her father. She rushed to the kitchen to prepare the coffee. All this silence excited her. On purpose she started to make lots of noise with the dishes. When she went into the sitting room, he had closed his eyes and he looked washed out. He felt her moving around, and said quickly:

"Imagine! I almost fell asleep. The last three nights I've hardly slept."

He sat up and asked her gently, "Are you depressed to be alone now?"

"No. I need to be alone."

"You're strange . . . Most women living alone complain a great deal."

"Not me."

"That's why he was happy with you."

"Who said he was happy?"

"That's what he had us understand."

The handed him the coffee and he began to talk about the war, and analyzed the reasons for the resumption and intensification of the fighting. Then he got up and said: "I'll drop around often. I need to talk to you."

"So do I."

When he had closed the door behind him, the air was filled with his smell and her father's sad face, and she decided to call and find out how he was.

After taking her father to the hospital, she hadn't even considered going down into the shelter. Most of the people kept insisting that she go down. But she didn't.

There, on her own, she could dream a lot about Manah, and a little about the future.

What would she do if the war were to end and life returned to its regular pace and he came back. And the school, and his friends' and family's stupid faces and eternal visits, and his anger and whims for what he wanted and didn't want. She felt incapable of touching him after today. In the past she had been content with him and submitted to his moods. But today the balance had been upset. He'd just escaped to Paris. What did he feel when he saw those beautiful, elegant Parisian women who were enjoying themselves while she was a prisoner of her responsibility, her loneliness and her death? Wouldn't he be confused by the comparison? At night whom would he hold? She well knew that he couldn't live without a woman, without touching, especially after the second drink. When his revolutionary friends had left he would sniff and lick her. Once she had fallen asleep with him kissing her body, content as a child, and she had heard him say frantically: "You're mine . . . mine . . . a thousand times mine."

It was that day that she realised that however much she submitted to him, he was never fully satisfied that she was his. He had said to her once that she wouldn't let him feel that she belonged to him, that she was like happiness: only felt after it was gone.

The sounds of the shells and the explosions returned, the daily blanket of the city which enfolded the inhabitants like a peasant woman's clothes enfolded her. She began to feel the warm pulse of her new life. The white space of time ahead was hers to contemplate. Again she took off her clothes in front of the mirror in the hallway. She saw Manah's face, and she felt embarrassed as she touched herself, as though he were actually watching. She felt a terrible longing for him. She knew his phone number. Why shouldn't she contact him, and use all her feminine tricks and wiles. Tell him that she was afraid and he would come over and hold her through the night. And she would drown in love in his body. But if that were to happen, how difficult it would be to return to the distant traveller. She knew that she couldn't maintain relationships with two men at the same time. She remembered that his uncle had brought her a letter from him two days ago and she hadn't yet looked at it. His writing was like his body: sensitive, supple and full of curves . . . reading handwriting is like making love to the writer.

"My darling, here, far away it's hard to forget, and it's hard to remember . . . I'm living like someone who is postponing his life. Beirut has not given us the space for expectation and hope. And yet, I am living it. My time and my space are defined by it, even though I'm far away in Paris . . .

"Peace-time Beirut is not as beautiful and passionate as war-torn Beirut. Because of her we become vicious in love with vice, and mystics in love with mysticism. I am filled with loneliness, longing and waiting. I recollect the city's face and yours, and feel that I am still intimately connected to it and to you. I feel that my amputation has been a kind of treachery. My darling, I am suspended between life and death. Every morning I am amazed that I can keep going. As I awake out of the confusion of my dreams I forget where I am, but am filled with the old joy, probably part of my childhood. This joy drives me to get up and wash my face, shave and dress. And as I go through the streets to work I discover the delusion of this joy, and I wonder why and I find it in Beirut and in your face. Both possess me to the point of suffocation. I walk through the streets like a lost child not knowing where the path is leading.

"The women of Paris are beautiful and they remind me of a phrase from Byron: 'If all the women of the world had but one mouth I would have kissed it and been happy.' How I miss your mouth, your long hair, my corner in front of the TV, my records, my bed, the smell of your cooking when I come home from work. How I long for the warmth of old! I'll be back when the war's over, that's what my director promised when he knew how I was suffering. Today he said to me laughing: 'You Beirutis, you're like fish out of water. I don't want you to die like a fish!'

"Pray for peace, so that I can return to you . . . Love always, Abdallah."

His last words revived all her anger at his departure. Was he only with her during times of peace, love, cooking, and warm beds? She hurried to the telephone and dialled Manah's number. He wasn't there. She'd try tomorrow and the day after and even when the war was over . . . And even if he returned from Paris . . .

★

★ ★ ★ ★

AUTHOR: *Prem Chand (1880–1936) was one of India's most highly regarded writers. Best known for his fiction, he wrote more than three hundred short stories and a dozen novels. His last novel,* Godan, *was translated as* The Gift of a Cow *in 1968 and is considered by many to be the finest novel in the Hindi language. He was a teacher and scholar, and was very active politically, joining Mahatma Gandhi's Non-Cooperation Movement in 1921. He later edited two literary journals, wrote screenplays, translated various literary works into Urdu and Hindi, and served as president of the All-India Progressive Writers' Association.*

SETTING: *India is a modern state with many nations – thirty-seven by some counts. The history of the subcontinent is one of constant battle among these nations, each group recording the history of its heroes and battles won. The result is a treasure-house of art and literature.*

Sati

Prem Chand

I

Two hundred years have passed, and yet the name of Chinta Devi is on everybody's lips. Thousands of men and women gather every Tuesday at Kalapi, an out-of-the-way place in Bundhelkhund, to pay homage to her memory. The multicoloured clothes of the women beautify even the mounds and hillocks. And the deserted place rings with soul-enchanting songs.

The Chinta Devi temple is built on so high a cliff that the red flag flying over its dome is visible from a long distance.

The temple, however, is small and cannot accommodate even two men at a time. Inside it there is no idol, but only a small altar. A flight of stairs, hewn out of stone, ascends to the temple. Lest members of the congregation should fall down in a stampede, a parapet has also been erected on either side of the staircase.

"Sati" is reprinted from *The Shroud and Other Stories* (New Delhi: SAGAR Publishing Co., 1971).

According to legend, it was at the site of this temple that Chinta Devi immolated herself, not by the side of the body of her husband, (for although he stood there with his hands folded, she would not even look at him), but for consummation with his soul. In fact, on that pyre, it was her husband's honour that was burnt to ashes.

II

Kalapi is a little village on the banks of the Yamuna. Chinta Devi was the daughter of the Bundela chief of this place. Her mother had died while she was still a child, and the burden of bringing her up had, therefore, fallen on the shoulders of the father. Those were the times when the warriors had no time to straighten their backs. They ate on horse back and slept in the saddle. Chinta Devi, therefore, spent her childhood with her father, who would hide her behind a wall, or leave her in a cave to go to the battlefield. Afraid of nothing in the world, she would make and unmake forts out of sand. Indeed, houses to her meant forts. The dolls she played with did not use headgear cover and she arranged dispositions on the battlefield. If her father did not return from the battlefield till late in the evening, she was not afraid and would sit up alone through the night without food or drink. She had not heard stories of the snake and the mongoose, but she certainly had heard tales of martyrdom and she had heard these tales from the lips of brave warriors themselves. No wonder then, she had become an idealist.

Once she had no news of her father for three days on end. Sitting in her cave on the mountainside, she built imaginary forts, *i.e.*, forts which the enemy could not even locate. All day long, she would draw up plans for the defences of the fort. And when she slept, she saw dreams of the fort.

Late in the evening of the third day then, several of her comrade-in-arms came up to her and started weeping. Bewildered, she asked them: "Where is father? And why do you weep?" None replied to her question. They began to weep louder. Chinta Devi understood that her father had attained martyrdom. The girl, then 13, did not, however, shed a single tear or heave a sigh; her countenance remained unruffled. She laughed. "If it is true that he has become a martyr," she asked, "why should you weep? What better fate could a warrior meet? What higher reward could he get for his valour? This is not an occasion to weep. It is rather one to rejoice."

"We are worried about you," said one of the warriors pensively. "Where now would you live?"

"On that score you need not worry," replied Chinta in a reflective tone. "I am the daughter of a brave father. I shall follow in his footsteps. He laid down his life to defend the freedom of the motherland. That is also the ideal which I have placed before myself. Go now, and take care of the men. Arrange for a horse and some weapons for me. God willing, you shall not find me lag behind anyone. And if you find me turning my back, do strike and put an end to this life of mine. This then is my only request to you. Go now and let there be no delay."

The warriors were not surprised at these brave words of Chinta Devi, but they did doubt whether this delicate girl could stand by her noble ideal.

III

Five years passed. All over the province, Chinta Devi's name became a synonym for valour. It symbolised victory. Enemies were uprooted. For, when she stood undaunted before the enemies' arrows and shots, she was an inspiration to her warriors. How could they turn their backs when she stood firm? (For when a delicate girl takes a step forward, how could the young take a step backward? When women watch, men's valour is redoubled. It becomes unconquerable. The verbal arrows of a young girl for the warriors are only a call to sacrifice themselves. A side glance from her could arouse manliness in their veins.)

Chinta Devi's fame attracted valiant fighters from all over to join her camp. She was like the flower round which hovered moths. Among the warriors was a Rajput youth, Ratan Singh by name. While every single soldier in Chinta Devi's army wielded a powerful sword and would sacrifice himself if she dropped a hint, or would jump into the fire if she raised her little finger, or would set out, at her command, to achieve the impossible, Ratan Singh stood in the front ranks. And Chinta Devi was secretly in love with him.

Unlike others, he wasn't obstinate. Though proud, he was outspoken. While people indulged in tall talk about themselves, and praised themselves to the skies, their object was not to reach their goal but to attract Chinta Devi's attention. Ratan Singh, on the other hand, was cool-headed. Far from boasting even if he had killed a lion, he would not even mention it to anyone. His humility and devotion verged on timidity. Thus while others' love for Chinta Devi had the element of lust in it, Ratan Singh's love consisted of sacrifice and penance. While others slept in peace, he passed the nights "counting the stars." While everyone else thought that Chinta Devi was his own, Ratan Singh entertained no such hope. It was for that reason, perhaps, that he was neither jealous of, nor unnecessarily friendly to, anyone. When he saw others singing their own praise before Chinta, he was simply amazed at how they could utter the words they did. With the passage of every second, his hopes became dimmer.

He was not an exhibitionist. At times he would be annoyed with his own helplessness. Why had God deprived him, he would say to himself, of the qualities for which women fall? Who would ever care for him? Who would fathom the pain in his heart . . . He cursed himself and there the matter ended.

Once when it was past midnight and Chinta Devi was resting in her tent — and her soldiers, having covered a difficult stage and having had subsequently a sumptuous meal, lay fast asleep – her force was threatened by an enemy patrol camping across a dense forest. Chinta Devi, who had received intelligence, was going round to arrange for an assault on the enemy the following morning. She firmly believed that the enemy was unaware of her arrival at the place it camped.

In fact, however, she was mistaken, because one of her own men was in league with the enemy and news of her force's movements reached the enemy's camp daily. The enemy had conspired this time to put an end to her life. The three brave and courageous soldiers, appointed to carry out the project, crawled through the forest and stood behind the trees to find out which was Chinta Devi's tent. The army being fast asleep, they had not the shadow of a doubt that they would succeed in their mission. They came out of their hiding place behind the trees, therefore, and crawling on the ground, like crocodiles in water, they advanced towards Chinta Devi's tent. While, however, the whole army, including the watchmen and the guards, who were all tired, lay in the lap of fast sleep, there was one who was on the alert. This was Ratan Singh, for whom there was nothing unusual in this, because, while encamping, he passed the nights sitting behind Chinta Devi's tent.

Hearing the footsteps of the assassins, he took out his sword and came forward. There were three men, bending forward and advancing. What course should he adopt? If he raised alarm, there would be panic in the whole army and, in the dark, his own people might attack one another. If, however, he did not do so, there was the risk of facing three men single-handed. Anyway, there wasn't much time to ponder over the situation. He had the warrior's gift of coming to a quick decision, drew his sword and attacked all the three. The clash of steels was followed by a death-like silence. While the three fell down dead, Ratan Singh himself lay unconscious.

When Chinta Devi got up next morning, she saw the four bodies lying on the ground outside her tent. Her heart-beat stopped. The blood in her veins froze. And as she went closer, she found that while the three assailants were dead, Ratan Singh was still alive. She understood the situation. For once the woman in her got the better of the soldier. The same eyes which had not shed one tear on her father's death, now showered a rain of tears. She put Ratan Singh's head on her own thighs and, in the *Swayamvar* ceremony held in her own heart, she put the garland of victory round his neck.

IV

For full one month, Ratan Singh did not open his eyes, neither did Chinta Devi close hers. She would not leave him even for a second. She worried neither about her dominions, nor about the enemy's advance. She had sacrificed all that was hers for Ratan Singh.

When, after a full one month, Ratan Singh opened his eyes, he found himself on the sick-bed and Chinta Devi standing in front of him with a fan in her hand. "Give me the fan, Chinta," he said in a voice, which was feeble. "You must be tired."

But Chinta Devi's heart at this time experienced heavenly happiness. Only a month earlier, she would weep, in utter hopelessness, by the side of this warrior's worn-out body. Now, when she saw him speaking to her, her joy knew no bounds. "If this is trouble, my Lord," she said softly and affectionately, "what constitutes joy I know not."

To be addressed as "My Lord," had the effect of a mantram on Ratan Singh. His eyes brightened up. In his veins coursed a new life — a life so delightful, so full of courage, so sweet, so full of joy that every pore of his body danced with joy. He felt that his arms had come by extraordinary strength, that he could conquer the whole world, could fly to the skies, could break the mountains. For a while, he felt contented, as though all his desires had been satiated. He wanted nothing more from anybody in the world. Indeed, he might even turn his face away from Lord Siva and not ask for any boon if he offered one. He desired nothing. He was proud and felt that there was none happier or luckier than himself in this world. But Chinta Devi, who had not completed her sentence, added: "You had to suffer unbearable hardship for my sake."

"None succeeds without effort," said Ratan Singh, making an effort to get up.

"There is no question of success in this case," said Chinta Devi, making him lie down with her soft hands. "What you did was to protect a woman. I am sure had it been some other woman, then too you would have protected her at the risk of your life. To tell you the truth, I had taken a vow of celibacy for life. Your devotion to me, however, has made me break my vow. Brought up in the lap of warriors, I can lay my heart only at the feet of a man who is a lion among men and could play with his life. The abandonment of the rake, the smartness of the clever, and the jugglery of the benevolent — these, according to me, have no place in life. I look upon such people as freaks of Nature. Only in your heart have I found true devotion. That is why I have been your slave, not only from today but since long past."

V

On the first night of love itself, while silence reigned everywhere and beautiful moonlight ruled the heart of the two lovers, advices were received that an enemy patrol was advancing. Caught unawares, Ratan Singh got up and grasped his sword. And brave Chinta Devi looked at him with the selfish love of a coward and said: "You can order some men to go and challenge the enemy. Why should you go yourself?"

"I am afraid, the enemy is in very large numbers this time," replied Ratan Singh, placing the rifle in position.

"Then I too shall go," said Chinta Devi.

"No," said Ratan Singh. "I am confident, they won't be able to withstand us. You watch. My first assault shall remove the foundations from beneath their feet. It appears to be the will of God that our first night of love should also be a night of our victory."

"I don't know why," said Chinta Devi, "but my heart is giving way. I don't want to allow you to go."

A little embarrassed at her simple and affectionate insistence, Ratan Singh pressed Chinta Devi to his heart and said, "I shall be back, my dear, before daybreak."

And putting her arms round his neck, with tears in her eyes, Chinta Devi remonstrated. "But I am afraid, lest you should not return for several days. My heart shall always be with you. Go now. But, do please send me advices every day. I kiss your feet. Please strike only when it is hot. I say this, because, at times, you have the weakness of allowing yourself to be swept off your feet. When you see the enemy and plan to pounce upon him with full force, my only request is that you should study the situation before you take a step forward. Go now, and come back with the same pride which you have now while you are going away."

Lust now took the place of the passion for victory which had once possessed her. The same tigress whose roar shook the hearts of the enemies had now become so feeble-hearted that, while Ratan Singh mounted his horse, she prayed to God for his safe return. And she kept on looking at him, til he disappeared from sight. In her heart there was nothing but a void. She climbed the highest minaret in her fort and kept gazing for hours on end in the direction in which he had gone. The hillocks hid Ratan Singh behind them. Chinta Devi, nevertheless, still thought that she saw him galloping. It was only after the red glow of the morning sun had peeped through the trees that her love-trance was broken. There appeared to be little life around. She descended from the tower, and lay on the bed weeping. She covered her face, and went on weeping.

VI

Hardly a hundred people had accompanied Ratan Singh, but each one of the hundred was a veteran who was indifferent both to the occasion and also to the number of the enemy, indeed, to his own life. While they spurred their horses, they sang songs of valour:

"Tilted is your turban, oh soldier;
Its honour is in thy hands,
Even if your sword, or your axe fails you,
And your coat of arms and your shield
Are rendered ineffective,
Let your heart not betray you;
Tilted is your turban, oh soldier
Its honour is in thy hands."

The hills rang with the echo of these brave words and the clap-trap of the horses also produced a rhythm of its own.

The night was over. The sun opened its blood-red eyes and showered its golden glory on the warriors. And it was in that glorious light that the enemy camp was sighted on the summit of a hill.

With his head bent and his heart hiding the pangs of separation, Ratan Singh advanced slowly. The farther he advanced, the farther back his heart pulled him. For the first time in his life he harboured troubled thoughts which made him apprehend danger. For, who knew how the battle would end?

Memories of the heavenly bliss that he had left behind troubled his mind. He remembered Chinta's wet eyes, and wanted to turn the horse back. As time passed, Ratan Singh's heart sank.

Suddenly then, one of his chiefs came closer. "You see, brother," he said, "the enemy is camping on that hill yonder. What is the course of action that we should adopt? In our opinion, we should attack them without delay, so that they are caught unawares and run helter-skelter. They are not less than a thousand in that camp. Delay on our part would only serve to alert them. The situation then might become delicate."

Ratan Singh looked at the enemy with looks of worry. "Yes, a thousand," he said. "At least that number."

"Should we attack?" asked the chief.

"Do as you wish," said Ratan Singh. "However, they are strong in numbers and we might think it over."

"It does not matter," said the chief. "We have defeated stronger enemies."

"True, we have," said Ratan Singh, "but it is no use jumping into the fire."

"Do you know, brother, what you are saying?" said the chief. "A soldier's life means jumping into the fire. You give us the word and then you shall see our valour."

"I am tired," said Ratan Singh. "Let's rest a little."

"No," said the chief. "If the enemy gets advices regarding our disposition, we shall be undone."

"If that be so," said Ratan Singh, "then you attack without further loss of time."

The soldiers pulled the reins of their horses and advanced against the enemy. When, however, they ascended the hill, they found that the enemy had not been taken unawares. It was, therefore, miscalculation by Ratan Singh's force. The enemy force was indeed prepared not only for defence but also for assaulting the fort.

When members of Ratan Singh's force saw the enemy advancing, they realized their own mistake. But it was too late. There was no way out, save to face the enemy.

Nevertheless, they were not despaired. Had a veteran like Ratan Singh been with them, they would not have been afraid; for through valour alone, he had triumphed in much worse situations. Wouldn't he demonstrate his mastery of the art of battle today also?

All eyes were looking out for Ratan Singh. But Ratan Singh was not to be seen anywhere. Where had he gone? Nobody knew. But then how could he go away? He was not the one to betray his comrades in a hopeless situation. No, he would certainly be there, devising means to turn the impending defeat into victory.

In no time, however, the enemy was upon them. After all, what could a handful of soldiers do in the face of a countless host?

From all sides Ratan Singh's followers called out for him.

"Where are you, brother?" they asked. "Give us the instructions. Don't you see, the enemy is already upon us? And still you are keeping quiet? Come out, and give us the lead."

But Ratan Singh could not be seen anywhere. The enemy forces were already upon them. The swords clashed. And with their lives "in the palms of their hands," the Bundelas started fighting in all their fury.

One Bundela soldier was more than a match for anyone. But here it was one against ten. This indeed was not a battle; it was a gamble with life. But the Bundelas had a name, because they fought hard, and would never retrace one step. Here in this case, however, they were not united. Each one advanced in the direction he could and as much as he could. None cared how it would end. One veteran cut his way through the ranks of the enemy and was even close to the commander; another one was killed while attempting to mount the commander's elephant. Indeed, even the enemy could not withhold praise at their superhuman courage.

But warriors in such situations only leave a name behind; they do not attain victories.

In about an hour's time the curtain dropped. The play was over. It was like a hurricane that came, uprooted the trees and was over. Had they been united, even this handful of Bundela warriors could have taught a lesson to their enemies. But then the one on whom lay the burden of organization was not to be seen anywhere.

The victorious Marathas identified each corpse on the battlefield. Ratan Singh had been an eyesore to them, for while he lived they could not sleep in peace. They wanted to finish him. They searched each and every stone of the hill, but could not lay their hands on Ratan Singh. Victory was theirs; but it was incomplete.

VII

Without any apparent reason doubts rose in Chinta Devi's heart. Never before had she felt so weak. She did not know how the Bundelas could ever lose. But this feeling of perturbation would not leave her.

If she had been destined to enjoy the bliss of love, she said to herself, her mother would not have left her, while she was yet an infant, to wander in forests and to live in caves and hideouts. And whatever slender protection she had did not last long, because even her father too turned his face away. Since his death she had not had even a day's respite. Would Destiny now put an end to her bewilderment?

A queer feeling now arose in her weak heart. If God should bring her lover back safely, she would take him away to a far-off village, settle down there and pass the rest of her life in the service of her beloved husband. She would turn her back on warfare. It was for the first time that femininity in her had been awakened.

Came the evening. The sun-god, like a vanquished soldier, appeared to be running to take refuge.

Then, suddenly, a soldier, bare-footed and bare-headed, came up and stood before her. Chinta Devi became dumb with surprise. She sat dazed, got up and, in great confusion, went to the soldier and asked him in a tone of anguish: "Which of them have come back alive?"

"None," replied the soldier.

"None, you say?" asked Chinta Devi. "None?" And she held her head in her hands and squatted on the ground.

"Marathas are approaching," added the soldier.

"Are they close at hand?" asked Chinta Devi. "Are they very close?"

"Very close," said the soldier.

"Get the funeral pyre ready," said Chinta Devi. "There is not much time left."

"But we are there to fight to the last," said the soldier.

"Do as you like," replied Chinta Devi. "My duty ends here."

"But we can certainly defend the fort from inside for months on end," repeated the soldier.

"Then go and do as you wish," replied Chinta Devi. "So far as I am concerned, I have no enemy left."

While darkness advanced, trampling light under its feet, the victorious Marathas also trampled the green fields under their feet, the green fields swaying in the breeze and advanced towards the fort.

The funeral pyre within the fort was being got ready. With the lighting of the lamps, the pyre too was set on fire. Chinta Devi, now in her best attire, and with an unusual glow on her face and a noble, smiling countenance, was immolating herself to reach the land where her husband was supposed to have reached.

VIII

Men and women had collected round the funeral pyre. And although the fort was surrounded by the enemy, none could care less. The faces of all and sundry were downcast and bent in grief. For it was only yesterday that, in this very place, nuptials were performed in great pomp and show. At the very spot where the funeral pyre was now burning, there had been the sacred fire. Yesterday also the flames had risen up, as they did now, and then too people had assembled. But how vitally different were the two scenes of today and yesterday! In fact, however, the difference was only superficial. It was the consummation of the same Yagna, the fulfillment of the same vow.

The thud of the horses was now heard. And it appeared that one soldier was goading his horse at full gallop. The thud then ceased. A soldier came running into the enclosure of Chinta Devi's apartment. And the people looked up in amazement, for it was Ratan Singh.

Gasping for breath, Ratan Singh went up to the pyre, and said: "But I am still alive, my darling. What have you done?"

The flames from Chinta Devi's saree were now leaping.

Like a drunkard, Ratan Singh advanced towards the pyre and tried to grab her by the hand. Others advanced to remove the half-burnt logs of wood.

But Chinta Devi did not even look at her husband. She merely motioned to him that he should get away.

Ratan Singh beat his head in shame. "What has happened to you, my darling? Why don't you look at me? You see, I am still alive."

"Your name may be Ratan Singh," came the voice from the pyre, "but you are not the Ratan Singh who was mine."

"Please look at me," said Ratan Singh. "I am the same Ratan Singh, your servant, your admirer, and your husband."

"My husband died a martyr," replied Chinta Devi.

"How could I make you understand?" asked Ratan Singh.

"Please put out the fire, gentlemen. Listen, darling, I am the Ratan Singh. Don't you recognize me?"

The flames had now swallowed up Chinta Devi's face. It looked as if in that fire a lotus had blossomed.

"I do recognize you," Chinta Devi was heard to say in a clear, unmistakable voice, "but then you are not *my* Ratan Singh. My Ratan Singh was brave, incredibly brave. He could not, for the sake of his life, for the sake of my body, ignore the warrior's credo. The man whose feet I kissed now graces the paradise. Please do not insult my Ratan Singh. He was a brave Rajput, not a coward to run away from the battlefield."

And as these last words had been uttered, the flames consumed Chinta Devi's head. In no time the precious lamp of beauty, the worshippers' idol of valour, the Sati was one with the fire. And there stood Ratan Singh — silent, blank, a mute witness to this tragic scene.

He took a deep breath and himself jumped into the funeral pyre.

★

★ ★ ★ ★

AUTHOR: *Gladys Thomas, one of the best known of African women writers, was born in Salt River, Cape Town, South Africa. She writes from her own experience – the experience of a black homemaker living with her family in a council house in Oceanview Township, a ghetto suburb of Cape Town. Thomas has published poems and stories in South Africa, Germany, France, Holland, Britain, Nigeria, China, and the United States and has been included in the Kwanzaa Honours List of South African black women writers for her contributions to the fight against apartheid.*

SETTING: *The violence inherent in South Africa's apartheid system is well known. Under the authority and military power of the state, thousands of black citizens have been deprived of life and liberty. Described either as genocide or civil war, the systematic mutilation of individuals and families by apartheid has been condemned by the international community. Between 1984 and 1986 alone, one thousand people died and two hundred and sixty-two thousand were arrested. Although there have been recent indications of political change in South Africa, the social and racial systems remain separate and violent.*

One Last Look at Paradise Road

Gladys Thomas

Miriam, not knowing where to start, looked wearily around the house at her duties for the day. Washing lay on the bedroom floor ready for the automatic washing machine. Dishes were piled high in the kitchen sink indicating that a good time was had by all at Madam's party. After she had served dinner to the guests last night, she had left the kitchen about nine o'clock. Most nights she would spend with her friend who worked across the road. They would talk about their families, their Madams and everything that affected their lives. Last night, however, Miriam had felt

---

too tired and just fell asleep in her tiny room. This morning she was back in the big house to do the cleaning up!

Today her heart felt heavy in her breast. She was nervous and had dropped things. Already she had broken a porcelain figurine when she was dusting. Tonight she would have to face the consequences. All she could do, as was usual after such a confrontation, was to return to the lonely maid's room in the back yard, and sulk.

She carried a transistor radio from room to room while doing her chores. She was listening expectantly for news of the worsening unrest in the townships. And it was a special day because of the call to march to Pollsmoor Prison to demand the release of Nelson Mandela. Why could she not be with her family and her people at a time like this? Instead she was compelled to spend her time cleaning for the rich and unconcerned.

At eleven-thirty she heard those special bleeps on the radio which preceded the news. Anxiously she turned up the sound for the urgent news flash. The police had taken over Athlone and the march on Pollsmoor had been put to an abrupt end! The police had used batons, quirts and teargas. There were many injured and detained.

Miriam stood stunned and shocked because some of the reported incidents had taken place near her home. After a while she decided that it would be best to return to the township where she lived, to where she felt that she would be needed by her family and neighbours. She filled the dog's water bowl, kicked the washing into a corner, locked all the doors, and left the big house in a hurry.

As she locked the gate she remembered that Madam would certainly telephone that afternoon to enquire, as she usually did, about what she would be cooking for supper that night. Now that was the least of her worries — she was on her way home!

She walked as quickly as her ungainly tired body could carry her. She turned into Paradise Road which was lined with tall green oak trees; birds flew about, and squirrels with their frenetic bushy tails jumped along the branches. The avenue, so peaceful with its beautiful spring-green trees stretching almost as far as the eye could see, was just like some fabled Eden.

Almost breathless, she arrived at the Claremont bus terminus and was just in time for a departing bus to her township. She had little time to waste as she had to return to her work before the white family arrived home that night. She sat down resolutely in a vacant seat at the window. As she stared out she thought about her husband, Amos. Yes, together they had been through hard times bringing up their three children; both working to make ends meet until three months ago when he was brought home in one of the construction company's trucks. The driver had to carry him inside the house! He had been employed by the company for ten years. Yet the day he injured himself the foreman said that he was too busy to fill in the compensation forms! Until now he had received just two weeks' pay and a pair of crutches.

These thoughts made her angry and, given the opportunity, she would have walked in the front row of that march! But she could not stay at home as she needed the job so badly. The family depended on the hundred-and-twenty rand a month which she earned as a maid. She thought about her daughter Winnie, the other breadwinner of the family. She worked at Groote Schuur Hospital as a trainee nurse. Every month Winnie would bring home her pay packet unopened. Miriam was very proud of her and loved her very much.

Her two sons were now both at high school. Ah, how she adored them! They never complained and were always satisfied. They wore patched pants and their shoes were often down at heel, but they never missed school. She really admired them and their dedication to their studies.

Steve was now in his final matriculation year and her baby, Fassie, now sixteen, was in Standard Eight. They were both so bright that she smiled as she thought about them. They would have joined the march that morning as they were supporters of the People's United Front. She remembered how her boys insisted on taking her to the mass political rally at the skating rink in Athlone. She had never seen such a crowd in her life! All were meeting for the struggle for freedom. The speeches were fiery and pertinent about the oppressive laws of her cruel country. She had felt pleased that her sons had brought her to the rally.

She was so deep in thought that she almost missed her stop. As she alighted, stones came smashing into the bus windows. The driver in great fear jumped out and ran for his life. Everyone scattered as the stones rained down upon the bus. Some of the youths were shouting slogans and angry words; "Down with the bus fares!", "We did not ask to be here!", "The government moved us to this ghetto!" They shouted at the empty bus as if it had ears! Missiles were aimed at the bright smiling face of a girl advertising toothpaste on the side of the bus. The stones smashed into the face with dull thuds. She saw flames quickly consume the smiling face leaving the side of the bus a blackened charred mass. Soon the whole bus was burning fiercely, as she hurried home, shocked at what she had witnessed.

The township looked like a battlefield. Clumsy-looking troop-carriers called Casspirs, army trucks filled with troops armed to the teeth and police with guns were to be seen everywhere. A soldier in full battledress and riot gear came towards her. Her heart began to pound fast and in a panic she half ran home. Children and adults were being chased like cornered animals. She turned a street corner; the teargas and burning tyres' smoke choked her as she stumbled into her home.

"Amos, Amos!" she cried and ran into the small dark bedroom. He stood at the window leaning on his crutches. They fell into each other's arms.

"I'm glad you're home, Mother. This all started this morning. It was going to be a peaceful march to Pollsmoor. Then came the batons and the guns. Standing here, and I'm unable to go out and help the injured, is driving me mad."

"Where are the children?" she asked anxiously.

"They joined the march this morning. I never saw them after that."

"Oh God, please bring them home safe. It is terrible out there and all we can do is just sit here while our children are fighting the whole army and all those guns. I feel so helpless, Amos."

"I feel exactly the same, Miriam. I wish I had died in that accident!"

"Oh Amos, my husband. Why do you talk like that? Soon you will be strong and on your feet again. We must not give in now. Our children need our support. Come, let's see what there is to eat. What you need is a nice cup of tea."

"Don't worry, my wife. You go and look for the boys. I can get something to eat for myself. Besides, I feel like being alone."

"Why do you want to be alone? I've just come in from work to be with you, and you want to be alone?"

"I know your heart is out there with the boys. You go and look for them. I'll be all right."

"Are you sure, Amos?" she asked tenderly.

She went to the kitchen to drink some water as her throat was irritated by the gas. She noticed that the boys had left in a great hurry — plates of half-eaten mealie meal still stood on the table. The large enamelled basin was filled with dirty dishes and the bucket that Fassie used to scrub the floor stood under the old wooden kitchen table. They had never before left for school before cleaning the house, but that morning was obviously an exception. She went back into the bedroom to tell Amos that she was leaving. As she turned away Amos looked sadly at her, thinking, "We live in such dangerous times that you don't know if you'll see your loved ones again once they leave the house. Bloody murderers!"

Miriam reached the gate and then turned quickly back into the house. She stood in the doorway and shouted, "Are you sure you're all right? Don't leave the house until I return. Do you hear me, Amos?"

"Go Wife, go! But take care. These people are out to kill us today."

She rushed out into the street. Stones rained from behind walls and bushes. She had to dodge and run to avoid the missiles. There were tyres burning in the streets, barricading the way of the Casspirs. But the iron monsters moved forward relentlessly. The faces of the men on the Casspirs, she noticed, were red with anger. Thick palls of tearsmoke filled the air and the tyres gave off acrid fumes which inflamed the eyes and throat. She heard gunshots in the next street and the piercing cries of the children. It was like a nightmare as she made her way to her sister's home a few streets away. She found herself running with the crowd at times. Perhaps her sons were at their Aunt Susan's home, hiding?

As she entered Susan's home she immediately felt that something was amiss. She found her in the kitchen shaking in a panic. Holding her ten-month-old baby over the kitchen sink she was blowing air into the child's mouth. This beautiful child with her large brown eyes, who was always gurgling with delight, now lay limp in her mother's arms!

"What happened?" Miriam asked very alarmed.

"They threw a teargas canister through the doorway. Little Dolly had just crawled there to sit in the sun," answered Susan, tears running down her cheeks. "My baby almost choked to death."

"Give her to me," said Miriam, and she held the child to her body. Slowly she rocked Dolly while her sister wiped the little face with a wet cold face cloth.

"I'm looking for Steve and Fassie. They didn't attend school today but joined the march. I thought they may be here with you, Sister."

"I didn't see them today, Miriam. Where can they be? Perhaps they're hiding someplace."

"But I want to find them before I go back to my work this evening."

"Are you off today?"

"I decided to come home when I heard the news of the beatings on the radio."

"Why didn't they allow this peaceful march?" Susan asked angrily.

"Yes, they want to shoot all of us," answered Miriam. "Here, I think she's sleeping," Miriam handed Dolly back to Susan. "You must watch her, anything can happen. I must leave now and search for the boys. Keep your door closed," she warned as she left.

Back on the streets she followed the crowd. By now her heavy body felt tired and sweaty. She ran along searching the crowd for her sons' faces amongst them. They were all singing freedom songs but nowhere did she see Steve or Fassie. The faces of the youth shocked her. She detected signs of hope, determination and defiance in them. On the way she met many mothers and stopped to talk to some of them that she knew.

"I'm looking for my sons," she tried to explain. They ignored her in their rush to get away.

"No time to talk," said one of the young men in the crowd.

"Come on, Mama. If you stand too long in one place they will shoot you," said another.

She joined the others, half running and half walking. Passing another woman she asked, "Are you also looking for your children?"

"Yes, yes!" several of the mothers in the crowd answered in great apprehension.

"Not one of them are at school today."

"They say that they are doing what we should have done years ago."

"That's true," approved several women.

When she approached her street she said goodbye to them and returned home very disappointed.

"Miriam, Miriam. Is it you?" Amos called from the bedroom. "Did you find them?"

"Oh, Amos. You'll never believe what's going on out there! It seems that all the high school students joined the march this morning. I tell you Amos, these children don't care about their lives!" She was now so overcome that she just sat down on the bed, crying.

"All right, Mother. Don't worry! It will turn out all right. I know it," he pacified her.

"I will not go back to work until I've found my sons," she said between her tears.

"What if you lose your job?"

"We will manage on Winnie's money. We've been through worse times before. But I'm going to stay here where I belong. Let the rich do their own work for a change. I'm tired of cooking, cleaning and picking up after them. I hate them all! They couldn't care a damn about us."

"My wife, you've been running around since this morning," said Amos looking at her with great concern. "Come let me make that cup of tea we were going to have this morning." He shuffled into the kitchen followed by Miriam.

"You must rest that leg of yours. Let me make the tea instead and I'll tell you what is going on out there. The children are all over the township. The roads are blocked with old mattresses and oil drums. I saw some of them making petrol bombs behind a wall. I can't believe it! There is a war going on out there, Amos."

"And no sign of our sons? I'm sure they will come home soon."

"Want some more tea?" she asked him. They continued to discuss the situation until late in the afternoon.

Suddenly the front door burst open and about six young people stormed inside breathlessly, seeking a place to hide. With them was Steve. When he saw his mother he was visibly surprised.

"Mama, why are you home from your work?"

"How can I stay at work with all this happening here?"

All Steve's friends seemed extremely nervous and fearful and cast anxious looks towards the front door.

"We must hide in here. Away from the police, Ma! They're after us and they are going to kill us, Ma!"

"Kill? Not while I'm around."

Amos suggested that two should hide behind the toilet in the back yard. They ran outside as fast as they could. Miriam pushed two boys into the bedroom. Steve and the last one jumped into the old fireplace which was covered by an old floral curtain. When they were safely in their hiding places, Miriam poked her head behind the curtain. "Where is your brother, Fassie?"

"I don't know. Shuh! Please go away, Mama. We'll go and look for him later. Please go, Ma." She returned to Amos and they stared at each other as a deathly silence fell over the house.

A loud crash preceded the front door being kicked open and in marched several policemen. They went straight into the kitchen without any invitation. Miriam's heart beat so fast that she could feel the colour warming her face, her hair soaked in sweat. Amos pretended that he was reading a book. It looked as if a blue-grey cloud of uniforms and hateful brown, black and red faces had invaded Miriam's kitchen. They confronted her and Amos with their guns at the ready. Miriam said a silent prayer.

"Where are they?" demanded the leader. "We saw them come in this house," he shouted at the two old people. His men backed him in unison.

"You saw wrong," Miriam shouted back in the same tone, surprising even Amos with her courage. "There is no one in this house but myself and my husband. How do you know they came here? All these council houses look the same."

"Search the whole place! And outside in the yard," the big red bull bellowed to his men.

They kicked over the dustbin in the yard. They threw everything around with absolute contempt. The men inside were deliberately knocking over chairs and one officer ripped the curtains from the windows, declaring, "This bloody house is as dark as hell!" Others went kicking open the inside doors of the house, searching everywhere. One even turned over the old zinc bath which the family used for their weekly bath. He flung it to the cement floor so that it made the sound of a bomb going off in the room. They appeared to be pleased with the chaos they were causing. But they did not discover any of the children! One of the policemen returned: "There is only that old stink shithouse out there."

"Where are they?" the sergeant shouted at Amos in anger and pulled at his crutch. Amos almost fell and a sharp pain shot up his bad leg. Miriam quickly held on to him.

"We don't know. We are alone here, my Baas," he whimpered.

On hearing the word "Baas" the sergeant looked pleased, thinking that he was in control of the situation. He called his men and ordered them to stop the search. The house was a shambles when they marched out. "We will be back," shouted the sergeant over his shoulder.

As a parting gift one of the policemen threw a teargas canister into the kitchen. Miriam and Amos struggled towards the bedroom to save themselves from choking. After shutting the bedroom door behind them they fell down on to the bed, bewildered. Every room in the house was soon filled with tearsmoke. Miriam had grabbed a wet facecloth from behind the bedroom door and held it over Amos's face as he had seemed to faint. Quickly she opened the bedroom window. "They are pigs. Just smell this house! Are you all right?" she asked Amos.

"We must live like this because we are of the wrong colour, Mother."

One by one the boys crept out of their hiding places and thanked Miriam and Amos politely, almost apologetically, for the trouble they had caused. Miriam ordered them to open all the windows and doors to get the smell out of the house. "It's our duty to protect you children," said Miriam.

The children discussed the events of the day in the backroom where Steve and Fassie slept. In their bedroom Miriam and Amos sat in silence. Finally she asked, "Where is our Fassie?"

"I hope he is safe," answered Amos. She started to weep softly. After a while she knelt down to pray at his side. Amos tenderly laid his hand on her while the young people continued their meeting. Their loud and angry voices filtered through to the bedroom.

"I saw them baton charge a young girl as she lay on the ground."

"That policeman hit her over the body with the strength of an ox!" said Steve.

"I saw them whip a priest full in the face, shattering his spectacles. I'm sure he's lost the sight in that eye. I've never seen anything so cruel," said another.

"What about the two old nuns they arrested!" someone complained angrily.

"All our leaders have been detained. Tomorrow we will meet at school and decide how to protest against this injustice," said Steve.

"One of you go outside and see if the police vans are still patrolling. We must search for my brother. We must find him!"

As they prepared to leave, their lookout returned to whisper, "It's all clear. They've left the area."

On the way out Steve went into his parents' room. His father was asleep but his mother was sitting next to him, just staring into space. "We are going to look for Fassie, Ma. You rest now, I can see that you are tired."

"God go with you, Son." She lay down next to her husband, but she was awake for a long time still. In the distance she heard the sound of gunshots, and people running and screaming.

The following morning she awoke with a headache and her body felt stiff all over. Quietly she tiptoed into the next room to see if Steve had returned home the previous night. On seeing the sleeping figure she murmured, "Thank God." Miriam shook him awake, asking softly, "Do you have any news about your brother?"

"We've looked all over, Ma. But he cannot be found."

Miriam went silently into the kitchen to cook a pot of mealie meal for breakfast. As she stirred the porridge she decided to go to Groote Schuur Hospital to tell Winnie about Fassie's disappearance.

"Maybe she can help," she said to herself. After they had had their breakfast Steve prepared to leave for school.

"I'm going to Winnie for help," Maybe Fassie is in the hospital," Miriam stated.

"Take care how you walk, Ma. Don't take chances out there," said Steve. "I'm off now. 'Bye Ma and Pa. Take care now," he shouted on his way out.

"I must be off too," Miriam said to Amos.

"Will you be all right or shall I come with you?"

"Now how can you come with your injured leg? No, you stay here. I won't be long." She pulled a scarf over her head, kissed him and left the house with feelings of anticipation that she would somehow find Fassie.

The streets were scattered with stones and the burnt-out tyres had left imprinted circles on the asphalt road from the previous day's unrest. As she passed the high school she saw massive army trucks parked outside the grounds with police and soldiers patrolling inside the fence. Their rifles were hanging down their sides. A helicopter hovered overhead. A Buffel troop carrier appeared from around a corner like an angry buffalo with a cannon for a nose, ready to attack. The township looked like a battlefield and a deathly atmosphere pervaded the scene which seemed to expect more violence. She hurried on and when she arrived at the hospital she climbed the stairs to Ward T2 where Winnie was on duty. They embraced each other.

"You look terrible, Ma. Are Steve and Fassie okay?" Winnie asked anxiously.

"That's why I'm here. They joined the march to Pollsmoor yesterday. Now Fassie is missing. We are sick with worry."

"Wait let me ask Matron for a few minutes off, then we can talk inside."

After a short while Winnie returned and took her mother's arm. They went through the male wards of the hospital. Winnie searched among the faces of the patients for her brother's, but without success.

"Come let's go to the out-patients, Ma," suggested Winnie. They found the corridors crowded with injured people from the townships. Inside the hall the benches were packed, and the doctors were busy attending to some people with gunshot wounds. A young boy howled for his mother. Winnie and Miriam walked amongst the injured people searching for Fassie but he was not to be found there.

Winnie saw her mother out, kissed her and promised to change her shift and come home as soon as possible. Miriam walked to the bus stop as if in a trance. After she had paid her fare, she counted the money in her purse. As there wasn't enough left for her to go straight home, she decided to collect her wages at the big house. However, to her surprise Steve was waiting for her at the Claremont bus terminus. Her heart started racing as he came towards her.

"What is it, Son?" she asked apprehensively.

"Fassie is on the run, Ma," he blurted out.

"Why, what happened?" she asked. "What does it mean?"

"He threw a petrol bomb at a police van. They saw his face and gave chase. He hid in someone's house and then jumped the fences. They followed him. If they find him he will go to jail. They know who he is! We will just have to wait for him to return home when the time is right."

"I thank the Lord, he is alive. When will this unrest end?" she cried.

"No one knows. Looks like it's only started." Steve looked grim-faced.

"Look Steve, I have no more money. We need food. I'm going to Madam to explain the situation to her. She will understand and give me my money. I'll go back to work when Fassie comes home. Now I must go to the big house. Are you coming with me, Steve?"

"No, Ma. I don't like it amongst those people. You go. I'll go home to Pa. But please bring some food home, Ma."

They each went their own way, she back to Paradise Road and Steve back to the township.

As she opened the gate of her employer's home, the dog ran to meet her. She went around to the back door and in the yard, to her surprise, she met a new maid with a bucket and rags hanging from her arm.

"Is the Madam home?"

"Yes. She is drinking her tea on the patio," the girl answered shyly.

Miriam walked through the huge house to the poolside. There she saw Madam sunbathing. She went closer. "Good afternoon, Madam," she said in a shaking voice. She didn't know how to go on.

Madam looked up and replied casually, "Oh, you finally arrived, Miriam."

In a defiant mood Miriam replied, "I've had a lot of trouble, Madam. My son is gone. My Fassie is missing!"

"I believe there is unrest in all the townships. Why are you people so violent? And where is your son? He is supposed to be at school, not so?"

"I see someone has already taken my place. Why the hurry?"

"Well, you let me down badly, Miriam. I had no alternative — if you can run home whenever you hear a gunshot sound in the township! Master and I have decided that it would be best if you stay home. Now let me pay you your month's wages. I have decided to deduct from your money the cost of the figurine you smashed. Is that okay, Miriam?"

"Yes, Madam. And my reference? I will have to look for other work. My husband is sick at home as you know," Miriam pleaded softly.

"I shall post your papers, or you can tell your new employer to phone me." Madam went inside and soon returned with Miriam's wages. "Now if you don't mind Miriam, my tea is getting cold."

Miriam walked away, her shoulders slumped. "Now that is appreciation for all the work I have done here!" she thought.

She walked through the large kitchen, opened the refrigerator and helped herself to a cool drink. On the table she saw a tempting cream cake topped with red cherries — Master's favourite nightcap! She cut a slice, then another and another — she could not stop eating. When she had had her fill she cut another large slice and wrapped it up to take home to Amos. She picked all the cherries off the topping and stuffed them into her mouth. Finally, feeling satisfied, she went out into the back yard.

Suddenly she remembered that Madam had a bad habit of accusing her servants of stealing. She had a pen in her handbag and she went back to the kitchen. She took a piece of writing paper from the kitchen cupboard drawer and wrote a message to Madam. "I ate the cake and enjoyed it, Madam." She pushed the note into the cream of the leftover cake. On her way out she greeted the new maid. "Poor girl," she said to herself.

As she walked down the avenue she felt good — even a little happy. "How foolish can one get! Why should I feel this way over a piece of cake?" she thought. The trees looked even greener than the day before. The birdsongs sounded louder and sweeter. She stopped to open her pay-packet to see how much Madam had taken for the figurine. Counting the money, she discovered that her carelessness had cost her ten rand. She swore to herself!

She decided that she must hurry home now, back to the gunshots and all the chaos. The avenue seemed longer today, or was it perhaps her tiredness? She stopped for a short rest, sitting on an old tree stump. A squirrel ran past her with an acorn in its mouth. As she admired the little creature which scrambled up a huge tree to feed its family, she remembered her family had eaten only one mealie meal that morning. She would have to go to the shops on her way through Claremont. The loss of the ten rand for the figurine had set her back financially, but they would manage somehow. She must also buy the daily newspapers for Amos as he was an avid reader. And some fruit and a chocolate for each one! "But what will I do with Fassie's bar? I will have to keep it until his return," she said to herself and then, without expecting any answer, "I wonder where my son is hiding now?" Suddenly she felt sad as she pictured Amos alone all day, wobbling around on crutches in the small dark council house. Miriam remembered that he had always brought her fruit and a chocolate bar on his pay-day. She got up from the old tree stump and continued down the road. At the bottom of the hill she turned back and could still see the big house in the distance. She wiped the sweat from her forehead and took one last look at Paradise Road.

★

★ ★ ★ ★

AUTHOR: *Andrei Platonov (1899-1951) served in the Red Army between 1919 and 1921 and was a war correspondent during the "Patriotic War" — World War II — 1941-1945. A popular writer, Platonov published more than one hundred short stories, nine novelettes, a novel, four plays, film scripts, and numerous articles. One of his favorite descriptions is of the changes that the revolution wrought in the minds and lives of people in Russia's most remote corners. He brought to his writing a sense of the possibility for moral regeneration even during war.*

SETTING: *After the Second World War, much of the Russian Army was demobilized. The rural economy had been neglected, and the country needed its peasants back on the land. Many men went back to villages and families that they had not seen for years. Although war causes incalculable suffering, it is well recognized that war also has a dimension of excitement, of movement, which daily peasant life lacks. This story portrays war as a mistress and depicts one man's reluctance to return to the once familiar, but dull, hearthside.*

The Homecoming
Andrei Platonov

Alexei Alexeyevich Ivanov, a sergeant in the Guards, had been demobilised from the army. In the unit where he had served all through the war they saw him off, as was only right and proper, with regret, affection, music and wine. His close friends and comrades went with him to the station, said their final farewells, and left. But the train was several long hours behind schedule, and after these hours had passed there was a further delay. The cold autumn night began to fall. The station building had been destroyed in the war and there was nowhere to spend the night, so Ivanov hitched a lift back to the unit. The next day they saw him off again, singing songs and embracing the departing sergeant as a token of their eternal friendship, but this time they expressed their feelings more briefly and only his closest friends were present.

Translated by B. Markevich. "The Homecoming" is reprinted from *Fro and Other Stories* (Moscow: Progress Publishers, 1933).

Ivanov set off for the station a second time. There he was told that the train had still not arrived and he might as well go back to the unit for the night. But not wanting to go through the awkward business of saying goodbye yet a third time and bothering his comrades, Ivanov stayed waiting miserably on the deserted asphalt of the platform.

By the main points there was an undamaged duty-box, and on a bench near the box sat a woman in a quilted jacket and a warm scarf. She had been sitting there with her things yesterday and was still sitting there now waiting for the train. As he was leaving yesterday to spend the night at the unit, Ivanov had thought of asking this lonely woman to come and stay with the nurses in their warm wooden house. Why should she be cold all night? There was no knowing whether she could keep warm in the duty-box. But while he was thinking, the car set off and Ivanov forgot about the woman.

Now this woman was sitting, motionless as before, in the same spot as yesterday. This constancy and patience bespoke a woman's faithful and unchanging heart, at least in relation to her possessions and home, to which this woman was probably returning. Ivanov went up to her: perhaps she, too, would prefer his company to being alone.

The woman turned her face to Ivanov and he recognised her. It was the girl they called "Masha, the bath attendant's daughter," because she had once called herself it, and really was the daughter of a man who worked in the steam baths. Ivanov had come across her once or twice at the airforce battalion station where this Masha, the bath attendant's daughter, worked as a volunteer helping the cook in the canteen.

The autumn landscape surrounding them was forlorn and sad at this time of day. The train that was supposed to take Masha and Ivanov home was somewhere out there in the grey expanse. The only thing that could possibly comfort and cheer a person's heart was the heart of another person.

Ivanov chatted to Masha and began to feel better. She was a comely lass, simple and kind with her big worker's hands and her healthy young body. She was also on her way home, wondering how she would live her new civilian life. She had got used to the girls at the aerodrome and the pilots, who loved her like their elder sister, gave her chocolate and called her "Ample Masha" because of her size and her big heart, which embraced all her brothers in one love, like real sisters always do, never just one of them. It was strange, even frightening to be going home to her relatives who seemed like strangers now.

Ivanov and Masha felt orphaned without the army. But Ivanov could never stay sad or despondent for long. He always felt that someone far away was laughing at him and being happy instead of him, while he was just moping like a silly fool. So Ivanov always got down to the business of living, that is, found himself some form of activity or comfort, or, as he put it, something nice and handy, and this cured his depression. He moved closer to Masha and asked her to let him give her a comradely kiss on the cheek.

"Just a little one," he said. "The train's late and it's miserable waiting for it."

"Only because the train's late?" asked Masha, gazing at his face alertly.

The ex-sergeant looked about thirty-five. The skin on his face was brown from being beaten by the wind and burnt by the sun, the grey eyes watching Masha were timid, almost shy, and his speech, although direct, was courteous and kind. Masha liked this elderly man's hollow, hoarse voice and his dark, coarse face with its look of strength and defencelessness. Ivanov put out his pipe with his thumb that did not feel the smouldering heat, and sighed as he waited for permission. Masha moved away from him slightly. He smelt strongly of tobacco, fried bread and a little wine — those clean things which come from fire or kindle it themselves. It was as if Ivanov lived on nothing but tobacco, rusks, beer and wine. He repeated his request.

"I'll be careful, just a light kiss, Masha. Imagine I'm your uncle."

"I've already imagined — that you're my father, not my uncle."

"I see. So it's all right, is it?"

"Fathers don't need to ask," laughed Masha.

Later Ivanov confessed to himself that Masha's hair smelled like fallen autumn leaves in the forest, and he would never be able to forget it.

Going a little way from the track, he lit a small fire to fry some eggs for his and Masha's supper.

The train arrived in the night and carried them off in the direction of home. For two days they travelled together, then on the third day Masha arrived at the town where she had been born twenty years ago. She gathered her things together and asked Ivanov to fix the bundle comfortably on her back, but Ivanov hoisted it onto his own shoulders and got out of the carriage after her, although he was still more than a day's journey from home. Masha was surprised and touched by his considerateness. She was afraid of suddenly being left alone in the town where she had been born and grown up, but which was now almost like a foreign land to her. Her mother and father had been driven into captivity by the Germans and had died in unknown circumstances. All Masha had left now was a cousin and two aunts, for whom she felt no real affection.

Ivanov arranged with the station-master to break his journey, and stayed with Masha. He should really have gone straight home to where his wife and two children, whom he had not seen for four years, were waiting for him. But he put off the joyful, anxious moment of meeting his family — why, he did not know. Perhaps because he wanted to enjoy his freedom a little longer.

Masha did not know whether Ivanov had a family and girlish shyness prevented her from asking him. She simply trusted him out of the goodness of her heart, with no thought for anything else.

Two days later Ivanov set off again on his journey home and Masha came to the station with him. He kissed her as a matter of course and promised to remember her forever.

In reply she smiled and said:

"Why remember me forever? There's no need, and anyway you're bound to forget. I don't ask anything of you. Just forget me."

"Dear Masha. . . . Where were you before? Why didn't we meet a long, long time ago?"

"Before the war I was at school, and a long, long time ago I wasn't even born."

The train arrived and they said goodbye. Ivanov went off and did not see the solitary Masha burst into tears because she could never forget anyone: not her girl friends, or the comrades with whom fate had once brought her together. Ivanov looked through the window at the small houses of the town which he was never likely to see again, thinking that in another town his wife Lyuba and children Petrushka and Nastya lived in a little house like these, and that they were waiting for him. He had sent his wife a telegram from the unit saying he was on his way home and longing to kiss her and the children as soon as possible.

Lyubov Vassilievna, Ivanov's wife, had met each train from the west for three days. She had got time off work, hadn't fulfilled her work quota, and could not sleep at night for joy, listening to the slow, indifferent swing of the pendulum on the wall clock. On the fourth day she sent the children, Petrushka and Nastya, to the station to meet their father if he arrived in the afternoon, and went again herself for the night train.

Ivanov arrived on the sixth day. He was met by his son. Petrushka was now eleven, and at first the father did not recognize this serious young lad who looked older than his years. What he saw was a skinny boy, small for his age, but with a big head, a broad forehead and a calm face that already seemed used to care and worry, while the small, brown eyes looked out on the world darkly and discontentedly as if they saw nothing but disorder everywhere. The boy was neatly dressed. His boots were worn but still wearable, and his trousers and jacket were old, made from his father's clothes, but without any holes. They had been darned here and patched there, and all in all Petrushka looked like a small, poor, but industrious peasant. His father was surprised and sighed.

"Are you father, then?" asked Petrushka, after Ivanov put his arms round him, kissed him and drew him close. "You must be."

"Yes. Hello, Pyotr Alexeyevich!"

"Hello. Why're you so late? We've been waiting for days."

"It was the train, Petrushka, a slow one. How're your mother and Nastya, fit and well?"

"Not bad," said Petrushka. "How many orders have you got?"

"Two, Petrushka, and three medals."

"Mother and I thought you'd be covered with them. Mother's got two medals as well, for helping with the war effort. Why've you got so few things — only one bag?"

"That's all I need."

"I suppose it's difficult to fight if you've got a big trunk?" asked the boy.

"Yes, it's easier with a bag," said his father. "You don't find anyone there with a trunk."

"I thought they'd all have them. I'd keep all my things in a trunk — they only get broken and crumpled in a bag."

He took his father's bag and set off home, with the father following him.

The mother met them on the porch; she had asked to be let off work again, as if her heart had told her that her husband would come today. She went home first from the factory before going to the station. She was afraid Semyon Yevseyevich might have come round: he liked dropping in occasionally in the afternoon; he would turn up in the middle of the day and sit with five-year-old Nastya and Petrushka. But he never came empty-handed. Always brought something for the children, a sweet, or some sugar or a white roll, or a coupon for something they needed at the shop. Lyubov Vassilievna had never had any cause to complain about Semyon Yevseyevich: in the two years they had known each other, he had been very kind to her, and he treated the children as if he were their own father, even more considerately than a father. But today she didn't want her husband to see Semyon Yevseyevich. She tidied the kitchen and their room — it must all be clean without anything that didn't belong there. And later on, tomorrow or the day after, she would tell her husband everything. Luckily Semyon Yevseyevich hadn't turned up today.

Ivanov walked up to his wife, embraced her and stood like that, not letting her go, feeling the forgotten yet familiar warmth of the woman he loved.

Little Nastya came out of the house and seeing her father whom she did not remember caught hold of his leg and tried to push him away from her mother, then burst out crying. Petrushka, who was standing silently by his father and mother, with the bag on his shoulders, waited a moment and then said:

"That's enough, you two. Nastya's crying, she don't understand."

The father let go of his wife and picked up Nastya who was crying with fright.

"Nastya," Petrushka called to her. "Stop that, I tell you. It's our father, he's one of the family!"

Inside Ivanov had a wash and sat down at the table. He stretched out his legs, closed his eyes and a feeling of quiet joy and calm contentment came over him. The war had ended. His legs had tramped thousands of miles in those years, his face was lined with fatigue, and his eyes ached beneath their closed lids — they wanted to rest now in dusk or darkness.

While he sat there the whole family got busy in the living room and kitchen preparing a special meat to celebrate his homecoming. Ivanov looked at all the things in the room one by one: the clock, the dresser, the thermometer on the wall, the chairs, the flowers on the windowsill, the Russian kitchen stove. They had lived here without him, missing him, for a long time. Now he had come back and he looked at them, getting to know them again, as if they were relatives who had been living a lonely, poor life without him. He breathed in the old, familiar scent of home: smouldering wood, his children's warm bodies, bits of charred food on the stove. The smell was the same as it had been four years ago. It had not drifted away or changed in his absence. Ivanov had never found it anywhere else, although he had been in hundreds of dwellings in different countries during the war. They all had their own odour, but it was different from his native home. Ivanov could still remember the scent of Masha, the scent of her hair; but it had smelt of forest leaves, an unfamiliar overgrown path, a life of fresh disquiet, not home. What was she doing now, Masha, the bath attendant's daughter, and how was she settling down to civilian life? Well, the best of luck to her. . . .

Ivanov could see that Petrushka was the most active person about the house. As well as working himself, he gave instructions to his mother and Nastya about what to do and what not to do and how to do things properly. Nastya obediently did what Petrushka said and was no longer afraid of her father as a strange man. She had the lively concentrated face of a child who does everything in life properly and seriously, and she was obviously sweet-natured because she never resented Petrushka.

"Clear the potato peelings out of that pot, Nastya. I need it."

Nastya obediently emptied the pot and washed it. Meanwhile the mother was quickly making a cake from dough without yeast to put in the stove which Petrushka had already lit.

"Get a move on, Mum! Hurry up!" Petrushka ordered. "You can see I've got the stove going. You're used to taking it easy, you old Stakhanovite."

"Won't be a minute, Petrushka," said his mother obediently. "I'll just put some raisins in, then it'll be ready. It must be quite a while since your father had raisins. I've been saving them up for a long time."

"He's had raisins, alright," said Petrushka. "Our soldiers get raisins, alright. They're well off for grub — just look at their fat faces. And why might you be sitting down, Nastya? Think you've come to tea or something? Peel some potatoes and we'll fry them up for supper. Can't feed a family on nothing but cake!"

While his mother was making the cake, Petrushka put an iron pot of cabbage soup into the stove with a big pair of tongs so as not to waste the fire, and proceeded to give orders to the fire itself:

"What are you burning all over the place like that for? Let's have a nice straight flame right under the food. Do you think the trees in the forest grew this wood for nothing? Nastya, why did you shove the kindling in the stove any old how? You should have laid it properly like I showed you. And why are you peeling half the potato away again. It's a waste of good food to cut the best part away. That's the last time I tell you. Next time you'll get what-for."

"What's the matter, Petrushka, ticking off Nastya all the time?" his mother said gently. "Leave her alone. How can she peel all those potatoes, if you keep going on about shaving them thin like a barber so nothing's wasted. Your father's just come home and all you can do is grumble!"

"I'm not grumbling. Just making sure everything's alright. Dad needs to be fed, he's just got back from the war and you're wasting good food. Think how much food we lose in a year from potato peelings. If we had a pig we could feed her for a whole year on nothing but potato peel and send her to a pig-show, and she'd win a medal there. Just think of that, but you don't care."

Ivanov didn't know his son had grown up to be like this, and now he sat there and marvelled at the lad's astuteness. But he preferred the gentle little Nastya, whose small hands were also busy with the housework and had already grown quick and deft. She must be used to working around the house.

"Why don't you talk to me, Lyuba?" he asked his wife. "Tell me how you got on when I was away, what your health's like and what sort of work you're doing."

Lyubov Vassilievna was as shy of her husband now as a young bride. She wasn't used to him anymore. She even blushed when he talked to her, and her face took on that timid, frightened expression that Ivanov had found so pleasing when she was a young woman.

"We managed, Alyosha. It wasn't too bad. The children weren't ill very often and I managed to bring them up. The trouble is I'm only home with them at night. I'm working at the brick place now, on a press, and it's a long walk from here . . ."

"Where are you working?" Ivanov hadn't understood.

"At the brick factory, on a press. I didn't have any training so at first I did odd jobs, then they trained me and put me on the press. It's not bad work, but the children are on their own all the time. See how they've turned out? Do everything themselves, just like grown-ups," said Lyubov Vassilievna quietly. "I don't know whether that's good or bad, Alyosha. . . ."

"We'll see about all that, Lyuba. Now we'll all be together again. There's plenty of time to work out what's good and bad. . . ."

"Everything'll be better now you're back. On my own I don't know what's right or wrong, and I used to get frightened. Now you must think how we should bring the children up. . . ."

Ivanov got up and paced around the room.

"So you didn't have such a bad time on the whole, eh?"

"Not too bad, Alyosha. We stuck it out somehow and it's all over now. But we missed you so much. It was terrible to think you might be killed out there like the others and never come back again. . . ."

She began crying over the cake which was already in a baking tin, and her tears fell into the dough. She had just brushed the top with egg and went on smoothing the dough with the palm of her hand, greasing the celebration cake with her tears.

Nastya clasped her mother's leg and pressed her face against her skirt, staring up at her father sternly.

He bent down towards her.

"What's the matter, Nastya, my love. Are you angry with me?"

He picked her up in his arms and stroked her small head.

"Ee, lass, you've quite forgotten me. You were only a little mite when I went off to the army. . . ."

Nastya put her head on his shoulder and began to cry too.

"What's up, my love?"

"Mummy's crying, so I'm going to as well."

Petrushka, who had been standing bewildered in front of the stove, did not approve of all this.

"What's the matter with all of you? While you've been blubbering, the heat in the stove's being wasted. And if we put some more wood on, who'll give us coupons for a new lot? We've nearly used up the last lot, except for a bit in the barn — about ten logs and that's only aspen. Give us the dough, mother, while there's still some heat left."

Petrushka took the large iron pot of cabbage soup out of the stove and raked the glowing embers in the hearth, while Lyubov Vassilievna hurriedly thrust two cake tins into the stove as if to pacify Petrushka, forgetting to brush the second with egg.

Ivanov's home felt strange to him and he still couldn't quite understand it. His wife was just the same, with her sweet, shy face, although it was drawn and tired now, and the children were his own, except that they had grown while he had been away in the army, which was only to be expected. But something was stopping Ivanov from feeling the full joy of his homecoming. Perhaps he was simply not used to family life anymore and could not quite understand even his nearest and dearest. He watched Petrushka, his grown-up first-born, listened to him giving orders and instructions to his mother and little sister, saw his serious, worried face and was ashamed to admit that he did not feel enough paternal warmth for the lad, did not feel drawn to him as a father should to his son. He was even more ashamed of this indifference towards Petrushka, since he realised that the boy needed his love and care more than the others, because he was so sad to look at. Ivanov did not know exactly how his family had lived without him and he could not understand properly, not yet, why Petrushka had got like that.

Sitting at the table in the family circle, Ivanov suddenly realised what his duty was. He must get on with things as quickly as possible, get a job to earn money and help his wife bring up their children properly — then things would gradually get better and Petrushka would go out to play with the other lads or read a book, instead of barking orders with a pair of tongs by the kitchen stove.

Petrushka ate less than anyone else, but scooped up all the crumbs and gobbled them down.

"What are you picking up crumbs for, Petrushka, when you haven't finished your slice of cake," said his father. "Eat it up and your mother will give you another slice."

"You can eat house and home, but I've had enough," said Petrushka frowning.

"He's afraid that if he starts to eat a lot, Nastya will too," said Lyubov Vassilievna simply. "And that worries him."

"Nothing worries you a lot," said Petrushka calmly. "I only want to see that there's more for you."

The father and mother exchanged glances and shuddered at their son's words.

"Why don't *you* eat?" the father asked little Nastya. "You copy Petrushka, do you? You'll have to eat properly, if you want to be a big girl."

"I am a big girl," said Nastya.

She ate one small piece of cake, and set aside another slightly larger one, covering it with a napkin.

"What are you doing that for?" asked her mother. "Would you like me to put some butter on it?"

"No, I'm full."

"Well, eat it like that, then. What have you put it away for?"

"Uncle Semyon will be coming. I'm saving it for him. It's not yours. It's mine and I haven't eaten it. I'll put it under a pillow so it doesn't get cold. . . ."

Nastya got down from the table, carried the slice of cake wrapped in a napkin over to the bed, and put it under a pillow.

Her mother remembered putting pillows over a cake she had made for the First of May celebrations, so it would not get cold before Semyon Yevseyevich came.

"Who's this Uncle Semyon, then?" Ivanov asked his wife.

Lyubov Vassilievna did not know what to say and said:

"I don't know who he is. . . . He comes to see the children. His wife and children were killed by the Germans. He's got fond of our children and comes to play with them."

"Play with them?" said Ivanov disbelievingly. "What do they play here? How old is he?"

Petrushka glanced swiftly at his mother and father. His mother did not reply and only looked sadly at Nastya, but his father gave a hard smile, got up from the table and lit a cigarette.

"Where are the toys you and this Uncle Semyon play with?" the father asked Petrushka.

Nastya got down from the table, clambered onto another chair by the chest of drawers, got some books out and brought them to her father.

"They're toy books," she said to him. "Uncle Semyon reads them out loud to me: 'Here's a funny bear, just look, He's a toy and he's a book.' . . ."

Ivanov took the toy books that his daughter handed him: about Misha the Bear, the toy cannon and the cottage where Grandma Domna lived and spun flax with her granddaughter. . . .

Petrushka remembered it was time to close the damper in the stove-pipe so the heat did not escape.

When he had closed it, he said to his father:

"He's older than you — Semyon Yevseyevich. He helps us out. Leave him alone."

Glancing out of the window just in case, Petrushka saw the clouds in the sky were the wrong ones for September.

"Take a look at them clouds. They're the colour of lead. Looks as if we'll have snow! Surely it can't be winter already? What'll we do? The potatoes haven't been dug up yet and we haven't got any fodder in for the winter! A right mess!"

Ivanov looked at his son, listened to his words and felt shy of him. He wanted to ask his wife exactly who this Semyon Yevseyevich was that had been visiting his family for two years now, and who it was he came to see — Nastya or his comely wife — but Petrushka was distracting Lyubov Vassilievna with household problems:

"Give me the bread cards for tomorrow, mother, and the coupons. And the paraffin coupons — tomorrow's the last day. We need charcoal, too, and you lost the sack, and they won't provide one. Have a good look for the sack or make a new one. We can't manage without a sack. And let's get Nastya to stop people coming to get water from our well tomorrow, or there won't be any left. Winter's coming and the level of the water drops, and our rope's not long enough to lower the bucket, and we don't want to eat snow instead — we'd need firewood to melt it. . . ."

While he was saying all this, Petrushka swept the floor by the stove and tidied the kitchen utensils. Then he took the bowl of cabbage soup out of the oven.

"You've had your cake, now it's time for cabbage soup and bread," he ordered everyone. "And tomorrow morning you'd better go to the District Soviet and Military Commissariat, father, and sign on so we can get coupons for you."

"Alright, lad," said his father meekly.

"Be sure to go. Mind you don't oversleep and forget about it."

"I won't forget," promised his father.

The family ate its first meal together after the war, cabbage soup with meat, in silence, even Petrushka sat quietly. It was as if the father, mother and children were afraid of destroying, with a chance word, the quiet happiness of a family sitting together.

Then Ivanov asked his wife:

"How are you all off for clothes, Lyuba? Could probably do with some new things, couldn't you?"

"We made do with the old ones, but now we'll see about getting something new," smiled Lyubov Vassilievna. "I mended what the children already had, then used your suit, two pairs of trousers and all your underwear to make things for them. We were very hard up, you see, and I had to clothe the children somehow."

"You were quite right," said Ivanov. "Never begrudge the children anything."

"I didn't. I sold the coat you bought me and I wear a quilted jacket now."

"It's too short for her. She could easily catch cold," Petrushka commented. "I'm going to work as a stoker at the steam baths and get her a coat with my wages. They're selling them in the market. I went along to see what they cost and there are some that aren't too expensive. . . ."

"We'll manage without you and your wages," said the father.

After dinner Nastya put on a big pair of glasses and sat down by the window to mend the gloves which her mother now wore under her mittens at work — it was autumn and the weather had turned cold. Petrushka got angry when he saw her:

"Why are you ruining your eyesight with Uncle Semyon's glasses?"

"I'm looking over the top, not through them."

"I can see what you're doing, alright! You'll ruin your eyesight and go blind, then you'll be a dependent for the rest of your life and live on a pension. Take them off at once. And stop darning the gloves. Mother'll do them herself, or I will when I have a moment. Get out your exercise book and practise your strokes. Goodness knows how long it is since you last practised."

"Does Nastya go to school, then?" asked the father.

The mother said she wasn't old enough for school yet but Petrushka made her do lessons every day. He had bought her an exercise book and she practised writing now. Petrushka was also teaching her to count with melon seeds and Lyubov Vassilievna was teaching her to read.

Nastya put down the mitten and took her exercise book and pen-holder out of the chest of drawers. Pleased that everything was being done properly, Petrushka put on his mother's quilted jacket and went into the yard to chop firewood for the next day. He usually brought the chopped logs inside at night and piled them behind the stove so they would dry out and burn more hotly and economically.

In the evening Lyubov Vassilievna made supper early. She wanted to get the children to sleep so she could sit and have a talk with her husband. But after supper it was a long time before the children dropped off: Nastya lay on the wooden divan peeping out from under the blanket for a long time at her father, and Petrushka lay on the shelf of the Russian stove where he always slept, summer and winter, tossing and turning, coughing and muttering something, unable to settle down. But then night came, Nastya closed her tired eyes and Petrushka began to snore on the stove.

Petrushka slept lightly, always on the alert: he was always afraid something would happen at night and he wouldn't hear it — a fire, or thieves breaking in or mother might forget to latch the door and it would swing open in the night letting all the warmth out. That night he was woken by the troubled voices of his parents talking in the room next to the kitchen. It could have been midnight or nearly daybreak for all he knew, but his mother and father were not asleep.

"Don't make a noise, Alyosha, or the children will wake up," said the mother quietly. "And don't say bad things about him. He's a good person and he loved your children. . . ."

"We don't need his love," said the father. "I love my children myself. . . . Fancy loving other people's children. I sent you money regularly and you had a job — why did you need this Semyon Yevseyevich? Still got the itch, eh? Oh Lyuba, Lyuba! I never thought you'd do a thing like that when I was away. So you've been making a fool of me. . . ."

He stopped talking and struck a match to light his pipe.

"How can you say such a thing, Alyosha!" the mother exclaimed loudly. "I looked after the children, they were hardly ever ill, they've grown up fit and strong. . . ."

"So what!" said the father. "Some women were left with four children and managed alright and the kids grew up as well as ours. And just look at

Petrushka now — talks like an old man but he's probably forgotten how to read."

Petrushka sighed on the stove and pretended to snore so he could go on listening. "Alright," he thought, "so I'm like an old man, but you didn't have to worry about grub out there."

"Yes, but he's learnt about the most difficult and important things in life," said the mother. "And he's not behind with reading and writing either."

"Just who is he, this Semyon of yours? Stop trying to talk me round," said the father angrily.

"He's a good person."

"Do you love him, then?"

"Alyosha, I'm the mother of your children. . . ."

"So what? Give me a straight answer!"

"I love you, Alyosha. I'm a mother. It's a long time since I was a woman, I've even forgotten when, and that was only with you."

The father said nothing and smoked his pipe in the darkness.

"I missed you, Alyosha. Of course I had the children, but they couldn't take your place. I waited and waited for you all those long, terrible years. I didn't even want to wake up of a morning."

"What's his job? Where does he work?"

"He works in the supplies department at our factory."

"I see. He's a crook."

"No, he's not. You see. . . . His whole family was killed in Mogilev, there were three children, the daughter was already grown up."

"Never mind, he soon found himself a new, ready-made family instead and a woman who's still young and not bad to look at, so he's done fine for himself."

The mother did not reply. Silence followed, but soon Petrushka heard her crying.

"He used to tell the children about you, Alyosha," she began, and Petrushka could tell there were big tears welling in her eyes. "He told them how you were fighting there for us and what you were going through. . . . They used to ask him why and he told them it was because you were a good person. . . ."

The father laughed and knocked the ash out of his pipe.

"So that's the sort he is, this Semyon of yours. Never even seen me, but thinks I'm a good bloke."

"He's never seen you, but he made it up just so the children would love you and not forget you."

"Why should he do that? To get round you? You just tell me what he wanted."

"Perhaps he's got a good heart, Alyosha, and that's why he does it. Why shouldn't he?"

"Don't mind my saying it, but you're a fool to believe that, Lyuba. Everyone's after something."

"But Semyon Yevseyevich often brought things for the children. He always came with sweets, or white flour, or sugar, and not long ago he brought Nastya a pair of felt boots, but they were no good — too small. And he never asked for anything from us. We didn't need anything either, Alyosha. We could have managed on our own, we were used to it. But he said he felt better when he was caring for other people, it helped him not to grieve so much for his dead family. You'll see him. It's not the way you think it is."

"That's all a load of rubbish," said the father. "Don't try to fool me. I'm fed up with you, Lyuba. I want to enjoy life."

"Enjoy it with us, Alyosha."

"Me with you, and you with Semyon?"

"No more, Alyosha. He won't ever come here again. I'll tell him not to."

"No more must mean there has been something. Ee, Lyuba, you women are all alike."

"And what about you men?" she asked bitterly. "What do you mean, we women are all alike? I'm not like that. I worked day and night. We were making fire bricks for railway engines. I got so thin in the face you could hardly recognise me. A beggar wouldn't have asked me for a farthing. Things were hard for me, too, and the children were at home with no one to look after them. I got back after work with the stove unlit, the supper to cook, and the children all alone in the dark. They couldn't help round the house like they can now. Petrushka was little in those days. Then Semyon Yevseyevich began to drop in. He came and sat with the children. He lived all on his own, you see. 'Mind if I come round and have a warm-up at your place?' he asked me. I told him our place was cold too and the firewood was damp, but he said 'Never mind, it's my heart that's chilled to the core. Just let me sit with your children for a bit — you don't need to light the stove for me.' So I said alright, he could come, the children wouldn't be so frightened if he was there. Then I got used to him as well and we all felt better when he came. I'd look at him and remember you, that we had you. It was so sad and hard without you. I was glad for anyone to come, so it wouldn't be so miserable and the time would go more quickly. We had no use for time when you weren't with us."

"Go on, what else?" the father urged her.

"There's nothing else. You're home now, Alyosha."

"Well, in that case everything's alright," said the father. "It's time for bed."

"Wait a bit," the mother said. "Let's talk some more. I'm so happy with you."

"Why don't they shut up and go to sleep," thought Petrushka on the stove. "They've made up and that's that. Mother's got to get up early for work tomorrow, but she's having herself a holiday now that she's stopped crying."

"Did this Semyon love you?" the father asked.

"Wait a minute, I'll just go and tuck up Nastya. She throws off the blanket in her sleep and gets frozen."

She drew the blanket over Nastya, went into the kitchen and stood listening for a moment by the stove to see if Petrushka was asleep. Petrushka realised this and began to snore. Then she went out and he heard her voice again.

"I suppose so. I used to catch a soft look in his eyes, and I'm not much to look at now, am I? He's had a hard time, Alyosha, he needed someone to love."

"You might at least have given him a kiss, if that's the way things were," said the father good-naturedly.

"Well, I never! He did kiss me twice, though I didn't want him to."

"Why did he do that, if you didn't want him to?"

"I don't know. He said he'd forgotten himself and remembered his wife, and I was a bit like her."

"Is he a bit like me?"

"No. There's nobody like you. There's only one Alyosha."

"Only one, eh? That's how it always begins — first one, then two."

"He only kissed me on the cheek, not the lips."

"Makes no difference where."

"Yes, it does, Alyosha. You don't know what things were like for us."

"What do you mean? I fought all through the war and was closer to death than I am to you now. . . ."

"You fought and I was dying for you here. My hands shook with unhappiness, but I had to work cheerfully to feed the children and help the government fight the fascists."

She was speaking calmly, but her heart was heavy, and Petrushka felt sorry for his mother: he knew she had learnt how to mend their shoes so as not to pay good money to the cobbler, and she had repaired people's electric fires in return for potatoes.

"I couldn't go on living like that, breaking my heart all the time," she said. "If I had, it would have been the end of me. I would have died, I know, but I had the children to think of. . . . I needed to feel something else, Alyosha, some sort of happiness, so that I could relax. There was a man who said he loved me and was as tender with me as you were once a long time ago. . . ."

"Who's that? Semyon again?" the father asked.

"No, someone else. He's the regional committee instructor in our trade union. He was evacuated here."

"To hell with him, whoever he is! So what happened? Did he make you happy?"

Petrushka did not know anything about the instructor and was surprised that he did not know him. "So our mother's been up to a spot of mischief too, fancy that," he muttered to himself.

She answered her husband's question.

"I didn't get anything from him, no happiness at all, and I felt even worse afterwards. My heart had reached out to him because it was dying, but when we got close, really close, I felt nothing. At that moment I thought about things to be done in the house and was sorry I had let him be close. I realised that I could only have peace and happiness with you and I would only rest when you were with me again. I can't go on without you. I wouldn't be any good for the children. Stay with us, Alyosha. We'll have a good life!"

Petrushka heard his father get out of bed without a word, light his pipe and sit down on a stool.

"How many times were you really close to him?" he asked.

"Only once," the mother replied. "It never happened again. Isn't that enough?"

"That's your business," the father remarked. "But why did you say you're the mother of our children and you'd only been a woman with me, a long time ago. . . ."

"It's true, Alyosha. . . ."

"How can it be true? You were a woman with him as well, weren't you?"

"No, I wasn't. I wanted to be but I couldn't. I felt I couldn't go on without you. I needed to be with someone. I was so worn out, everything seemed so hopeless, that I couldn't even love my children and you know I'd put up with anything for them."

"Just a minute!" said the father. "You say you made a mistake with this new Semyon of yours and didn't find any happiness with him, yet you managed to go on and you're still in one piece?"

"Yes, I managed to go on," she whispered, "I'm still alive."

"So you're lying to me about that as well. How can you talk about telling me the truth?"

"I don't know," she whispered, "I don't know anything."

"Well I do. I know a lot. I've been through more than you have," the father said. "You're a whore, that's what you are."

The mother was silent. You could hear the father's heavy, fast breathing.

"So I've come home," he said. "The war's over and now you've wounded me in the heart. Well, go and live with your Semyons. You've made a laughing-stock of me, but I'm flesh and blood, too, not just a plaything."

He began to get dressed in the dark, then lit the paraffin lamp, sat down at the table and wound the watch on his wrist.

"Four o'clock," he said to himself. "Still dark. It's true what they say, that there are lots of wenches but no true wife."

It was quiet in the house. Nastya was breathing evenly asleep on the wooden divan. Petrushka snuggled up against the pillow on the warm stove and forgot that he should be snoring.

"Alyosha!" said the mother lovingly. "Alyosha, forgive me."

Petrushka heard his father grunt, then there was the sound of breaking glass. Through the chinks in the curtain he saw it had got darker in the room where his father and mother were, but there was still a light burning. "He's broken the lamp glass," thought Petrushka. "You can't get them anywhere."

"You've cut your hand," said the mother. "It's bleeding. Get a towel from the chest of drawers."

"Shut up!" he shouted at her. "I can't stand the sound of your voice. . . . Wake up the children. Wake them up at once, I tell you. I'll let them know what sort of mother they've got!"

Nastya gave a frightened scream and woke up.

"Mother!" she cried. "Can I come into your bed?"

She liked creeping into her mother's bed at night and snuggling up against her warm body under the blanket.

Petrushka sat up, his legs dangling over the edge of the stove, and said to everyone:

"It's time you were asleep. Why have you woken me up? It's not morning yet. It's still dark outside. Why are you making such a noise, with the light on too?"

"Go back to sleep, Nastya, it's early yet. I'll come and tuck you up in a minute," his mother replied. "And you lie down and stop talking, Petrushka."

"Why are you talking then? What does father want?" said Petrushka.

"What's it got to do with you, what I want!" his father retorted. "Regular little sergeant major, you are."

"Why did you go and break the lamp glass? What are you frightening mother for? She's thin enough as it is. Eats her potatoes without butter and gives it to Nastya instead."

"Do you know what your mother got up to here?" cried the father plaintively, like a little boy.

"Alyosha!" Lyubov Vassilievna beseeched her husband.

"Yes, I do, I know everything." Petrushka said. "She cried for you and waited for you, but now you're back and she's still crying. You're the one who doesn't know!"

"You don't understand a thing yet!" shouted his father angrily. "Look what a son we've got."

"I understand everything inside-out," Petrushka answered from the stove. "You're the one that doesn't understand. We've got work to do. We've got to go on living, and all you two can do is quarrel like stupid idiots."

Petrushka broke off, lay down on his pillow and began to cry suddenly and silently.

"A fine person you are to have in charge," said the father. "Still, who cares now? You can rule the roost instead of me. . . ."

Wiping his tears, Petrushka answered.

"What sort of a father are you, saying things like that, even though you're grown up and fought in the war. . . . Just you go into the disabled servicemen's co-op tomorrow and take a look at Uncle Khariton. He serves behind the counter there, cutting bread, and never cheats anyone. He fought in the war as well and came back. Go and ask him. He's always talking and joking. I've heard him myself. His wife Aniuta learnt to drive and now she delivers the bread. She's a good woman — never steals it. She had a friend, too, used to go to see him and he used to feed her. This friend of hers had a medal, he's lost an arm and he's in charge of a shop where they sell manufactured goods."

"Stop all that talking and go to sleep. It'll soon be daylight," said the mother.

"You wouldn't let me sleep either. . . . It won't be light for a bit. This bloke with one arm got friendly with Aniuta and that made life easier for them. Khariton was away fighting. Then one day he comes home and starts cursing Aniuta. Curses her all day long, then drinks wine and eats snacks all through the night, but Aniuta just cries and doesn't eat anything. He goes on and on cursing her till he's had enough, then stops going on at her and says: 'Fancy you just having one bloke with one arm, you silly woman. I had Glashka, Aproska, Maruska, another Aniuta, and then there was Magdalinka.' And he's a-laughing and Aunt Aniuta's a-laughing as well. And then she goes around boasting that there's still no one to beat Khariton and that he killed hundreds of fascists and the women were all crazy about him. Uncle Khariton tells us about it in the shop when he's handing out the bread ration. And now they're living together quietly and happily. But Uncle Khariton laughs and says: 'I was fooling my Aniuta. There weren't any Glashkas, Aproskas, or Aniutas, not even a Magdalinka. A soldier's job is to serve his country. He spends his time fighting the enemy, not mucking about. I just wanted to give Aniuta a fright.' Go to bed, father, and put out the light. It's smoking without the glass."

Ivanov listened in amazement to the story his Petrushka was telling. "The little beggar!" he thought to himself. "I expected him to come out any moment with something about my Masha. . . ."

Petrushka fell asleep at once and began to snore — this time he was not pretending.

It was broad daylight when he woke up and he immediately started worrying because he had slept too long and not done anything around the house yet.

The only person at home was Nastya. She was sitting on the floor looking through a picture book that her mother had bought her a long time ago. She looked at it every day because it was the only book she had, and traced the letters with her finger as if she was reading.

"What are you doing with your book so early in the morning, messing it about? Put it back where it belongs!" Petrushka said to his sister. "Where's mother? Gone to work?"

"Yes," said Nastya quietly and closed the book.

"What about father?" Petrushka looked for him round the house, in the kitchen and the living room. "Has he taken his bag?"

"Yes," said Nastya.

"What did he say to you?"

"Nothing. He kissed me on the eyes and mouth."

"Did he then?" said Petrushka thoughtfully. "Get up off the floor," he ordered her. "I'll wash and dress you, then we'll go out together."

At that moment their father was sitting in the railway station. He had already drunk a big glass of vodka and had a hot meal on a voucher in the station buffet. Last night he had decided to go to the town where he left Masha and see her, perhaps, never to leave her again. It was a pity that he was much older than this bath attendant's daughter with the hair that smelt of autumn leaves. Still, they'd see how things worked out. You could never tell in advance. All the same he hoped Masha would at least be a bit pleased to see him again. That was all he asked. It would mean he had someone new who was close to him, and also pretty, gay and kind-hearted. They'd see how it worked out.

Soon a train arrived which was travelling in the direction Ivanov had come from only yesterday evening. He picked up his bag and went on to the platform. "Masha's not expecting me," he thought. "She told me I'd forget her and we'd never see each other again, but here I am going back to her forever."

He climbed into the end platform of the carriage and stood there, so as to have a last look when the train moved off at the small town where he had lived before the war and where his children had been born. . . . He wanted to look once more at the house he had left; you could see it from the train because the street it was in ran up to the level crossing which the train would pass.

The train moved off and slid quietly over the station points into the empty autumn fields. Ivanov grabbed hold of the rails by the door and looked out at the small houses, buildings, barns and fire-tower of what had been his native town. He recognized two tall chimneys in the distance: the soap works and the brick factory where Lyuba was working her press now. Let her go her own way now, and he would go his. Perhaps he could have forgiven her, but what would be the good of it? His heart had hardened against her and had no forgiveness for a person who had kissed and been close to another, just so the war and the separation from her husband would not make her so lonely and miserable. And the fact that Lyuba had drawn close to her Semyons because life was hard, because she was tormented by need and longing, was no excuse. It simply proved her feeling. All love springs from need and longing; if people never needed anything or longed for anything, they would never fall in love.

Ivanov decided to go into the carriage to sleep, and not take a last look at the house where he had lived and left his children: why upset yourself unnecessarily. He looked ahead to see how far it was to the crossing, and there it was in front of him. At this point the railway track crossed the dirt road leading to the town; on the road were wisps of straw and hay that had fallen off carts, willow twigs and horse dung. The road was generally empty except for the two market days each week; occasionally you would see a peasant driving past on his way to town with a full cartload of hay or returning to the village. So it was now; the village road was empty, except for two children in the distance running from the direction of the town, along the street which joined the road. One was a little larger than the other, and had taken the small one by the hand pulling it along after him, but hurry as the small one did, trotting along fast on its little legs, it kept falling behind. So then the larger child dragged it along after him. At the last house they stopped and looked in the direction of the railway station, as if they were trying to decide whether to go there or not. Then they saw the passenger train on the crossing and began to run along the road towards the train as if they wanted to catch it up.

The carriage in which Ivanov was standing rushed over the crossing. He picked his bag up from the floor to go inside and sleep on the rack where he would not be disturbed by other passengers. But had those two children managed to reach the last carriage or not? He leaned out and looked back.

The two children, holding hands, were still running along the road to the crossing. They both fell down together, scrambled up and were off again. The larger one raised his empty hand, and, turning his face with the movement of the train in Ivanov's direction, waved it as if he were calling someone to come back to him. Then immediately the two of them fell down again. Ivanov noticed that the larger one had a felt boot on one foot and a rubber overshoe on the other, which was why he tripped so often.

Ivanov closed his eyes not wishing to see or feel the pain of these tripping, exhausted children, and suddenly felt a hotness in his chest as if his heart, imprisoned and languishing inside him, had been beating slowly and pointlessly all his life, and had only now beaten its way through to freedom filling his whole being with warmth and shuddering. He suddenly knew everything he had known before much more precisely and really. Before he had felt life through a barrier of pride and selfishness, but now he had touched it with his naked heart.

From the steps of the carriage he looked again at the distant children. He knew now that they were his children — Petrushka and Nastya. They must have seen him when the carriage was passing over the crossing, and Petrushka had called him home to their mother, but he had looked at them casually thinking about something else, and had not recognized his own children.

Now Petrushka and Nastya were running a long way behind the train on the sandy strip alongside the track. Petrushka was still holding Nastya by the hand, dragging her after him when she could not keep up.

Ivanov threw his bag out of the carriage onto the ground, then climbed down to the bottom step and jumped off the train onto the sandy strip along which his children were running towards him.

★

★ ★ ★ ★

AUTHOR: *Ama Ata Aidoo (1942--) is one of Ghana's best-known writers. She has written a collection of short stories,* No Sweetness Here; *a novel,* Our Sister Killjoy; *and the plays* Anowa *and* Dilemma of a Ghost.

SETTING: *The story takes place in the West African country of Ghana. Under colonialism, men were asked, or required, to fight alongside their colonial masters in European wars. In this story, a mother tells her daughter how her husband had gone south to the capital of Ghana (Accra) to join the English forces during the Second World War. As she explains, the Ghanese, ruled by the "Anglis-people," were required to fight the "German-people." The daughter then sees her husband go south to fight a yet-unknown enemy. A new baby – a future husband – has just been born.*

Certain Winds From the South

Ama Ata Aidoo

M'ma Asana eyed the wretched pile of cola-nuts, spat, and picked up the reed-bowl. Then she put down the bowl, picked up one of the nuts, bit at it, threw it back, spat again, and stood up. First, a sharp little ache, just a sharp little one, shot up from somewhere under her left ear. Then her eyes became misty.

"I must check on those logs," she thought, thinking this misting of her eyes was due to the chill in the air. She stooped over the nuts.

"You never know what evil eyes are prowling this dust over these grasslands, I must pick them up quickly."

On the way back to the kraal her eyes fell on the especially patchy circles that marked where the old pits had been. At this time, in the old days, they would have been nearly bursting and as one scratched out the remains of the out-going season, one felt a near-sexual thrill of pleasure

---

"Certain Winds From the South" is reprinted from *African Short Stories*, ed. Chinua Achebe and C. L. Innes (London: Heinemann, 1985) by permission of the author.

looking at these pits, just as one imagines a man might feel who looks upon his wife in the ninth month of pregnancy.

Pregnancy and birth and death and pain; and death again . . . when there are no more pregnancies, there are no more births, and therefore, no more deaths. But there is only one death and only one pain.

Show me a fresh corpse, my sister, so I can weep you old tears.

The pit of her belly went cold, then her womb moved and she had to lean by the doorway. In twenty years Fuseni's has been the only pregnancy and the only birth. Twenty years and the first child and a male! In the old days, there would have been bucks and you got scolded for serving a woman in maternity a duicker. But these days those mean poachers on the government reserves sneak away their miserable duickers, such wretched hinds! Yes they sneak away even the duickers to the houses of those sweet-toothed southerners.

In the old days, how time goes, and how quickly age comes. But then does one expect to grow younger when one starts getting grandchildren? Allah be praised for a grandson.

The fire was still strong when she returned to the room. M'ma Asana put the nuts down. She craned her neck into the corner. At least those logs should take them to the following week. For the rest of the evening, she sat about preparing for the morrow's marketing.

The evening prayers were done. The money was in the bag. The grassland was still, Hawa was sleeping and so was Fuseni. M'ma came out to the main gate, first to check up if all was well outside and then to draw the door across. It was not the figure, but rather the soft rustle of light footsteps trying to move still more lightly over the grass, that caught her attention.

"If only it could be my husband."

But of course it was not her husband!

"Who comes?"

"It is me, M'ma."

"You, Issa, my son?"

"Yes, M'ma."

"They are asleep."

"I thought so. That is why I am coming now."

There was a long pause in the conversation as they both hesitated about whether the son-in-law should go in to see Hawa and the baby or not. Nothing was said about this struggle but then one does not say everything.

M'ma Asana did not see but felt him win the battle. She crossed the threshold outside and drew the door behind her. Issa led the way. They did not walk far, however. They just turned into a corner between two of the projecting pillars in the wall of the kraal. It was as it should have been for it was he who needed the comforting coolness of it for his backbone.

"M'ma, is Fuseni well?"

"Yes."

"M'ma, is Hawa well?"

"Yes."

"Ma'ma please tell me, is Fuseni very well?"

"A-ah, my son. For what are you troubling yourself so much? Fuseni is a new baby who was born not more than ten days ago. How can I tell you he is very well? When a grown-up goes to live in other people's village . . ."

"M'ma?"

"What is it?"

"No. Please, it is nothing."

"My son, I cannot understand you this evening . . . yes, if you, a grown-up person, go to live in another village, will you say after the first few days that you are perfectly well?"

"No."

"Shall you not get yourself used to their food? Shall you not find first where you can get water for yourself and your sheep?"

"Yes, M'ma."

"Then how is it you ask me if Fuseni is very well? The navel is healing very fast . . . and how would it not? Not a single navel of all that I have cut here got infected. Shall I now cut my grandson's and then sit and see it rot? But it is his male that I can't say. Mallam did it neat and proper and it must be all right. Your family is not noted for males that rot, is it now?"

"No, Ma'ma."

"Then let your heart lie quiet in your breast. Fuseni is well but we cannot say how well yet."

"I have heard you, M'ma. M'ma?"

"Yes, my son."

"M'ma, I am going south."

"Where did you say?"

"South."

"How far?"

"As far as the sea, M'ma, I thought you would understand."

"Have I spoken yet?"

"No, you have not."

"Then why did you say that?"

"That was not well said."

"And what are you going to do there?"

"Find some work."

"What work?"

"I do not know."

"Yes, you know. You are going to cut grass."

"Perhaps."

"But my son, why must you travel that far just to cut grass. Is there not enough of it all round here? Around this kraal, your father's and all the others in the village? Why do you not cut these?"

"M'ma, you know it is not the same. If I did that here people would think I was mad. But over there, I have heard that not only do they like it but the government pays you to do it."

"Even so, our men do not go south to cut grass. This is for those further north. They of the wilderness, it is they who go south to cut grass. This is not for our men."

"Please M'ma, already time is going. Hawa is a new mother and Fuseni my first child."

"And yet you are leaving them to go south and cut grass."

"But M'ma, what will be the use of my staying here and watching them starve? You yourself know that all the cola went bad, and even if they had not, with trade as it is, how much money do you think I would have got from them? And that is why I am going. Trade is broken and since we do not know when things will be good again, I think it will be better for me to go away."

"Does Hawa know?"

"No, she does not."

"Are you coming to wake her up at this late hour to tell her?"

"No."

"You are wise."

"M'ma, I have left everything in the hands of Amadu. He will come and see Hawa tomorrow."

"Good."

"When shall we expect you back?"

"Issa."

"M'ma."

"When shall we expect you back?"

"M'ma, I do not know. Perhaps next Ramadan."

"Good."

"So I go now."

"Allah go with you."

"And may His prophet look after you all."

M'ma went straight back to bed, but not to sleep. And how could she sleep? At dawn, her eyes were still wide open.

"Is his family noted for males that rot? No, certainly not. It is us who are noted for our unlucky females. There must be something wrong with them . . . Or how is it we cannot hold our men? Allah, how is it?

"Twenty years ago. Twenty years, perhaps more than twenty years . . . perhaps more than twenty years and Allah, please, give me strength to tell Hawa.

"Or shall I go to the market now and then tell her when I come back? No. Hawa, Hawa, now look at how you are stretched down there like a log! Does a mother sleep like this? Hawa, H-a-a-w-a! Oh, I shall not leave you alone . . . and how can you hear your baby when it cries in the night since you die when you sleep?

"Listen to her asking me questions! Yes, it is broad daylight! I thought you really were dead. If it is cold, draw your blanket round you and listen to me for I have something to tell you.

"Hawa, Issa has gone south."

"And why do you stare at me with such shining eyes. I am telling you that Issa is gone south.

"And what question do you think you are asking me? How could he take you along when you have a baby whose navel wound has not even healed yet?

"He went away last night.

"Don't ask me why I did not come and wake you up. What should I have woken you up for? Listen, Issa said he could not stay here and just watch you and Fuseni starve.

"He is going south to find work, and . . . Hawa, where do you think you are getting up to go? Issa is not at the door waiting for you. The whole neighborhood is not up yet, so do not let me shout . . . and why are you behaving like a baby? Now you are a mother and you must decide to grow up . . . where are you getting up to go? Listen to me telling you this. Issa is gone. He went last night because he wants to catch the government bus that leaves Tamale very early in the morning. So . . .

"Hawa, ah-ah, are you crying? Why are you crying? That your husband has left you to go and work? Go on weeping, for he will bring the money to look after me and not you . . .

"I do not understand, you say? Maybe I do not . . . See, now you have woken up Fuseni. Sit down and feed him and listen to me.

"Listen to me and I will tell you of another man who left his newborn child and went away.

"Did he come back? No, he did not come back. But do not ask me any more questions for I will tell you all.

"He used to go and come, then one day he went away and never came back. Not that he had to go like the rest of them . . .

"Oh, they were soldiers. I am talking of a soldier. He need not have gone to be a soldier. After all, his father was one of the richest men of this land. He was not the eldest son, that is true, but still there were so many things he could have done to look after himself and his wife when he came to marry. But he would not listen to anybody. How could he sit by and have other boys out-do him in smartness?

"Their clothes that shone and shone with pressing . . . I say, you could have looked into any of them and put khole under your eyes. And their shoes, how they roared! You know soldiers for yourself. Oh, the stir on the land when they came in from the south! Mothers spoke hard and long to daughters about the excellencies of proper marriages, while fathers hurried through with betrothals. Most of them were afraid of getting a case like that of Memunat on their hands. Her father had taken the cattle and everything and then Memunat goes and plays with a soldier. Oh, the scandal she caused herself then!

"Who was this Memunat? No, she is not your friend's mother. No, this Memunat in the end ran away south herself. We hear she became a bad woman in the city and made a lot of money.

"No, we do not hear of her now. She is not dead either, for we hear such women usually go to their homes to die, and she has not come back here yet.

"But us, we are different. I had not been betrothed.

"Do you ask me why I say 'we'? Because this man was your father. Ah-ah, you open your mouth and eyes wide? Yes, my child, it is of your father I am speaking.

"No, I was not lying when I told you that he died. But keep quiet and listen. He was going south to get himself a house for married soldiers.

"No, it was not that time he did not come back. He came here, but not to fetch me.

"He asked us if we had heard of the war.

"Had we not heard of the war? Was it not difficult to get things like tinned fish, kerosene and cloth?

"Yes, we said, but we thought it was only because the traders were not bringing them in.

"Well, yes, he said, but the traders do not get them even in the south.

"And why? we asked.

"Oh you people, have you not heard of the German people? He had no patience with us. He told us that in the south they were singing dirty songs with their name.

"But when are we going, I asked him?

"What he told me was that that was why he had come. He could not take me along with him. You see, he said we were under the Anglis-people's rule and they were fighting with the German-people.

"Ask me, my child, for that was exactly what I asked him. What has all that got to do with you and me? Why can I not come south with you?

"Because I have to travel to the lands beyond the sea and fight.

"In other people's war? My child, it is as if you were there, that is what I asked him.

"But it is not as simple as that, he said.

"We could not understand him. You shall not go, said his father. You shall not go, for it is not us fighting with the Grunshies or the Gonjas.

"I know about the Anglis-people but not about any German-people, but anyway they are in their country.

"Of course his father was playing, and so was I.

"A soldier must obey at all times, he said.

"I wanted to give him so many things to take with him but he said he could only take cola.

"Then the news came. It did not enter my head, for it was all empty. Everything went into my womb. You were just three days old.

"The news was like fire which settled in the pit of my belly. And from time to time, some will shoot up, searing my womb, singeing my intestines and burning up and up and up until I screamed with madness when it got into my head.

"I had told myself when you were born that it did not matter you were a girl. All gifts from Allah are good and anyway he was coming back and we were going to have many more children, lots of sons.

"But Hawa, you had a lot of strength, for how you managed to live I do not know. Three days you were and suddenly like a rivulet that is hit by an early harmattan, my breasts went dry. Hawa, you have a lot of strength.

"Later they told me that if I could go south and prove to the government's people that I was his wife I would get a lot of money.

"But I did not go. It was him I wanted not his body turned into gold.

"I never saw the south.

"Do you say 'oh'? My child I am always telling you that the world was created a long while ago and it is old-age one has seen but not youth. So do not say 'oh'.

"Those people, the government's people, who come and go, tell us trade is bad now, and once again there is no tinned fish and no cloth. But this time they say this is because our children are going to get them in abundance one day.

"Issa has gone south now because he cannot afford even goat flesh for his wife in maternity. This has to be, so that Fuseni can stay with his wife and eat cow-meat with her? Hmm. And he will come back alive . . . perhaps not next Ramadan but the next. Now my daughter, you know of another man who went to fight. And he went to fight in other people's war and he never came back.

"I am going to the market now. Get up early to wash Fuseni. I hope to get something for those miserable colas. There is enough rice for two, is there not?

"Good. Today even if it takes all the money, I hope to get us some smoked fish, the biggest I can find, to make us a real good sauce."

★

★ ★ ★ ★

AUTHOR: *Chinua Achebe (1930–) is known as Nigeria's, and perhaps Africa's, foremost novelist. A Biafran (Ibo), he was the director of the External Service of the Nigerian Broadcasting Corporation at Lagos before the Nigerian Civil War. During the Nigerian Civil War, he saw and experienced firsthand both the universal, human dimension of war and the uniqueness of the African experience of war. Some of his well-known works include* Things Fall Apart, Arrow of God, No Longer at Ease, *and the book of verse,* Beware, Soul Brother.

SETTING: *The war, also called the Nigerian-Biafran War, was fought between 1967 and 1970. Three distinct ethnic groups – the Hausa of the north, the Yoruba of the east, and the Ibo (or Biafrans) – fought for control of Nigeria. The Hausa and Yoruba, supported by Britain, the Soviet Union, and Italy, ultimately defeated the Ibo, who had been supported by the French. The two million casualties and seeming futility of the war captured the world's attention.*

Girls at War

Chinua Achebe

The first time their paths crossed nothing happened. That was in the first heady days of warlike preparation when thousands of young men (and sometimes women too) were daily turned away from enlistment centres because far too many of them were coming forward burning with readiness to bear arms in defence of the exciting new nation.

The second time they met was at a check-point at Awka. Then the war had started and was slowly moving southwards from the distant northern sector. He was driving from Onitsha to Enugu and was in a hurry. Although intellectually he approved of thorough searches at road-blocks, emotionally he was always offended whenever he had to submit to them.

He would probably not admit it but the feeling people got was that if you were put through a search then you could not really be one of the big people. Generally he got away without a search by pronouncing in his deep

"Girls at War" reprinted from Chinua Achebe, *Girls at War and Other Stories* (London: Heinemann, 1972) by permission of the author.

authoritative voice: "Reginald Nwankwo, Ministry of Justice." That almost always did it. But sometimes either through ignorance or sheer cussedness the crowd at the odd check-point would refuse to be impressed. As happened now at Awka. Two constables carrying heavy Mark 4 rifles were watching distantly from the roadside leaving the actual searching to local vigilantes.

"I am in a hurry," he said to the girl who now came up to his car. "My name is Reginald Nwankwo, Ministry of Justice."

"Good afternoon, sir. I want to see your boot."

"Oh Christ! What do you think is in the boot?"

"I don't know sir."

He got out of the car in suppressed rage, stalked to the back, opened the boot and holding the lid up with his left hand he motioned with the right as if to say: After you!

"Are you satisfied?" he demanded.

"Yes sir. Can I see your pigeon-hole?"

"Christ Almighty!"

"Sorry to delay you, sir. But you people gave us this job to do."

"Never mind. You are damn right. It's just that I happen to be in a hurry. But never mind. That's the glove-box. Nothing there as you can see."

"All right sir, close it." Then she opened the rear door and bent down to inspect under the seats. It was then he took the first real look at her, starting from behind. She was a beautiful girl in a breasty blue jersey, khaki jeans and canvas shoes with the new-style hair-plait which gave a girl a defiant look and which they called — for reasons of their own — 'air force base'; and she looked vaguely familiar.

"I am all right, sir," she said at last meaning she was through with her task. "You don't recognize me?"

"No. Should I?"

"You gave me a lift to Enugu that time I left my school to go and join the militia."

"Ah, yes, you were the girl. I told you, didn't I, to go back to school because girls were not required in the militia. What happened?"

"They told me to go back to my school or join the Red Cross."

"You see I was right. So, what are you doing now?"

"Just patching up with Civil Defense."

"Well, good luck to you. Believe me you are a great girl."

That was the day he finally believed there might be something in this talk about revolution. He had seen plenty of girls and women marching and demonstrating before now. But somehow he had never been able to give it much thought. He didn't doubt that the girls and the women took themselves seriously, they obviously did. But so did the little kids who marched up and down the streets at the time drilling with sticks and wearing their mothers' soup bowls for steel helmets. The prime joke of the time among his friends was the contingent of girls from a local secondary school marching behind a banner: WE ARE IMPREGNABLE!

But after that encounter at the Awka check-point he simply could not sneer at the girls again, nor at the talk of revolution, for he had seen it in action in that young woman whose devotion had simply and without self-righteousness convicted him of gross levity. What were her words? We are doing the work you asked us to do. She wasn't going to make an exception even for one who once did her a favour. He was sure she would have searched her own father just as rigorously.

When their paths crossed a third time, at least eighteen months later, things had got very bad. Death and starvation having long chased out the headiness of the early days, now left in some places blank resignation, in others a rock-like, even suicidal, defiance. But surprisingly enough there were many at this time who had no other desire than to corner whatever good things were still going and to enjoy themselves to the limit. For such people a strange normalcy had returned to the world. All those nervous check-points disappeared. Girls became girls once more and boys boys. It was a tight, blockaded and desperate world but none the less a world — with some goodness and some badness and plenty of heroism which, however, happened most times far, far below the eye-level of the people in this story — in out-of-the-way refugee camps, in the damp tatters, in the hungry and bare-handed courage of the first line of fire.

Reginald Nwankwo lived in Owerri then. But that day he had gone to Nkwerri in search of relief. He had got from Caritas in Owerri a few heads of stock-fish, some tinned meat, and the dreadful American stuff called Formula Two which he felt certain was some kind of animal feed. But he always had a vague suspicion that not being a Catholic put one at a disadvantage with Caritas. So he went now to see an old friend who ran the WCC depot at Nkwerri to get other items like rice, beans and that excellent cereal commonly called Gabon gari.

He left Owerri at six in the morning so as to catch his friend at the depot where he was known never to linger beyond 8:30 for fear of air-raids. Nwankwo was very fortunate that day. The depot had received on the previous day large supplies of new stock as a result of an unusual number of plane landings a few nights earlier. As his driver loaded tins and bags and cartons into his car the starved crowds that perpetually hung around

relief centres made crude, ungracious remarks like "War Can Continue!"
meaning the WCC! Somebody else shouted "Irevolu!" and his friends
replied "shum!" "Irevolu!" "shum!" "Isofeli?" "shum!" "Isofeli?" "Mba!"

Nwankwo was deeply embarrassed not by the jeers of this scarecrow
crowd of rags and floating ribs but by the independent accusation of their
wasted bodies and sunken eyes. Indeed he would probably have felt much
worse had they said nothing, simply looked on in silence, as his boot was
loaded with milk, and powdered egg and oats and tinned meat and
stock-fish. By nature such singular good fortune in the midst of a general
desolation was certain to embarrass him. But what could a man do? He
had a wife and four children living in the remote village of Ogbu and
completely dependent on what relief he could find and send them. He
couldn't abandon them to kwashiokor. The best he could do — and did do
as a matter of fact — was to make sure that whenever he got sizeable
supplies like now he made over some of it to his driver, Johnson, with a
wife and six, or was it seven? children and a salary of ten pounds a month
when gari in the market was climbing to one pound per cigarette cup. In
such a situation one could do nothing at all for crowds; at best one could
try to be of some use to one's immediate neighbours. That was all.

On his way back to Owerri a very attractive girl by the roadside waved
for a lift. He ordered the driver to stop. Scores of pedestrians, dusty and
exhausted, some military, some civil, swooped down on the car from all
directions.

"No, no, no," said Nwankwo firmly. "It's the young woman I stopped
for. I have had a bad tyre and can only take one person. Sorry."

"My son, please," cried one old woman in despair, gripping the door-
handle.

"Old woman, you want to be killed?" shouted the driver as he pulled
away, shaking her off. Nwankwo had already opened a book and sunk his
eyes there. For at least a mile after that he did not even look at the girl
until she finding, perhaps, the silence too heavy said:

"You've saved me today. Thank you."

"Not at all. Where are you going?"

"To Owerri. You don't recognize me?"

"Oh yes, of course. What a fool I am . . . You are . . ."

"Gladys."

"That's right, the militia girl. You've changed, Gladys. You were
always beautiful of course, but now you are a beauty queen. What do you
do these days?"

"I am in the Fuel Directorate."

"That's wonderful."

It was wonderful, he thought, but even more it was tragic. She wore a high-tinted wig and a very expensive skirt and low-cut blouse. Her shoes, obviously from Gabon, must have cost a fortune. In short, thought Nwankwo, she had to be in the keep of some well-placed gentleman, one of those piling up money out of the war.

"I broke my rule today to give you a lift. I never give lifts these days."

"Why?"

"How many people can you carry? It is better not to try at all. Look at that old woman."

"I thought you would carry her."

He said nothing to that and after another spell of silence. Gladys thought maybe he was offended and so added: "Thank you for breaking your rule for me." She was scanning his face, turned slightly away. He smiled, turned, and tapped her on the lap.

"What are you going to Owerri to do?"

"I am going to visit my girl friend."

"Girl friend? You sure?"

"Why not? . . . If you drop me at her house you can see her. Only I pray God she hasn't gone on weekend today; it will be serious."

"Why?"

"Because if she is not at home I will sleep on the road today."

"I pray to God that she is not at home."

"Why?"

"Because if she is not at home I will offer you bed and breakfast . . . What is that?" he asked the driver who had brought the car to an abrupt stop. There was no need for an answer. The small crowd ahead was looking upwards. The three scrambled out of the car and stumbled for the bush, necks twisted in a backward search of the sky. But the alarm was false. The sky was silent and clear except for two high-flying vultures. A humorist in the crowd called them Fighter and Bomber and everyone laughed in relief. The three climbed into their car again and continued their journey.

"It is much too early for raids," he said to Gladys who had both her palms on her breast as though to still a thumping heart. "They rarely come before ten o'clock."

But she remained tongue-tied from her recent fright. Nwankwo saw an opportunity there and took it at once.

"Where does your friend live?"

"250 Douglas Road."

"Ah! that's the very centre of town — a terrible place. No bunkers, nothing. I won't advise you to go there before 6 p.m.; it's not safe. If you don't mind I will take you to my place where there is a good bunker and then as soon as it is safe, around six, I shall drive you to your friend. How's that?"

"It's all right," she said lifelessly. "I am so frightened of this thing. That's why I refused to work in Owerri. I don't even know who asked me to come out today."

"You'll be all right. We are used to it."

"But your family is not there with you?"

"No," he said. "Nobody has his family there. We like to say it is because of air-raids, but I can assure you there is more to it. Owerri is a real swinging town and we live the life of gay bachelors."

"That is what I have heard."

"You will not just hear it; you will see it today. I shall take you to a real swinging party. A friend of mine, a Lieutenant-Colonel, is having a birthday party. He's hired the Sound Smashers to play. I'm sure you'll enjoy it."

He was immediately and thoroughly ashamed of himself. He hated the parties and frivolities to which his friends clung like drowning men. And to talk so approvingly of them because he wanted to take a girl home! And this particular girl too, who had once had such beautiful faith in the struggle and was betrayed (no doubt about it) by some man like him out for a good time. He shook his head sadly.

"What is it?" asked Gladys.

"Nothing. Just my thoughts."

They made the rest of the journey to Owerri practically in silence.

She made herself at home very quickly as if she was a regular girl friend of his. She changed into a house dress and put away her auburn wig.

"That is a lovely hair-do. Why do you hide it with a wig?"

"Thank you," she said leaving his question unanswered for a while. Then she said: "Men are funny."

"Why do you say that?"

"You are now a beauty queen," she mimicked.

"Oh that! I mean every word of it." He pulled her to him and kissed her. She neither refused nor yielded fully, which he liked for a start. Too many girls were simply too easy those days. War sickness, some called it.

He drove off a little later to look in at the office and she busied herself in the kitchen helping his boy with lunch. It must have been literally a look-in, for he was back within half an hour, rubbing his hands and saying he could not stay away too long from his beauty queen.

As they sat down to lunch she said: "You have nothing in your fridge."

"Like what?" he asked, half-offended.

"Like meat," she replied undaunted.

"Do you still eat meat?" he challenged.

"Who am I? But other big men like you eat."

"I don't know which big men you have in mind. But they are not like me. I don't make money trading with the enemy or selling relief or . . ."

"Augusta's boy friend doesn't do that. He just gets foreign exchange."

"How does he get it? He swindles the government — that's how he gets foreign exchange, whoever he is. Who is Augusta, by the way?"

"My girl friend."

"I see."

"She gave me three dollars last time which I changed to forty-five pounds. The man gave her fifty dollars."

"Well, my dear girl, I don't traffic in foreign exchange and I don't have meat in my fridge. We are fighting a war and I happen to know that some young boys at the front drink gari and water once in three days."

"It is true," she said simply. "Monkey de work, baboon de chop."

"It is not even that; it is worse," he said, his voice beginning to shake. "People are dying every day. As we talk now somebody is dying."

"It is true," she said again.

"Plane!" screamed his boy from the kitchen.

"My mother!" screamed Gladys. As they scuttled towards the bunker of palm stems and red earth, covering their heads with their hands and stooping slightly in their flight, the entire sky was exploding with the clamour of jets and the huge noise of home-made anti-aircraft rockets.

Inside the bunker she clung to him even after the plane had gone and the guns, late to start and also to end, had all died down again.

"It was only passing," he told her, his voice a little shaky. "It didn't drop anything. From its direction I should say it was going to the war front. Perhaps our people are pressing them. That's what they always do. Whenever our boys press them, they send an SOS to the Russians and Egyptians to bring the planes." He drew a long breath.

She said nothing, just clung to him. They could hear his boy telling the servant from the next house that there were two of them and one dived like this and the other dived like that.

"I see dem well well," said the other with equal excitement, "If no to say de ting de kill porson e for sweet for eye. To God."

"Imagine!" said Gladys, finding her voice at last. She had a way, he thought, of conveying with a few words or even a single word whole layers of meaning. Now it was at once her astonishment as well as reproof, tinged perhaps with grudging admiration for people who could be so light-hearted about these bringers of death.

"Don't be so scared," he said. She moved closer and he began to kiss her and squeeze her breasts. She yielded more and more and then fully. The bunker was dark and upswept and might harbour crawling things. He thought of bringing a mat from the main house but reluctantly decided against it. Another plane might pass and send a neighbour or simply a chance passer-by crashing into them. That would be only slightly better than a certain gentleman in another air-raid who was seen in broad daylight fleeing his bedroom for his bunker stark-naked pursued by a woman in a similar state!

Just as Gladys had feared, her friend was not in town. It would seem her powerful boy friend had wangled for her a flight to Libreville to shop. So her neighbours thought anyway.

"Great!" said Nwankwo as they drove away. "She will come back on an arms plane loaded with shoes, wigs, pants, bras, cosmetics and what have you, which she will then sell and make thousands of pounds. You girls are really at war, aren't you?"

She said nothing and he thought he had got through at last to her. Then suddenly she said, "That is what you men want us to do."

"Well," he said, "here is one man who doesn't want you to do that. Do you remember that girl in khaki jeans who searched me without mercy at the check-point?"

She began to laugh.

"That is the girl I want you to become again. Do you remember her? No wig. I don't even think she had any earrings . . ."

"Ah, na lie-o. I had earrings."

"All right. But you know what I mean."

"That time done pass. Now everybody want survival. They call it number six. You put your number six; I put my number six. Everything all right."

The Lieutenant-Colonel's party turned into something quite unexpected. But before it did things had been going well enough. There was goat-meat, some chicken and rice and plenty of home-made spirits. There was one fiery brand nicknamed "tracer" which indeed sent a flame down your gullet. The funny thing was looking at it in the bottle it had the innocent appearance of an orange drink. But the thing that caused the greatest stir was the bread — one little roll for each person! It was the size of a golf-ball and about the same consistency too! But it was real bread. The band was good too and there were many girls. And to improve matters even further two white Red Cross people soon arrived with a bottle of Courvoisier and a bottle of Scotch! The party gave them a standing ovation and then scrambled to get a drop. It soon turned out from his general behaviour, however, that one of the white men had probably drunk too much already. And the reason it would seem was that a pilot he knew well had been killed in a crash at the airport last night, flying in relief in awful weather.

Few people at the party had heard of the crash by then, so there was an immediate damping of the air. Some dancing couples went back to their seats and the band stopped. Then for some strange reason the drunken Red Cross man just exploded.

"Why should a man, a decent man, throw away his life? For nothing! Charley didn't need to die. Not for this stinking place. Yes, everything stinks here. Even these girls who come here all dolled up and smiling, what are they worth? Don't I know? A head of stock-fish, that's all, or one American dollar and they are ready to tumble into bed."

In the threatening silence following the explosion one of the young officers walked up to him and gave him three thundering slaps — right! left! right! — pulled him up from his seat and (there were things like tears in his eye) shoved him outside. His friend, who had tried in vain to shut him up, followed him out and the silenced party heard them drive off. The officer who did the job returned dusting his palms.

"Fucking beast!" said he with an impressive coolness. And all the girls showed with their eyes that they rated him a man and a hero.

"Do you know him?" Gladys asked Nwankwo.

He didn't answer her. Instead he spoke generally to the party:

"The fellow was clearly drunk," he said.

"I don't care," said the officer. "It is when a man is drunk that he speaks what is on his mind."

"So you beat him for what was on his mind," said the host, "that is the spirit, Joe."

"Thank you, sir," said Joe, saluting.

"His name is Joe," Gladys and the girl on her left said in unison, turning to each other.

At the same time Nwankwo and a friend on the other side of him were saying quietly, very quietly, that although the man had been rude and offensive, what he had said about the girls was unfortunately the bitter truth, only he was the wrong man to say it.

When the dancing resumed Captain Joe came to Gladys for a dance. She sprang to her feet even before the word was out of his mouth. Then she remembered immediately and turned round to take permission from Nwankwo. At the same time the Captain also turned to him and said, "Excuse me."

"Go ahead," said Nwankwo, looking somewhere between the two.

It was a long dance and he followed them with his eyes without appearing to do so. Occasionally a relief plane passed overhead and somebody immediately switched off the lights saying it might be the Intruder. But it was only an excuse to dance in the dark and make the girls giggle, for the sound of the Intruder was well known.

Gladys came back feeling very self-conscious and asked Nwankwo to dance with her. But he wouldn't. "Don't bother about me," he said, "I am enjoying myself perfectly sitting here and watching those of you who dance."

"Then let's go," she said, "if you won't dance."

"But I never dance, believe me. So please enjoy yourself."

She danced next with the Lieutenant-Colonel and again with Captain Joe, and then Nwankwo agreed to take her home.

"I am sorry I didn't dance," he said as they drove away. "But I swore never to dance as long as this war lasts."

She said nothing.

"When I think of somebody like that pilot who got killed last night. And he had no hand whatever in the quarrel. All his concern was to bring us food . . ."

"I hope that his friend is not like him," said Gladys.

"The man was just upset by his friend's death. But what I am saying is that with people like that getting killed and our own boys suffering and dying at the war fronts I don't see why we should sit around throwing parties and dancing."

"You took me there," said she in final revolt. "They are your friends. I don't know them before."

"Look, my dear, I am not blaming you. I am merely telling you why I personally refuse to dance. Anyway, let's change the subject . . . Do you still say you want to go back tomorrow? My driver can take you early enough on Monday morning for you to go to work. No? All right, just as you wish. You are the boss."

She gave him a shock by the readiness with which she followed him to bed and by her language.

"You want to shell?" she asked. And without waiting for an answer said, "Go ahead but don't pour in troops!"

He didn't want to pour in troops either and so it was all right. But she wanted visual assurance and so he showed her.

One of the ingenious economies taught by the war was that a rubber condom could be used over and over again. All you had to do was wash it out, dry it and shake a lot of talcum powder over it to prevent its sticking; and it was as good as new. It had to be the real British thing, though, not some of the cheap stuff they brought in from Lisbon which was about as strong as a dry cocoyam leaf in the harmattan.

He had his pleasure but wrote the girl off. He might just as well have slept with a prostitute, he thought. It was clear as daylight to him now that she was kept by some army officer. What a terrible transformation in the short period of less than two years! Wasn't it a miracle that she still had memories of the other life, that she even remembered her name? If the affair of the drunken Red Cross man should happen again now, he said to himself, he would stand up beside the fellow and tell the party that here was a man of truth. What a terrible fate to befall a whole generation! The mothers of tomorrow!

By morning he was feeling a little better and more generous in his judgments. Gladys, he thought, was just a mirror reflecting a society that had gone completely rotten and maggotty at the centre. The mirror itself was intact; a lot of smudge but no more. All that was needed was a clean duster. "I have a duty to her," he told himself, "the little girl that once revealed to me our situation. Now she is in danger, under some terrible influence."

He wanted to get to the bottom of this deadly influence. It was clearly not just her good-time girl friend, Augusta, or whatever her name was. There must be some man at the centre of it, perhaps one of these heartless attack-traders who traffic in foreign currencies and make their hundreds of thousands by sending young men to hazard their lives bartering looted goods for cigarettes behind enemy lines, or one of those contractors who receive piles of money daily for food they never deliver to the army. Or perhaps some vulgar and cowardly army officer full of filthy barrack talk and fictitious stories of heroism. He decided he had to find out. Last night he had thought of sending his driver alone to take her home. But no, he must go and see for himself where she lived. Something was bound to reveal itself there. Something on which he could anchor his saving operation. As he prepared for the trip his feeling towards her softened with every passing minute. He assembled for her half of the food he had received at the relief centre the day before. Difficult as things were, he thought, a girl who had something to eat would be spared, not all, but some of the temptation. He would arrange with his friend at the WCC to deliver something to her every fortnight.

Tears came to Gladys's eyes when she saw the gifts. Nwankwo didn't have too much cash on him but he got together twenty pounds and handed it over to her.

"I don't have foreign exchange, and I know this won't go far at all, but . . ."

She just came and threw herself at him, sobbing. He kissed her lips and eyes and mumbled something about victims of circumstance, which went over her head. In deference to him, he thought with exultation, she had put away her high-tinted wig in her bag.

"I want you to promise me something," he said.

"What?"

"Never use that expression about shelling again."

She smiled with tears in her eyes. "You don't like it? That's what all the girls call it."

"Well, you are different from all the girls. Will you promise?"

"O.K."

Naturally their departure had become a little delayed. And when they got into the car it refused to start. After poking around the engine the driver decided that the battery was flat. Nwankwo was aghast. He had that very week paid 34 pounds to change two of the cells and the mechanic who performed it had promised him six months' service. A new battery, which was then running at two hundred and fifty pounds was simply out of the question. The driver must have been careless with something, he thought.

"It must be because of last night," said the driver.

"What happened last night?" asked Nwankwo sharply; wondering what insolence was on the way. But none was intended.

"Because we use the head light."

"Am I supposed not to use my light then? Go and get some people and try pushing it." He got out again with Gladys and returned to the house while the driver went over to neighbouring houses to seek the help of other servants.

After at least half an hour of pushing it up and down the street, and a lot of noisy advice from the pushers, the car finally spluttered to life shooting out enormous clouds of black smoke from the exhaust.

It was eight-thirty by his watch when they set out. A few miles away a disabled soldier waved for a lift.

"Stop!" screamed Nwankwo. The driver jammed his foot on the brakes and then turned his head towards his master in bewilderment.

"Don't you see the soldier waving? Reverse and pick him up!"

"Sorry, sir," said the driver. "I don't know Master wan to pick him."

"If you don't know you should ask. Reverse back."

The soldier, a mere boy, in filthy khaki drenched in sweat lacked his right leg from the knee down. He seemed not only grateful that a car should stop for him but greatly surprised. He first handed in his crude wooden crutches which the driver arranged between the two front seats, then painfully he levered himself in.

"Thanks sir," he said turning his neck to look at the back and completely out of breath.

"I am very grateful. Madame, thank you."

"The pleasure is ours," said Nwankwo. "Where did you get your wound?"

"At Azumini, sir. On tenth of January."

"Never mind. Everything will be all right. We are proud of you boys and will make sure you receive your due reward when it is all over."

"I pray God, sir."

They drove on in silence for the next half-hour or so. Then as the car sped down a slope towards a bridge somebody screamed — perhaps the driver, perhaps the soldier — "They have come!" The screech of the brakes merged into the scream and the shattering of the sky overhead. The doors flew open even before the car had come to a stop and they were fleeing blindly to the bush. Gladys was a little ahead of Nwankwo when they heard through the drowning tumult the soldier's voice crying: "Please come and open for me!" Vaguely he saw Gladys stop; he pushed past her shouting to her at the same time to come on. Then a high whistle descended like a spear through the chaos and exploded in a vast noise and motion that smashed up everything. A tree he had embraced flung him away through the bush. Then another terrible whistle starting high up and ending again in a monumental crash of the world; and then another, and Nwankwo heard no more.

He woke up to human noises and weeping and the smell and smoke of a charred world. He dragged himself up and staggered towards the source of the sounds.

From afar he saw his driver running towards him in tears and blood. He saw the remains of his car smoking and the entangled remains of the girl and the soldier. And he let out a piercing cry and fell down again.

★

★ ★ ★ ★

AUTHOR: *Kay Boyle (1903–1992) has been a writer of novels, short stories, poetry, children's fiction, biographies, translations, and was even a foreign correspondent for the* New Yorker *(1946–1953). Considered one of the left bank writers of France during the pre–World War II era, her pre-war fiction includes* Wedding Day and Other Stories *(1930),* Plagued by the Nightingale *(1931),* Gentlemen, I Address You Privately *(1933), and* Monday Night *(1938). She moved to Germany in 1948 to join her Austrian-born husband, who had a post in the American Occupational Government as an official of the United States War Department. Searching for another face of Germany – one other than the Nazi face – and describing the bitter agony of defeat and humiliation, she nevertheless wrote with a delicate style and mood. She continued her career as a professor of English at San Francisco State University and is now Professor Emeritus. Her latest major work,* This Is Not a Letter and Other Poems *(1985), was well received.*

SETTING: *Germany was divided into four zones of occupation after it surrendered on May 7, 1945, each zone to be controlled by one of the victors: France, Great Britain, the United States, and the Soviet Union. In this story, a German Jew – returning from exile – and an American employee of the occupation government come to terms with the war's aftermath.*

Frankfurt in Our Blood

Kay Boyle

It was the half bottles of wine which made them speak. Without them, the two women seated at a small table at the end of the dining-car might have had nothing to say. Paris lay barely twenty minutes behind them, but already the gently sloping green hills and the luxuriant fields of France were there, streaming swiftly past the windows: the villages, the feathery trees, the fluid country dimmed now to the quality of ancient murals by the veil of dusk which lay across the land. But inside the crowded diner of the Orient Express, the illumination was as hard as brass, and the waiters swayed down the aisle between the tables, bearing their trays as if upon the current of a stream.

Behind the diner swung the nimble links of the long racing train, the sleeping-cars for Prague and Frankfurt coupled with those for Warsaw and Budapest, or with sleepers for Bratislava, Vienna, Munich, Bucharest. By morning, these cars, which roared through the pastoral stillness of the continent, would have taken their separate ways, shunted off at Bar-le-Duc while the travellers slept within them, and the people who shared tables for the evening meal would have forgotten the look of one another in a little while. The two women were strangers to each other, and the one who rode in the direction in which the train was going was young and soft-skinned, and she wore a blue cotton short-sleeved dress, as simple as a schoolgirl's dress. She sat with her face turned toward the window, and her chin held in the cushion of her ringless left hand. The small stooped aging woman who sat opposite had also turned her head to watch the deepening twilight, her flesh, hair, clothing, eyes, all of the same worn faded gray. But there were the half bottles of red wine before them, and it was the faded little woman who made the first move, and who leaned forward toward the girl.

"Perhaps we could divide a half bottle between us?" she began, her diffidence coming meekly, patiently, to speech. "We could share the expense of it," she said, her accent not quite English and not quite American.

The girl turned back from the window, her wide eyes startled, and she looked at the woman as if waking from a dream.

"Yes, indeed. Yes," she said, and that might have been the end of it. It was the other woman who motioned the waiter to pull the cork of one of the two little bottles of red wine. Once he had done this, and wiped the bottle's dark mouth clean, it was her hand, reaching, narrow and ivory-knuckled, from the suit's gray sleeve, which poured the wine into their glasses with care. The girl had turned to the window again, her hands clasped on the table before her, her soft dark hair hanging long across the shoulders of her dress. "How I hate it," she said, and she looked out at the sight of the fleeing country as she spoke. "How I hate going back to Germany," she said, and she reached quickly and blindly out and took her glass up, and drank down the first swallow of red wine.

"Yes, going back," said the little woman, but she did not drink. Instead, she picked up her gray cotton gloves from where they lay beside her plate, and she laid the wrinkled fingers of them carefully together, and she smoothed them gently, reflectively, out upon her knees. "Yes, going back," she said.

When the woman began to eat the split pea soup, the girl turned away from the window again, and she pushed the metal bowl of her own soup aside. It could be seen that her mouth was bright with lipstick, and blemished by discontent, and that her glossy hair was cut in a fringe above blue baleful eyes. The faded little woman watched her young hand, her bare arm, lift to fill their glasses with the strong good wine.

"Every time it's a little bit harder than it was the time before," the girl was saying quickly. She sat with her arms resting on the table, turning the glass of wine between her fingers on the cloth. "You see, I go to Paris perhaps once a month, just for the week end. And every time I have to go back it's like cutting my heart out and throwing it away."

"And you can't stay in Paris?" the woman said quietly.

"Well, I have a job," the girl said, still watching the glass turn on the cloth. "I'm a War Department civilian in Frankfurt." The waiter had carried the bowls away, the full one inside the empty one, and the girl took another swallow of the wine. "I took the job just to get over. Just to get on the same continent with France," she said, and she lifted one hand to the side of her face as if to shield it, as though there might be tears in her eyes and she did not want a stranger to see them fall.

"Yes, Frankfurt," said the faded little woman. "It's been a long time, but I could tell you the name of almost every street still. You know, I went there as a bride once!" she said, and she lifted her glass of wine again and drank a little, trying to make it sound, even after all the years that had passed, festive and jaunty and gay. "My husband taught in the university there," she said, with a sociable smile on her lips, but her hand as it set the glass down on the cloth again was trembling like a leaf in the high wind of emotion that came sweeping through her heart. She looked at the ham in gravy which the waiter set before her, but she made no move to eat. "We lived there twenty-five years together," she said.

"You have memories. That's a certain kind of wealth," the girl said, seeming to begrudge them to her. "I have absolutely nothing except the things I want to be."

"Well, let's make this into a little celebration," said the woman, and she raised her glass as if they might drink a toast together, but the girl drank quickly, without acknowledging the woman's lifted glass or the tentative smile that hung upon her mouth.

"Six months ago, I didn't believe that Germany would remain for me this alien, evil thing," the girl said, and across the table, the woman looked meekly up at her young face. "I thought I would be able to get close to what it really is, or was," the girl said, speaking quickly, while outside the

windows the lights of the villages and the rural stations of France were cast
behind them in the dark. "But I see Germany like some isolated territory,
like a lepers' colony, an infected island which free men conquered, and
who have, because of this, become ailing and evil and no longer free."

"Yes," said the woman, "but, you know, there is a strange thing that
can happen to people. Or perhaps when people get older, this is the thing
that always happens." The waiter bore the plates away, and the woman sat
smiling, smiling almost in apology across the cloth. "I can only think of
Germany now as it was when I was a child, and of Frankfurt as I knew it as
a bride," she said. And now an unexpected look of audacity, an almost
devilish look of mischief came into her worn faded eyes. "You know, I have
a little French money left, not much, but enough," she said; "and I would
like to spend it on another half bottle of wine!"

The waiter uncorked the second half bottle, and wiped its mouth
clean, and then he put the plates of lamb and peas before them. And now
that the woman's voice had ceased to speak, the girl turned to the window
again, and to the sight of the deepening darkness through which the
country flowed swiftly, irretrievably past. Tomorrow there would be
Frankfurt, and the bomb-gutted station in the early morning, and the
houses laid open to the elements still bearing within their rubble
outlandish bits and pieces of what had once been comfort and security.
There would be the radiator hanging by its pipes through a floor that had
capsized beneath it five years before, and the bathtub standing two stories
high above the dead magnolia trees, its clawed feet resting on nothing, and
the panelled door behind it still standing ajar.

"Or perhaps the place you began life in as a bride is a place that can
never change for you," the woman was saying now, and the girl turned
abruptly away from the window, and she poured their glasses full with
wine. "There was my husband's work in the university, and there were
other professors, and there were artists, too, writers, countless friends," said
the little woman smiling as she spoke. "There we had meetings,
discussions, and not only among intellectuals, but among men of the free
crafts, the guilds, the unions. For Frankfurt was once the heart of liberal
Germany. And then, in 1934, my husband died. He was very wise to
choose that year to die in," she said, still smiling, but her hand was
shaking as if with palsy as she took the glass of wine. "We are a Jewish
family," she said, "so in one way or another we had to go."

"And you, where did you go?" the girl asked, and the turmoil, the
protest, seemed to halt within her for a moment.

"We went to China. My sons and I left for China that year," said the woman. "We carried what we could of Frankfurt in our blood with us — its culture, its wisdom, its democratic history. Or perhaps the only thing we really took with us was the sound of Goethe's words saying many things to us who were also the German people, saying very clearly that wisdom's last decree is that freedom and life are deserved only by those who conquer them anew each day." The girl and the woman both finished the wine in their glasses, and the girl sat turning the glass in her fingers while opposite her the woman's voice went on speaking gently and patiently of a town that had been Frankfurt once, and a country that had been Germany. "That was a gift I had to give my children," the woman said; "a belief in free men which free men themselves had communicated to me."

And, as the girl listened to the woman's voice going on with this, the city they travelled toward took on another aspect, and the sound of the familiar German voices perished, no longer saying, as they had said to her for six months now: "I lost everything in the bombings, everything — my house, my furniture, my business," for the woman was speaking of the Taunus hills, and of the walks they had taken there in the springtime, she and the others, the professors, the artists, the writers, the free men of Frankfurt who had seen freedom die.

"And now you are going back? After fifteen years, you are going back?" the girl said, looking at her, and forgetting to turn the wine glass on the cloth.

"Yes," said the little woman. "No choice was offered. The women and children of foreigners were being evacuated. I was flown out of China last week. I am going back to Frankfurt," she said, the smile hanging on her mouth again, "because there does not seem any other place for me to go."

"How many children did you have?" the girl asked, for it was the members of this family which mattered, as the rest of Germany had never mattered. It was what they had been, and how they had spoken, and what answer they had given when the questions had been asked.

"I had four sons," the woman said, and her hand had begun to tremble again as she lifted her glass again to drink. "Two of them left Germany with me, the two younger ones. We went to China together," she said, having wet her lips with the wine. "The two others," she went on saying after a moment, but she could not go on with it at once. "The two others," she began again, and there was no hint of crying, nothing that even resembled anguish in the words she said. "The two others died with their countrymen and women in Dachau," was what she was saying, but even the strength of the wine she drank was not enough to lean on now, and her lips, her chin, her empty hands, were trembling as if stricken with the plague.

"Now it is my turn to order another half bottle," the girl said quickly, and she made the sign to the waiter as he passed with the *bombes glacées*. And then she reached across the table, and she touched the woman's worn aged hand that lay, like a forgotten object, on the cloth.

"I am afraid to go back," the woman said, and her teeth bit hard into her shaking lip. "I am not afraid of my memories. I am afraid of hearing what the living now have to say."

"We can listen to other things," the girl said, and their hands held to each other's as the waiter set the plates of crackers and cheese before them, and poured the fresh wine out. And then the stooped little woman shouldered the burden of patience and resignation again, and she smiled across the table at the girl.

"I shall make out very well," she said, and their hands drew apart, and they lifted their glasses and drank. "I have a widow's pension accumulated at the university. It will be enough to begin again on," she said, and an unsteady look of recklessness or tipsiness came into her face. "It will be enough to pay my way into the Palm Garden in the afternoons, and there'll still be the orchid hothouse, with orchids as different as people, with wise faces, and foolish ones," she said, and she giggled as if she were a young giddy woman now. "I don't remember how many species there were, but I knew them all by name once. And in the tropical conservatory, there'll be the camellias flowering, reddish and white and waxy, as they flowered in China so profusely —" And then she stopped talking. "Unless," she said quickly. "I mean, was the Palm Garden bombed — are the greenhouses there still?"

"Yes, they are there," said the girl, and then the two women began to laugh across the table at each other.

"I must write to my sons at once, to my two boys in China," the woman said, wiping the tears of laughter away, "and tell them how tall the banana trees have grown."

★

★ ★ ★ ★

AUTHOR: *Bui Ngoc Tan published this story in March 1958, at the conclusion of the French-Indochina War. The story uses many of the cultural stereotypes fostered by war situations: the beautiful, sincere peasant girl; the uncomprehending foreigners; and the cynical, observant commentator. The story clearly indicates that foreigners do not, and cannot, understand Vietnam – neither the land nor the people. And, in not comprehending, neither can foreigners understand the devastation of the war.*

SETTING: *After the withdrawal of the Japanese from Vietnam near the end of World War II, the French attempted to reassert their authority over their former colony, French Indochina. In the north, the Vietminh, led by Ho Chi Minh, proclaimed the independent Democratic Republic of Vietnam. Fighting continued until May 7, 1954, when the French finally lost to General Vo Nguyen Giap at Dien Bien Phu. An international conference in Geneva worked out an agreement whereby the fighting would cease and the French would withdraw. The Vietminh set up a government north of the 17th Parallel, the Democratic Republic of Vietnam, while the Vietnamese non-Communists set up a government south of the demarcation line, the Republic of Vietnam.*

Sao

Bui Ngoc Tan

The prisoner was about 6 ft. 3 ins. tall. He had curly fair hair, deep-set eyes, ash-blue in colour, a broad forehead and a two days' beard which made him look a little older than his age of twenty-two as stated in the paper of escort.

The five prisoners who made up the convoy were Adiotti, an Italian native of a small village in the Alps, Pierre, a French farmer from the Loire department, Mohamed, a Moroccan, Hectmad, a German, native of Hamburg, and the man referred to above. We were attracted to him at first sight. We did not remember the reason for such a feeling: was it because he was taller than the other prisoners, or because he was the youngest of the five, because of his stubbornness or because he was a pilot; we didn't know.

"Sao" was published in North Vietnam during the Vietnam War without publication information. The author's name may be a pseudonym.

The paper of escort described him in a few lines: "De Labéri, born on August 4, 1931 in Paris, into an official's family; a law student, trained as pilot in 1950, landed in Vietnam in February 1952." He was taken prisoner five months after he had arrived in Vietnam.

Thach and I were entrusted with the task of escorting the five prisoners from Quang Yen to Thai Nguyen. After two days, they began talking to us, except Labéri who always lagged far behind the others. When he was in shirt-sleeves, one could see his strong hairy arms. A U.S.–made knapsack was flung on his back and a bag containing five Nestlé tins of milk slung over his shoulders.

Paying no attention to our conversation, he walked with his lips continually glued to a tin of milk. Now and then his comrades looked greedily at him, but he didn't take any notice of them. Thach flew into a rage, "Let me deal with him," he said and called: "Labéri! Vite, vite!"

The French prisoner raised his head but continued shuffling along, his hand on his bag of milk.

"You see, he doesn't care a straw for any one," fumed Thach. "With this fellow we can't use sweet words."

Thach was in a very dark mood because his mother, wife and children had been blown to pieces by a bomb falling into their trench. When Thach returned home, it was to see three graves freshly raised.

I knew very well that Thach was doing his best to suppress his anger.

I couldn't bear this haughty POW either, so I said to Labéri acrimoniously, "You are invited to walk faster, sir!"

In our absence, he was much more lively. Once Hectmad whispered to me, "Labéri lectured us for having lost our soldier-like demeanour and surrendered to yellow-skinned people."

Once he struck Mohamed.

I shouted, "Labéri" and not waiting for his answer, rushed to him, bursting with anger. He stood to attention and raised his hand in salute, "Captain?"

I asked, "What have you just done?"

Ashamed, he lowered his head to avoid my fierce look.

"Carry Mohamed's knapsack!"

The Moroccan looked at me in awe. Labéri violently snatched the knapsack from him and became more taciturn.

It was swelteringly hot. The trees lining the road withered. The sun shone through their foliage in golden spots, dazzling our eyes.

Labéri gasped for breath.

Once when he came to a narrow street, he took a rest in a café apart from ours. When he saw me coming he hid a bottle behind him, uneasy.

"Spirits?" I exclaimed.

"Yes, Captain," he said.

I looked casually at his wrist and could not see his gold watch. Realizing that he had paid for his drink with it, I began to pity him. I defrayed his expenditure and told the café-keeper to give him back his watch. His eyes wide open, he looked at me, astonished, and shook hands with me respectfully.

"I do not understand, Captain, but I thank you."

"You are a drinker, Labéri?"

"That's my vice."

"Don't do that anymore," I said gravely.

He bowed his head and scratched the earth with the tip of his sandal.

"A gold watch against a bottle of spirits!" I went on, shrugging my shoulders.

"Well, when one is in need . . . This watch was given me by my mother before I left for Vietnam." Labéri said, also shrugging his shoulders.

I smiled sarcastically: "This was a keepsake. A fine sort of fellow you are!"

"I know that I was wrong, but I couldn't help it."

And he told me about his family. He lived in Paris with his mother and a little sister. Before his captivity, he had received a letter from them every month wishing him good health and prompt return . . .

"Five months have elapsed," he said sadly, "but to me, they are as long as a century."

"Perhaps you miss Paris badly!"

He looked out into the distance and did not reply directly to my question. "In summer, we used to walk along the bank of the Seine," he said. "I was petted by my mother but was angry because she liked to treat me as a child."

His face brightened as he remembered the halcyon days in that fashionable city far away in the West.

These prisoners were people who squandered money. Labéri could eat a whole chicken. The five cigarettes given him each day were smoked in no time. Once I threw away a cigarette stump. Pierre rushed in and gave it a long puff. Labéri turned his face away.

I flung Labéri a cigarette. He smoothed it, put it to his lips then opened his hands and looked at me appealingly. I threw him a lighter. He looked at the effigy of a tank on it, lit his cigarette and thanked me.

* * *

We resumed our journey. Before us was a young woman in a brown jacket and black trousers walking clumsily with a big bag hanging on her shoulders. Sunshine made her white palm-leaf hat glitter.

"A girl from the area controlled by the puppet administration, you see!" I told Thach.

We walked more quickly. When we caught up with her, we saw at a glance that she was still in her teens, and had very long curling eye-lashes; her cheeks were reddened by the sun and her hair, damp with sweat, fell on her broad forehead.

It seemed that I had met her somewhere! But I did not remember who she was.

She looked at the prisoners of war, bewildered, and walked more slowly. Perhaps she was afraid. I also slowed down my pace. Her round shoulders were bent under the weight of her heavy bag. Her thin brown jacket, open at the sides showed her white underwear, and was tight over her firmly moulded breasts.

Forgetting their fatigue, the POWs began talking merrily, except Labéri who dazed with alcohol, did not utter a word.

She frowned and slackened her pace. I boldly started the conversation:

"It seems that I've seen you somewhere."

She looked intently at me and asked, "Are you Tan?"

"Yes, I am," I replied, astonished. "How do you know my name?"

"You came to my house once," she said with joy.

"Are you from Thuy Nguyen?"

"No," she replied, turning her face away.

"Sorry, I'm mistaken."

But she turned round and looked at me, laughing, "Yes, I live at Thuy Nguyen. You came with Chau."

"Oh! Sao. I remember you now. What are you doing here? Why are you alone?"

"I am on my way to see an old acquaintance of mine."

"Where?"

"At Vo Nhai."

"I am going to Vo Nhai, too."

"How lucky I am! I was afraid I shouldn't know the way."

"Keep us company."

When they heard me talk to the girl, all the POWs, including Labéri, turned round to have a look. Sao lowered her hat.

"Don't frighten," I said, laughing. "We are in the free zone, and not at Thuy Nguyen."

"Where are you taking them?" she asked me.

"To the concentration camp."

After a pause, she shifted to another subject, "Con is dead," she said. "Do you remember him, a member of the guerilla district committee?"

Her word gave me a start. "Con dead, when?"

"At the beginning of this year."

Mopping her face, she told me that after having captured Con, the enemy beat him with a rifle butt. Con opened his eyes wide, saying, "Don't be disrespectful to me. I want to see your lieutenant."

The lieutenant served him a drink and gave him a roasted leg of chicken.

Con emptied the spirits at a gulp and threw the cup and the chicken into the lieutenant's face. "They killed Con at Giai Vu." Sao said, "I was there; I was very frightened because Con's body was so contorted before he died."

Then she pointed to Mohamed, saying, "The killer looked like that fellow." Pointing to Labéri she said, "The lieutenant, a Corsican, was like that one. The enemy combed Con's hair with brilliantine and exhibited his head at the market place."

Anger choked me and prevented me breathing properly. I could not bear the presence of these two fellows and told Thach to march them far ahead.

"They deserve to be killed at once to atone for their crimes," Thach said, gnashing his teeth.

Sao and I walked more slowly.

"How do you like living here?" I started another subject.

"Very much indeed! Before I came away I felt sure I should meet with death. Only outside the enemy controlled zone, can I feel I am alive."

"By the way, how is your mother? Have you received news from your husband?"

"My mother is very well, thanks, and I've already heard from my husband."

"Where is he now?"

"At Vo Nhai."

I burst out laughing. "So that's it. I have been wondering who could induce you to come from Thuy Nguyen despite so many difficulties."

I knew very well the love she and Vu, her husband had for each other. Last year when I lived in her house, I frequently caught her gazing in the direction of Ang Son where cannons were roaring. But she would pretend not to think of anything special and, to dispel my suspicion, would take a broom and sweep the house. I would immediately go away to allow her to indulge in her meditations about the man from whom she had been separated seven days after the wedding.

In winter it was cold and dry. The earth was parched, the vegetation shrivelled. The roses shed their leaves which littered the ground. Sao was alone at home. She watered vegetables; from time to time, she stopped and looked up into the leaden sky. Far away stood the Dau Cau post; overhead some kites were hovering and shrieking.

Nobody knew why Vu was so loath to write letters.

Then came the rumour that he had died in a battle on Highway 18. That piece of gossip retailed from mouth to mouth was without foundation, but it made Sao weep bitterly.

We tried to comfort her, but it was of no avail. She spent the night repairing our underground shelter and would not go to sleep though we begged her to go many times.

It transpired that the more she thought of her husband the more she took care of us. She used to like very much to hear about my wife who lived in the rear of the enemy line in Hadong province . . .

"Since last year, haven't you had any occasion to see your wife?" she asked me.

I shook my head. She heaved a sigh.

When there was nobody in the house, she used to take out Vu's letters to read. The letters were very short and generally did not convey any affection but she read them passionately, grasping other meanings between the lines. When the reading was over, she sat still and sighed. We kept quiet, respecting her sufferings.

Now, her happiness seemed to communicate itself to me while we were walking side by side.

"How did you know his address?" I asked her.

"My uncle who works at the town military command, wrote to me that when he went to Vu Nhai for a conference, he met my husband in the street quite unexpectedly."

"How lucky you are!"

She smiled and shifted to another topic. "When we had crossed the Van river, we all jumped for joy as we were in the free zone. My joy was so great that I kept on singing and when a policeman asked my papers I forgot that they were . . . in my hand. The river is very large . . . How beautiful the banknotes are here with President Ho's picture on them!"

I remembered the road from Thuy Nguyen. How dangerous it was! To come here we had to pass through Nam Tao and Bac Dau, two important posts built on a hill at the roadside. We had to prepare ourselves for all eventualities. At Luc Dau Giang, the most dangerous but the last stronghold, the river was so wide that it looked like a sea. The enemy motor boats from Pha Lai patrolled this section all night long. We were told that to be safe a mother had to stifle the cries of her baby until it fainted for lack of breath.

"Aren't you afraid on your journey?" I asked Sao. Thach replied in her stead, "Why should she be afraid? Even if the road were ten times more dangerous she could get through easily; only we, have to be careful."

She smiled.

Arriving at an inn, she fished in her bag a packet of cigarettes and gave them to us. I declined, saying, "It's better to keep it for your husband."

But she entreated us each to take a cigarette. The POWs cried, "French cigarettes!" and looked at Sao and us, astonished.

Sao turned away and put the packet of cigarettes back in her bag.

I told her that the POWs will be repatriated soon.

She looked at them a long while and handed the cigarettes to Thach saying, "Give them to them to smoke."

With delight the POWs grasped the cigarettes. Labéri received his share with both hands. He was a slave to the cigarette. He politely bowed his head towards Sao, saying, "Thank you."

The cigarette smoke gave him much ecstasy. From that time on he was more taciturn. Sometimes he stole a glance at Sao and gazed at the sunny horizon.

I asked Sao, "Why did you give them cigarettes?"

"I don't know why. I begin to pity them," she replied shyly.

I suddenly remembered the moments she had stood at a corner of the house, thinking of her husband, the night she was alone, the enemy's raids during which her life hung on a thread, the days she had to sit in a flooded trench or her forced march to Giai Vu before the rifles of the enemy.

Now the enemy were here, sad and despondent — because they could no longer live the lives of drunkards and homicides — and they were smoking Sao's cigarettes.

We resumed our march on the hot dusty road. Sometimes Sao lagged behind, wet with perspiration as it was sweltering hot.

When I saw how tired she was, I asked, "Can I carry the bag for you?"

She refused saying, "I can carry it, though I am not accustomed to. It'll be better if I have a carrying pole."

At another café, she managed to get a pole and wanted to carry also my knapsack, but I thanked her.

Labéri looked at her, amazed. He limped along far behind and in the end could not take another step: he fell ill. His face reddened, his nose ran and he perspired profusely.

"Why am I condemned to make such a long trip?" he cried and lay at the foot of a tree. "No, I cannot go further. Let me die here. Oh Yvonne!"

We all stopped and did not know what to do.

"Give me a bullet rather than to torture me like that," he said.

I gave him some tablets of quinine, the only medicine we had, but he refused, "I do not suffer from malaria and could not take this hateful drug."

We could not stop there for the night as the date of concentration was drawing near.

"Surely he has a sunstroke," whispered Thach. I tried to comfort him, "Make an effort to walk, I'll buy medicine for you if it is available on the road."

He did not answer and lay motionless.

Sao called me to a corner and said, "I'm having some medicines, but do not know their use."

Under the watchful eyes of Labéri and the other POWs, Sao searched among the bundles of white cloth, underwear and towels and took out a small packet containing some quinine vials, Ganidan and Aspirin tablets. Thach cried aloud as the required medicine was found.

The POWs flocked in. Labéri sat up and swallowed the drug as docilely as does any patient. Then he looked at Sao saying, "Thank you very much."

She cooked for Labéri a rice gruel; when he saw the hot bowl of food, he sat up immediately. But he did not eat at once and looked intently at Sao, full of astonishment and gratitude.

Sao became very gentle and played with the children. Labéri ate slowly.

He was well again after some more potions of drug and could walk more quickly. Sometimes he peeped at Sao and lowered his head in a pensive mood. He whispered to himself, "Oh darling! . . ."

He told me, "The Vietnamese women have many special qualities which cannot be found in any French women. Sao treated me as a sister though I am her enemy."

In a sunny mood I told Labéri of the love between Vu and her, adding that the drug she had given him was bought for her husband in the army. Labéri looked at the young girl from head to toes, as surprised as if he first met her. Then he signed, "Oh, Yvonne!"

"Have you seen that love is something wonderful?" he told me. "It laughs at all dangers. After seven days living together they were separated for two years and now they will meet again. What happiness! For me I never hope to see my Yvonne again."

"Is Yvonne your wife?"

"She is my fiancée."

I fancied a young French girl, in her teens, slim, with silky curly hair falling on the forehead, smiling lips but thoughtful and sad looking eyes.

"Yvonne and I loved each other for more than a year," he said. "I liked to lie in a park and hear her ask me, 'Have you surrendered to me?' as she put one foot on my chest."

How many remembrances there were in his mind! He looked very childish and pitiful. To give full swing to his thoughts, I let him alone and turned to Sao who was looking vacantly at the quiet river. At a sluice where the water fell in a torrent, she told me, "Here field work is very easy. Irrigation is not necessary; drain pipes bring water direct to the fields. In my locality irrigation is a problem."

"Here only oxen are used for tilling," she said on seeing some tillers at work. "In my country, where clay soil predominates we need very strong buffaloes." Everything amazed her: the herds of buffaloes which were grazing freely in the meadow, each animal with a wooden bell at the neck, the firewood which found no gatherers, and myrtle trees with their sweet fruit.

After Thai Nguyen town, I told her, "We are nearing our destination."

"How many kilometers are left?" she asked.

"Quicken your steps, you'll arrive soon," Thach replied, imitating the Tho accent.

We all laughed heartily. Sao mopped her hair and face and, unable to control her joy, walked more swiftly.

"Slow down your pace and wait for us," Thach said. "Why are you in such a hurry, we'll arrive to-night, be sure!"

Sao smiled.

The sinking sun tinged the valley and plain in yellow. What a splendid scenery indeed! The buffaloes grazed peacefully, the green leaves of cassava roots planted on the mountain range rose in waves.

On the mountain slope, some Tho girls were busy tending their cassava plants, making indigo spots on an immense blue background. Two carts were running towards the other side of the hill. A unit of soldiers was stationed at the roadside, camouflaged with leaves. Here and there the scent of grass pervaded the atmosphere.

This familiar scene made us forget our fatigue and announced the end of our journey. Mohamed's and Labéri's faces brightened up.

We stopped at Long Giang bridge. Aware of her impatience, we said, "Go ahead, we stay here for a while."

As she hesitated, we urged her, "There's nothing to fear. From here the road is very easy. If you walk without a stop you will arrive this evening. You cannot wait us. If engaged we'll start tomorrow."

Sao bade us farewell. Labéri wished her, "Good luck and happiness!"

We followed her from afar. Arriving at a tiny stream some scores of metres from us, she laid down her bag on the bank and washed her face in the stream. She took out of her pocket and raised to her face something which we guessed to be a mirror.

From afar, Thach warned her, "Hurry up, or you will make him wait."

She looked at us. Thach's happiness had been shattered and he appreciated all the more the happiness of others. He waved his helmet and Sao responded with her conical hat. The POWs gazed at her. Labéri murmured, "Good bye! Good bye!"

Sao went off. Alone in this region of mountains and forests, at nightfall, her graceful walk enhanced the beauty of the scenery. She vanished in the forest of pine-trees gilded by the last sun rays . . .

Only then did Labéri stop looking at her; he turned to me and said, "I missed my Yvonne badly. She is as kind as Sao."

He took a diary out of his knapsack.

The first page had a red lip-print bearing below the mention, "Many kisses to you, your unfortunate Yvonne."

The second page read, "Yvonne's letter has been received with great joy. She is always well. One month away from her is as long as one year. Her letters are read again and again. She reminds me of the evenings of July, of the holidays, of the nights we walked hand in hand along the Seine river.

"I miss Paris more and more, the city of light and Yvonne, my darling Parisian girl . . . On the day we parted, she rouged her lips. I asked her why but she kept secret. A little later she took out a note-book, applied her lips on the first sheet of paper and offered me this kiss . . .

"Arrive at Cat Bi. Haiphong is small and narrow, but swarming with beautiful girls. They are all slim, have black hair and jet black eyes, very exotic.

". . . First flight in a Hellcat in Vietnam sky and dropping of the first bomb. A whole village burns like a sea of flames as picturesque as a painting. The rebels live deep in the jungle. The country teems with mountains and forests. Bombing and strafing at random; don't know whether the targets are hit . . ."

". . . Receive another letter from Yvonne, in which she reproaches me because my letters to her were short and few. She asks how she could be forgotten. Perhaps the yellow-skinned angels have overshadowed 'your' Yvonne! Yvonne says she has heard stories of good soldiers spoiled after a stay in Vietnam. Why does that happen?

"Paul is right. What can I do? Should there be no drink and girls and air trips! The airfield is surrounded by barbed wire and one lives inside like a detainee.

"Paul tells me to go to a brothel. A herd of despicable girls. Oh, Blessed Virgin, save my soul! . . ."

I was fed up after running over a few pages and handed the diary back to Labéri.

"You are all tarred with the same brush," I said.

"Yes. Everyone has a sweetheart beyond the ocean," his prompt reply connoted that he had misunderstood my hint.

"But here, there are husbands and wives who are separated by an immense ocean because of the war."

"That is the case of beautiful Sao. But she will reach the other side of the ocean very soon."

After a short stop at Long Giang bridge we resumed our march. An army unit which had rested by the roadside set off. Labéri looked at the soldiers saying, "You rely on mountains and forest to win."

I made up my mind to tell him the decisive factor of our victories when the tearing humming of an airplane was heard overhead. We had just the time to lie flat on the ground and saw a Hellcat flying as low as the top of the mountain. It fired some bullets at random. Labéri craned his neck and followed the direction of the plane, most envious . . .

Only when the airplane was reduced to a tiny pinpoint and disappeared behind the mountain range, did we stand up. Night was falling. We guessed that Sao had arrived at destination and met her husband. We tried to imagine the happiness of this couple! Maybe Vu's teammates would have surrounded him and his wife. He would have become the target for the jokes of some merry-makers. In a hut reserved for the couple, Vu would have flung his arm around his wife's neck. That night they would be more happy than the night of the wedding.

Darkness changed the scenery. The road along which we were trudging became a whitish track. The mountains and forests around us darkened and were full of mystery. In a few huts built on the mountain slope, light was on, glittering as stars in the immense sky. The weather became mild again; it was windy and less hot.

We drew near a bright torch and saw on the road a big crowd surrounding a corpse.

Many voices rose:

"The plane fired some shots only."

"Nobody knows where her family lives. She is not from our country."

"I was working in the field when I saw her lying down. After the strafing, she did not stand up."

We worked our way through the crowd and saw a bloodstained woman with broken legs and a pair of trousers torn to pieces. I uncovered the towel hiding her face and was so horror struck that my legs would not hold me upright, because the unfortunate woman was Sao. Her face was ghastly, her eyes lifeless and her hair unkempt and caked with blood. I looked intently at her and closed my lips so that no curses would come out.

Late in the afternoon Sao had been still talking merrily to us and now Death had carried her off. What a terrifying death! Sao would be forgotten for ever. Here Death was incarnated in the person of an airman, a fellow laden with crimes, who considered a burning village a beautiful picture.

Sao had travelled with us for several days. From Thuy Nguyen near the seacoast she had to cover hundreds of kilometres and pass by scores of military posts to come to her husband. Now she lay for ever in a locality not far from where he was living but separated by two worlds. How much love and affection she had had for him, how many hopes she had expected from him and how many worries had she wanted to tell him after two long years of separation? Alas, she had taken all this with her to the grave.

A coffin was brought in and a voice rose, "Dress her in her new clothes."

They searched her bag and saw that the clothes contained therein were either soaked with blood or rent by bullets: the packet of cigarettes was bloodstained.

When two men put her body in the coffin, Thach shouted, "Wait a minute! Her husband is not far from here. Let him see her for the last time."

I did not know what they talked to each other, but they laid Sao's body back at the first place, and stared at us. I felt my cheeks flame. I shed tears. I wept in front of the POWs, and glared at them.

Thach also looked daggers at them. However one of them could understand that we were looking askance at them. Hectmad, Adiotti, Pierre and Mohamed were gathering around a tree, holding a silent but awful conversation. Hectmad broke out of the crowd, sat on the pavement and exclaimed in German, "Terrifying!"

I happened to see that Labéri was looking intently at me. I thought to myself why at this time that damned fellow was so light-hearted. I was in tears and wanted to burn him alive but I couldn't catch his eye. Maybe he was not really looking at me, but away in the distance. He did not notice that my anger might drive me into committing a murder. He stared at the loosened bag, at the blood-stained cigarettes, at the Aspirin tablets laying higgledy-piggledy on the roadside. He peered at Sao's body lying inert like a charred tree.

There was a deathly silence except for the crackling of the fire. The POWs withdrew in secret towards Hectmad who sat despondently. Only Labéri was unmoved.

Thach groaned, "This crime is committed by a Hellcat. Oh, the murderer!"

Then he grasped Labéri's arms and led him away. "This is the deed of one of your friends, understand!"

While he was dragged away, Labéri did not stop gazing at Sao.

Suddenly he looked up into the sky in the direction of the criminal airplane: he looked up as if he was saying a prayer; he uttered jerky groans and had a lump in his throat.

"Paul . . . I've understood, sure I have . . ."

And burying his face in his hands he sobbed bitterly.

Yen Bai, March 1958

★

★ ★ ★ ★

AUTHOR: *Tim O'Brien (1946-) was born in Austin, Minnesota. His socialization in a small, midwestern town played a major role in the moral conflict he experienced when he was drafted into the army just after finishing college in 1968. O'Brien felt that the war in Vietnam was morally and politically wrong; yet he allowed what he once called the "gravity" of his upbringing to draw him into the war. His guilt and confusion over having served as an infantryman in Vietnam surface in nearly all of his writing. O'Brien wrote a memoir of his war experiences (from which "Mori" was taken) shortly after the war, while he was a graduate student at Harvard. In 1978 his brilliant novel* Going After Cacciato *won the prestigious National Book Award.*

SETTING: *In the late 1950s and early 1960s, the United States became increasingly involved in the conflict in Indochina. By 1968, the year in which this story takes place, the United States was no longer simply "advising" South Vietnam: U.S. troop levels had risen to more than 500,000. When the United States withdrew, it was estimated that more than 50,000 Americans had been killed and 300,000 wounded. The South Vietnamese lost more than 500,000 soldiers and the Army of the North and Vietcong guerillas lost an estimated 924,048 lives. This story relates the death of one victim.*

Mori

Tim O'Brien

She had been shot once. The bullet tore through her green uniform and into her buttock and out through her groin. She lay on her side, sprawled against a paddy dike. She never opened her eyes.

She moaned a little, not much, but she screamed when the medic touched at her wound. Blood gushed out of the holes, front and back.

Her face lay in dirt. Flies were all over her. There was no shade. It was mid-afternoon of a hot day. The medic said he did not dare squirt morphine into her, it would kill her before the wound did. He tried to patch the holes, but she squirmed and twisted, rocked and swayed, never opening her eyes. She flickered in and out of consciousness.

"She's a pretty woman, pretty for a gook. You don't see many pretty gooks, that's damn sure."

"Yes. Trouble is, she's shot dead through the wrong place." A dozen GI's hovered over her.

"Look at that blood come, Jesus. Like a fuckin' waterfall, like fuckin' Niagara Falls. She's gonna die quick. Can't mend up them bullet holes, no way."

"Fuckin'-aye. She's wasted."

"I wish I could help her." The man who shot her knelt down. "Didn't know she was a woman, she just looked like any dink. God, she must hurt. Get the damn flies off her, give her some peace."

She stretched her arms out above her head. She spread her fingers wide and put her hands into the dirt and squeezed in a sort of rhythm. Her forehead was wrinkled in a dozen long, flushed creases; her eyes were closed.

The man who shot her peered into her face. He asked if she couldn't be given shade.

"She's going to die," one soldier said.

"But can't we give her some shade?" He swatted at a cloud of flies over her head.

"Can't carry her, she won't let us. She's NVA, green uniform and everything. Hell, she's probably an NVA nurse, she probably *knows* she's just going to die. Look at her squeeze her hands. Trying to hurry and press all the blood out of herself."

We called for a dustoff helicopter and the company spread out in a wide perimeter around the shot woman. It was a long wait, partly because she was going to die, helicopter or no helicopter, and partly because she was with the enemy.

Her hair was lustrous black. The man who shot her stroked her hair. Two other soldiers and a medic stood beside her, fanning her and waving at the flies. Her uniform was crusted an almost black color from her blood, and the wound hadn't clotted much. The man who shot her held his canteen to her lips and she drank some Kool-Aid.

Then she twisted her head from side to side. She pulled her legs up to her chest and rocked, her whole body swaying. The man who shot her poured a trickle of water onto her forehead.

Soon she stopped swaying. She lay still and seemed either dead or unconscious. The medic felt her pulse and shrugged and said she was still going, just barely. She moaned now and then, almost talking in her sleep, but she was not being shrill or hysterical. The medic said she was not feeling any more pain.

"Damn, she is pretty. It's a crime. We could have shot an ugly old man instead."

When the helicopter came, she was still. Some soldiers lifted her onto a poncho and took her to the chopper. She lay curled up on the floor of the helicopter, then the bird roared and went into the air. Soon the pilot radioed down and asked what we were doing, making him risk his neck for a dead gook.

★

★ ★ ★ ★

AUTHOR: *Hsiao Hung (1911-1942) was the daughter of a landlord in Harbin, northeast China. During the Sino-Japanese War, she lived in Chungking and Japan. She finally fled to Hong Kong in 1940. Her first, and perhaps finest, novel,* The Field of Life and Death, *was published when she was only twenty-three.*

SETTING: *There were three major periods of Japanese-Chinese warfare between 1894 and 1945: the First Sino-Japanese War (1894-1895), the Russo-Japanese War (1904-1905), and the Second Sino-Japanese War of 1937-1945. Each was related to an attempt by Japan to be a major international power. The era culminated in World War II in the Pacific and involved all the Asian countries, including Japan, the Soviet Union, China, Korea, plus the United States.*

The Chinese literature of the era has a consistent theme: the Chinese peasant, innocent and brave, but steeped in tradition and unable (because of an ineffective national regime) to mount effective resistance, is victimized by organized, ruthless foreign aggression. This is the story of a traditional Chinese woman who is frightened and confused by the events that unsettle her personal life. Her husband (symbolizing the old order) is killed for desertion from the army (a symbol of the traditional regimes' brutality), and she flees — to an unknown destination — symbolic of the requirement for change in China.

On the Oxcart

Hsiao Hung

Late March. Clover covers the banks of the streams. In the early light of the morning our cart crushes the red and green grasses at the foot of the hill as it rumbles through the outskirts of Alter-grandfather's1 village. The carter is a distant uncle on Mother's side. He flicks his whip, but not to strike the rump of the ox; the tip merely dances back and forth in the air.

"Are you sleepy already? We've only just left the village! Drink some plum cider now, and after we've crossed the stream you can sleep." Alter-grandfather's maid is on her way to town to visit her son.

Translated by Howard Goldblatt. "On the Oxcart" reprinted from *Born of the Same Roots*, by Vivian Ling Hsu (Bloomington, Ind.: Indiana Univ. Press, 1981) by permission of the publisher.

"What stream? Didn't we just cross one?" The yellow cat we're bringing back from Grandfather's house has fallen asleep in my lap.

"The Hou-t'ang Stream."

"What Hou-t'ang Stream?" My mind is wandering. The only things from Alter-grandfather's village still visible in the distance are the two gold balls topping the red flagpole in front of the ancestral temple.

"Drink a cup of plum cider, it'll perk you up." She is holding a cup of the dark yellow liquid in one hand as she puts the lid back on the bottle.

"I don't need anything . . . perk me up? You perk yourself up!"

They both laugh as the carter suddenly cracks his whip.

"You young lady, you . . . you sharp-tongued little scamp . . . I, I . . ." He walks over from alongside the axle and reaches out to grab hold of my hair. Drawing my shoulders back, I clamber to the rear of the cart. Every kid in the village is scared of him. They say he used to be a soldier, and when he pinches your ear it hurts like the dickens. Wu-yün Sao[2] has gotten down off the cart to gather a lot of different kinds of flowers for me. Now the wind blowing in from the woods has picked up a bit, and her scarf is flapping around her head. It reminds me of a raven or a magpie, like the ones I saw in the village. Look at her jumpin' up and down, just like a kid! She's back in the cart now, singing out the names of all kinds of flowers. I've never seen her so happy and carefree.

I can't tell what those low, coarse, grunting noises from the crater mean. Puffs of smoke from his short pipe float back on the wind. As we start off on our journey, our hopes and expectations are far off in the distance.

I must have fallen asleep. I remember waking up once, somewhere after we crossed Hou-t'ang Stream — I don't know exactly where — and through the cobwebs of my mind I thought I saw the boy who watches over the ducks beckon to me. There was also the parting scene between me and Hsiao-ken as he straddled the ox. And I could see Alter-grandfather again taking me by the hand and saying, "When you get home tell your grandpa to come on over during the cool autumn season and visit the countryside. You tell him that his old in-law's quail and his best sorghum wine are waiting here for us to enjoy together. You tell him that I can't get around so well anymore; otherwise the past couple of years I would have gone."

The hollow sound of the wheels wakes me up. The first thing I see if the yellow ox plodding along the road. The carter isn't sitting there by the axle where he should be — there he is, on the back of the cart. Instead of the whip, he's holding a pipe in his hand. He keeps stroking his jaw with his other hand; he is staring off into the horizon. Wu-yün Sao is holding the yellow cat in her lap and stroking its tail. The blue cotton scarf around her head has dipped below her eyebrows, and the creases on her nose are more distinct than usual because of the dust that has gathered around them.

They don't know I'm awake.

"By the third year there were no more letters from him. You soldiers . . ."

"Was your husband a soldier too?" I couldn't hold back. My carter-uncle pulls me backwards by my pigtail.

"And no more letters at all after that?" he asks.

"Since you asked me, I'll tell you. It was just after the Mid-Autumn Festival — I forget which year it was. I had just finished eating breakfast and was slopping the pigs in front of the house. 'Soo-ee, soo-ee!' I didn't even hear Second Mistress from the Wang family of South Village as she came running up, shouting, 'Wu-yün Sao, Wu-yün Sao! My mother says it's probably a letter from Brother Wu-yün.' She held a letter right under my nose. 'Here let me have it. I want to see . . .' I don't know why, but I felt sick at heart. Was he still alive? He . . . A tear dropped on the red-lined stationery, but when I tried to wipe it off, all I did was make a red smudge on the white paper. I threw the slop down in the middle of the yard and went into my room to change into some clean clothes. Then I ran as fast as I could to the school in South Village to see the schoolmaster. I was laughing through my tears. 'I've got a letter here from someone far away; would you please read it to me? I haven't had a single word from him for a year.' But after he read the letter he said it was for someone else. I left the letter in the school and ran home. I didn't go back to feed the pigs or put the chickens to roost; I just went inside and lay down on the brick bed. For days I was like someone whose soul had left her."

"And no more letters from him since then?"

"None." She unscrews the lid from the bottle of plum cider and drinks a cupful, then another.

"You soldiers, you go away for two or three years, you say, but do you return home? How many of you ever do? You ought to at least send your ghosts for us to see."

"You mean . . . ?" the carter bursts out. "Then he was killed in battle somewhere?"

"That's what it amounted to; not a word for more than a year."

"Well, was he killed in battle or wasn't he?" Jumping down from the cart, he grabs his whip and snaps it in the air a couple of times, making sounds like little explosions.

"What difference does it make? The bitter life of a soldier doesn't allow for much good fortune." Her wrinkled lips look like pieces of torn silk, a sure sign of an unrooted nature and a life of misfortune.

As we pass Huang Village the sun begins to set and magpies are flying over the green wheat fields.

"Did you cry when you learned that Brother Wu-yün had died in battle?" As I look at her, I continue stroking the yellow cat's tail. But she ignores me and busies herself with straightening her scarf.

The carter scrambles up into the cart by holding on to the handrail and jumping in, landing right above the axle. He is about to smoke; his thick lips are sealed as tightly as the mouth of the bottle.

The flow of words from Wu-yün Sao's mouth is like the gentle patter of rain; I stretch out alongside the handrail and before long I've dozed off again.

I awake to discover that the cart is stopped alongside a small village well — the ox is drinking by the well. Wu-yün Sao must have been crying, because her sunken eyes are all puffed up and the crow's feet at the sides of her eyes are spread open. The carter scoops up a bucketful of water from the well and carries it over to the cart.

"Have some — it's nice and cool."

"No thanks," she replies.

"Go ahead and drink some. If you're not thirsty, at least use some of it to wash your face." He takes a hand towel from his waistband and soaks it in the water. "Here, wipe your face. Your eyes are all dusty."

I can't believe it, a soldier actually offering his towel to someone! That strikes me as peculiar, since the soldiers I've known only know how to fight battles, beat women, and pinch children's ears.

"That winter I traveled to the year-end market to sell hog bristles. I stood there shouting, 'Good stiff hog bristles . . . fine long hog bristles . . .'" By the next year I had just about forgotten my husband . . . didn't let him tear at my heart anymore. What good was there in thinking of him, I told myself. After all these years, he's got to be long gone! The following autumn I went into the fields with the others to harvest kaoliang . . . here, look at my hands — they've done their share of work.

"The next spring I hired myself out for a season's work, so I took the baby with me, and the household was broken up for two or three months. But I pulled it back together the next winter. All kinds of ox hairs . . . hog bristles . . . even some bird feathers, I gathered them up. During the winter I sorted them, cleaned them, and took them into town to sell whenever there was a thaw. If I could catch a ride on a cart, I took Little Baldy into town with me.

"But this one time I went in alone. The weather that day was awful — it had been snowing almost every day — and the year-end market lacked its usual bustle. I'd only brought a few bundles of hog bristles but I couldn't sell them off. I squatted there in the marketplace from early morning till the sun was setting in the west. Someone had put a poster up on the wall of a large store at the intersection, which everyone stopped to read. I heard that the 'proclamation' had been put up early in the morning, or maybe it had only been there since around noontime. Some of the people read part of it aloud. I didn't know what it was all about. They were saying, 'proclamation this' and 'proclamation that,' but I couldn't figure out just what was being 'proclaimed.' I only knew that a proclamation was the business of officials and had nothing to do with us common folk, so I couldn't figure out why there were so many people interested in it. Someone said it was a proclamation about the capture of some army deserters. I overheard a few other tidbits here and there . . . in a few days the deserters were going to be delivered to the county seat to be shot."

"What year was that? Was that the execution of the twenty-odd deserters in 1921?" The carter absent-mindedly lets down his rolled-up sleeves, and strokes his jaw.

"How should I know what year it was? Besides, execution or not, what business was it of mine? Anyway, my hog bristles weren't selling so well and things were looking bleak." She rubs her hands together briefly and suddenly stretches out her hand as though she were catching a mosquito.

"Someone was reading out the names of the deserters. I saw a man in a black gown and said to him, 'Read those names again for me!' I was holding the hog bristles when I heard him say Chiang Wu-yün . . . Chiang Wu-yün . . . the name seemed to be echoing in my ears. After a moment or two, I felt like throwing up, like some foul-smelling thing was stuck in my throat; I wanted to swallow it, but couldn't. My eyes were burning. The people looking at the 'proclamation' crowded up in front of it, so I backed off to the side. I tried to move up again and take a look, but my leg wouldn't hold me. More and more people came to look at the 'proclamation,' and I kept backing up . . . farther . . . farther . . ."

I can see that her forehead and the tip of her nose are beaded with perspiration.

"When I returned to the village it was already late at night. Only when I was getting down from the cart did I remember the hog bristles . . . they'd been the farthest thing from my mind at the time. My ears had turned as stiff as two chips of wood . . . my scarf had fallen off, maybe on the road, maybe in the city . . ."

She lifts up her scarf to show us and, sure enough, her earlobes are missing.

"Just look at these; that's what it means to be a soldier's wife . . ."

The ends of her scarf, which she has fixed tightly over her head again, flutter slightly when she speaks.

"So Wu-yün was still alive, and I wanted to see him; after all we had been husband and wife for a time.

"In February I strapped Little Baldy on my back and went into town every day. I heard that the 'proclamation' had been put up several more times, though I never went to see the God-awful thing again. I went to the yamen to ask around, but they only said, 'That's none of our business!' They sent me to the military garrison . . . ever since I was a kid I've had a fear of officials . . . a country girl like me, I'd never seen a single one. Those sentries with their bayonets sent shivers up and down my spine. *Oh, go ahead! After all, they don't just kill people on sight.* Later on, after I'd gone to see them lots of times, I wasn't afraid any longer. What more was there to lose? After all, out of the three people in our family, they already had one in their clutches. They told me that the deserters hadn't been sent over yet. When I asked them when they would be, they told me, 'Wait another month or so!' But when I got back to the village I heard that the deserters had already come from some county seat or other — even today I can't remember which county seat it was, since the only thing that mattered to me was that they had been sent over — and they said if I didn't hurry and go see him, it'd be too late. So I strapped Little Baldy on my back and went back to town, where I asked around again at the military garrison. 'Why all the impatience?' they asked me. 'How many dozens of times are you going to ask? Who knows, maybe they won't be sent over at all.' One day I spotted some big official riding in a horsedrawn carriage with its bells jingling as it came out from the garrison buildings. I put Little Baldy down on the ground and ran over; the carriage was heading straight toward me, so I knelt down in front of it . . . I didn't even care if the horse trampled me.

"'Venerable sir, my husband . . . Chiang Wu- . . .' Before I even got his name out I felt a heavy blow on my shoulders . . . the carriage driver had pushed me over backwards. I must've been knocked over . . . I crawled over to the side of the road. All I could see was that the driver too was wearing a military cap.

"I picked myself up and strapped Little Baldy on my back again. There was river in front of the garrison, and for the rest of the afternoon I just sat there on the bank looking at the water. Some people were fishing and some women were washing clothes. Farther off, at the bend in the river, the water was much deeper, and the crests of waves passed in front of me, one after the other. I don't know how many hundreds of waves I saw passing by as I sat there. I felt like putting Little Baldy down on the bank and jumping straight to the bottom. Just leave that little life behind; as soon as he started crying, someone would surely come and pick him up.

"I rubbed his little chest and said something like, 'Little Baldy, you go to sleep.' Then I stroked his little round ears . . . those ears of his, honestly, they're so long and full, just like his daddy's. Looking at his ears, I was seeing his daddy."

A smile of maternal pride spreads across her face.

"I kept on patting his chest and said again, 'You go to sleep, Little Baldy.' Then I remembered that I still had a few strings of cash on me, so I decided to put them on his chest. As I reached over . . . reached over to put . . . when I was putting them on his . . . he opened his eyes . . . just then a sailboat came around the bend, and when I heard a child on the boat shouting 'Mama,' I quickly picked up Little Baldy and held him against my bosom."

Her tears fall as she tightens the scarf under her chin.

"But then . . . then, I knew I had to carry him back home. Even if I had to go begging, at least he would have his mother . . . he deserved a mother."

The corners of her blue scarf quiver with the movements of her jaw.

A flock of sheep cross our path; the shepherd boy is playing a willow whistle. The grass and the flowers in the woods all blend together in the slanting rays of the sun, so that all we can see is a vast jumbled patch of yellow.

The carter is now walking alongside the cart, raising trails of dust on the road with the tip of his whip.

"It wasn't until May that the people at the garrison finally told me, 'They'll be coming soon.'

"Toward the end of the month a big steamship pulled up to the wharf in front of the garrison. God, there were a lot of people! Even on the July Fifteenth Festival you don't have that many people coming out to watch the river-lanterns."

Her sleeves were waving in the air.

"The families of the deserters were standing over to the right, so I moved over there with them. A man in a military cap came over and pinned a kind of badge on each of us. I had no idea what the badge said, since I can't read.

"When they were about to lower the gangplank, a troop of soldiers came up to those of us who were wearing the badges and herded us into a circle. 'Move a little farther back from the river, move a little farther . . .' They pushed us back some thirty or forty feet from the steamship with their rifle butts. An old man with a white beard stood next to me, holding a bundle in each hand. 'Uncle, why did you bring those things along?' I asked him. 'Huh? Oh, I have a son and a nephew . . . one bundle for each . . . When they get to the next world it wouldn't be right for them not to have clean clothes to wear.'

"They lowered the gangplank. Some of the people began to cry as soon as they saw the gangplank being lowered. Me, I wasn't crying. I planted my feet squarely on the ground and kept my eyes on the ship, but no one came out. After a while, an officer wearing a foreign sword leaned over the railing and said, 'Have the families move farther back; they're going to be leaving the ship now.' As soon as they heard him bark out the order, the soldiers herded us even farther back with their rifle butts, all the way back to the bean field by the edge of the road, until we were standing there on top of the bean shoots. A rumble sounded on the gangplank, and out they came, led by an officer, their leg-irons clanking along. I can still see it: the first one out was a little short man . . . then five or six more . . . not one of them with broad shoulders like Little Baldy's daddy . . . really, they looked wretched, their arms hanging stiffly in front of them. I watched for a long time before I realized that they were all wearing manacles. The harder the people around me cried, the calmer I became. I just kept my eyes on the gangplank . . . I wanted to ask Little Baldy's daddy, 'Why couldn't you just be a good soldier? Why did you have to desert? Look here at your son; how can you face him?'

"About twenty of them came down, but I couldn't spot the man I was looking for; from where I stood they all looked the same. A young woman in a green dress lost control and burst through the rifles holding us back. Naturally the guards didn't allow her to pass; no, they went out and grabbed her, and she started rolling in the dirt and crying, 'He hadn't even been a soldier for three months . . . not even . . .' Two of them carried her back. Her hair was all mussed up and hanging over her face. After God knows how long they finally led those of us wearing badges over. The more we walked, the closer we got, and the closer we got, the harder it was for me to spot Little Baldy's daddy. My eyes started to blur . . . the weeping all around made me panicky . . .

"Some of them had cigarettes dangling from their mouths, some were cursing, some were even laughing. So this was the stuff soldiers are made of. I guess you could say that soldiers don't give a damn what happens to them.

"I looked them over; Little Baldy's daddy wasn't there for sure. *That's strange!* I grabbed hold of an officer's belt: 'What about Chiang Wu-yün?' 'What's he to you?' 'He's my husband.' I put Little Baldy down on the ground and the little pest started to cry. Pah! I slapped him across the mouth, then I began hitting the officer: 'You've destroyed him! What have you done with him?'

"'Good for you, lady, we're with you.' The prisoners shouted as one, stamping their feet. When the officer saw what was happening, he quickly called some soldiers over to drag me away. 'It's not only Chiang Wu-yün,' they said. 'There are a couple of others who haven't been sent over yet; they'll be over in a day or two on the next ship. Those three were the ringleaders of the deserters.'

"I put the child on my back and left the riverbank, with the badge still pinned on, and walked off. My legs were all rubbery. The streets were filled with people who had come over to watch the excitement. I was walking behind the garrison buildings, and there at the base of the garrison wall sat the old man with the bundle, but now he had only one left. 'Uncle, didn't your son come either?' I asked him. He just arched his back, chewed on the ends of his beard, and wept.

"He told me, 'Since he was one of the ringleaders, they carried out their capital punishment on the spot.' At the time I didn't know what 'capital punishment' meant."

At this point she begins to ramble.

"Three years later, when Little Baldy was eight. I sent him to the beancurd shop . . . That's what I did. I go to see him twice a year and he comes home once every two years, but then only for ten days or a couple of weeks."

The carter has left the side of the cart and is walking along the berm, his hands clasped behind his back. With the sun off to the side, he casts a long shadow which makes a huge fork with every step he takes.

"I have a family too . . ." The words seem to fall from his lips, as though he is speaking to the woods.

"Huh?" As Wu-yün Sao loosens her scarf a little, the wrinkles above her nose quiver momentarily. "Really? You're out of the army, and still you don't go home?"

"What's that? Go home, you say! You mean go home with nothing but the clothes on my back?" The carter sneers as he rubs his nose hard with his coarse hand.

"Haven't you put a little something away these past few years?"

"That's exactly why I deserted, to make a little money if I could." He cinches his belt tighter.

I put on another cotton jacket and Wu-yün Sao throws a blanket over her shoulders.

"Um! Still another mile to go. Now if we had a cart horse . . . um! We could be there in no time flat! An ox is something else. This beast just plods along with no spirit, and it's no good at all on a battlefield."

The carter opens his straw bag and takes out a padded jacket. Pieces of straw fall off and swirl in the wind. He puts it on.

The winds at dusk are just like February winds. In the rear of the cart the carter opens the jug of wine that my mother's father had brought for Grandfather.

"Here, drink! As they say, 'In the midst of a journey open a jug of wine, for the poor love to gamble.' Now have some." After drinking several cups, he opens his shirt and exposes his chest. He is chewing on some pieces of jerky, causing froth to gather at the corners of his mouth. Whenever a gust of wind blows across his face, the bubbles on his lips expand a little.

As we near the town, through the gray overcast we can tell only that it is not a patch of open country, or a mountain range, or the seashore, or a forest. The closer our cart comes, the more the town seems to recede. Our hands and faces feel sticky. Another look ahead, and this time even the end of the road is lost from view.

The carter puts the wine jug away and picks up his whip. By now even the ox's horns have become indistinct.

"Haven't you returned home even once since you left? And you don't hear from them either?" Apparently the carter doesn't hear her. He whistles to urge the ox on. Then he jumps down from the cart and walks along up front with the animal. An empty cart with a red lantern hanging from its axle comes rolling up to us.

"A heavy fog!"

"You said it!"

The carters thus hail each other in passing.

"A heavy fog in March . . . that means either a war or a year of famine . . ." The two carts pass on the road.

★

Notes

1. The distinction between maternal and paternal relations is marked in Chinese kinship terms. In this translation, the prefix "alter-" is used to distinguish maternal grandfather from paternal grandfather.

2. The term *sao* designates the wife of one's older brother, but it is also used loosely in informal familiar address to any middle-aged woman.

★

Part III

Children and War

The stories in this section are about the ways children experience war, but they are thematically similar to the stories of war's impact on men and women, which implies that war's impact crosses all lines of age and gender.

In the first story we are shown how easily human beings in war can kill — even when the victim is a child — and how simple it seems to kill the "enemy." Vsevolod Ivanov's "The Child" tells the story of a group of Red Army soldiers trying to raise a small baby on the rugged Mongolian steppe. Shortly after the story opens, these soldiers kill an army officer and his wife. They decide to spare the couple's infant because it is "innocent." They forgive the baby for having a bourgeois father but later have absolutely no qualms about sending a Mongolian peasant's child to its death so that the mother can better breast feed their "little Christian Russian lad." Ironically, the Mongolian-Kirghiz peasant baby is taken out into the country and left to die by a character who is referred to as the "tenderest of them all," the detachment's paymaster. The Russian soldiers in this story demonstrate great affection and concern for the baby they have adopted, but they see nothing wrong with declaring another life expendable if its skin color and nationality differ.

"Children of the War," by Ninotchka Rosca, is narrated by a Filipino doctor who worked in a hospital near Saigon during the Vietnam War. Toward the end of the story, the doctor recalls that he was raised to believe that serving in war was expected and acceptable. However, the eyes of the Vietnamese children constantly haunt him, and he comes to believe that the only just battle in war is the battle against war. In an effort to shatter the image of the children staring at him, the doctor takes the Sophoclean route of ensuring his own blindness.

The next story in this section is one of the most poignant in the entire collection. In it, Pinchas Kagonovitch depicts the anxieties, humiliation, and degradation of a Polish-Jewish family during the Nazi occupation. Rather than stressing the Nazis' physical brutality, "Meyer Landshaft" explores the fears of a Jewish father for the fate of his most coveted possession — his virgin daughter. He fears that she is about to fall victim to the sexual desires of a group of SS officers. The daughter is portrayed as innocent, unsuspecting, but wise beyond her years. The Nazis represent "not only his own doom, but the doom of the entire world"; the daughter represents the innocent, unsuspecting community.

The same theme of parents' concern for their children appears in Luigi Pirandello's story of World War I, "War." A group of Italian civilians, travelling together in a train compartment, converse about the war and their children's involvement in it. The children are never directly portrayed. Instead, they emerge for the reader out of their parents' grief. The children fight and die for their country as their parents attempt to deal with reality by consoling themselves with all the clichés. Nevertheless, by the close of this brief sketch, it becomes clear that nothing compensates for the loss of a child in war. Both parents and children become sacrifices to the gods of war.

"Rats Do Sleep at Night," a gentle but powerful story, was written by Wolfgang Borchert. In this story, a nine-year-old boy stands guard for days over the rubble of a bombed-out building in order to keep the rats away from the corpse of his four-year-old brother. Borchert belonged to the so-called lost generation of postwar German writers, a generation suspicious of language's ability to express the futility of war, a generation critical of chauvinism and heroism. It is thus understandable that he chose a small boy to embody the stoicism and bravery normally associated with men. The rats in the story convey far beyond any words the predatory nature of war.

In "The Imprint of Blackness," by Muhammad Salih Haydara of Yemen, a young boy is required to assume adult roles as a result of losing his father. The story opens with a description of the Yemenese countryside. Throughout the story, natural resources (especially life-giving, scarce water) serve as symbols of the ways in which human beings compete for resources, destroying one another and the environment in the process. The narrator tells us that as a youth he had "paid no attention to the natural environment of which I was a part." In a gradual but painful process of politicalization, he finally comes to believe that soldiers and the governments that they represent should not have the power to control nature, which provides sustenance to the people. The boy's initiation culminates with his final understanding of his father's rebellion and sacrifice.

The acceleration of maturation under the pressures of war underlies Ghassan Kanafani's story, "The Land of Sad Oranges." The story is told by a narrator who looks back on his childhood, when his family fled their home and became refugees. War and persecution are portrayed as distortions of the natural order. This is symbolized by the orange groves at the beginning and by a withered orange at the story's end. Even though it is set in a time of tragic upheaval and was written by an author who was personally affected by the turmoil, the story does not devolve into inflammatory accusations and political rhetoric. Instead, the sad portrayal of a family — a father's despair and impotency, the children's loss of their childhood, and the mother's helplessness — evokes compassion for the universal suffering of "displaced persons" or refugees.

In Mahmoud Diab's "A House for My Children," an Egyptian man reveals the deep mental scars that a childhood experience of an air raid has left on him. The house, representing personal and family stability, is the pregnant symbol in this story. When he was a boy, the narrator's house was destroyed, his family uprooted, and his community terrified by German aerial strafing. As the story unfolds, the reader is given the impression that the house the narrator has just purchased embodies a new beginning, new hope, and an effort to bury the terrible memories of the past. And yet, one is left with the impression of war's inevitable return.

War's dehumanizing effect is the theme of "My Being," a story by Mykola Khvylovy in which the local communist death squad commander decides whether or not to pronounce sentence on his own mother and a group of nuns. The mother represents Ukrainian nationalism; the nuns, the church. Like so many of the stories in this volume, this tale of war's perversion of the natural order opens and closes with powerful images of nature. The new political order for which the protagonist is fighting is referred to in the opening paragraph as the "quiet lakes of untouchable communism." In the story's closing paragraph it becomes "the quiet lakes of unreachable communism." This change suggests that the protagonist's act of matricide in the name of politics has made true community impossible.

The last story in this section, "The Children's Campaign," was first published in 1935, between the two world wars. Pär Lagerkvist, in bitter satire, depicts a war wherein "childlike" becomes "childishness." The children in a fictitious society become warriors: they fight, earn war medals for illustrious deeds, have parades that their parents watch with pride, sing patriotic anthems loudly, and win and lose battles, all the while forgetting even their Christmas parcels. The story ends with a picture of small graves under whose small white crosses the child heroes rest.

★

★ ★ ★ ★

AUTHOR: *Vsevolod Ivanov (1895–1963) was born in Siberia. Considered the epic poet of the Russian Civil War, Ivanov wrote of the conflict from his own experiences as a soldier, first with the White Army and later with the Red forces. His best-known work, Armored Train 14-69, was based on an actual incident in the Civil War. The breadth of his experiences — as a circus clown, a sorter in the emerald mines, a sailor, and a news correspondent at the Nuremburg war crimes trials — provided him with the knowledge needed to write on a broad spectrum of topics. His works include: The Taking of Berlin, Sands, Journey to a Country That Does Not Yet Exist, I Live a Queer Life, and Patched Breeches.*

SETTING: *In 1921 the People's Republic of Mongolia was established under the political and military tutelage of the Soviet Union. When Japan invaded Manchuria in 1931, this seemed to threaten Mongolia, and the Red Guards were called upon to turn them back, which they did. The Red Guard in Mongolia was usually composed of two types of units: the so-called regulars and non-regulars. The non-regulars were most often conscripted peasants, illiterate and unsophisticated. They seldom understood why they were fighting or the rules of war. There was great antipathy for the regulars, especially for the officer corps who, to the peasants, represented the old aristocracy. Non-regulars were unpaid or underpaid and, therefore, were known for looting, pillaging, and mistreating the people wherever they were fighting. This story takes place in one of those areas: Mongolia.*

The Child

Vsevolod Ivanov

I

Mongolia — a wild and joyless beast! The rock is a beast, the water is a beast; even the butterfly, even it tries to sting.

What kind of heart the Mongolian has, no one knows. People say he goes about in animal skins, looks like a Chinaman, and took to living far from the Russians across the desert, Nor-Koi. And, another thing they say,

"The Child" by Vsevolod Ivanov, translated by Thomas Bradley, from *Great Soviet Short Stories* by Franklin D. Reeve, Richard S. Ravenal and Thompson Bradly. Copyright 1962 by Dell, a division of Bantam Doubleday Dell Publishing Group, Inc. Used by permission of Dell Books, a division of Bantam Doubleday Dell Publishing Group, Inc.

he'll go off beyond China and India to deep-blue, unknowable lands on seven shores. . . .

Those Kirghiz from around the Irtysh River, who had fled from the Russian war to Mongolia, flourished here near the Russians. Everyone knows that their heart is like mica, worthless, transparent through and through. They came here without hurrying and brought with them their herds, their children and even their sick.

But the Russians had been driven here unmercifully — they were strong and healthy peasants. They had left their excess weakness behind on the rocks and mountains: some died, some were killed. Families and tools and cattle were abandoned to the Whites. The peasants were as evil-tempered as wolves in spring. In ravines, in tents, they lay and thought about the steppe, about the Irtysh. . . .

There were some fifty of them with Sergei Selivanov at their head, and the detachment was known as "Comrade Selivanov's partisan detachment of the Red Guard."

They were bored and lonesome.

While the Whites were driving them across the mountains, there was terror in their hearts from the rock, immense and dark, but when they came to the steppe, it was dull and sad. Because the steppe was like the Irtysh steppe: sand, stiff grasses, a firmly forged sky. Everything was strange, not your own, unplowed, wild.

And, moreover, it was hard without women.

At night they told obscene soldiers' stories about women, and when it became unbearable, they saddled the horses and went out after Kirghiz girls on the steppe.

And the Kirghiz girls, seeing the Russians, fell submissively on their backs.

It was bad, repulsive to take them — motionless with tightly closed eyes, as if they were sinning with cattle.

The Kirghiz — they feared the Russians — moved far off into the steppe. Seeing a Russian, they would threaten with rifles and bows, whoop, but not shoot. Maybe, they didn't know how to.

II

The detachment's paymaster Afanasy Petrovich Trubachov was a regular cry baby, and, like a baby's his face was small, beardless and ruddy. Only his legs were long and powerful like a camel's.

But when he mounted a horse, he became stern. His face grew distant, and he sat there gray, angry and terrible.

On Whitsunday three men were sent on detail — Selivanov, paymaster Afanasy Petrovich, and secretary Drevesinin — to look for good forage grass on the steppe.

The sands steamed under the sun.

A wind blew from above, from the sky, the sultry heat rose from the earth to the quivering sky. The bodies of the men and animals were hard and heavy as rocks. Melancholy.

And Selivanov said hoarsely:

"What kind of meadows are over there?"

They all knew. He was speaking about the Irtysh. But the sparsely bearded faces were silent, as if the hair had been seared by the sun like the grasses on the steppe. Their eyes, slitted like a fishhook wound, burned red. Heat.

Only Afanasy Petrovich responded plaintively:

"Is there really drought there, too, boys?"

The small voice was tearful, but the face did not cry, and only the tired and panting horse under him had aching tears in its big, long eyes.

Thus one after another the partisans went off into the steppe along paths beaten by wild goats. . . .

. . . The sands glowed dully. A suffocating, sand-smelling wind stuck to one's shoulders and head. Sweat burns in the body, but cannot force its way out through the dry skin. . . .

Toward evening, as they rode up out of a hollow, Selivanov said, pointing toward the west:

"Here come some travelers on the move."

To be sure, right on the horizon the sands were tossing a red-hued dust.

"Kirghiz, probably."

They started arguing about it: Drevesinin said that the Kirghiz lived far off and did not come near Selivanov's ravines. Afanasy Petrovich said it was Kirghiz for certain, it was Kirghiz dust, thick.

But when the sand had rolled the dust up close, everyone decided:

"Strangers . . ."

The horses sensed it from their masters' voices — something alien was being carried on the wind. They pricked up their ears and fell to the ground long before the command. Gray and yellow horse carcasses lay in the gully helpless and absurd with legs thin as poles. Was it from shame that they had closed their big frightened eyes and breathed fitfully?

Selivanov and paymaster Afanasy Petrovich lay on the edge of the gully. The paymaster cried, sniffling. So as not to feel frightened, Selivanov always kept him nearby, and from that childish crying his heavy peasant's heart was almost gladdened and strengthened.

The path unfurled dust. The wheels clattered intermittently. Like dust the long black manes curled and wreathed in the collars.

Selivanov said confidently:

"Russians . . . Officers."

And he called Drevesinin out of the gully.

Two persons in peaked caps with red bands sat in a new little wicker cart. Their faces were imperceptible in the dust, as if the red bands were floating in a yellow cloud. A rifle — the muzzle sticks out when the hand with the whip emerges from the dust.

Drevesinin reflected a minute and said:

"Officers . . . on business, probably. An expedition . . . That's clear."

He winked mischievously:

"We'll show them, Selivanov, old boy."

The cart carried the people along, bore them along sturdily. The horses. They were having a fine time of it, and behind, like a fox with its tail, the cart covered up the tracks with Mongolian dust.

Afanasy Petrovich drawled tearfully:

"Don't boys. . . . Better take them prisoners. . . . Let's wait about killing them."

"You aren't afraid . . . are ya? . . ."

Selivanov became irritated and, as one unbuttons a button, threw back his rifle bolt noiselessly.

"This is no place for tears, paymaster."

What enraged them most of all — the officers appeared on the steppe alone, without an escort, as if there were a host of them, as if they were death to the peasants. There, for example, an officer was standing up straight, gazing around the steppe, but he could not see much: dust. The evening wind blew red on the scorched grasses, on two rocks near the ravine, like horses' carcasses. . . . Which rocks? Carcasses?

In the red dust the cart, wheels, people and their thoughts . . . whirling along.

They fired. . . . Whooped. Fired again.

Simultaneously knocking against one another, the caps fell into the cart.

The reins went slack, as if snapped. . . .

The horses darted . . . nearly bolted. But suddenly their withers foamed milk-white. . . . Shuddering along the powerful knots of their muscles, they lowered their heads and stopped.

Afanasy Petrovich spoke:

"They're dead. . . ."

The peasants came up and took a look.

The red bands were dead. They sat shoulder to shoulder, their heads thrown back, but one of the dead was a woman. Her hair fell undone in the dust — half yellow, half black, and the soldier's tunic was raised high by a woman's breasts.

"Strange," said Drevesinin. "It's her own fault . . . shouldn't put a cap on. Who wants to kill a woman? Society needs women."

Afanasy Petrovich spat:

"You bourgeois beast . . . You don't have any feeling, you bastard. . . ."

"Hold on," Selivanov interrupted them. "We're not thieves — we have to make a list of the people's property. Give me some paper."

Under the front compartment in a small Chinese wicker basket, among the rest of the "people's property," lay a little white-eyed, white-haired child. A corner of a brown blanket was clutched in his tiny hand. Unweaned, small, he whimpered slightly.

Tenderly Afanasy Petrovich said:

"You see now . . . probably he's telling in his own way how . . ."

Once again they felt sorry for the woman and did not take her clothes off, but the man they buried naked in the sand.

III

Afanasy Petrovich rode back in the captured cart, holding the child in his arms and, rocking him, crooned very softly:

Nightingale, nightingale-pipit . . .
Little canary . . .
Who sings so plaintively . . .

He remembered the little village of Lebyazhy — his home, the stables with the cattle, his family, the little children — and wept softly.

The baby cried, too.

The loose, crumbling, scorched sands raced along and cried softly. The partisans raced along on the low, firm-fleshed Mongolian horses. They were scorched-faced and scorched-hearted partisans.

Sun-stifled wormwood drifted along the path, like sand, fine and imperceptible.

And the sands were like wormwood — fine and bitter.

You paths, goats' paths! You sands, bitter sands! Mongolia — the wild and joyless beast!

They examined the officer's belongings. Books, a suitcase filled with tobacco, shiny steel instruments — among them, on three long legs, a square brass box with compartments.

The partisans came near and examined, touched and weighed them in their hands.

They smelled of sheep fat. They ate a lot from nothing else to do, and their clothes became all greasy. High cheekboned ones with soft thin lips, from the Don Cossack villages; swarthy ones with long black hair, from the lime pits. And all of them had legs curved like shaft bows and throaty steppe voices.

Afanasy Petrovich picked up a brass-headed tripod and said:

"A telescope," and screwed up his eyes. "A good telescope. It must have cost a pretty bit. They looked at the moon with it, boys, and discovered gold fields there. . . . You don't have to pan it, it's like flour, the purest gold. Chuck it in the bag. . . ."

One of the young city boys guffawed:

"Listen to those tales, for God's sake. . . ."

Afanasy Petrovich lost his temper:

"So I'm lying, huh, you stupid bastard? You better watch it. . . ."

"Who're you telling to watch it?"

Afanasy grabbed his revolver.

"All right, cut it out," said Selivanov.

They divided up the tobacco, but the instruments were handed over to Afanasy Petrovich — as paymaster he might, when the opportunity arose, be able to barter them for something with the Kirghiz.

He laid the instruments in front of the child.

"Here, play. . . ."

The child did not see: he whimpered. Afanasy tried everything, he even broke out in a sweat. Still the child whimpered and would not play.

The cooks brought dinner. There rose a heavy smell of butter, porridge and cabbage soup. Broad Semipalatinsk spoons were fished out of boot tops. Around the camp the grass was trampled down. Up above on the cliffs a sentry shouted:

"How much longer for me? I want some grub . . . Send . . . send the relief!"

They finished eating and remembered — they had to feed the baby.
The child was whimpering incessantly.

Afanasy Petrovich chewed up some bread. He shoved the soggy lump
into the moist opened little mouth and smacked his lips:

"Try — try it . . . little one . . . eat it up, little goblin . . . 's good."

But he closed his tiny mouth and turned his head away — he would
not take it. He cried through his nose, thinly, shrilly.

The peasants came over; they stood around him. Over the heads they
peered at the child. They were silent.

It was hot. Cheek bones and lips shone from mutton. Shirts were
unbuttoned, feet bare, yellow, like the Mongolian soil.

Someone suggested:

"He wants some cabbage soup. . . . Let's try some cabbage soup for
him. . . ."

Some soup was cooled, Afanasy Petrovich dipped a finger into the
soup and put it into the baby's mouth. The good greasy cabbage soup ran
down his little lips onto his little pink shirt and onto the blanket.

He would not take it. He whimpered.

"A pup's smarter — it'll eat from your finger. . . ."

"What do you mean a dog, this's a human being. . . ."

"What next! . . ."

There was no cow's milk in the detachment. They thought of giving it
some mare's milk, they had plenty of mares. It was no good — kumiss gets
you drunk. He might fall sick.

They broke up into groups among the carts and talked the matter
over. They were worried. And Afanasy Petrovich rushed around among the
carts, a tattered Caucasian coat over his shoulders, his eyes small, also
tattered. His small voice was thin, troubled, childish, as if the child itself
were running around, complaining.

"What's going to happen? But he's got to eat, doesn't he? Do
something, why don't you, you bastards. . . ."

They stood there broad, powerful-bodied, with a helpless look.

"It's woman's work. . . ."

"Of course it is. . . ."

"From a woman he'd have eaten a ram. . . ."

"Well, now, that's right."

Selivanov called a meeting and declared:

"You can't let a little Christian lad die like a beast. The father, let's
say, was a bourgeois, but what about the child? It's innocent."

The peasants agreed:

"It's not the child's fault. It's innocent."

Drevesinin guffawed:

"Grow, kiddy. He'll grow up with us and fly to the moon . . . to the gold fields."

The peasants did not laugh. Afanasy Petrovich raised his fist and shouted:

"What a bastard you are. The only scoffer in the detachment."

He shuffled around a bit, swung his arms and suddenly cried out shrilly:

"A cow . . . He needs a cow! . . ."

They responded unanimously:

"Without a cow — it's death. . . ."

"We got to have a cow. . . ."

"Without a cow he'll conk out."

Resolutely Afanasy Petrovich said:

"Boys, I'll go get some cows. . . ."

Drevesinin interrupted him insolently:

"To the Irtysh, to Lebyazhy? . . ."

"No point in my going to the Irtysh, you prize ass. I'll go to the Kirghiz."

"To swap for the telescope? Go, benefactor."

Afanasy Petrovich lunged at him: he bawled angrily:

"You carrion dog! You want to get it in the puss?"

But seeing that their swearing got out of hand, the chairman of the meeting, Selivanov, cut them short:

"That's enough. . . ."

And they voted as follows: Drevesinin, Afanasy Petrovich, and three others were to go to the Kirghiz villages on the steppe and drive back a cow. If possible two or five, since the cooks were running out of meat.

They hung their rifles on the saddles and put on fox-lined Kirghiz jackets so as to look like Kirghiz from a distance.

"Good luck."

They wrapped the child up in a blanket and laid him in the shade under a cart. A young lad sat by him and every now and then for his and the baby's amusement fired off his revolver into a wormwood bush.

IV

Oh, you Mongolian sands, you joyless sands! Oh, you rock — you sad blue rock, you deep-earthed hands, you evil hands!

The Russians cross the sands. Night.

The sands smell of heat, wormwood.

In the village dogs bay at a wolf, at the darkness.

In the dark wolves howl at hunger, at death.

The Kirghiz fled from death.

"Will we drive the herds away from death?"

A green, suffocating darkness shivers over the sands, the sands barely retain it — now it breaks off and flutters toward the west.

The village smells of burning dung and straw, of sour milk. Gaunt, hungry Kirghiz children sit by yellow campfires. Beside the children lie bare-ribbed, sharp-faced dogs. The *yurts*[1] rise like hayricks. Beyond the *yurts* in a lake, rushes.

Suddenly from the rushes hollow shots rang out into the yellow campfires:

"O-o-a-at! . . ."

At once the Kirghiz sprang out of the felt *yurts*. They shouted fearfully:

"Ui-boi . . . Ui-boi, the Red Russians are coming. . . . Ui-boi . . ."

They leaped on their horses. The horses were kept saddled day and night. The *yurts* thumped. The steppe thumped. The rushes shrieked like a wild duck:

"Ai-ai, Red Russian — White Russian, ai-ai . . ."

One graybeard fell head first off his horse into a kettle, a cauldron, and tipped it over. Scalded, he howled in a deep full voice and nearby a shaggy dog, his tail between his legs, timidly poked his hungry mug into the hot milk.

The mares whinnied softly. As if frightened by wolves the sheep thrashed about in the sheepfold. The cows panted as if short of breath.

And the submissive Kirghiz women, seeing the Russians, submissively lay back upon the felt rugs. . . .

Drevesinin guffawed lasciviously:

"Are we stallions, or something? . . . We don't always want to. . . ."

He hastily strained some milk into a small flat Austrian flask, and, cracking his whip, herded the cows with their calves toward the *yurts*. The untethered calves, swiftly nudging the soft udder with their heads, joyfully seized the teats in their large soft lips.

"Well, how do you like that, they're hungry, the little bullocks. . . ."

And Drevesinin fired his revolver at the calves.

Afanasy Petrovich was still riding around the village and was about to go off after Drevesinin, when suddenly he remembered:

"Gotta have a feeder. The idiots, they forgot a nipple! . . ."

He rushed from *yurt* to *yurt* looking for a nipple. The fires in the *yurts* had been put out. Afanasy Petrovich seized a firebrand and, scattering sparks, coughing from the smoke, searched for a nipple. The torch was sputtering in one hand, and in the other he held a revolver. The nipple was nowhere to be found.

The submissive Kirghiz women, covered with coats, lay out on felt rugs. The babies were squalling.

Afanasy Petrovich lost his temper and in one *yurt* shouted at a young Kirghiz woman:

"A nipple, you dumb bitch, give me a tit!"

The woman began to weep and quickly started undoing her silk coat and then pulling off her shift.

"Don't hurt me . . . Ai . . . Ai . . . Take me. . . ."

And beside her on the felt rug wailed a baby swaddled in rags. The woman was already spreading her legs.

"Ai . . . Ai . . . take me. . . ."

But just then Afanasy Petrovich seized her breast, squeezed it and whistled joyfully:

"Hey . . . Now there's a tit. Eh! What a sturdy one!"

"Don't hurt me. . . . Don't . . ."

"All right, don't quack. Come on! What a sturdy one!"

And he dragged her by the hand after him.

The torch fell — it went dark in the *yurt*.

In the dark he sat the woman on the saddle and, every once in a while feeling her breasts, raced back to the Selivanov ravines, back to the detachment.

"I found her, boys, eh," he said happily and he had tears in his eyes. "I'll find her, brother, if I have to dig her up from under the ground."

V

But at the camp it turned out — Afanasy Petrovich had not noticed in the dark — that the woman had brought her own baby with her.

"Let her keep it," the peasants said, "There'll be enough milk for both of them. We have cows, and she's a sturdy one."

The Kirghiz woman was silent and stern and nursed the babies out of everyone's sight. They lay beside her on a felt rug in the tent — one white, the other yellow — and wailed as one.

Only a week later, Afanasy Petrovich lodged a complaint at the general meeting:

"She's cheating us, Comrades: that Kirghiz woman's a hussy, she nurses unfairly — she gives the whole breast to her own, but ours gets what's left over. I spied on her, men. You just take a look. . . ."

The peasants went over and looked: they were babies like all babies; one white, the other yellow, like a ripe melon. But it looked as if the Russian were thinner than the Kirghiz.

Afanasy Petrovich spread his arms:

"I gave him a name, Vaska . . . and you see what happens. . . . What a trick."

Drevesinin said without so much as a grin:

"But you're a sickly one, Vaska, you're half dead. . . ."

They found a pole and measured it on a shaft so that one side would not overbalance the other.

The babies were suspended from the ends to see which one was heavier. Swaddled in rags and suspended on hair ropes, the babies whined. They smelled of that delicate baby's smell. The woman stood by a cart and, not understanding anything, cried.

The peasants were silent. They were watching.

"Let 'em go," said Selivanov. "Let go of the scales."

Afanasy Petrovich took his hands off the pole and immediately the Russian child went up.

"See, the little yellow-mouthed bastard," said Afanasy angrily, "he stuffed himself."

He picked up a dried-out ram's skull which had been lying around and put it on top of the Russian baby. The babies were then evenly balanced.

The peasants raised a cry and shouted:

"By a whole head, boys, she overfed hers, eh? . . ."

"It's hard to keep track of her. . . ."

"What a beast . . . See how she's fed him."

"Who was supposed to watch her? . . ."

"We have other things to do than look after babies!"

Some of the staid peasants supported this:

"How can you keep track!"

"After all, she's his mother. . . ."

Afanasy Petrovich stamped and shrieked:

"So you think a Russian should die because of some foreigner . . . Vaska die? My Vaska?"

They looked at Vaska — he lay there white and thin.

The peasants felt bad.

Selivanov said to Afanasy Petrovich:

"Then you take him . . . and . . . a . . . perhaps let him go . . . let him die . . . that Kirghiz brat. A lot of them were killed anyway. It's all one. . . ."

The peasants glanced at Vaska and went off silently.

Afanasy Petrovich seized the Kirghiz baby and wrapped him in a ripped bag.

The mother wailed. Afanasy punched her lightly in the teeth and went out of the camp into the steppe. . . .

VI

A day or two later the peasants were standing on tiptoes beside the entrance to the tent and looking over each other's shoulders inside where the Kirghiz woman was nursing the white child on a felt rug.

She had a submissive face with narrow eyes, like oat seeds; she wore a violet silk coat and small morocco boots.

The child was pounding his little face into her breast and patting her coat with his tiny hands; his legs were kicking comically and clumsily, as if he were hopping.

The peasants looked on with a mighty laugh.

The tenderest of them all was Afanasy Petrovich. Sniffling, he said tearfully:

"See, he really likes it! . . ."

But beyond the canvas tent ran the ravines, cliffs, steppe, alien Mongolia — no one knew where.

No one knew where Mongolia ran — Mongolia, the wild and joyless beast.

★

Note

1. A tent made of skin.

★ ★ ★ ★

AUTHOR: *Ninotchka Rosca was born in Manila, the Philippines. She began to write in 1966 and won first prize in the Free Press Annual Short Story Contest for 1967 as well as several other prizes for short stories in 1969. She later became associate editor of* The Graphic *magazine.*

SETTING: *The Philippines played an important role in the Vietnam conflict. Clark Air Base and Subic Naval Base provided the "staging area" from which U.S. attacks were launched. The Philippines also sent 1,576 men under the Many Flags Program and served as a listening post for Asian responses to the war. In return, the Philippine government under Ferdinand Marcos received some $39 million as well as military equipment and support. This story is told from the viewpoint of a Philippine doctor serving in South Vietnam. The author carefully and methodically writes of cultural and racial tensions, class distinctions, political and moral corruption, and clashes between men and women, all the while focusing the reader's attention on children as the ultimate victims of war. In 1985, during the presidency of Gerald R. Ford, Operation Babylift evacuated 2,678 Vietnamese and Cambodian babies. The first C-5 planeload crashed, killing 138 of the 314 children aboard and bringing war's victimization of children to the public's attention.*

Children of the War

Ninotchka Rosca

You too have seen our city's affliction, caught
In a tide of death from which there is no escaping —
Death in the fruitful flowering of her soil;
Death in the pastures; death in the womb of woman,
And pestilence, a fiery demon gripping the city,
Stripping the house of Cadmus, to fatten hell
With profusion of lamentation.

— Sophocles

"Children of the War" is reprinted from Ninotchka Rosca, *Bitter Country and Other Stories* (Queen City, Philippines: Malaya Books, 1970) by permission of the author.

Nothing now but darkness about me: a night of that malignant disease which has come to roost within the interlaces of my soul. What had I sought to accomplish with that act, that decision to black out the sun with those twin slices of pain ramming into my eyeballs, the world suddenly dissolved, smashed into a thousand splinters of color without form, sound without image, touch without presence? I strive to limit the span of my attention, concentrating only upon the great vine of that sickness entwined about my conscience, hoping to discover, in its obscene embrace, the exculpation of my guilt. The past reels before me constantly, in that shrinking of the world, while I, agonized spectator, examine each little scene — from the imagined taste of the innocent milk flowing from my mother's breasts to the first soft coiling of a woman's arm around my neck. Where and at what point had I chosen wrongly? When did the original bruise occur, the first sin from which all this agony had sprung? Whose was its guilt?

I dare not question any one in the house, though they treat me with a deference afforded only the ill; I wonder, at dusk, when the cricket-cries drumbeat a symphony intruding upon my internal darkness, whether they too can smell the canker in the core, the secret rot and deterioration, the stink of which gags my nostrils constantly. To sever all communication — that had been my intent, in that moment of intense pain, so that, with the light turned nowhere but into the night of the spirit, I may understand; and understanding, forgive myself.

The world continues to press in upon me; those little sounds of normality, the odors of everyday life in this peace, the peace of this world, while I rest my weary mind in the cradle of happy voices about me. Pepito, the littlest son of the house, quick on his feet, muttering to himself while he plays alone in the afternoon, dragging his wooden sword after him; Maria, the daughter of the house, whose passing disturbs the air lightly with its smell of crushed flowers; and the mother of the house who sits beside me in the afternoons while I listen, both to the forced casualness of her tone and the rustle of the cloth she sews between her hands.

She tells me, struggling to be calm with her words, of how my father, the father of this house, marched away, in the middle of an afternoon while falling bombs were echoing all over the city; and before him, his own father, and his father's father, down to the dim memories of the first generation of this race, uttering their war cries upon the shore, brandishing their *kampilans*. I know — does she think she can deceive me? — the purpose of this constant renewal of ties with the dead — the heroic dead who now appear to have had only that sole intent in living; to die that others may remember them and the manner of their dying.

"War," she tells me, her voice barely quavering, "is the essence of peace."

I turn over that sentence in my mind, recalling how, in the far land of my father's death the soil is dark green and dewy with new-born grass. And suddenly, I am a boy again, parting the verdant blades, to discover two armies of ants, with pincers for weapons and skin for armor, locked in a confrontation with death.

Pepito disturbs the quiet afternoon with his mock war-cries and his feet, thudding upon the fallen enemy, resounds through the house. I tell myself that it will never leave me again — this war — not while jets shriek overhead, nor children play; not even when I try to drown myself in music and switch on the radio with groping fingers, only to hear a funereal voice blaring out the last news of the war: a hundred cities attacked, hundreds dead, Hue shattered, an ally shocked at the discovery of its own weakness.

It is not new to me; I switch off the radio and hear voices outside raised in violent argument — it is Maria and the Mother. Maria, child, barely-woman, quick to find in things she can only feel but not thoroughly understand, her own kind of heroes. She has been moving about me quietly, since my return and I feel — no, it could not be denied — in the elaborate politeness of her voice, the contempt in her eyes. Once, asking her to read to me for my rest, she had, before I could be aware of it, opened a book and recited Sophocles to me, her voice passionate and taut, her breathing strained.

Aye; the truth. One is supposed to see it in darkness; but I saw it before the merciful night came. It is time; I tell myself that escape is impossible and, following the running footsteps of my sister to her room, I carry, like a cane before me, the inevitable.

SAIGON — it blooms in the mind like a great Asian calyx, its indescribable cacophony of commerce, its women with their bird-like voices and their pink, green and purple ao-dai floating in the summer sun. It was the first Asian city I had seen, the first true city of the war I had lived in, with the white men standing at street corners bargaining with little boys over the tiny porcelain buddhas they sold, over their smudged photographs and dingy postcards, over their younger and elder sisters, and finally, over their own hardly fleshed-out little bodies.

The mind pales before this huge corruption of the war which hanged over the city as surely as the blue dome of the sky — this city of frantic pleasure where everyone burned up his and his brother's flesh for that small piece of paper that would feed the body until the day when flesh had to be sold again. Each man was bringing, into the market, no more and no less than his own soul and the flesh of his brother. The stranger coming to this city soon loses his anonymity and his innocence, and becomes a trafficker in the city's soul.

So it was with us after that flag-strewn, flower-filled ceremony of our coming. What had I expected to be, in this city ravaged by the barbarity of men? A compassionate man, an aider, a benefactor, or, at the most, a liberator. The gaiety and nonchalance of life had shocked me, who expected to find a city swooning at his feet — until I learned of the hidden hysteria beneath the casualness of its pleasures. And this, Maria, was how I discovered it.

Dusk found the three of us — Paul, the Vietnamese interpreter, Joe the GI whose name I had not caught, and myself, the uniformed civilian — making our way through the crooked, shop-lined and bar-studded backstreets of the city. Women in their western clothes stood at the bardoors, showing thighs and half their globular breasts. The white gentle flesh screamed in the subtle torture of the falling light; the women's sharp, small voices called out to us in chirps of broken English and French. I stood there bewildered by their presence — the women of the war, so unlike other women I had met before but who were, strangely, familiar — by the mixed odor of pungent perfume and alcohol and the stale vomit lining the gutter and hugging the front doors of the bars. Men in uniform leaned against walls, the sound of their retching piercing through the music and the screams of women pouring out promises of joy in all the languages of the world.

An American staggered by, borne by two brown women who let out a crescendo of giggles as the American threw them back and waded through a mound of vomit, the wide swath of his sailor's trousers tumbling the tops off the little piles of human reject.

I stood there smelling the East with my nose, the surfeit of sounds clogging my ears while my doctor's hands hanged trembling and loose from the cuffs of my shirt. Paul — his mouth slit open in a wide grin — pulled my arm and steered me towards a red-lit door through which shadows could be seen jerking across a bare, dark dance-floor while a golden-clothed woman poured out an incomprehensible song into the microphone she clutched tightly in one long, fine-skinned hand which threw back the smoulder of the spotlight under which she stood. We sidled our way past tables where couples sat — the women idly staring at us appraisingly, as though bored with the companions they had.

The woman who sat with us at the table was small and light-footed. She seemed to have appeared out of nowhere. Even the slight light could not conceal the dark circles beneath her eyes as she looked us over, one by one, smiling wearily while her hands played tap-tap on the table. Joe — we called him that, though he must have had some distinct name in his home — placed an arm around her shoulder and I was surprised by the sudden squeal she let out. She slapped his hand away, her mouth pulled open in a ragged laugh while her eyes were two daggerpoints digging into his face. She spoke to Paul in Vietnamese and he shook his head, motioning in some way I could not understand, at the American. Her face then turned to me, the bright eyes dancing with steely grace as she extended one limp cold hand for me to touch.

"Hello," she sighed, rather than spoke the word out. I took her hand and felt the callouses growing upon her palm. Her hand stung the fine grains of my hand and I let it go as her eyes drew mocking circles about my head.

"Her name is Mei," said Paul, his teeth suddenly red in the light. "Mei, our good friend here is a doctor. He has come to cure our people, to be of help to the children."

She peered at me slyly. "All doctors only want this," she said, making an obscene gesture and before I could protest, she had let out a thin, racking laugh. I saw then that she was drunk.

"When did Doctor arrive? Only today?" she smiled at my nod. "Then you missed the most beautiful sight in Saigon — an execution."

Paul looked at her sharply and spoke some words in a cracking voice. Mei laughed into his face and suddenly raised the wineglass the waiter had placed before her.

"Bottoms up," she brayed while I looked at Paul questioningly.

"He was a bad man," the interpreter said stiffly. "I was there . . ."

I could only feel the hidden crevices of their words, the sheathed fang of danger that fringed Paul's glances as he turned away from Mei. The American, who had paid no attention to us, was singing loudly — a song from way back home, he had explained — smacking his beerglass down for accompaniment. I turned my eyes away from them, already feeling the stifling heat, as my fingers tugged at my tie and unbuttoned the stiff collar of my uniform.

"She's drunk," said Paul, his voice suddenly sly, "if she gets drunk enough, you can get her for free. Some of them get sentimental when drunk."

Mei, I saw, was draining glass after glass, tossing down the liquid as though it were water. I could see the red color, deeper than the light that now swayed overhead, creeping up the wasted cheek of the girl and nestling in the fragile curve of her ear. She shrugged off the waiters hovering behind her, now touching her shoulder, now whispering at her ear.

"Goddamn country," said the American who had turned beet-red. "Yesterday we discovered something terrifying. These people — peasants — had been asking for mortar shells. To make into pots and pans, they said; so we gave them — the dirty s.o.b.'s. Yesterday, while digging for a new building, we discovered this tunnel, full of empty mortar shells. They'd been giving them to the guerrillas to reload and shoot back at us. Goddamn country."

Mei let out a squeal of delight and the American turned to her.

"What are you laughing at?" he shouted. "Don't you know me? Don't you know us? We're the liberators!"

He sat back in his chair, muttering goddamns, sulking in his sweat-stained uniform while Mei rolled her eyes at him.

"Liberator," her tiny voice shrilled. "Cheers!"

Joe looked at her resentfully and for a moment I could see him, back in his home — a boy hardly out of his teens, licking his wounds and hating obstacles.

"I could shoot you," he said slowly, drawing his pistol and aiming it at her. "I could shoot you right here for being a goddamn traitor."

Mei stuck her tongue out at him. "Shoot, shoot," she squealed.

Paul put an arm around the American's shoulder; a pair of soft hands pulled at him and he sank back, cradled by giggling women. The American laughed and patted Mei's arm with a hairy paw.

"You're just a whore, goddamn it," he muttered, his eyelids falling. "Am sorry. You're just a goddamn whore."

I looked over at Mei and saw that her eyes were as steady and as cold as before, her face red with something more than alcohol.

"What does Mei mean?" I asked, feeling slightly ridiculous in that room of violence. "Is that your real name?"

"No," she answered. "Names, names, names. I have lots of them. So had the man who was shot this afternoon."

"Was he a relative?" I asked and was surprised by the sudden look she darted at me. "Why are you so worked up about him?"

"No," she laughed again, and then continued to honk beneath her breath: "names, names, names."

Suddenly, she began to cry; softly at first, and then louder, keening thinly through the noise of the bar. "I am just a whore," she said, between small wails, her eyes overflowing with red teardrops.

"See," Paul whispered. "They do get sentimental. Now you work on her."

Suddenly, the American stood up and swore loudly — just one snapping word — and it was then that I saw with terrifying clarity, the fall of the gunbutt in the soldier's hand and the sudden welling of blood along the woman's dark hair. I stood up, hypnotized by the blood, feeling myself called to duty but inept while Mei sat there, slumped in her chair, her head upon the table, blood dripping from the strands of her hair. I felt a hand pulling me away from the spectacle and we stumbled out — the three of us — suddenly laughing while Joe aimed his gun at the black night and fired three shots: one, two, three.

THE NEXT DAY I was in the country, miles away from the city, hovering over the dull white beds that moaned with a slow, monotonous insistence, as though to keep in cadence with the heavy throb of pain. A vast wing of human suffering hanged over that small, white-painted hospital where the wounded spilled out of the rooms into the corridors where they lay blanketed upon the cold, dirty floor. I watched the children being brought in, children whose flesh crumbled at the slightest touch of the finger, children who writhed in unimaginable tortures, the contorted figures of their bodies revealing the broken outlines of their pain. The children of the war were strange children.

They would come shrieking in shrill, thin voices, wordless except for the grating sound of their pain melting away the flesh and laying the gangrenous veins and white bones open to the sight. Later, swathed in bandages, their bodies soaked in ineffective drugs, they would lie silent in their little beds, surrounded by palpitating mothers, grandmothers, and their little relatives. All through that hall of bandaged children lay a silence so heavy, so fraught with the question of pain that all of us avoided the place. They never seemed to sleep. Sometimes, in the early morning hours, I would pace along that long room, touching a forehead here, arranging a dressing there and the eyelids beneath my hand would fly open and those eyes would look at me with that dark suffering look. I would turn away from the bed only to discover that the children in the other beds had awakened and, with their heads lifted, were looking at me in the same portentous questioning way. I would leave the ward, brooding over the black sheen of the children's eyes, only to encounter the same look from the wounded and the relatives who lay along the dirty, mud-smudged corridor. I would curse the Enemy, he who had done all these and who was even now doing these things to me.

In my sleep, the children would come on their silent feet, footsteps muffled by bandages, waving their missing arms and limbs. They would look at me silently, with those black eyes tinged with some evil, and flap their broken arms in my dreams, as though blessing me with the wounds of the war. I would wake up covered with sweat, only to face the same nightmare in my waking hours as the shriek of rockets continued, as the thud of bombs echoed, and the shrill screams of jets and planes tore through the land. I would curse and curse, spitting into the dust, as though it were the Enemy's face. Pity was strangling me to death; I felt as though the flap of reality had lifted to reveal an insane world of suffering underneath.

Time flew fast enough in the midst of those eyes, of the heat and dust, in the midst of the continuing struggle to lessen the fragile bodies that piled up in the morgue. The same flies that hovered over our dinner grew fat in the feast upon the dead. Into the front door of the hospital poured a steady stream of screaming children held tightly in their mother's arms while at the back door, they either walked out on a missing leg or were pitched into the cold slabs of the morgue where they waited, white squares of cloth stuck to their foreheads like butterflies. And all of us cursed, cursed heartily, unbrokenly, cursed at the Enemy who lay somewhere undefined in the open wound of the country. The days were a long chain of children's eyes — from morning to morning.

Outside, in the dusty yard, small children, tinier than can be imagined of normal children, terribly emaciated, their bones sticking through their gas-wrinkled skin, would play in a corner. The siren of an ambulance would sound through the quiet of the day and they would drop their little toys of bullet shells and run to the entrance, crowding about the blood-stained stretchers. And then, they would turn back silently to their games, with only the glances they threw across their shoulders with that same look which no one could define, revealing the emotions that shuddered through their bodies. Time marched on in a series of bomb flares and burnt human flesh. I would sit beside the hospital window,

looking at the silver eagles soaring in the sky, exhaustion drenching my
bones, my throat dry, my eyes blind with the continuous death of children.
I would sit there alone, brooding upon the fragility of the human body and
this most monstrous of human games: the war, the war which surrounded
us like the green forest encircling the clearing where the building stood.

PAUL CAME to visit me once — a man who suddenly detached
himself from a green jeep and walked to the hospital door, his green
camouflage uniform and ranger hat impeccably clean in the afternoon
light. The smart slap of his boots raised little whorls of dust that clung to
his feet. The children stopped playing and scampered away from his path.
They stood like tiny monkeys, clinging to the barbed wire that marked off
the hospital from the vile, green forest encircling the clearing.

At dinner, Paul sat across from me, his face a knife-edge in the light of
the single bulb in that mess hall. He had toured the ward, laughing at first,
growing more and more morose as the children's eyes had followed his
every movement. He sat now before me, gnawing on a scraggly chicken leg.
He leaned forward while talking, dropping his French and English as
though the words were some tiny secret that was meant for me alone.

"What happened to the girl?" I asked him.

"Who? Oh! That one!" he jerked back at the sudden remembrance.
"Why, they got her, I suppose."

"They? Who?"

Paul leaned back and swept my face with his eyes. He smiled and
threw a quick glance at the others who were bent over their plates.

"My country is at war, Doctor. It is very difficult to understand. They
— the secret police; got her — shot her. I suppose."

"You suppose?" I looked at him with dismay, "but didn't you bother
to find out? How did you know they could have arrested her?"

He smiled again, his teeth very square and proper in his mouth.

"I had to report the incident, of course," he said very calmly.

I could not, for a moment, understand his words and had to stare at
him, turning it over in my mind.

"But she was only a bar girl," I said and was surprised to hear the
note of pleading in my voice. "That's ridiculous. She was only a bar girl
who was sentimental. You said so yourself."

His eyes had a strange and forbidding look when he threw them at my
face.

"You do not understand, Doctor," he repeated. "We are at war. Your
country — it is very nice; all quiet and peaceful. But here . . ."

I leaned on the table and looked at him. I could not understand why my hands clutched at the table edge with some frantic fury.

"We have been at war; several times, in the past . . ."

"Then," he raised a quieting hand, "you understand. Haven't people been executed for things like that before?"

"Yes, but . . ."

"Then, you agree; we have to protect ourselves."

"But Paul," my throat was just a squeal — of despair perhaps? I could not know. "Those were done, not by us, but by the Enemy. The invaders . . . not the people . . . not . . ."

"Doctor," he rasped out, "this is a different war; it is our war: between my people and me. You understand?"

He stood up, dropping the chicken leg to the plate while I followed him with horrified eyes. Quite irrelevantly, I noticed just then, how well-tailored his uniform was; how well the trousers hugged his hips and slipped down to the trim ankles of his feet.

"Surely," I said to him, "that would make care and mercy even more needed: that the war is between you and your people, though the Americans are here."

"The war is the same in any part of the world, Doctor," he stepped away from the table and moved to a window. "You know the dictum: he who is not with us is against us. You are a doctor and it is very hard for you to understand. We appreciate your kindness in coming here to help us. As for other people, they are vermin and deserve to be exterminated."

"Paul, Paul," I moved to his side. "You saw the children. They are not vermin, you know that."

"Those are accidents of the war," he snapped at me. "I was talking of the necessities of the war."

"Necessities? Like executing a bar girl?"

"Yes," he said harshly and for a moment, stood there as though he were guarding the window against me. Then he smiled and turning back to the view before us, he waved a hand towards the forest. "Don't take a walk over there. It is not safe. They say the guerillas are all over these jungles. I don't know how they can survive."

"But, what about the girl?" I insisted, feeling myself choked by this different man before me.

"I do not wish to discuss it any further," he said slowly. "And anyway, I am not at liberty to discuss that part of my work. I have to go now."

I led him to the door, silenced by his curtness and watched him walk to the jeep that would bring him tomorrow to the city, away from the testimony that was the hospital. I stood there dumb, as his jeep roared away, leaving only the awakened dust. In the failing light, the forest loomed and it seemed to me, for a moment, that a very young face had peered through some parted bushes — a face so young it took my breath away — and two eyes looked at me through the dusk. I stood there staring back for a moment and then it was gone, only the brief shadow was left behind and I could not be sure whether it was my own mind playing with me or whether the jungle was, in truth, teeming with more than animal life.

THE HEAT in my room was a thin noose about my neck. The Enemy had taken away a friend and had left me nothing but the heat. A nurse came running on her white, rubber-soled shoes, the emergency alarm sounding behind her. I followed the quick motion of her back, stopping only to slip a sterile mask about my face. Body after body streamed on to the operating table. In between operations, my small, dark-haired assistant would haul a pail of water and throw it over the table which dripped with blood. Our feet sank in the filthy red water that ran to the floor. My trousers were spotted with blood to the knees. The whole hospital echoed the panic of the emergency siren.

As a body was brought in or taken out of the room, I would see the children standing outside, their white bandages gleaming in the dim light, their eyes like daggers aimed at the operating table that stood in the middle of the room. The night shook with bombs while the whole hospital trembled with the explosions and the nurses braced themselves on the table where another thrashing body lay. The light of flares threw shadows upon the walls as the bulbs flickered out and flickered on again, struggling with the bursts that made the very foundations of the earth shudder.

I stood there with scalpels in my hand, cutting off flesh, cutting off veins, cutting, cutting, cutting all through that insane night while my mind trembled as I removed a forearm shielding a face, afraid to find a familiar face, though I knew that I was far from the country of my birth. I stood there slicing off flesh and limbs for the simple expediency of it until the last siren sounded and the night grew quiet and was reclaimed by the songs of crickets and the swish of batwings. Still I stood there, quaking inside my doctor's gown, remembering my father and all the other faces which had been so precious to me, thinking them before me now, stretched upon this blood-drenched table, screaming into my unhearing ears, the intensity of their pain. I stood there until a nurse tapped my shoulder and led me outside.

Dropping my wet and exhausted body into a chair, I suffered the screams all over again — only now, in the silence that followed the madness, did those screams penetrate my ear. They had lodged in my brain without my noticing and now played back, like a phonograph record, echoing and reechoing in the labyrinths of my mind. I felt the veins on my temple throbbing with pain; a groan tore itself from my throat and I dropped my head into my palms, digging my fingers into the flesh, trying to squeeze out the memory of those screams. Someone removed my blood-spotted gown. I could no longer see from exhaustion; fat rolls of sweat dropped from my brow to my shoulders, wetting my shirt. A cool hand pressed a towel to my face and I grabbed at it like a man drowning, only to find myself holding a nurse's hand. Her eyes were swimming with something more than fatigue. She shook her head.

"It was very bad, Doctor," she said softly. "We lost three-fourths of them."

I looked at her, the image of the full morgue in my eyes.

"Why," I asked, my voice hoarse and unfamiliar to my ears, "why do you do this to yourselves? Your people — everyone of you."

She looked at me, the tears hanging at the edge of her lashes.

"These were wounds of bombs, Doctor," her voice was soft with reproach. "Wounds of napalm, shrapnel bombs, bullets. We do not have them, Doctor. We have only our hands."

I rose from the chair, infinitely weary, a taste so bitter in my mouth that I wanted to spill my guts out there in the dust.

"Yes," I said to her. "Yes, I am sorry."

Suddenly, I saw that the children had crowded around the door; they stood in the corridor, ready to spring with their eyes; the muzzle of the black pupils aimed with deadly accuracy at my body. They flattened themselves against the walls, their faces turning, following my back as I began to walk down the corridor. A sea of children was in my way; a sea of tiny bodies mutilated by the war, a movement rippling like waves through their bodies as I approached and they fell back, clinging to the walls, merely looking at me with their eyes aged beyond their years. It seemed to me that the multitude was endless; and not only the children of the present looked at me from those walls but even the children of the past and future.

I stopped and stood there gaping at them, trying to shield myself from their eyes. For suddenly, I had heard the slight whisper of their voices, those voices that spoke only in silence, in the face of human suffering; those voices that spoke only with the language of the eyes: *you, too, have kept silence, have tacitly approved, have tried to deny the scream of the open flesh that lay under your hands.*

I read, felt, the accusation, the white-hot anger that burned in their eyes at my betrayal. I gasped, stepped back and turned away from those eyes, still pursued by the damning looks, and ran out of that hospital, out of that clearing, out, out into the black night muffling the forest. Somewhere behind me someone called but I could no longer answer for I knew, I knew that the enemy was at last discovered; he was no longer in the forest but had entered the hospital and taken lodging in my soul. I ran on, twigs breaking under my foot, my breath rasping in my ear until the ground gave to the black darkness of a pit. And in the middle of that long fall, I heard the horror-filled scream of my voice and saw the bamboo thorns gleaming like bared fangs in the darkness.

They assumed I was ambushed or fell accidentally. I do not know what they thought of in the private rooms of their minds. They gave me a medal which they pinned on my chest in some ceremony I could only hear. They hanged flowers around my neck — it was, I suppose, a splendid farce and I stood there while the President of the country hugged me delicately. Women kissed me while all the while, I could only see the children's eyes in the darkness that now completely surrounded me. I could only remember my own voice as I lay there on that same blood-stinking operating table, repeating over and over again: *why hast thou forsaken me?* And I felt I was asking the question not of God but of my father.

PEACE — that was promised to me in this world and I look for it constantly now, moving between its walls, touching this furniture and that shelf. How many times have I run a finger along the heavy frame of our father's portrait in this sala? There is honor, mother tells me, in marching like your father. Alas, I cannot tell her that he was not there to guide me in my choice.

At night I hear you quarreling — you, Maria, and the mother of the house and it seems to me that some other presence watches you with me: that Other who plays with Pepito for hours, who walks with mother to the store where she struggles with the smaller problems of living. It sits here now with me, while I talk to you, a different darkness spilling from its eye-sockets, its face scraped tight by a knife, its mouth stretched into a hideous grin. You quarrel over the war, contending with mother where the honor shall lie while I sit here, watching the Other smirking at your hushed voices.

I was born before the war in this country; you were born after. But to the one who gave us her breasts to suck, there could be nothing but peace for us in the morrow. I sit here, useless and broken, wishing to tell her that this was true — but the voices of invisible children reassure me that war is the essence of living and I keep quiet, feeling that everything is too late. Too late, too late, for the war has already floated in, is indeed already in the houses and crouches, leering at us, while we make futile gestures of peace.

★

★ ★ ★ ★

AUTHOR: *Pinchas Kagonovitch (Der Nister, 1884–1950) was one of the Soviet Yiddish writers in Kiev in the 1920s. The Hebrew-Yiddish pseudonym Der Nister ("the hidden one") characterizes Kagonovitch, who was considered to be the finest Yiddish symbolist novelist and poet. He intermingled Jewish, Christian, and Olympian supernatural creatures and produced allegories, mystic visions, and other forms of impressionist writing. More than half of the Yiddish-speaking Jews perished in the Nazi holocaust, and the dictatorship of Joseph Stalin liquidated most Yiddish Soviet writers, but Der Nister somehow survived. Although he was considered a romantic, nonpolitical writer, this story combines nostalgia for the world of his childhood — its unhurried pace, shabby respectability, and wasteful aimlessness — with the political events of the early 1930s. It is one of his strongest and best-remembered works.*

SETTING: *Shtetls were and are small, self-contained Jewish communities in Eastern Europe. Although their economic and social viability was historically marginal, the shtetls of western Russia became targets for the Russian revolutionaries in 1917. Those that somehow survived were easy targets for the Nazis in the mid-1930s. Following World War II, whatever was left of the shtetl was under siege by the new governments of Poland, Rumania, and the Baltic States. As a result, most of their inhabitants were killed outright, fled to urban areas, or emigrated to Western Europe and to non-European lands. Because the shtetl represented a culture within a culture, accurate records of the number of shtetls destroyed or the numbers of people killed are unavailable. We know enough to say that the wars and revolutions of the first part of this century were the direct and indirect cause of the temporary disappearance of a people and their culture.*

Meyer Landshaft

Pinchas Kagonovitch
A fragment about an incident in today's occupied Poland.

I

It was a few days after they marched in. . . . There were rumors that the town *Kommandant* had already summoned the Jewish community elders, empowering them to carry out all orders and commands that the

Translated by Joachim Neugroschel. "Meyer Landshaft" is reprinted from Joachim Neugroschel, ed. *The Shtetl* (New York: G. P. Putnam's Sons, 1979) by permission of Joachim Neugroschel.occupying force would issue specifically for the Jewish population.

occupying force would issue specifically for the Jewish population.

In Meyer Landshaft's home, as in all Jewish homes, the family was utterly distraught. Meyer Landshaft — an unusual sort of Polish-Jewish businessman, a man of few words, well-versed in the holy texts and of a good family, a good stock, and a pious man as well; whose piety, however, never prevented him, in his younger days or now, in his early fifties, from looking into books by Luzzato, by Nakhman Krokhmal, and even by non-Jews, authors whom he knew rather well, for instance Klopstock or Schiller; this Meyer Landshaft — a tallish man, with a large, wide, blond beard, with blondish eyebrows over grayish eyes, that peered out from between his lashes like silent lakes surrounded by reeds; this Meyer Landshaft, whose tidy clothing alone required everyone in his presence to remain more quiet than at home and which, whenever he came in either from the street or from another room to someone waiting for him, compelled that person to straighten up respectfully; this Meyer Landshaft, who, in all situations, even terribly difficult ones, for example, when a child was sick or some other trouble was afflicting the house, never showed the slightest change in his face, because his inner faith would not permit him to doubt or lose his conviction that even the worst predicament would be happily resolved; this Meyer Landshaft, who now, after reading his fill of newspaper stories about what the new occupiers had done, first with the Jews in their own country, and especially after attacking Poland, when people found out what they were doing with Jews in the Polish towns and shtetls that they had conquered and subjugated now, when this Meyer Landshaft, like so many others, had failed to leave town after the enemy's sudden entrance before anyone could even think about whether or not to stay — now, even this Meyer Landshaft felt he was caught in a trap, and he began to forsake his normal rule — of believing that things would get better. . . .

You could see this in his grayish eyes, peering out from between his lashes, as though struck by a powerful tempest that gathers in even the quietest lakes, surrounded by reeds; you could tell by his nervous, staccato answers if you asked him anything upon his returns from town, where he went, not to do business — buying or selling — but merely to get the latest news, to hear what people were saying about the things they were so terrified of. . . . And as for his wife Hanna-Gitl, who had always gone along with him, hand in hand, always so greatly honored him, loved him, and hung on his every word, ready to satisfy his every wish, even forestall his wishes — whenever she asked: "What are people saying in town? What's the latest news?" he would answer: "Nothing, nothing. . . . No talk, no news.

. . ." And he would look away, avoiding her eyes, and turn and do things in the house, the kind of things you do before moving from a house or going on a trip, when you're confused and don't quite know what you're about.

He was not behaving now as he usually did in the past, when, unless he was taking a meal or dealing with people, he would always be seen holding a book in his right hand, tilting it slightly, a bit myopically, towards his right eye and the right side of his face, and peering into it. But not now. His mind wasn't on books now. And if at some point he did manage, for a brief instant, to emerge from the personal anxieties that had attacked him, Meyer Landshaft, like all the Jewish inhabitants in the town, he used that instant to walk about, isolated, sharing his thoughts with no one, walk from wall to wall and from corner to corner in the room, twisting his hands when no one was watching, and constantly whispering the Hebrew phrase, "Oh Lord, art Thou hastening Thy destruction?" That is to say: "Had God really, heaven forbid, decided to end everything and wipe out the Jews? . . ."

But no, he didn't even have time for that because chiefly and above all he was busy worrying about himself and his family, over whose heads he saw the hovering sword. . . . But there again his mind focused on no one in the family — not himself, who was as imperiled as any of them, not his wife, Hanna-Gitl, who had always gone along with him, hand in hand, always hung on his every word, ready to satisfy his every wish, even forestall his wishes; not his married sons and daughters and their spouses and children, his grandchildren — no, his mind focused on no one when he hunted for air and an escape from the cage he was caught in, that is to say, the various rumors, each more horrifying, that came to his ears — no, his mind focused on no one so much as his youngest daughter, his baby, Vittl, or Wanda in Polish, as they called her in high school, where she was studying and about to graduate.

II

She had long, delicate fingers, Wanda, the sign of a highly refined ancestry, and perhaps also the sign of a late birth to parents who had already borne many children before her, the very last. She differed from all the other children in her great resemblance to her father, in her fine, quiet, well-mannered ways — while the other children were more like the mother, Hanna-Gitl, who was not from such a lofty background and whose uneducated father, it was said, had paid a tidy sum to get a son-in-law like Meyer Landshaft.

She was also her father's favorite because she was the baby and also because the father saw her somewhat as a reflection of himself, and even though he outwardly didn't show her more affection than the other children, everyone in the house nevertheless viewed her as an exception, to whom the father gave more, if not in words then with quiet, loving eyes, that he rested on her from time to time.

Naturally, neither the mother nor even the children were jealous of her, on the contrary — to their father's exceptional love they added their own, and they weren't jealous when their father allowed her to do something that the other children weren't allowed to do: go to the Polish high school, where, incidentally, they got the priest, the religion teacher, to excuse her from classes on Saturdays, since she worked hard enough to do everything she had to during the week.

In short, Wanda: an exception at home, and also among her friends, with whom she was very retiring, very moral — an effigy of her father's behavior, which was well-known both in the family and in the town. All the businessmen, all her girl friends said that Wanda would never put up with a free word from any of the boys, her fellow classmates, never put up with foolish liberties from them. And furthermore: she even concealed and drew in her girlish form as though ashamed, as though regretful that she hadn't been born in armor.

And now she, Vittl/Wanda, the slim, blond seventeen-year-old creature, with a great measure of childhood innocence, which peered from her eyes, thoughtful eyes that were covered with a thin, thin veil of dreaming, she weighed heaviest on her father's mind, caused him the worst anxiety, because she was in the greatest danger — of being noticed by them, appealing to those whom she shouldn't, absolutely mustn't appeal to under any circumstances.

Now her father's eyes rested on her very often, and if someone addressed him on any important matter, he would turn away in the middle of the conversation and look at her, as though fearful of losing her, of losing sight of her.

Why? Because, aside from the rumors about the fine things that the new occupiers had already done in all the places they had reached earlier, and about the same things they had already started in the town where Meyer Landshaft lived — aside from all those things, which were already horrible enough, Meyer Landshaft, like other involved fathers, had heard a rumor that made him tremble: a rumor about certain houses where young women were brought: unmarried girls, young wives, for the shameful pleasure of the officers or the ordinary soldiers. . . .

Soon, it was no longer a rumor. It was told with all certainty that the Jewish administration had already received a clear order to contribute a number of Jewish women for that shame. They were still keeping it a secret, not leaking any details to the greater public, thinking they could appeal to the occupiers and get them to rescind the edict. But it didn't work. And now the Jews were already trudging about, devastated, and among them, and, as we can imagine, more devastated than anyone, Meyer Landshaft, who looked so dazed, who never uttered a word, but who could be seen twisting his fingers quietly. . . . That was one thing. And the second: In the morning, in the evening, at night, if someone had listened to his prayers to heaven, he would have heard only one desire, expressed in the words of a biblical verse that was not in any prayer: The eagle hath no fear of any predatory fowl, for she flieth higher; but she feareth the huntsmen, so she carrieth her eaglets above and not below herself, saying: 'It is better for the arrow to pierce me than my children.'" And that was what Meyer Landshaft wished: "Better me than my children" — meaning Wanda.

III

In his great bewilderment, Meyer Landshaft stopped associating with other people, he remained at home for days on end, and just to keep in his mind occupied with something, anything, he began sharpening the kitchen knives, which he normally did only on Fridays, for the Sabbath — an old custom of his.

"What's this all of a sudden?" asked Hanna-Gitl and also the older children, seeing him do this unusual chore in the middle of the week.

"Nothing. . . . Just. . . ." he answered, not looking in their faces, as during the past few days when anyone spoke to him. And in their great respect and esteem, neither Hanna-Gitl nor the children asked him anything further, realizing why he was occupying his mind with such useless things and why he was so sparing of words and answers.

Sitting there, sharpening the knives, he most certainly had no thoughts, except perhaps only about what he, as a knowledgeable man, had once read, namely, that in hard times, similar to these, hard times for the nation, fathers had once been forced to execute their own children — like strangers: to kill them in order to prevent them from falling into the hands of others. . . . He didn't know how that had been done, or what had happened to the "compassionate father" (for it is written in Psalms: "As a father hath compassion upon his children, so hath the Lord compassion upon them that fear Him"). But as in those earlier times — he thought to himself — compassion is the most merciless thing of all, which a man has to tear out and destroy in himself.

He must have trembled at that thought. . . . But he trembled even harder when, sitting at the table, doing his sharpening, he suddenly heard his doorbell ring, and he was certain it wasn't a familiar hand, which they would surely have recognized, but some alien hand, which pressed the button hard and long, letting the bell quaver, urgent and demanding.

It must be either a mailman, a telegraph boy, in a hurry, or members of the occupation force, who demand an instant response, an instant admission, with no respect for the people whose bell they are ringing.

Meyer Landshaft was so alarmed by the ringing that he made an awkward movement and cut his hand, and blood began running from the cut. But he noticed neither the cut nor the blood. He then heard one of the family hurrying to the door and opening it. And from the silence of the opening and the encounter with him, or with them who had rung, Meyer Landshaft concluded that these were certainly no ordinary visitors crossing the threshold and entering his home.

From the corridor leading to the dining room, where Meyer Landshaft was sitting, he could hear the thud of military feet, heavy-soled boots, and the surprised silence of his family — and, as it turned out, the frightened encounter of the person who had let them in was palpable through all the rooms.

The family came and gathered in the dining room, where they felt the soldiers would come first, the first room visible from the corridor, without a door. And that was what happened. The entire family was at home, as generally on all those days that were ruled by the physiognomy of the occupying force, still undefined for the non-Jewish population, but already very sharply defined for the Jewish population, who felt forsaken and three-quarters condemned.

Meyer Landshaft's entire family, pale, frightened, collected in the dining room. And no sooner had they come in, no sooner had the soldiers marched in, than all of them, both the soldiers and Meyer Landshaft's family, watched Meyer Landshaft, as though he had been expecting this, get up from his chair, as pale as the others, and, seeing them all gathered in the room, he suddenly had only one word to blurt out: "Wanda," which meant that of all his family Wanda was to come over and stand at his side.

IV

"Hände hoch! Hands up!" came a second voice, louder than Meyer Landshaft's, the voice of the officer commanding the squad, and right after that order, the same officer shouted again: "Get in a row! Men and women separate! And nobody try to move!"

They obeyed. Silently. Meyer Landshaft saw the men in the house line up to his left, his sons and sons-in-law; and to his right, the women, with Wanda closest to him, after he had called her over, when the soldiers had appeared, and next to Wanda — his wife, and next to his wife — his daughters and daughters-in-law.

The commanding officer, a lieutenant, at first glared silently at the file of people to make sure that it was orderly and that they had obeyed him properly and that no one moved. . . . *"In Ordnung!"* Then he turned to some man, not a military person, who had marched in with the soldiers — an administrative official, empowered by the Jewish elders, and forced by the occupiers to come along to all the Jewish homes, like now to Meyer Landshaft's home, and to do what they demanded of him: this time for some kind of registration that the occupiers considered necessary.

"Zähl! Count!" the lieutenant ordered the man. "Wait! No!" He changed his mind after glancing at the row of men and then the row of women, fixing his delighted gaze on Wanda, and dwelling on her for a long time.

Any of the family who still had some wits about them in their terror at this degrading ceremony could see that the lieutenant, the commander of the squad, was more drunk than sober. And they noticed this in his dangling blue eyes, which were shiny and seemed virtually to be floating in grease, and they noticed this too in his uncertain movements, his precarious equilibrium.

He began counting from the left row, the men, pointing a finger into each chest: one, two, three, until he came to the chest of Meyer Landshaft himself, who, like all the others, was holding up his hands, but who was turning his head, not to the row of men at his left, but to Wanda, who was at his right.

The lieutenant, before passing on with his finger to the line of women, remained in front of Meyer Landshaft for a while. Then he stretched his counting hand to Wanda, peering with a silly grin at what his finger had so lightly grazed — Wanda's breasts, as though he were sticking his finger in honey that he was about to lick.

A cry came from Meyer Landshaft — from him, the man of few words, who had never in his life said a loud word to anyone, and who probably wasn't even capable of saying a loud word.

"Hände weg! Hands off!" came from Meyer Landshaft's mouth, a strict order, which made all the others, except for him, lower their hands in

terror, forgetting that they had to hold them up, according to the lieutenant's order.

"What?!" The lieutenant almost didn't understand who was meant by that disrespectful, threatening cry — he, he himself, the *Herr Offizier*, was supposed to remove his unclean hands from that which was not for him and from which he was to remain far away.

"What?!" he roared, glaring at Meyer Landshaft and taking a few steps back from where he was standing, in order to have a better look at that man from the distance. "What did he say? What did he dare to say to a German officer?"

And he glared drunkenly at Meyer Landshaft through half-closed eyes and saw him standing with his hands up and with blood running from one hand into his sleeve.

"Blood?!" he roared again, as though viewing it on his own hand, as though his own hand had been wounded. "What's that blood?" he shouted, peering around the room suspiciously, at all the people, as though, before his arrival, they had planned some evil and sharpened some kind of weapon, thereby wounding themselves.

Really: He glanced at the table and saw knives and a whetstone, which apparently someone, before his arrival, had held in his hands and prepared for a suspicious use — so it seemed to the officer.

"Who did this, who was sharpening knives?" the lieutenant asked, pointing at the knives on the table.

"I was!" replied Meyer Landshaft, and the others sensed a great satisfaction in his reply, apparently because the knives were averting the lieutenant's eyes from the girl whom he had just noticed and at whom he had so pleasurably thrust his honeyed finger.

It took a few seconds for the lieutenant to figure out how to act. . . . (Incidentally, we ought to say that these things happened back then, when the occupiers had not unloosed their right hand to carry out their plans for Jews in those areas they had only just invaded and gained control of, they were still keeping within certain, almost legal bounds — not like now, at the time we are writing, when such a lieutenant would not have hesitated with a man like Meyer Landshaft, killing him on the spot, without a second thought, for the least word he didn't care for, like any Jew, guilty or not, like a rat carrying the plague: to be wiped out. . . .)

V

"Arrest him!" screamed the lieutenant as soon as he realized what had to be done. "Arrest this bloodthirsty Jew, who sharpens knives to use against us!" he screamed to the soldiers accompanying him.

"Oh, no," Meyer Landshaft's daughter, Wanda, suddenly stepped out of the line. . . . And, modest as her behavior may have been with her own people, the students at school, whom she had never permitted a free word, or the least hint about herself, as a member of the female sex, she now, however, in the moment of danger for her father, who was obviously as dear to her as she to him — she, never giving voice to her feelings, but carrying them in girlish concealment, just as her father carried his love for her in his gazes. . . . Modest as Wanda's behavior may have been previously, when she never exploited her ability to attract men, she now, however, coming to the lieutenant and trying to save her father from the terrible situation caused by his powerful stance against the lieutenant — she now, suddenly — who knows how? — played up that ability, peculiar to all women at certain moments, when they have to charm someone and attain something for their charm. . . .

"Oh, no, Herr Lieutenant," she said, behaving like an adult for her family, this first time in her life — for the members of the household, for her father and mother. She was inspired with fluent speech, and lowering her eyes in her normal modesty, as whenever she faced a strange man, and then raising her eyes to this strange man, she said, with a smile that she had acquired from somewhere:

"Oh, no, Herr Lieutenant, it's a mistake. Those aren't knives for the occupiers. My father isn't like that. It's a custom here, my father always does it on Friday for the Sabbath, and now there's no business because of the confusion in town, and so he's started doing it during the week, you can look at them, Herr Lieutenant, they're ordinary kitchen knives."

And with lowered eyes, Wanda just barely smiled and continued to play up that ability which was supposed to make the man she was talking to, the lieutenant, forget the insult he had gotten from her father, who had told him to remove the hands with which he had taken indecent liberties. . . . She stepped over to her father and caressed him affectionately to demonstrate his innocence, vouching for it with her proximity, and to risk her life for him, that is to say, for the business of the knives, which, as the Herr Lieutenant could see, was really a bagatelle, not worth wasting any breath on.

Wanda was successful. They could see small fires, mixed with small shadows, in the lieutenant's eyes, as he looked at her, first when she stepped out of line, and then when she stood opposite him, defending her father, and especially afterwards, when, upon finishing her defense, she tenderly went over to her father and gently caressed him.

The somewhat drunken lieutenant was giving in, and the situation was almost resolved: If Wanda had just said a few more words about her father in that same defending tone, and if her father, Meyer Landshaft, had silently continued to let her defend him, then, almost, almost, the lieutenant would have forgotten all his anger and taken back his order to arrest Meyer Landshaft.

But that wasn't what happened. Because the moment Wanda affectionately joined her father, and he, the father, saw the devices she, his Wanda, was using to woo the lieutenant's favor and avert his anger from him; when he saw the manner in which Wanda wanted to save him, he pushed her away, and, just as the lieutenant, for Wanda's vouching and for her sake, was about to free the father of any suspicions and not accuse him of anything else — at that moment, Meyer Landshaft, his reason incomprehensible, suddenly stepped out of the line, and, even more suddenly and unexpected, he said something absurd and repeated the same words he had spoken earlier, when the lieutenant had asked the people: "Who was sharpening knives?" and he, Meyer Landshaft had spoken up in front of everyone, had taken the blame and said: "I was!"

"I was!" he now repeated the same words: "I was!" — as though trying to remind the lieutenant that no one else, only he, Meyer Landshaft had said it, and that he was standing by what he had said, refusing to back off from it, unrepenting, not accepting any efforts by anyone to intercede on his behalf with the lieutenant, not even his daughter Wanda, whom he loved so much.

"What?!" cried the lieutenant, utterly amazed, upon seeing Meyer Landshaft's defiance and gazing at him as though he had just caught sight of him appearing out of nowhere. He couldn't believe his ears when hearing the man who had been on the verge of release from his predicament, and who had now, for no reason whatsoever, as the lieutenant assumed, brought back his predicament and taken it upon himself. It was as though a man with a healthy, innocent head had slipped it into a hangman's noose.

"Meyer!" his wife, Hanna-Gitl, cried in terror and amazement, upon seeing her husband, for the first time in his life, committing such a senseless act, as now, saying something that could endanger both him and all the others, God forbid.

"What's he doing?!" These words were blurted out reluctantly and with great but concealed fear by the Jewish administration official (who had witnessed the entire scene) when he heard Meyer Landshaft's defiant words, which virtually sealed his doom, drawing the misfortune upon himself, the reason being incomprehensible: It could have been resolved happily, in the best way, which seldom happens in such cases.

"What's he doing?" said the administration man to himself, turning away, unable to look at Meyer or his senseless act. "Criminal," he said almost aloud, "suicide" (the latter in Hebrew), at a loss to grasp what was happening in that man, who didn't understand the whole thing, who didn't understand the simple facts of life in dealing with the authorities, especially such authorities, when they suspect you of something, even some foolish act which can become very serious, and which you have to clear yourself of — and not only was that man not defending himself, but he was refusing the possibility of help from his daughter, who very nearly could have pulled him out of the pitfall.

Those were the thoughts of the administration man, and those were likewise the thoughts of Meyer's wife, Hanna-Gitl, and likewise of all the other people in the household, who, looking at him, were stunned and speechless, unable to comprehend why he was drawing the calamity on like a beloved piece of clothing.

But Meyer Landshaft himself did understand and he had a reason and justification for his deed, being unwilling to allow the lieutenant's amorous eyes to fall upon Wanda, seeing how the lieutenant was leering at her and sizing her up and delightedly resting his insolent, gaping, filthy officer's eyes on every part of her. . . .

VI

"Arrest him!" shouted the furious lieutenant at the soldiers after Meyer Landshaft had aroused his anger a second time, even making him forget about Wanda, whom he had only just been leering at with such desire, and whom, had he only been permitted to approach her even slightly, he would have exonerated of any suspicions and accusations.

"Arrest him!" the lieutenant said, harsh, resolute, no longer eyeing Wanda, doing his officer's duty — to wipe away the open enemy, this Jew, who was sharpening knives to use against the occupiers.

"Please don't, *Herr Offizier!*" begged first Hanna-Gitl, then her and Meyer Landshaft's older children, then Wanda, who said to the lieutenant: "Take me, Herr Lieutenant, take me instead of him!"

"Arrest him!" the lieutenant commanded for the third time, ignoring, refusing to see, all the people who were surrounding him with their entreaties.

They seized him, Meyer Landshaft. . . . Wanda and also the other children tried to accompany him to the *Kommandantur*, running alongside him the whole time, refusing to leave him. But when they were approaching that destination — the high, broad building the length of a block — and they came to a glass entrance, which was flung wide open by a sentry to let the soldiers in, and finally, after the children had stood out on the sidewalk, for a long time, opposite that building, waiting for him to come back out, and he did not appear, they despaired of seeing him released today and they went to do the kind of things you do in cases like that: look for some way to intercede, run to find help from the Jewish administration and private individuals, Jews, and non-Jews, from whom they believed they could get assistance.

A foolish act. . . . One would think offhand, a trifle. . . . But the very fact that Meyer Landshaft was taken to the *Kommandantur* and accused of defying the authorities, even worse, sharpening knives in broad daylight, something a man like him does not normally do; that very fact alone and the lieutenant's testimony, confirming that when he found him sharpening knives and asked him what he was doing, the Jew had not denied anything, on the contrary, he had even defiantly retorted that he was indeed doing that — that alone and all that was enough for the authorities to deal earnestly with Meyer Landshaft and hand him over immediately to a certain interrogator, to whom he was led in a secret room, out of the way, in the huge, dense *Kommandantur* building.

The interrogator was a tall, aristocratic-looking man with deeply pitted cheeks indicative of sinful nights and years of revelry, and now a severe, a stubbornly taciturn man, with a sidelong glare, like a rooster, and a monocle in his eye. It cannot be said that Meyer Landshaft was dreadfully tortured there. But just the isolated and out-of-the-way room in the long, hollow corridor of the *Kommandantur* building, the taciturn demeanor and sidelong glare of the interrogator, whose one eye looked like that of an old sick golden eagle with a bad conscience — those things alone were enough for Meyer Landshaft, a man of few words, a scholar from a fine background, who had never had any dealings with government authorities, and who had never found himself having to be interrogated, especially by such an interrogator — those things alone were enough for him to feel from the very start that he was in some division of hell. . . .

True, at first he had tried to act free and unrestrained in front of the interrogator, being alone here and out of the danger that had only just faced his Wanda at home. . . . The so-called accusation was something he regarded as trivial, something he could easily upset and invalidate. Coming before the interrogator, he mustered his skimpy knowledge, gathered from the books in the language that the interrogator used as he addressed him now — Meyer Landshaft was hoping, both modestly and also a little boastfully, to show that he, the interrogator, was dealing not with just anybody, but with a man who was not only eminent in town, but also was well-versed in the works of a Klopstock, a Spielhagen, a Schiller, so that he, the interrogator, could understand that such knowledge, such experience were obviously enough of a guaranty and could serve as something of a protection against any kind of misinterpretation, any sort of suspicion. . . .

The interrogator eyed him indifferently. He allowed him to have his say and virtually let him believe that everything he, Meyer Landshaft, said, was being taken at its full face value — as proof of his innocence, and that the lieutenant who had brought him here had apparently made a mistake, suspecting a man who was above suspicion.

The interrogator listened to everything he said, he gazed at him, taciturn, as though counting every word, until the very last, which made Meyer Landshaft think they would even apologize to him, give him back his freedom, as a man who had truly been brought here for nothing, here, where he didn't belong.

That was what he thought, and then all at once the interrogator stood up from his chair and forced Meyer Landshaft — who didn't know why — likewise to stand up and face him, and Meyer sensed in the last minute that the interrogator's action did not bode good. Really. . . .

It cannot be said that even now the interrogator's behavior towards Meyer Landshaft was like that of all the occupier's interrogators, according to the normal practice, after an interrogation. He was not thrown into a side room for certain Gestapo men to "work him over": by ordering him to climb up on a table and sit down on a chair there and then knocking the chair out from under him so that he would fall and break his back; he was not beaten with a rubber truncheon; nor was he punched in the chin, the teeth, and forced to push back his head, further and further, until his neck was on the verge of breaking.

No, this time the interrogator did it alone, unassisted, and not all that harshly. . . . He merely walked over to Meyer, quietly, wordlessly, and as Meyer stood before him, surprised and already frightened, the interrogator grabbed Meyer's beard with both hands and suddenly and hastily pulled and tore it, so that the interrogator's hands clutched two dense tangles of hair, and Meyer Landshaft's cheeks, with a meager remainder of tufts, looked like a stubble field after the harvest — that was all.

"Go away!" said the tall, aristocratic-looking interrogator to Meyer Landshaft, gazing at the victim like a sick golden eagle and with a bad conscience. "Go away. That's what you get for the knives you were sharpening, as you say, for your filthy Jewish sabbath. Go about your business, and if we need you we'll call you, with your plucked face."

VII

He left. . . . But if any of his family or friends would have encountered him as he trudged home from the *Kommandantur,* they would most certainly not have recognized him: He had changed too much between the time of his arrival there and his departure, both because most of the hair was gone from his beard and because his normal silence was so intensified that his tallish stature and his silent and pensive walk almost made him look like the famous mournful knight, as he is depicted, that is to say, like a man who has burned out inwardly and now looks like the chimney of what once was his house.

Upon his arrival home, he was spared any questions about what had happened, they saw without asking, and they immediately understood his dissembled and unspoken intention: to remain alone in his isolated room until the shame was gone and until the hair had grown back in his beard.

They never went into the room, none of them, except for Hanna-Gitl, his wife, to bring him food and take care of him, and even she, when she went in, during the first few hours and even the first few days, she couldn't draw a single word out of him. Apparently, the pull on the outside had torn something from inside him. He remained mute. And the only thing that maintained him, strengthened him, and comforted him in his isolation was, perhaps, the thought that by taking upon himself the shame of the *Kommandantur* and that interrogator with the pitted cheeks, with the long legs, and the monocle — by taking upon himself the shame of feeling the pull by that man's hands, he, Meyer Landshaft, had actually saved the honor of his child, Wanda, who was on the verge of being violated far more horribly than he.

"Thank God," he must have thought whenever Hanna-Gitl came in to him and he asked her: "Is there any news in town, what are people saying, and . . . How is Wanda?" That was always his last question, as he withdrew into his isolation again, refusing to show himself to the world, to other people, without his normal stately appearance.

But even this solace did not last long: The lieutenant had had a good reason for coming to his home with his soldiers that time. They had registered many women in many Jewish and Gentile homes, except pregnant women and those who were nursing babies, and in Meyer Landshaft's home, they registered Wanda in the list. . . . The way they did this and the way they took the women for unspeakable, shameful things is another story, which is unparalleled in the chronicles of evil that the world is familiar with. The way children were torn from homes, the way they were jammed into freight cars, with only a tiny grated window at the top of one side; the number that was stuffed into one car, the way they were collected at the railroad station, with no parents, no relatives allowed to come and say good-bye to them; and the way the jammed trains with these prisoners lumbered out of the stations; and how many tears, sobs, and quiet swoons could be heard from the sealed railroad cars, through the tiny grated windows — there is no need to say anything further about these things, what we know is enough.

We have to imagine what went on in all these homes when children crossed the parental threshold for the first time, never to come back again; and if they were to come, it would probably be better if neither side were to experience it, not the children and not those to whom they were dear.

We have to imagine what went on in the home of Meyer Landshaft — with everyone, with Hanna-Gitl, with the older children, with the sisters and brothers, not to mention — Wanda herself, but more than anyone else, the father, Meyer Landshaft. He, Meyer, during all the days when they prepared Wanda for the journey (according to regulations, the women had to take along shoes, clothing, and food for several days, as though going to some kind of work), when occasional cries could be heard in the home, a cry from one and then from someone else in the house, letting go in hysterical outbursts; during all those days, Meyer Landshaft did not appear. Not even on the last day, not even at the last hour, nor in the last few minutes, when Wanda was saying good-bye to everyone, accompanied by wild sobs from her mother, Hanna-Gitl, as well as from her brothers, sisters, and other relatives — not even when Wanda went up to her father's door, and her voice, among all the cries in the house, could be heard pleading: "Daddy, open up. I want to say good-bye to you" — not even then did Meyer Landshaft open the door, or throw his arms around Wanda. During the first few moments, he remained silent, then he said: "No, daughter, I can't." Not out of cruelty, to be sure, but because he simply didn't have the heart. Standing at the door, Wanda seemed to hear a weeping, which accompanied her and afflicted her for a long time en route — the weeping of a man lamenting not only his own doom, but the doom of an entire world.

Wanda couldn't endure it and she left. . . . But that evening, at the station, when the train was transferred to a distant line and when several of the prisoners, unaccompanied by anyone, stood in the car where Wanda was, stood under the high window, which they could barely reach, saying good-bye, with their last looks, to their home, from which they were being torn away — at that time, Wanda, like others, also stretched her head to that little window. . . . She wasn't thinking of anyone then, not even her mother, whose last loving kisses she could still feel on her jacket, right by her breast, when her mother, upon saying good-bye, had wept into her breast, burying her face there for a long time, unable to tear herself away — no, not the mother, she was thinking of no one else, only her father, imagining him behind the locked door, as he stood and listened to her pleading, the pleading of his youngest child, his baby, Wanda, and he did not have the heart to open the door, to come out and take a final look at her.

★

And there was warfare among all kings.
And the whole earth collapsed.

And nothing was left of the demons.
They became nothing.

Amen.

— Rabbi Nakhman

★ ★ ★ ★

AUTHOR: *Luigi Pirandello (1867–1936) won the Nobel Prize for literature in 1934. Born on the island of Sicily, he was a prodigious writer, best known for his play* Six Characters in Search of an Author. *The short story of war reprinted here is one of the best known in European literature.*

SETTING: *During the First World War, Italy was an ally of Germany and Austria. However, the Italian Revolution of 1848–1849 had laid the groundwork for continual internal conflict, and by 1914 Italy was so preoccupied with its own problems that it declared neutrality. Not before, however, sending thousands of young men to fight "for their country." Through a conversation among nameless characters on a train leaving Rome, Pirandello portrays not only the chasm between what people say and how they may feel about honor, duty, and patriotism, but how war affects relationships between husbands and wives, fathers and sons, friends and strangers.*

War

Luigi Pirandello

The passengers who had left Rome by the night express had had to stop until dawn at the small station of Fabriano in order to continue their journey by the small old-fashioned local joining the main line with Sulmona.

At dawn, in a stuffy and smoky second-class carriage in which five people had already spent the night, a bulky woman in deep mourning was hoisted in — almost like a shapeless bundle. Behind her — puffing and moaning, followed her husband — a tiny man, thin and weakly, his face death-white, his eyes small and bright and looking shy and uneasy. Having at last taken a seat, he politely thanked the passengers who had helped his wife and who had made room for her; then he turned around to the woman trying to pull down the collar of her coat, and politely inquired:

"Are you all right, dear?"

The wife, instead of answering, pulled up her collar again to her eyes, so as to hide her face.

"War" is reprinted from *21 Great Short Stories*, translated by Michael Pettinati.

"Nasty world," muttered the husband with a sad smile.

And he felt it his duty to explain to his traveling companions that the poor woman was to be pitied, for the war was taking away from her her only son, a boy of twenty to whom both had devoted their entire life, even breaking up their home at Sulmona to follow him to Rome, where he had to go as a student, then allowing him to volunteer for war with an assurance, however, that at least for six months he would not be sent to the front and now, all of a sudden, receiving a wire saying that he was due to leave in three days' time and asking them to go and see him off.

The woman under the big coat was twisting and wriggling, at times growling like a wild animal, feeling certain that all those explanations would not have aroused even a shadow of sympathy from those people who — most likely — were in the same plight as herself. One of them, who had been listening with particular attention, said:

"You should thank God that your son is only leaving now for the front. Mine has been sent there the first day of the war. He has already come back twice wounded and been sent back again to the front."

"What about me? I have two sons and three nephews at the front," said another passenger.

"Maybe, but in our case it is our *only* son," ventured the husband.

"What difference can it make? You may spoil your only son with excessive attention, but you cannot love him more than you would all your other children if you had any. Paternal love is not like bread that can be broken into pieces and split amongst the children in equal shares. A father gives *all* his love to each one of his children without discrimination, whether it be one or ten, and if I am suffering now for my two sons, I am not suffering half for each of them but double. . . ."

"True . . . true . . . ," sighed the embarrassed husband, "but suppose (of course we all hope it will never be your case) a father has two sons at the front and he loses one of them, there is still one left to console him . . . while. . . ."

"Yes," answered the other, getting cross, "a son left to console him but also a son left for whom he must survive, while in the case of the father of an only son if the son dies the father can die too and put an end to his distress. Which of the two positions is worse? Don't you see how my case would be worse than yours?"

"Nonsense," interrupted another traveler, a fat, red-faced man with bloodshot eyes of the palest gray.

He was panting. From his bulging eyes seemed to spurt inner violence of an uncontrolled vitality which his weakened body could hardly contain.

"Nonsense," he repeated, trying to cover his mouth with his hand so as to hide the two missing front teeth. "Nonsense. Do we give life to our children for our own benefit?"

The other travelers stared at him in distress. The one who had had his son at the front since the first day of the war sighed: "You are right. Our children do not belong to us; they belong to the Country. . . ."

"Bosh," retorted the fat traveler. "Do we think of the Country when we give life to our children? Our sons are born because . . . well, because they must be born, and when they come to life they take our own life with them. This is the truth. We belong to them but they never belong to us. And when they reach twenty they are exactly what we were at their age. We too had a father and a mother, but there were so many other things as well . . . girls, cigarettes, illusions, new ties . . . and the Country, of course, whose call we would have answered — when we were twenty — even if father and mother had said no. Now at our age, the love of our Country is still great, of course, but stronger than it is the love for our children. Is there any one of us here who wouldn't gladly take his son's place at the front if he could?"

There was a silence all round, everybody nodding as to approve.

"Why then," continued the fat man, "shouldn't we consider the feelings of our children when they are twenty? Isn't it natural that at their age they should consider the love for their Country (I am speaking of decent boys, of course) even greater than the love for us? Isn't it natural that it should be so, as after all they must look upon us as upon old boys who cannot move any more and must stay at home? If Country exists, if Country is a natural necessity, like bread, of which each of us must eat in order not to die of hunger, somebody must go to defend it. And our sons go, when they are twenty, and they don't want tears, because if they die, they die inflamed and happy (I am speaking, of course, of decent boys). Now, if one dies young and happy without having the ugly sides of life, the boredom of it, the pettiness, the bitterness of disillusion . . . what more can we ask for him? Everyone should stop crying; every one should laugh, as I do . . . or at least thank God — as I do — because my son, before dying, sent me a message saying that he was dying satisfied at having ended his life in the best way he could have wished. That is why, as you see, I do not even wear mourning. . . ."

He shook his light fawn coat so as to show it; his livid lip over his missing teeth was trembling, his eyes were watery and motionless, and soon after he ended with a shrill laugh which might well have been a sob.

"Quite so . . . quite so . . ." agreed the others.

The woman who, bundled in a corner under her coat, had been sitting and listening had — for the last three months — tried to find in the words of her husband and her friends something to console her in her deep sorrow, something that might show her how a mother should resign herself to send her son not even to death but to a probable danger of life. Yet not a word had she found amongst the many which had been said . . . and her grief had been greater in seeing that nobody — as she thought — could share her feelings.

But now the words of the traveler amazed and almost stunned her. She suddenly realized that it wasn't the others who were wrong and who could not understand her but herself who could not rise up to the same height of those fathers and mothers willing to resign themselves, without crying, not only to the departure of their sons but even to their death.

She lifted her head, she bent over from her corner trying to listen with great attention to the details which the fat man was giving to his companions about the way his son had fallen as a hero, for his King and his Country, happy and without regrets. It seemed to her that she had stumbled into a world she had never dreamed of, a world so far unknown to her, and she was so pleased to hear everyone joining in congratulating that brave father who could so stoically speak of his child's death.

Then suddenly, just as if she had heard nothing of what had been said and almost as if waking up from a dream, she turned to the old man, asking him:

"Then . . . is your son really dead?"

Everybody stared at her. The old man, too, turned to look at her, fixing his great, bulging, horribly watery light-gray eyes, deep in her face. For some little time he tried to answer, but words failed him. He looked and looked at her, almost as if only then — at that silly, incongruous question — he had suddenly realized at last that his son was really dead — gone forever — forever. His face contracted, became horribly distorted; then he snatched in haste a handkerchief from his pocket and, to the amazement of everyone, broke into harrowing, heart-rending, uncontrollable sobs.

★

★ ★ ★ ★

AUTHOR: *Wolfgang Borchert (1921–1947) was born in Hamburg, Germany, and was a private in the Germany army that invaded Russia in 1941. He was wounded, bitter, and was imprisoned for his anti-war sentiments, but he nevertheless returned to the Russian front in 1944. He died shortly after the war of an unknown fever at the age of twenty-six. His stories tell of individuals facing the apocalypse of war.*

SETTING: *This story takes place in the ruins of a bombed-out German city during the Second World War. It may have been the small city of Dresden, which was bombed during the last part of the war. On February 13, 1945, 650,000 incendiary bombs were dropped by 764 Royal Air Force Lancasters and 450 American Flying Fortresses; 135,000 people perished. This "strategic bombing" of a lovely medieval town with little military value was meant to undermine the morale of the Germans. It also demonstrated the possibilities of men's evilness. In this story the cost is counted in the lives of one man and one child.*

Rats Do Sleep at Night

Wolfgang Borchert

The empty window in the lonely wall yawned blue-red, full of early evening sun. Dust clouds shimmered between the steep-stretched remains of chimneys. The ruined wilderness was dozing. His eyes were shut. Suddenly it grew still darker. He knew that someone had come and was now standing in front of him, darkly, quietly. Now they've got me! he thought. But when he blinked a little, he only saw two somewhat poorly clad legs. They were standing in front of him, rather bandy, so that he could see through between them. He risked a little blink up the trouser-legs and saw an elderly man. Who had a knife and a basket in his hand. And a little soil on his finger-tips.

This is where you sleep, eh? asked the man and looked down at the tumble of hair. Jürgen blinked at the sun between the man's legs and said:

No, I don't sleep. I have to keep guard here. The man nodded: I see, that's why you've got the big stick there I suppose? Yes, replied Jürgen bravely, and held fast to the stick.

What are you guarding, then?

I can't tell you that. He held his hands tight round the stick.

Money, I'll bet, eh? The man set the basket down and wiped the knife to and fro on the seat of his trousers.

No, not money at all, said Jürgen contemptuously. Something quite different.

Well, what then?

I can't tell you. Just something different.

Well, don't then. And of course I won't tell you what I have here in the basket. The man kicked the basket with his foot and clicked the knife shut.

Pah, I can just imagine what's in the basket, observed Jürgen disdainfully, rabbit food.

By jiminy, you're right! said the man, you're a smart lad. How old are you, then?

Nine.

Aha, think of that, so you're nine. Then you certainly know what three times nine are, eh?

Sure, said Jürgen, and to gain time he added: That's quite easy. And he looked through the man's legs. Three times nine, eh? he asked again, twenty-seven. I knew it at once.

Correct, said the man, and that's exactly the number of rabbits I've got.

Jürgen made a round mouth: Twenty-seven?

You can see them. Lots of them are still quite young. Would you like to?

But I can't. I have to keep guard, said Jürgen uncertainly.

All the time? asked the man, at night, too?

At night too. All the time. Always. Jürgen looked up the bandy legs. I've been here since Saturday, he whispered.

But don't you ever go home at all? You must eat, mustn't you?

Jürgen lifted up a stone. There was half a loaf lying there. And a tin box.

You smoke? asked the man, have you a pipe then?

Jürgen firmly clutched his stick and said timidly: I roll cigarettes. Don't like a pipe.

Pity. The man stooped towards his basket. You'd have been welcome to look at the rabbits. Specially the young ones. Perhaps you'd have chosen one for yourself. But you can't get away from here.

No, said Jürgen sadly, no, no.

The man picked up his basket and straightened up.

Well, if you *must* stay here — pity. And he turned round. Then Jürgen said quickly: if you won't give me away, it's because of the rats.

The bandy legs came back a pace: Because of the rats?

Yes, they eat dead bodies, you know. Of people. That's how they live.

Who says so?

Our teacher.

And now you're guarding the rats? asked the man.

No, not them! And then he said quite softly: My brother, he's lying under there. There. Jürgen pointed with his stick at the fallen-in walls. Our house got a bomb. All at once the light in the cellar went out. And he went, too. We shouted and shouted. He was much smaller than me. Only four. He must be here still. He's so much smaller than me.

The man looked down on the tumble of hair. And then he said suddenly: Yes, but didn't your teacher tell you that rats sleep at night?

No, whispered Jürgen and all at once looked quite tired, he didn't say that.

Well, said the man, he's a fine teacher, if he doesn't even know that. Of course the rats sleep at night. You can safely go home at night. They always sleep nights. As soon as it gets dark.

With his stick Jürgen made little holes in the rubble.

Lots of little beds those are, he thought, all little beds.

Then the man said (and his bandy legs moved restlessly): Do you know what? I'll just go and feed my rabbits now, and as soon as it's dark I'll call for you. Perhaps I can bring one with me. A little one, or what do you think?

Jürgen made little holes in the rubble. Lots of little rabbits. White, grey, white-grey. I don't know, he said softly, and looked up the bandy legs, if they *really* sleep at night.

The man climbed over the remains of the wall out on to the street. Of course they do, he said from there, your teacher ought to pack it in, if he doesn't even know that.

Then Jürgen stood up and asked: Can I really have one? A white one perhaps?

I'll see what I can do, shouted the man, already walking away, but you'll have to wait for me here. Then I'll come home with you, see? I'll

have to tell your father how to build a rabbit hutch. For you'd have to
know how.

Yes, shouted Jürgen. I'll wait. I'll have to keep guard anyway, till it
gets dark. I'll wait for certain. And he shouted: We've still got some boards
at home. Boxboards, he shouted.

But the man was already out of earshot. With his bandy legs he was
running towards the sun. It was already red with evening and Jürgen could
see how it shone through his legs, they were so bandy. And the basket
swung excitedly to and fro. There was rabbit food in it. Green rabbit food,
a little grey from the rubble.

★

★ ★ ★ ★

AUTHOR: *Muhammad Salih Haydara, like many of Yemen's writers, is deeply involved with politics. His works portray the past as a time of great suffering and the present as a time of struggle. The future is, however, a vision of hopefulness. Individuals are warm and liberated, somehow immune to the vagaries and costs of war.*

SETTING: *In 1962 rebellious army officers overthrew the monarchy of Yemen, starting a war that lasted until 1970. In 1978 the pro-Western Yemen Arab Republic (North Yemen) accused the Soviet-backed People's Democratic Republic of Yemen (South Yemen) of murdering its president, which precipitated the 1979 Yemenite Civil War. There was very little peace until the two countries were reunited in 1991. This story is not only a story of the war era but also a reminder of the political importance of natural resources — in this case, water.*

The Imprint of Blackness
Muhammad Salih Haydara

In the distance rose the lofty peaks of a wide circle of mountains. From the core of these mountains issued relatively high hills that stretched across the intervening space. Numerous valleys opened into one valley in which the torrents that poured from the high ground when it rained collected and were channelled towards irrigation-outlets for extensive farm lands.

This was the natural world on which my eyes first opened. By the time I was just over three years old, I had not grasped its true nature. I observed it simple-mindedly. The abundance of the milk I drank, which came from the udders of goats, depended on rainfall and the flourishing of the pastures; the little bits of bread I was used to eating came from the earth; when rain did not fall and drought prevailed, the ground became arid, and widespread famine and destitution was the result: all this I came to comprehend at a later date; but, at the age of three, I was concerned only with having enough to eat. I paid no attention to the natural environment

---

Translated by Lorne M. Kenny and Thomas G. Ezzy. "The Imprint of Blackness" is reprinted from *The Literature of Modern Arabia: An Anthology,* ed. Salma Khadra Jayyusi (Austin, Tex.: Univ. of Texas Press, 1988) by permission of the author and publisher.

of which I was a part.

Our village was a collection of box-like houses, one or two storeys high, that lay at the foot of one of the hills. Some of them resembled, architecturally, fortified citadels, while others were made of clay or goats' hair. These architectural distinctions did not reflect the tastes or desires of the occupants; rather, they gave clear testimony to their varying material and social conditions. Wealth called for the building of fortresses and two-storey homes, while poverty dictated clay and goats' hair. The village had not been set up this way originally, for our people, tribal in nature, once possessed rights over equal amounts of property. Need had forced some of them to sell or mortgage part of their land to those who, anticipating times of famine, possessed money or seed. One outsider, for example, had come to our village with money and cunning, and had made it a practice to lie in wait for those in need. Thus, he came to dwell in a large, castle-like house, and owned scores of acres of fertile land. I was not aware of these facts at that time.

When I was four years old, violent rains fell on the mountains and slopes, sending heavy floods down the valley. It was my first experience of this natural force. People rushed towards the fields with a joy and energy I had not noticed before, and I did not understand why they were behaving this way. I found myself and a band of village children racing along with the people, each of us holding on to his father's or mother's gown, paying no attention to the threat of injury in this rushing tide of humanity, and joyful in this happy, boisterous procession.

Our childish joyfulness, however, disappeared, followed by shock, at our first sight of the colour of blood. The red drops that flowed from the head of one of the men jolted our tender and innocent sensibilities. Two men had been arguing fiercely at one of the sluice-gates; one of them had struck the other on the head with a stone, and the latter had drawn a knife and buried it in the former's back. Blood gushed out and he had fallen unconscious into the torrent. People gathered to lift him out before the rushing water carried him away.

Instinctively, I hurried toward my father, who was busy repairing an outlet through which the flooding water had broken. The owner of the adjacent land was widening this outlet and taking away the mud which my father was putting back in place. It was a ludicrous sight.

People were intervening to prevent what had happened a few moments earlier from happening again, when some men who were wearing coarse, unfamiliar clothes came on the scene. They carried long wooden rods with holes in the upper ends (I learned later that these were rifles), and some of them were leading the man who'd stabbed the other. One of them pointed at my father. At this, cries arose and hands reached out but, finally, my father was led away, while the owner of the neighbouring land was left free. Angrily, I hung on to my mother's skirt. I felt an overpowering urge to go after my father as he left, but my mother held on to me tightly. Meanwhile our neighbour, paying no attention to the armed strangers, widened the outlet as he wished, until our own land was left completely without water.

I became tormented by an inner compulsion, an urgent need to understand the meaning of what I'd seen that afternoon: my father's leaving with the armed men and his failure to return. My mother's anxiety and sorrowful silence gave me no rest. They doubled my bewilderment and kindled my desire to get to the bottom of what had been taking place around me. As she was preparing supper, my mother noticed my anxiety and wondered at it. By the time supper was ready I had gone to bed. Amazed at my going to sleep so early, she woke me up. I said I would not get up until I knew what had happened to my father. She tried to mollify me with a few words, adding that the time had not come for me to know, that I would understand it later. I refused supper and pretended to go to sleep. A demon raged in my mind — a sudden insomnia kept my nerves on edge.

I heard my mother talking to herself and understood that she was giving vent to her anger:

"It's like this every rainy season! The land can't enjoy the rain, and now my man has been taken to prison! The authorities are hypocrites! They give judgements that favour whoever pays the most! They won't even give us a chance to feel happy at the rain — they snatch the joy out of our hearts! It is a tyranny that never ends!"

An unfamiliar agony took me over: my little frame trembled, and tears poured from my eyes, but there was no insight to help me understand the situation. All my efforts to grasp precisely what was going on were in vain; they were like speaking into a void. My brain was wrapped up in a dark, mysterious cloud, which left an imprint of blackness on it . . .

The wizened face of the mountains and rolling foothills vanished, covered by a mantle of green — a glorious display of our natural environment's radiance and splendour. My mother would go out early in the day to take the flocks of sheep to high ground, leaving her small baby on the floor. I pitied the little one's condition: swarms of flies gathered on his little mouth while he slept and, when awake, he would cry ceaselessly. He would eat dirt and whatever else fell within his grasp.

I saw children somewhat older than I taking on the task of shepherding the flocks, often at the insistence of their families. I no longer remember how I came to the decision to follow their example. My mother was startled when I told her that I was going to do the shepherding in her place. She disagreed on the grounds that the time had not yet come for that. When she saw she could not dissuade me, she entrusted me to the rest of the children.

In time I became accustomed to it, and learned to love deeply my fellow-shepherds. We would go out together in the morning and, at noon, would divide up the dry, round loaves of bread and make tea beside some stream. Before evening we would be on our way home to the village. Those were days of cloudless happiness. We wore only a knee-length garment (most of us had only one) for months on end. On moonlit nights we would get together, late into the night, and play various games. Then we would sleep and set out again before dawn . . .

Time imparted a severity — or, more accurately, a stubborn patience — to my mother. The lack of news of my father gave rise to uneasiness in the village, in my mother and in myself.

One night, when the village was peaceful as usual, with no sign of life other than the faint glow of lamps that issued from the narrow windows and died out one by one, and while we children were playing as usual, a company of armed soldiers encircled the village. Having left their vehicles at the bottom of the slope, they invaded the village on foot. Groups of them took up positions at the entrances to the village, while others surrounded our house. Carrying a light in their hands, they knocked loudly on the door. We youngsters scattered amongst them. The door opened and there stood my mother.

"Where is he?" one of them asked, several times.

Close up, I could see my mother's astonishment. Mindful of the soldier's irate arrogance, she pointed to me and said:

"I have no man except him, and a suckling infant inside! As for my husband, *you* took him by force — you, or others like you!"

"You're lying!" retorted the man sharply. "He is hiding inside!"

All together they burst through the door, almost knocking my mother to the ground. I was seized by a furious anger. I thought of picking up a stone to crash down on the head of one of those roughnecks. My mother put her arms about me and looked at them in amazement. She was truly baffled that they should be searching for a man they had put in prison.

The soldiers withdrew and those who had blocked off the entrances to the village went away with them. They left, however, a huge unanswered question in our home. We could not settle down all night, plunged as we were into a wide sea of anxiety and confusion. The impact of these events on my limited imagination was to thrust me into a whirlpool that seemed truly impenetrable. But all this translated itself in my mind into a protest against a wrong, that I did not understand, being perpetrated on us.

Gradually, this undefined resentment would advance towards a more precise awareness of its object. In retrospect, I later came to realize that such a quest for awareness is an element of basic intelligence which, if a child acquires it early in life, will have important consequences: resentment, hatred, even love, should not be allowed to subside into the unconscious without having been subjected to the ordeal of a long and exhaustive examination, which may take years, in order to find answers to the question of *why* we resent, or hate, or love. This, along with just reasoning, ensures the soundness and legitimacy of one's emotions, and results in stability and constancy . . .

My ordeal increased in severity. I became more and more concerned about my father, felt more attached to him. In my imagination I pictured him as a great man and listened in on various conversations to learn more about him. I decided to go to the city, where the authorities and the prison were located. I did not know how to begin, but no one would listen to me, for in our tradition, no one pays any attention to what children say: the general rule followed by grown-ups is to brush them off harshly.

Leaving the narrow confines of our village for the city, which seemed to me another world despite the fact that it was only a country town, was my first venture. I then decided to break into the prison, but the difficult question was, how?

As I was searching for a means to this end, somehow my feet led me up to the prison wall at a spot where I was able to climb up to look in at a window. I fell against it, however, and smashed the glass. I ran, but could not evade the guards. Powerful blows fell on my face and I was put in jail where I was greeted with great surprise. One of the inmates told me that my father and a few others had escaped from the prison and had probably headed north.

The setting sun was tinging the horizon with yellow when the door opened and I was released. My ear was pinched several times and I was threatened with some very forceful advice.

I wandered through the city as darkness fell. Ordinarily, a child my age would not dare to undertake the long distance between the city and our village while night ruled the highway. But I was feeling strangled by the strangeness of the city and it would have been unbearable for me to remain there.

Fighting back my fear of what the pitch darkness might be hiding, I decided to take the risk and left. The trees took on frightening shapes for me, which made my imagination run wild. From time to time I lost my way, bumping into a tree or boulder or falling into a ditch.

My mother, anxious as she'd been, met me with a painful beating, even before offering me any food. But her anger did not last long for, once she knew everything, she realized her error of hastiness. In her joy at my escape from the wild animals which, it was said, prowled the valley under cover of night, she had a ram slaughtered.

The meat was very tasty.

We had not finished supper when we heard a light knock on the door.

"Who's knocking?" she asked, in a loud voice.

Bidding her to keep her voice down, he opened the door.

It might not be possible for me to describe our feelings exactly, so I shall content myself by saying that the warmth of our joy compensated for the lack of burning coals in our hearth on that very chilly winter's night.

Father did not pay much attention to us or to news about the land or the people. Most of his concern was focused on the little one who had been born in his absence. A fountain of love had burst forth inside him: he examined the baby's features as though to engrave them on his mind, in view of possible future eventualities.

Before I went to bed, he embraced me:

"Plant the seeds of jasmine and sweet flowers in your soul for the motherland," he said. "Water them constantly with the life blood that flows through your veins so that they may blossom to spread a pure fragrance within you for the sake of our land, honour and freedom. Let your heart be a skilful and vigilant gardener, tending the motherland's flowers inside you, watering them lest they wither away. You must show yourself mature, for you are the man of the house and of our land. You represent me to others."

My young breast swarmed with fervent emotions so that I could not speak.

"My little son, we have dedicated ourselves to the motherland.[1] We have taken our lives into our own hands and do not know whether we shall die from one moment to the next, or whether we shall live to a ripe old age and see our struggle crowned with shining success. I am entrusting you with everything — with my weapons and the convictions that lie deep within me. I am telling you all this now because I will be leaving with the dawn, while you are still asleep. Goodbye!"

Conflicting feelings, which I had never before experienced, struggled deep inside me, along with a powerful love for the man who would be going away in a few hours and who possibly would never return. This generated a powerful insomnia that kept sleep away.

In the following days, things seemed different to me. I possessed the germ of a strong conviction which was, inevitably, to become clearer to me: through it, the rancour that had appeared as a small imprint on my mind was transformed, took on new dimensions and a rational character which justified its existence. I dared not act except in accordance with his parting admonitions, because his shadow dominated my movements and thoughts. I conducted myself as though he were present among us.

And when the news that he had been killed in a cruel fashion finally reached us, I was not filled with fear or grief for a single moment. Instead, I fired several shots from his rifle — a resonant kind of weeping which was, at the same time, an expression of pride. I kept my father's admonitions before my eyes, feeling them in every cell of my body and putting them into practice with scrupulous attention. And at their head I added another principle of my own, defined by my initial imprint of blackness: namely, that no piece of land should ever, under the protection of armed soldiers, have its fill of water while another piece of land remained thirsty.

★

Note

1. He is speaking here of the long political struggle in Yemen against the Imam prior to the 1962 revolution.

★ ★ ★ ★

AUTHOR: *Ghassan Kanafani (1936–1972), spokesman for the Popular Front for the Liberation of Palestine and supporter of the Arab Nationalist Movement, will probably be remembered less for his political activism than for his literary works. He wrote of the personal and social problems of the Palestinian refugee community, of which he was a part. At the age of twelve, he fled Acre, his birthplace, with his family, joining thousands of others in Damascus, Syria. He worked as a teacher, journalist, political spokesman, and writer in Damascus and Beirut. In 1972 he was killed by a booby-trapped car. His best-known works include* Men in the Sun, The Deceived, *and* Umm Saad.

SETTING: *The Arab-Israeli War of 1948–1949 was a direct consequence of the Balfour Amendment, which established the state of Israel. Arab armed forces from Egypt, Syria, Transjordan, Lebanon, and Iraq invaded Israel on May 14, 1948, and took control of territory in southern and eastern Palestine. The Israelis managed to halt the Arab advance, and the United Nations secured a four-week truce in June. Fighting resumed in July, and the Israeli forces gained territory until another truce went into effect for about three months. Israeli forces then pushed back the Arab armies on all fronts and gained possession of the Negev desert region. At the end of the war, Israel occupied most of the disputed areas in Palestine, had increased its territory by about one-half, and had developed a formidable standing army. Approximately four hundred thousand Palestinians fled Israel – in response to the war itself, in fear of retribution, or because of fear tactics and propaganda. They sought refuge in the surrounding Arab states. Some were integrated into local economies; others lived the remainder of their lives in refugee camps.*

The Land of Sad Oranges

Ghassan Kanafani

When we set out from Jaffa for Acre there was nothing tragic about our departure. We were just like anybody who goes to spend the festival season every year in another city. Our time in Acre passed as usual, with nothing untoward. I was young then, and so I probably enjoyed those days because they kept me from going to school. But whatever the fact of

---

Translated by Hilary Kilpatrick. "The Land of Sad Oranges" is reprinted from *Men in the Sun* (Washington, D.C.: Three Continents Press, 1983) by permission of the publisher.

the matter, the picture gradually became clearer on the night of the great attack on Acre. That night passed, cruel and bitter, amidst the despondency of the men and the prayers of the women. You and I and the others of our age were too young to understand what the story meant from beginning to end, but that night the threads began to grow clearer. In the morning, when the Jews withdrew, threatening and fuming, a big lorry was standing at the door of our house. A simple collection of bedding was being thrown into it, from here and there, quickly and feverishly. I was standing leaning against the ancient wall of the house when I saw your mother climb into the lorry, followed by your aunt and the children. Your father started tossing you and your brothers and sisters into the lorry, and on top of the belongings, and then he seized me from my corner and lifted me over his head into the iron rack on the roof of the driver's cab, where I found my brother Riyad sitting quietly. The lorry was already moving off before I had settled myself into a comfortable position. Beloved Acre was already disappearing behind the bends in the road going up to Ras Naqoura.

It was rather cloudy, and a chilly feeling invaded my body. Riyad was sitting quite quietly, with his legs hanging over the edge of the rack, leaning his back against the luggage, as he stared into the sky. I sat silently, with my chin between my knees and my arms wrapped round them. The groves of orange trees followed each other in succession along the side of the road. We were all eaten up with fear. The lorry panted over the damp earth, and the sound of distant shots rang out like a farewell.

When Ras Naqoura came into sight in the distance, cloudy on the blue horizon, the lorry stopped. The women climbed down over the luggage and made for a peasant sitting cross-legged with a basket of oranges just in front of him. They picked up the oranges, and the sound of their weeping reached our ears. I thought then that oranges were something dear and these big, clean fruits were beloved objects in our eyes. When the women had bought some oranges, they brought them over to the lorry and your father climbed down from the driver's side and stretched out his hand to take one. He began to gaze at it in silence, and then burst into tears like a despairing child.

In Ras Naqoura our lorry stopped beside many others. The men began handing their weapons to the policeman stationed there for the purpose, and as our turn came and I saw the rifles and machine-guns lying on the table and looked towards the long line of lorries entering Lebanon, rounding the bends in the roads and putting more and more distance between themselves and the land of the oranges, I too burst into a storm of weeping. Your mother was still looking silently at the orange. And all the orange trees which your father had abandoned to the Jews shone in his eyes, all the well-tended orange trees which he had bought one by one were printed on his face and reflected in the tears which he could not control in front of the officer at the police post.

In the afternoon, when we reached Sidon, we had become refugees.

We were among those swallowed up by the road. Your father looked as though it was a long time since he had slept. He was standing in the street in front of the belongings heaped on the ground, and I quite imagined that if I ran over to say something to him he would explode in my face: "Damn your father! Damn . . . !" Those two oaths were clearly etched on his face. I myself, a child educated in a strict religious school, at that moment doubted whether this God really wanted to make men happy. I also doubted whether this God could hear and see everything. The coloured pictures which were handed out to us in the school chapel showing the Lord having compassion on children and smiling in their faces seemed like another of the lies made up by people who open strict schools in order to get higher fees. I was sure that the God we had known in Palestine had left it too, and was a refugee in some place which I did not know, unable to find a solution to his own problems. And we, human refugees, sitting on the pavement waiting for a new Fate to bring some solution, were responsible for providing a roof under which to spend the night. Pain had begun to undermine the child's simple mind.

Night is a fearful thing. The darkness which gradually came down over us cast terror into my heart. The mere thought that I would spend the night on the pavement aroused all kinds of fears within me. They were cruel and harsh. No one was prepared to have pity on me. I could not find anyone to console me. Your father's silent glance cast fresh terror into my breast. The orange which your mother held in her hand set my head on fire. Everyone was silent, staring at the black road, keen for Fate to appear round the corner and hand out solutions to our difficulties, so that we could follow him to some shelter. Suddenly Fate did come; your uncle had reached the town before us, and he was our fate.

Your uncle never had great faith in ethics, and when he found himself on the pavement like us he lost it entirely. He made for a house occupied by a Jewish family, opened the door, threw his belongings inside and jerked his round face at them, saying very distinctly: "Go to Palestine!" It is certain that they did not go, but they were frightened by his desperation, and they went into the next room, leaving him to enjoy the roof and tiled floor.

Your uncle led us to that shelter of his and pitched us into it with his belongings and family. During the night we slept on the floor, and it was completely taken up with our small bodies. We used the men's coats for coverings, and when we got up in the morning we found that the men had passed the night sitting up. The tragedy had begun to eat into our very souls.

We did not stay long in Sidon. Your uncle's room was not large enough for half of us, but it held us for three nights. Then your mother asked your father to look for some job, or let us return to the orange trees. Your father shouted in her face, the rancour trembling in his voice, and she fell silent. Our family problems had begun. The happy, united family we had left behind, with the land, the house, and the martyrs killed defending them.

I don't know where your father got the money from. I know that he sold the gold he had bought for your mother when he wanted to make her happy and proud that she was his wife. But the gold did not bring in a sum large enough to solve our problems. There must have been another source. Did he borrow at all? Did he sell something else he had brought away without us noticing? I don't know. But I do remember that we moved to a village on the outskirts of Sidon, and there your father sat on the high stone balcony, smiling for the first time and waiting for the fifteenth of May in order to return in the wake of the victorious armies.

The fifteenth of May came, after a bitter period of waiting. At exactly midnight your father poked me with his foot as I lay asleep and said in a voice vibrant with hope: "Get up and see for yourself as the Arab armies enter Palestine." I was up like a shot, and we clambered down barefoot over the hills to the main road, which lay a full kilometer from the village. All of us, young and old, panted as we ran like madmen. The lights of the lorries climbing to Ras Naqoura shone in the distance. When we got to the road we felt cold but your father's shout drove everything else from our minds. He had begun to race after the lorries like a small boy. He was calling out to them. He was giving hoarse shouts and gasping for breath, but still he raced along after the string of lorries like a little boy. We ran along beside him, shouting in unison with him. The friendly soldiers were looking at us from under their helmets, silent and motionless. We were gasping for breath. Meanwhile your father, racing along despite his fifty years, pulled cigarettes out of his pocket to throw to the soldiers and went on shouting to them. We were still running along beside him, like a little flock of goats.

Suddenly the lorries were at an end. We went back to the house exhausted, our breathing coming with a low whistle as we gasped for air. Your father was absolutely silent, and we too were incapable of speech. When the lights of a passing car fell on your father's face his cheeks were wet with tears.

Things dragged past extremely slowly after that. The communiqués deceived us, and then the truth in all its bitterness cheated us. Despondency found its way back to people's faces. Your father began to find enormous difficulty in mentioning Palestine and talking of the happy past spent in his plantations and houses. And we were the ones who formed the massive walls of the tragedy which dominated his new life, as well as being the wretches who discovered, without any difficulty at all, that the idea behind climbing the hills in the early morning, as your father ordered, was to distract us from demanding breakfast.

Complications set in. In some extraordinary way the simplest thing was enough to rouse your father. I remember perfectly the time when someone asked him for something — I neither know nor recall what. He shuddered, and then began trembling as though he had received an electric shock. His eyes glittered as they roamed over our faces. A diabolical thought had implanted itself in his brain, and he jumped up like a man who has found a satisfactory conclusion. Overwhelmed by his awareness that he was able to put an end to his difficulties, and by the dread of someone who is about to undertake a momentous action, he began to mutter to himself as he turned round and round, looking for something we could not see. Then he pounced on a chest which had accompanied us from Acre and started to scatter its contents with terrible nervous movements. Your mother had understood everything in an instant and, caught up in the agitation which mothers feel when their children are exposed to danger, she set about pushing us out of the room and telling us to run away to the mountain. But we stayed by the window. We plastered our little ears to its shutters, and heard your father's voice: "I want to kill them. I want to kill myself. I want to be done with . . . I want . . ."

Your father fell silent. When we looked into the room again, through the cracks in the door, we saw him lying on the ground, gasping for breath and grinding his teeth as he wept, while your mother sat at one side watching him anxiously.

We did not understand. But I remember that when I saw the black revolver lying on the floor beside him I understood everything. Driven by the mortal terror of a child who has suddenly caught sight of an ogre, I ran off towards the mountain, fleeing from the house.

As I left the house behind, I left my childhood behind too. I realized that our life had ceased to be pleasant, and it was no longer easy for us to live in peace. Things had reached the point where the only solution was a bullet in the head of each one of us. So we must take care to behave suitably in all that we did, not asking for something to eat even when we were hungry, keeping silent when your father spoke of his difficulties and nodding and smiling when he said to us: "Go and climb the mountain, and don't come back till midday."

I returned home in the evening, when dusk had fallen. Your father was still ill and your mother was sitting beside him. Your eyes all had a cat-like glitter and your lips were sealed as though they had never been opened, as though they were the scars left by an old wound not properly healed.

You were huddled there, as far from your childhood as you were from the land of the oranges — the oranges which, according to a peasant who used to cultivate them until he left, would shrivel up if a change occurred and they were watered by a strange hand.

Your father was still ill in bed. Your mother was choking back the tears of a tragedy which has not left her eyes till now. I slipped into the room like a pariah. When my glance fell on your father's face which was twitching with impotent fury I saw at the same moment the black revolver lying on the low table, and beside it an orange.

The orange was dried-up and shrivelled.

★

★ ★ ★ ★

AUTHOR: *Mahmoud Diab (1932--) was born in Ismailiyya, Egypt. Although he was educated in law, he is best known for his plays. His play* The Storm *represented Egypt at a UNESCO competition.*

SETTING: *The country of Egypt has had a long history, one in which the periods of war and peace seem to follow each other with predictable regularity. In this century, Egypt has been a participant in two world wars, in at least four wars with neighboring countries, and has experienced almost unremitting internal conflict. Each war has meant the destruction of the lives and homes of both rich and poor. The storyteller remembers his childhood home – his father's modest home in Ismailiyya – destroyed by a bomb in an air raid during World War II.*

A House for My Children

Mahmoud Diab

It isn't possible that the idea occurred to me suddenly, for I had always dreamed of having a house. Though in my dreams its features were not sharply defined, it was characterized by a general enveloping air of warmth and serenity. When, therefore, the chance presented itself I grasped it as though my life depended on it.

While the idea was not a sudden one to me, it came as a surprise to my wife, who was unable to hold back her tears for excitement. I didn't in fact surprise her with it as an idea, which would not have caused her such excitement, but in the form of an actual contract for a vacant plot of land on a new housing estate in the eastern part of the city.

This was on the birthday of my children, Hala and Hisham. The former was four years old and the latter three. Born in the same month, though not on the same day, we used to celebrate their birthdays together.

On returning home that day my wife asked me:

"Have you forgotten that today's the children's birthday?"

"No, I haven't forgotten," I said softly, attempting to conceal my restlessness.

"Don't tell me you're broke," she said slyly.

"No, I'm not broke."

"They've been waiting for you and yet I see you've come back without even troubling to buy them a piastre's worth of sweets," she said, indicating my empty hands.

"I'm fed up with getting them only toys and sweets."

Unable to prepare the way for the surprise any better than this, I produced a large envelope from under my arm and handed it to her.

"My present's in the envelope," I said, and she took out the contract and ran her eyes over it while I watched her in an ecstasy of pride. Failing to understand what it was about at first glance, she raised her beautiful face inquiringly.

"What's this?" she cried.

"It's a house for them," I said smiling.

Hisham crept out from behind, and buried his face between my legs and gave a soft laugh. I bent over, picked him up and began kissing him, oblivious of the unexpected results my surprise had wrought in my wife.

From that moment great changes came over her. No longer did she bring up the old story of my love affair which she had found out about some days ago. Whether she had forgotten about it or merely pretended to have done so I don't know. She also became more tender and gay and there wasn't a relative or friend of hers to whom she didn't announce the news of the house we'd be building. In fact she no longer enjoyed talking to me about anything else.

We went, the four of us, to the plot of land the following day, in order, as she put it, "to give it the once over." We stood by one corner of it, she beside me, radiant with smiles, while Hala and Hisham ran races nearby, shouting and stirring up little eddies of dust.

My wife was outlining what the house would be like and went on unconsciously repeating herself, "It'll be a single storey, won't it? But when the children get bigger we'll add another one. We'll surround it with a large garden. I'd love a house of mine to have a garden. I'll look after it myself. I'll fill it with flowers. What sort of flowers do you like, darling? Isn't it funny that for five whole years I've never known what flowers you liked?"

"I like jasmine," I said.

"We'll cover the garden with jasmine," she cried. Then: "Living in a house like this so far away from the smoke and din of the city is beautifully healthy for the children. My grandfather used to have a lovely house in

Mansoura — it had an acre of garden. Imagine! By the way, you must make provision for a laundry room on the roof, also a servants' room . . ."

"What do you mean by a servants' room?" I cut her short. "I've spent precious years of my life turning a dream into reality and I'd ask you not to turn it into a nonsense!"

"All right — and the garage, the house must have a garage."

"But I don't own a car."

"You'll have a car some time and where would you put it if the house didn't have a garage?"

She called out to Hala to bring back her brother, then she let out a shrill laugh and raced after her children with the gaiety of a young girl.

My thoughts wandered far afield as I watched the three of them in the middle of the plot of land. Only when my wife returned and was standing by me did I come to. She repeated what she had told me before, embroidering on it, while I replied to her in between my thoughts with "yes" or "no," without paying any attention to what she was saying.

I remembered an old house, far away in both time and place. The place was the town of Ismailiyya; as to the time, I am able to fix in terms of my age, for at that time I was eight or nine years old. We owned a house in that town, a modest single-storey house surrounded by a small but beautiful garden. It did not, however, possess a servants' room, for we had no servants; nor did it have a garage, for my father had never been in a private motorcar in his life. I remember that there was a trellis of vines in our garden, and two mango trees, a lemon tree, and a large hen house. I also remember that my father would not be in the house for a minute before he'd take up the hoe and wield it in the garden, the fence of which was covered in strands of jasmine. I don't remember when it was we came to own that house or when we moved into it. I do remember, though, that my father was extremely proud if it, while my mother regarded our coming into possession of it as a stupendous and historic event. She had thus made of it a set date by which she fixed the events of her life and those of the whole family. Many is the time I have heard her say:

"When we moved to the house I was pregnant with so-and-so-" or "when we bought the house my husband's salary was so much . . ." and similar expressions which I still smile at when I recollect them.

I don't remember any particular happenings that occurred at home during that period other than the birth of one of my brothers, the fifth of us all and the third male child. No doubt the other incidents were all so commonplace that they have left no special impression on my mind. I do remember, though, that when evening came a group of our neighbors would turn up to see my father and they'd gather out in the garden and converse on various topics, while we children would play around them, and the breezes of spring would blow drowsily, made sluggish with the aroma of jasmine. It must be that it was ever spring in our house in those days, for I can scarcely imagine it now without games in the garden and the smell of jasmine.

Then some events occurred which did not immediately break the monotony of life. For this reason I can scarcely remember them now in detail though I do remember vague echoes of them, as for instance that I began hearing the word "war", a word new to me being repeated at home far more frequently than the word "bread"; it was also constantly used by the grown-ups in our street without my understanding its meaning to begin with. There were other words I learned by heart despite their difficulty and strangeness because of the way they were repeated: "The Allies — the Axis — the Germans — the Maginot Line" and others, all of which were mere words that I chanced to hear.

My father and our neighbors gathered in the garden would talk only about such matters. They would divide up into two opposing factions, one wanting victory for the English and the other praying that the Germans would win. My father belonged to the latter faction, and I, in my turn, prayed for a German victory. Often I would hear my father say, "A German victory means that the English would get out of Egypt," though Uncle Hassan, our nearest neighbour, believed that if the English got out of Egypt it would mean the Germans entering it. The grown-ups would carry on long animated discussions which would end on one night, only to begin again on another, while we children, in our games, would divide ourselves up into two groups, one "the English" and the other "the Germans". I naturally belonged to the latter. We would then indulge in childish warfare which left us puffing and blowing to the point of exhaustion.

When it was time to go to sleep I would slip into bed and lie there for a time listening to the voices of the grown-ups in the garden. I would single out my father's voice among them and would then try to conjure up a picture of the Germans. I did not picture the Germans as being the same size as the English or as looking like them, but saw them as both larger and more magnificent.

One night the air raid warning sounded. That, too, was something new and exciting in those days. The lights in the street and the houses went out and darkness, weighed down with tense silence, ruled. Ghostly forms gathered at the doorways and the scent of jasmine was diffused more strongly than on any previous night.

"German aeroplanes!" shouted my father. Gazing up at the sky and listening intently, I was able to make out a disjointed humming that cut through the solid darkness at the horizon's end and drew nearer.

"Will they bomb the town?" I asked my mother in terror. "No," my father answered her in the tones of someone well-informed on such matters. "Hitler wouldn't do that. They're merely making for the English camps."

English camps surrounded our small town on all sides, indeed were almost touching it. We heard terrible explosions which I don't remember ceasing for an instant. An aeroplane burst into flames in the sky; then ghostly forms with heavy tread passed by announcing to the rushing people that the planes were laying waste the town and advising them to keep away from the houses.

Bands of phantom figures rushed out, running and stumbling in the street. Our parents got up and hurried us off with the terrified crowds towards the desert which stretched to the northeast of the city; there was no other place of escape.

That night seemed like nothing so much as the gathering of the dead at the end of the world. This was how father expressed it and my mother later repeated his words. People were pushing one another about crazily, barefoot in their night-gowns, calling out to one another in the midst of that solid darkness. "Where are you Muhsin? Where are the children? Did you close the door? Let the house go to hell! Hurry up, Lawahiz! Wait for me, father," while the barking of dogs rang out in every direction. I cried as I ran, with three of my brothers and sisters — many were the children that cried in the midst of that solid darkness.

I am unable to say exactly how many people took refuge in the desert on that confused night. All I know is that the black desert was filled with them so that we were like people "at an anniversary feast of some saint — at the anniversary feast of Sheikh Hitler," as Uncle Hassan said ironically.

"Help me dig," said my father to my mother in the voice of an expert on these matters. "Dig, children! Hassan Effendi, make a hole for your children to protect them from the shrapnel."

We dug a large hole in which my father fitted us tightly together, while explosions thundered in the town and the disjointed humming filled the sky and sudden flashes of light burst forth like lightning from time to time. Then the aeroplanes were circling above us.

"They're right over our heads," shouted my father. My mother gave an anguished scream and threw herself on to us to cover us with her body. My father did likewise. Voices were raised throughout the desert ordering the people to be silent, followed by other voices telling them to shut up. I craned my neck, thrust up my head, and took a look, over my father's shoulder, at the sky in the hope of seeing a German in his aeroplane so that I might verify the picture I had stored up in my head of the Germans. However, my father violently pushed my head back into the sand.

"Why are they bombing us if it's the English they're fighting?" whispered my mother.

My father answered not a word.

"Aren't we their friends?" I asked.

"God's curse be on both of them!" my father shouted angrily.

The aeroplanes came so close to the ground that I could feel the reverberation of their engines shaking my body. Then sudden, fearful lights that whistled stripped bare the desert and were followed by shots that "sprayed the people like rain" as Uncle Hassan's wife said the day we met her for the first time two years after that night.

The shouts that rose up from the ground mingled with the explosions coming from the sky, forming an inferno of clamor that still echoes in my ears despite the passage of years. When morning came my mother gave herself up to a fit of hysterics, as did all the women around us, and it was in vain that my father attempted to bring her back to her senses.

Eventually the slaughter came to an end, the aeroplanes dissolved from our skies and the explosions and all the other noises from the heavens ceased, making way for the crazed noises of the earth, until the blackness of night melted away before the first thread of daylight.

We got up out of our hole and followed our parents in utter exhaustion, our eyes tightly closed as ordered by them lest we should see the carnage around us. We made our way to our house but didn't find it; nor did we find Uncle Hassan's house, nor a third house and half a fourth in the same street: they had all become heaps of rubble. On the heap that had been our house one of our geese roamed around in bewilderment; she was followed by one of her young of whom there had been five. There was not a trace of the scent of jasmine in the air.

Like someone in a daze my father stood looking first at the ruins, then at my mother who had been rendered speechless by the unexpected sight. The final and ghastly event of the day was to see my father crying, something I had never seen in all my life.

"A whole life's hard work gone in an instant," my mother muttered through tears.

"Thanks be to God," mumbled my father, drying his tears, "we weren't inside it." Silence enveloped us for a while, then he said, "You must emigrate into the country . . ." and in "emigrate" I learned a new word that day.

"Let's go now to your aunt's house," my father resumed, "if it too hasn't been destroyed, until we arrange our affairs."

The melancholy procession re-formed and off we went with miserable gait, "as though at a funeral" — as I used to say whenever I recounted the story to my friends when I had grown up. Before moving away from the ruins of our house I saw my father pick up a protruding piece of stone and hurl it at the big heap of rubble.

"When the war ends," I heard him say, "we'll return and build it again."

And the war ended. . . .

My reverie was broken by a jog at my shoulder and my wife's voice saying, "What's wrong with you? Aren't you listening? When shall we start building?"

The spectre of the ruins of our house still filled my head.

"Those people who invented all these terrible means of destruction," I said, "why didn't they think of inventing something to protect houses against them?"

Surprise appeared on my wife's face. She stared into mine with questioning tenderness. I smiled and added, sighing and waving my hand as though to chase away my thoughts, "It doesn't matter, because I don't believe there'll be another war."

Which only increased the signs of surprise on my dear wife's face.

★

★ ★ ★ ★

AUTHOR: *In the 1920s, Mykola Khvylovy (1893–1933) was one of the most strident members of the Ukrainian cultural renaissance. An ardent Communist and Ukrainian nationalist, he resisted the Russianization of Ukrainian literature. He wrote short stories, poems, and novels, many of which have been translated into English. The following story was first published in 1924.*

SETTING: *This story takes place in the Ukraine during the revolutionary upheavals that followed the First World War. It presents a situation that typifies the conflict between nationalism (identified with the church) and communism in Eastern Europe. The Ukrainian Autocephalous Church, which had been established by Ukrainian nationalists in 1921, tried to ensure its own survival by deciding not to oppose the Soviet government. In 1924 it petitioned for legal status and called on Bolshevik leaders to recognize it as part of the professed Bolshevik program on national and cultural autonomy. Lenin's government, however, distrusted the church because of its earlier connections and its support of Ukrainian nationalism. In the end, all associated with it were declared anti-Soviet and anti-Revolutionary and were required to confess in writing to having engaged in anti-Soviet propaganda. The Cheka, or secret police, headed by the notorious Felix Dzerzhinski, was in charge of the purge. A Ukrainian Bolshevik official, a member of the Cheka, is the focus of this story. His very "being," or identity, is torn between all that is Ukrainian (his mother, village, and religion) and the new communist order. He makes his decision when his mother is arrested and her life is in his hands.*

My Being

Mykola Khvylovy
"To the Apple Blossom"

Out of the distant mist, out of the quiet lakes of untouchable communism, a rustling sound is heard: the Virgin Mary is walking. I reach the endless plains, cross ditches, and there, where the mounds are smouldering, I finally lean on a solitary desert cliff. I stare into darkness. Then my thoughts ride around me like Amazons. And everything

Translated by G. Tarnawsky. "My Being" by Mykola Khvylovy is reprinted from *Modern Ukrainian Short Stories*, ed. George S.N. Luckyj (Ukrainian Academic Press, 1973) by permission of the publisher: P.O. Box 6633, Englewood, CO 80155-6633.

disappears. . . . The mysterious riders gallop toward the foothills, swaying rhythmically, and the day goes out like a flame; the road winds between the ancient grave-mounds into the silent steppe. I raise my eyelashes and reminisce: . . . truly, my mother is the incarnation of this enigmatic, timeless Mary. My mother is naiveté, quiet sorrow, and endless goodness. (I remember this very well!) And my incredible pain and my unbearable torture burn in the votive lamp of fanaticism, in front of this image full of anguish.

. . . .

Mother says that I (her rebellious son) have tired myself out completely. . . . Then I take in my hands her beloved head covered with silver hair and press it to my chest . . . Behind the windowpanes, the mornings full of dew were passing, and mother-of-pearl light was descending. The impossible days were going by. In the distance, wanderers were coming out of the dark forest, halting near the blue well at the crossroads, where an ancient crucifix stood. These are young communist idealists.

But the nights pass, the evenings rustle beside the poplars, the poplars walk into the endlessness of highways, together with years and my violent youth. Then come the days before the storm. There, behind the foothills of a bluish forest, the lightnings boil and flash, and the waves of mountains foam. The heavy sultry thunder cannot manage to come through from India, from the east. And nature grows tired waiting for the storm. But one can also hear another thundering behind the boiling of the clouds — a dull cannonade. Two storms are approaching.

— Alarm! Mother says that she was watering the mint in the garden, and that the mint is dying in sorrow. Mother says: "The storm is approaching!" And I can see two crystal tears in her eyes.

I

Attack follows attack. The enemy's forces press furiously. Then our cavalry attacks from the flank, and long rows of insurgents advance into counterattack, and the storm is nearing, and my thoughts are like an incredibly tight-stretched wire.

I spend my nights and days in the *Cheka*.[1]

Our quarters are in the fantastic palace of an executed prince: exquisite curtains, ancient designs, family portraits — all these look at me from every corner of this, my accidental office.

Somewhere in the distance the telephone sounds its painful alarming melody that reminds me of the distant whistle of a train.

On the lofty couch, an armed Tatar soldier sings his monotonous Asiatic: "ala-la-la," his legs crossed under him.

I look at the portraits: the prince scowls, the princess is full of high airs and disdain, the children are hidden in the shade of the ancient oak trees.

In this weird feeling of sternness, I can sense the world of yesterday, the forceless grandeur and beauty of the youth of the bygone nobility.

This looks like a clear mother-of-pearl surface soiled by the banquet of a wild and hungry mob.

And I, a completely strange person, a bandit to one man and an insurgent to another — I just look simply and with clear vision upon these portraits, and there is no anger in my soul; and I know that there will be no anger in my soul; this is quite simple: I am a Chekist, but I am also a man.

In the dark night, when behind the windowpanes the city evenings saunter high on a mountain, the palace reigns over the city, when the blue smoke rises above the smokestacks of the brick kilns, and when the citizens are being brought into the palace, seized easily like mice — in the dark night, in my strange office, my comrades gather. This is a new Sanhedrin, the black tribunal of communism.

Then, out of every corner, the true and truly hair-raising death watches.

The citizen speaks: "This is a council of sadists!"

I remain silent.

On the city tower behind the mounds, the brass resounds alarmingly. Then the clock strikes. Out of the dark steppe comes the dull sound of artillery.

My comrades sit behind the wide black wooden table. Silence. Only the distant telephone in the railway station rings its painful alarming melody. From time to time the partisans pass under the window. My comrades are easily recognized: Dr. Tahabat, Andriy, and the third — the degenerate one, the monster (the faithful sentinel always at his post). The black tribunal is complete.

Then I speak:

"Attention! Our first case today is that of merchant X!"

Out of the adjoining rooms the servants come bowing, as if before their lord, looking attentively at this new Sanhedrin, bringing the tea and putting it on the table. Then they disappear noiselessly into the labyrinth of high-ceilinged rooms, walking on the soft carpets.

The candelabrum with two candles sheds its dim light. The light is too weak to brighten even a quarter of the room. Up above looms the girandole. The city is in darkness. So are we: the powerhouse has been blown up.

Dr. Tahabat sprawls on the wide couch, far away from the candelabrum, and I can see only his white bald skull and his very high forehead. Behind him, even deeper in the darkness, I see the faithful sentinel with the degenerate skull structure. I can discern only his almost insane eyes, but I know that he has a low forehead, a mop of black disheveled hair on his head, and a flat nose. He reminds me of a convict, and I am sure that he has a long record.

Andriy sits on my right side with an "inattentive" face, glancing from time to time at the doctor with a frightened look. I know what is happening to him.

Andriy, my poor Andriy, was sent here by the merciless revolutionary committee, against his weak will. And he, this gloomy communist, at the moment one has to sign one's name energetically under the dark sentence — "to be shot"

— he always hesitates, and does not sign his full name on this fierce document, but puts down a strange, illegible sign that looks like a hieroglyph.

I speak: "Well, this is all. What do you think, Dr. Tahabat?"

Doctor (speaking with force): "Shoot him!"

Andriy, frightened, looks at Tahabat and hesitates. Then, in a trembling and timid voice, he says:

"I don't agree with you, doctor."

"You don't agree with me?" and into the dark rooms rolls the peal of hoarse laughter.

I was waiting for this laughter; it was always like that. But as always, I shudder and I have a feeling that I am sinking into a cold mire. My thoughts reach their maximum speed.

And, at that moment, the image of my mother suddenly appears before me.

"Shoot him?"

And she stares at me silently and with sorrowful eyes.

. . . Again in the distant city tower the brass is resounding: the clock strikes. The northern darkness. Into the prince's home come the sounds of

the distant cannonade. The telephone report said that our forces had
made a counterattack. Through the curtain on the glass doors, one can see
the conflagration: the villages are burning, the steppes are burning, the
dogs are howling, staring at the flames out of the dark corners of the city
gates. In the city, quiet reigns, and the silent chiming of people's hearts.

. . . Dr. Tahabat pressed the button.

Then the butler brings in a tray of old wines. And then he goes away,
and his footsteps grow faint and die away on the leopard skins.

I stare at the candelabrum but instinctively my eyes waft toward the
place where Dr. Tahabat is sitting with the sentinel. They hold the wine
bottles in their hands, drinking greedily, voraciously.

This is the way, I think.

But Andriy strides nervously back and forth, trying to speak up. I
know what he is thinking about: he wants to say that this isn't honest, that
communists don't do such things, that this is an orgy, etc., etc.

Ah, what a strange person he is, this communist Andriy!

But when Dr. Tahabat threw the empty bottle on the velvet rug and
signed his name very legibly under the verdict:

"to be shot"

all of a sudden I was seized by despair. This man, with a wide forehead
and white bald skull, with his cold reasoning and a stone in place of his
heart — he was my lord whom I could not escape. He was my animal
instinct. And I, the chairman of the black tribunal of communism — I was
a puppet in his hands, obeying the desires of the fierce animal.

"But where is the solution?"

— Where is the solution? — I could see no solution.

Then in front of my eyes passes the dark history of civilization, and
the nations wade, and eras, and time itself . . .

— But I could see no solution!

Really, Dr. Tahabat must be right.

. . . Andriy hurriedly put his hieroglyph under the verdict, and the
monster kept staring at the letters with an expression of extreme pleasure.

Then I thought: if the doctor is my evil genius, my evil mind, then the
monster is the blade of the guillotine.

But I thought again: what nonsense! He is no blade! It was to him that
I, during moments of great exaltation had sung my hymns.

And then my mother slowly walking, stealing away from me, like an
image of the untouchable Virgin Mary, loomed in the darkness, waiting.

. . . The candles were melting. The sullen austere figures of the prince and the princess were disappearing in the blue of the cigarette smoke.

. . . There were

six

persons sentenced to be shot!

Enough! This is enough for tonight!

The Tatar again sings his Asiatic "ala-la-la."

I look at the curtain on the glass door and at the conflagration seen through it. Andriy is already gone. Tahabat and the sentinel are drinking old wines. I hang my gun on my shoulder and leave the palace. I walk through the deserted sulky streets of the besieged city.

The city is dead. The inhabitants know that in another three or four days we will be gone, that our counterattacks are in vain; very soon our wagons will roll creaking toward the far northern land. The city lurks. Darkness.

Like a dark hairy silhouette the prince's palace looms in the east; now it is the black tribunal of communism.

I turn around and look at it, and then, all of a sudden I remember that I have six people on my conscience.

. . . Six on my conscience?

No, not six! Six hundred,

six thousand, six million —

infinity on my conscience!

— Infinity?

And I squeeze my head in my hands.

. . . But again before my eyes passes the dark history of civilization, and the nations wade, and eras, and time itself . . .

Then I, completely exhausted, lean on the fence, kneel down, and from the bottom of my heart I thank God for my meeting with Dr. Tahabat and the sentinel with the degenerate skull structure. Then I turn around and, as though in prayer, stare at the hairy silhouette of the east.

I am lost in the narrow streets. Finally I reach the solitary little house where my mother lives. In the yard there's the smell of mint. Behind the hut in the back yard, lightning flashes and the distant weak thunder may be heard.

Infinity!

I enter the house, take off the gun, and light a candle.

"Are you asleep?"

But mother was awake.

She comes up to me, takes my tired face in her thin old hands, and rests her head on my chest. Again she says that I, her rebellious son, have tired myself out completely.

And I can feel on my hands her crystal tears.

I speak:

"Oh, how tired I am, mother!"

She leads me toward the candle and looks at my exhausted face.

Then she stands in front of the dim votive lamp and, full of sorrow, stares at the image of the Virgin. — I know: my mother will go to the monastery tomorrow; she cannot stand our alarms and the ferocious surrounding atmosphere.

"Ferocious atmosphere? How can she think like that? Only reactionaries think this way!"

So I, confused, assure myself that this isn't true, that there is no mother in front of me, that this is nothing more than a phantom.

— Phantom? and I jump up again.

No, this is just what is wrong! Here, in this silent room, my mother is not a phantom, but a part of my own criminal being which was set free by me. Here in this dark corner, on the edge of the city, I hide a part of my soul away from the guillotine.

And then I, like an animal in a wild fit, close my eyes and, like a male animal in the springtime, choking, I whisper:

"Who cares about the details of my inner experiences?"

I am a real communist. Who dares to say otherwise? Don't I have the right to rest for a while?

The votive lamp in front of the Virgin's icon burns dimly. In front of it my worried mother stands like a statue. But I stop thinking. My head is caressed by a peaceful, blue dream.

II

Our forces retreat, leaving position after position: panic seizes the front lines as well as the rear. My company is all alert. In two days I too will throw myself into the roar of cannons. My company is well-chosen — these are all young communist fanatics.

But at the present time I am needed here just as much. I know how it is in the rear when the enemy is outside the city's walls. These muddled rumors spread with every day and creep like snakes in all directions along the streets. These rumors agitate even the garrison troops.

I am told that:

there are hidden complaints

and that revolt is possible.

Oh yes! I know: revolt is possible, and my faithful agents roam around
the city's dark streets and by now there is no room in the prisons to take up
all this guilty and almost unguilty scum of society.

The thundering of the artillery grows louder and louder. Messengers
from the front lines appear more and more often. The dust gathers into
clouds which hang above the city, shadowing the muddy, fiery sun.
Lightning flashes from time to time. The long columns of wagons drag
along, the locomotives emit frightened sounds, the cavalry flees.

Only at the black tribunal of communism the oppressive quiet
remains.

Yes:

hundreds are going to be shot, and I am completely exhausted!

The reactionaries hear the clear, short shots bursting in the dead
silence of the palace reigning over the city; the reactionaries know that this
is General Dukhonin's late staff!

And the mornings bloom like white mother-of-pearl and their stars fall
into the fog of the distant forest. The cannonade grows louder. The storm
is approaching.

. . . .

I enter the palace.

Dr. Tahabat and the sentinel drink wine. Andriy sits in the corner,
scowling. Then he comes up to me and speaks in a naive, painful voice:

"Listen, friend! Let me go!"

"Where to?" I ask.

"To the front," says Andriy, "I can't stand it here any longer."

So, he can't stand it here any longer! And anger blows up in me all of
a sudden. Finally it is out. I have been holding myself back for a long time.
— So he wants to go to the front lines! He wants to be as far away as
possible from our dirty business. He wants to wipe his hands and be as
pure as a dove. He gives me his privilege to bathe in the puddles of blood.

Then I shout:

"Comrade, you forget yourself! Do you hear me? If you say this once
more, I will blow your brains out!"

"That's the way! That's the way!" laughs Dr. Tahabat violently, and his laughter rolls through the empty labyrinths of the palace halls. "That's the way! That's the way!"

Andriy grew confused and pale and then left the room.

"That's enough of that!" the doctor said. "Now I will rest! You go on!"

"Who is the next one?" I asked.

"Case Number 282."

"Bring them in," I said.

The sentinel left the room silently, like a robot.

(Yes, he was irreplaceable, this sentinel. Not only Andriy sinned sometimes, but also the doctor and I. We very often failed to supervise the executions. But he, this monster, always remained a soldier of the revolution, and he used to leave the execution place only when the last of the smoke dispersed and when the bodies were being buried.)

. . . The curtain parted and two persons entered: a woman in a black mourning veil, and a man with glasses. They were apparently completely frightened by the interior: the aristocratic luxury, the portraits of the prince's family, and the clutter: empty bottles, pistols, and the blue cigarette smoke.

I speak: "Your name?"

"Z"

"And your name?"

"Y"

The man's thin lips grew pale and his voice soft and full of tears: he asked for mercy. The woman was drying her eyes with a handkerchief.

I speak: "Where were you taken?"

"In such and such a place!"

"For what?"

"For this and this!"

"Oh! So you were at a meeting! Don't you know that there should be no meetings in such a dangerous time, at night, in somebody's home?

"Oh, so you are theosophists! You search for truth! . . . For new truth? . . . Oh, yes! . . . Well, where is it? . . . In Christ? . . . No? . . . In some other saviour? . . . Oh, yes! You are not satisfied with Confucius, nor with Lao-tse, nor with Buddha, nor with Mohammed, nor with the devil himself! Yes, I understand: the vacuum has to be filled."

I speak again: "So you think that now is the time for the new Messiah to come, eh?"

The man and woman: "Yes!"

I speak: "You think that this psychological crisis is everywhere — in Asia, and in Europe, and in all other parts of the world?"

The man and the woman: "Yes!"

I speak: "So why the hell, you sons of bitches, don't you find this your Messiah in *Cheka?*"

The woman started to cry. The man grew even paler.

The stern portraits of the prince and the princess stared frowning down from the walls. The artillery firing could be heard, together with the alarming whistling from the railroad station. The telephone reports that the enemy's armored train is attacking our station. From the city comes the noise of wagons thundering over the bridge.

. . . The man fell on his knees begging for mercy. I pushed him with my foot and he sprawled upon the floor.

The woman pressed the black veil to her temples and stooped over the table in despair.

She said in a deep dead voice:

"Listen, I have three children! . . ."

"Shoot them!" I say.

The sentinel jumped up and in a few seconds my office was empty.

Then I went up to the table, filled my glass with wine and hastily gulped it down. Then I put my hand on my cold forehead and said:

"Next one!"

The monster entered. He says I should stop my regular cases and investigate an exceptionally important one. He says that they have just brought in a group of reactionaries, all nuns: yesterday they were demonstrating in the city, preaching against communism.

I assumed my role. Haze was covering my eyes, and I was in a state of ecstasy. I think that the Christian fanatics fought the Crusades in such a state.

I went to the window and said:

"Bring them in!"

. . . A whole crowd of nuns filled my office. But I
did not see nor feel this. I was looking at the city.
It was getting dark. — I did not turn around for a
long while, enjoying the thought: in a couple of hours
they will all cease to exist! — It was getting
dark. — And again lightning flashes, foreboding storm.
. . . On the far horizon behind the brickyard the smoke
rises slowly . . . The reactionaries press violently and fiercely, as
the telephone reports. On the desert roads, wagon

caravans appear from time to time, retreating toward
the north. In the steppe the cavalry guard regiments wait, like
legendary ancient heroes. Alarm! The shop windows in
the city are nailed up with boards. The city is dead,
disappearing in the savage time of the Middle Ages. The
stars grow on the sky, pouring onto the ground their
green muddy light. Then they die out, disappear.

But I must hurry, I have a whole mob of nuns behind my back! Yes, I have to hurry: the cellars are full up.

I turn around, determined and ready to say the inexorable:

"Shoot them!" . . .

. . . .

but as I turn around, I see — just before my eyes — my mother, my suffering mother, with her eyes of the Virgin Mary.

I jumped aside in consternation: what is this? Hallucination? I jumped aside in consternation and shouted:

"You?"

Out of the crowd I can hear the sorrowful:

"My son! My rebellious son!"

I feel that I am going to faint any minute. I feel dizzy, I grabbed the back of the chair and stooped toward the ground.

But at this moment a wave of laughter burst toward the ceiling and disappeared. This is Dr. Tahabat.

— "Mama?!" Oh, you lousy bastard! "You want pee-pee? Mama?!"

I took hold of myself and grabbed my gun.

"The hell with you!" — and I jumped at the doctor.

But he looked at me calmly and said:

"Steady, steady, you traitor to communism! Why don't you do with your 'mom' (and he distinctly said 'mom') what you did with the others?"

I turned around silently.

. . . I was stupefied. Pale, almost dead, I stood in front of the crowd of nuns, confused and derided. (I could see myself in the huge mirror hanging in front of me.)

. . . Yes! — they have finally gotten hold of the other part of my soul! I shall never hide myself again like a criminal in the suburbs of the city! I have only one right left:

— *not to say anything to anybody about how "my being" was split in two.*

And I did not lose my head.

Thoughts were cutting my brain. What must I do? Is it possible that I, a soldier of the revolution, will yield in this responsible moment? Is it possible that I will leave my post and become a shameless traitor to communism?

I bit my teeth, looked at my mother with a sullen look, and said harshly:

"Put them all in the cellar. I will stay here for a while."

But as soon as I said that, the room again shook with laughter.

Then I turned around and said clearly to the doctor:

"Dr. Tahabat! You apparently have forgotten with whom you are dealing. Or maybe you too want to join General Dukhonin's late staff . . . together with this trash!" — I gestured with my hand in the direction where my mother stood and left the room without saying a word.

There was silence behind my back.

. . . .

. . . I was walking into nowhere, away from the palace, strolling along like a drunk through the shadows of the evening stuffy before storm. The artillery grew louder. The smoke was rising again above the distant brick kilns. Behind the mound, the armored trains thundered: a decisive duel was taking place. The enemy forces were fiercely fighting the insurgents. There was a smell of execution.

I was walking into nowhere. Nearby the columns were dragging, the cavalry was fleeing, the wagons were thundering over the bridge. The city was smothering in the dust, and the evening did not shoot off the ammunition of the oncoming storm.

I was walking into nowhere. Without thoughts, with dull vacuity, with a heavy weight on my stooping shoulders.

I was walking into nowhere.

III

. . . Yes, those were impossible moments. That was a torture! — But I knew what I was going to do.

I knew this even at the time I left the palace. Otherwise I wouldn't have left it that fast.

. . . Well, I have to be consistent!

. . . So I worked all night.

Then for a few dark hours the short clear shots flashed periodically:

— I, the chairman of the black tribunal of communism, was carrying out the duties entrusted to me by the revolution.

. . . Was it my fault, then, that the image of my mother did not leave me that night, not for one moment?

Was it my fault?

. . . .

. . . During dinner time Andriy came to me and said gloomily:

"Listen! Release her!"

"Whom?" I asked.

"Your mother!"

I don't say anything. Then I feel that I have a tremendous urge to laugh. I can't hold myself back any longer and I burst out with laughter, filling all the rooms with it.

Andriy stares at me very coldly. I cannot recognize him at all.

"Listen. Why this melodramatic situation?"

My naive Andriy wanted to be very penetrating this time. But he was wrong.

I speak very roughly:

"Beat it!"

Andriy grew pale this time too.

Oh, this naive communist — he just does not understand anything. He literally does not know what this absurd, animal-like cruelty is for. He cannot see anything behind my cold and wooden face.

I speak:

"Ring them up! Find out where the enemy is!"

Andriy:

"Listen! . . ."

I:

"Ring them up! Find out where the enemy is!"

At the moment I said that, a hissing artillery shell whizzed over the palace and exploded nearby. The windows rattled and the noise echoed through the empty resonant rooms.

Over the telephone they say that the reactionaries are close, only about two miles away. The Cossack scouts have reached the station: the insurgents retreat — the distant whistle in the station calls for help.

. . . Andriy ran out. I followed him.

. . . The whole expanse was reeking. Again the smoke was exploding over the horizon. Above the city there was a cloud of dust. The sun was the color of copper, and one could not see the sky. Only far away, high above, the turbid cloud of dust was spreading with great speed. The dust phantoms rose up from the roads into the firmament, invaded the pure space, flew over the villages, and galloped in the distance. The atmosphere of oncoming storm waited as if hypnotized.

. . . Around us the shells thudded. Cavalry was fleeing. Columns of wagons were retreating to the north.

. . . I forgot about everything. I did not hear anything, and I don't know how I got to the cellar.

Like a bell, shrapnel exploded behind my back, and emptiness and silence ensued. I went to the door, and as I tried to look into the cell through the small door-window to see if my mother was there, I felt somebody touch my hand. I turned around.

— It was the monster.

"Look at those guards," he laughed — "they all ran away."

"And you?" I said.

He said:

"Me? Oh, I stay here!" and he tapped with his finger on the door.

Yes, this was the faithful watch dog of the revolution. He will always remain at his post, even under stronger fire. I remember how at that moment a thought flashed through my mind:

— "he is the guard of my soul" and without thinking any more, I dragged myself into the empty city.

. . . .

. . . But toward evening the southern part of the city was taken. We have to retreat to the north and to leave the city. But the insurgents were given orders to hold the city until the night came and they were dying heroically on the earthworks, in the tunnels, on crossroads and in silent corners of the city gates.

. . . But what about me?

. . . We were evacuating very hastily, amid the clear whistling of bullets. I was tiring myself out completely! Documents were burning, the hostages were being shipped away. The ransacking of the city was continuing.

. . . I was tiring myself out completely!

. . . But suddenly my mother's face would appear in my eyes and I could hear again the worried, persistent voice. I push my hair back and with wide-opened eyes stare at the city tower. It was getting dark again, and the villages were still burning.

. . . The black tribunal of communism is getting ready for the flight. The wagons are being loaded, some of them pull away, the crowds are pushing to the north. Only our single armored train is slowly dying in the depth of the forest, holding back the right flank of the enemy's forces.

. . . Andriy disappeared somewhere. Dr. Tahabat sits leisurely on the couch, drinking wine. He silently watches what I do, and from time to time glances ironically at the prince's portrait. But I can feel this same kind of look on my body and this makes me nervous and disturbed.

. . . The sun went down. The evening is dying. Night is approaching. On the earthworks, rifle shots and machine guns rattle monotonously. The deserted rooms of the palace look dead, as if waiting for something.

I look at the doctor and I cannot stand the way he stares at the portrait of the prince.

I speak harshly:

"Dr. Tahabat! In another hour I have to execute the last party of the condemned. I have to take charge of the company."

Then he says indifferently and ironically:

"Well? All right!"

I am nervous, but the doctor looks at me with an obsequious smile on his face. — Oh, he certainly understands what this is all about! My mother is in this last party.

I speak:

"Leave the room, please!"

The doctor:

"Well! All right."

Then I lose control of myself and blurt out:

"Dr. Tahabat! I remind you for the last time; do not joke with me!"

But my voice breaks down and my throat bubbles with words. I want to grab my gun and finish with the doctor, but all of a sudden I feel very pitiable and worthless, and I understand that the rest of my will power is leaving me. I sit down on the couch like a dog who has been beaten, and look at Tahabat.

. . . But time flies. I have to go.

I take hold of myself again and look for the last time at the lofty-aired portrait of the princess.

Darkness.

"The guard!" I shout.

The sentinel entered and reported: — They have taken them out. The execution will take place outside the city: at the edge of the woods.

*   *   *

The moon emerged from behind the distant foothills. Then she flew on the quiet blue waters, splashing with lemon-like squirts of waves. At midnight she punctured the zenith and hung over the abyss.

. . . There was heavy firing in the city.

. . . We were walking on the north road.

I shall never forget this murky procession — this dark crowd of people doomed to die.

Behind my back the wagons were creaking.

The front consisted of our guards. Then came the party of nuns; I was in the rear with some more guards and Dr. Tahabat.

. . . But we have come across some real reactionaries: during the whole walk, not one of the nuns opened her mouth. They are real fanatics.

I was walking, like the other time, into nowhere; at either side of me the guardians of my soul are walking: the doctor and the monster. I was looking at the crowd of nuns but I could see nothing there.

But I felt:

— my mother was walking

there with a bowed head. I could sense the smell of mint.

I caressed her beloved head covered with silver hair.

But suddenly I could see before me the untouchable distance. Then I had a desire to fall on my knees again and pray to the black tribunal of communism.

I squeezed my head in my hands and walked the dead road. Behind my back the wagons were creaking.

. . . .

But what is this, a hallucination? All of a sudden I heard a voice. Is this the voice of my mother?

And again I know that I am a contemptible person, and there is an unpleasant feeling inside my breast. And I did not want to cry, but just to shed my tears, as in my childhood, on somebody's warm chest.

Then I burst out:

"Am I going to have her shot?

What is this: reality or a dream?"

But this was reality: true reality of life — fierce and ravenous, like a pack of hungry wolves. This was reality without solution, inescapable like death itself.

. . . But maybe this is a mistake?

Maybe I should not do it?

But this is cowardice, the result of being uncertain. There is a rule in life: *errare humanum est.* So what do you care? Make mistakes! and make this mistake and not that one! . . . there are no mistakes!

Truly, this was reality, like a pack of hungry wolves. But this was the only way to the distant untouchable lakes of the beautiful unknown communism.

. . . And then I was full of the fanatic fire and my footsteps thundered on the northern road.

. . . The silent procession reached the forest. I don't remember where they took the nuns; I only remember:

how the doctor came up to me and put his hand on my shoulder:

"Your mother is there! Do what you want!"

I looked in the direction of the nuns: a lonely figure

departed from the crowd and walked toward the forest.

. . . The moon hung over the abyss in the zenith of the sky. The dead road was slowly escaping into the lemon-green distance. On my right stood the guard platoon of my company. And at that moment the city lighted up with heavy firing — the bullets were again sounding the alarm. The enemy has noticed the retreat of the insurgents.

A shell exploded nearby.

. . . I took the pistol out of its case and ran up to the lonely figure. And I remember how then the night lit up with short bright shots: the nuns were being shot.

And I also remember:

out of the woods our armored train sounded the alarm. The forest moaned. The fire flashed — once,

twice —

and again, and again!

The enemy is approaching. I have to hurry. Oh, I have to hurry!

And I walk, and walk, and the solitary figure of my mother remains on the same spot. She stands with uplifted arms staring at me with a worried look. I hurry toward that incredible charmed place, and the solitary figure remains always in the same place.

There is no one around. Only the moon sheds its green light from the punctured sky. I hold my gun in my hand, but my hand grows weak, and I have a feeling that I will start crying soon, as in my childhood, on somebody's warm chest. I want to shout:

— Mother! Come here, I tell you! I have to kill you.

And my brain is being sliced by the sorrowful voice. I can hear again my mother say that I (her rebellious son) have tired myself out completely.

. . . What is this? Is this hallucination again?

I throw my head back.

Yes, this was hallucination: I have been standing all this time on the edge of the forest, facing my mother and looking at her:

She was silent.

. . . The armored train bellowed in the woods.

The flowers became brighter. Storm was approaching. The enemy attacked. The insurgents are retreating.

. . . Then I, not knowing what I was doing, seized by a strange fit of happiness, put my arm around my mother's neck and pressed her head to my chest. Then I brought my gun to her temple and pulled the trigger.

She leaned on me like a cut stalk of grain. I put her on the ground and looked around in consternation. — There was no one around. Only the black warm bodies of the nuns were lying nearby. — Not far away the cannons were pounding.

. . . I put my hand in my pocket and remembered that I had forgotten something in the palace.

What an idiot I am, I thought.

. . . Then I remembered:

— where are the people?

"I have to hurry, to catch up with my company," and I turned around.

But I have hardly taken a step when I feel something stopping me.

I stopped and ran back to my mother's body.

I knelt down and looked at her face with great care. But she was dead. I remember the dark streak of blood on her face.

Then I lifted this head which I could not make alive again and greedily pressed my lips on her white forehead. — Darkness.

And then, all of a sudden, I hear:

"Well, communist, get up! Time to go!"

I turned around quickly and saw:

The monster standing again before my eyes.

"Oh, just a moment! Just a moment! Yes, I am late!" — Then I adjusted my belt and started walking.

. . . In the steppe, like those legendary ancient heroes, the insurgent cavalry was waiting. I ran toward them, holding my head in my hands.

. . . Storm was roaring. The flecks of dawn grew in some places. The moon was dying quietly in the punctured sky. Clouds were coming from the west. The shots were numerous and clear.

. . . .

I stopped in the dead steppe:
— there, in the far somewhere, the quiet lakes of unreachable communism, the distant mountains were burning quietly.

★

Note

1. *Cheka:* Secret police.

★ ★ ★ ★

AUTHOR: *Pär Lagerkvist (1891–1974) was one of Sweden's foremost writers, winning the Nobel Prize for* Barabbas *in 1951. He was a lyric poet, dramatist, satirist, and novelist. His writing is carefully constructed, reflecting both an appreciation of beauty and an existentialist philosophy.*

SETTING: *First published in 1935, this story was set in the then-distant future – 1978 – in a country that might be Sweden, although it could be any time or place. It is an unsettling satire of the childishness of the military and of the war game itself.*

The Children's Campaign

Pär Lagerkvist

Even the children at that time received military training, were assembled in army units and exercised just as though on active service, had their own headquarters and annual manoeuvres when everything was conducted as in a real state of war. The grown-ups had nothing directly to do with this training; the children actually exercised themselves and all command was entrusted to them. The only use made of adult experience was to arrange officers' training courses for specially suitable boys, who were chosen with the greatest care and who were then put in charge of the military education of their comrades in the ranks.

These schools were of high standing and there was hardly a boy throughout the land who did not dream of going to them. But the entrance tests were particularly hard; not only a perfect physique was required but also a highly developed intelligence and character. The age of admission was six to seven years and the small cadets then received an excellent training, both purely military and in all other respects, chiefly the further moulding of character. It was also greatly to one's credit in after life to have passed through one of these schools. It was really on the splendid foundation laid here that the quality, organization and efficiency of the child army rested.

Translated by Alan Blair. "The Children's Campaign" originally appeared in Pär Lagerkvist, *Den Tilden* copyright Albert Bonniers Förlag 1935. Reprinted by permission of the publisher.

Thereafter, as already mentioned, the grown-ups in no way interfered but everything was entrusted to the children themselves. No adult might meddle in the command, in organizational details or matters of promotion. Everything was managed and supervised by the children; all decisions, even the most vital, being reached by their own little general staff. No one over fourteen was allowed. The boys then passed automatically into the first age-group of the regular troops with no mean military training already behind them.

The large child army, which was the object of the whole nation's love and admiration, amounted to three army corps of four divisions: infantry, light field artillery, medical and service corps. All physically fit boys were enrolled in it and a large number of girls belonged to it as nurses, all volunteers.

Now it so happened that a smaller, quite insignificant nation behaved in a high-handed and unseemly way toward its powerful neighbour, and the insult was all the greater since this nation was by no means an equal. Indignation was great and general and, since people's feelings were running high, it was necessary to rebuke the malapert and at the same time take the chance to subjugate the country in question. In this situation the child army came forward and through its high command asked to be charged with the crushing and subduing of the foe. The news of this caused a sensation and wave of fervour throughout the country. The proposal was given serious consideration in supreme quarters and as a result the commission was given, with some hesitation, to the children. It was in fact a task well suited to this army, and the people's obvious wishes in the matter had also to be met, if possible.

The Foreign Office therefore sent the defiant country an unacceptable ultimatum and, pending the reply, the child army was mobilized within twenty-four hours. The reply was found to be unsatisfactory and war was declared immediately.

Unparalleled enthusiasm marked the departure for the front. The intrepid little youngsters had green sprigs in the barrels of their rifles and were pelted with flowers. As is so often the case, the campaign was begun in the spring, and this time the general opinion was that there was something symbolic in it. In the capital the little commander-in-chief and chief of general staff, in the presence of huge crowds, made a passionate speech to the troops in which he expressed the gravity of the hour and his conviction of their unswerving valour and willingness to offer their lives for their country.

The speech, made in a strong voice, aroused the greatest ecstasy. The boy — who had a brilliant career behind him and had reached his exalted position at the age of only twelve and a half — was acclaimed with wild rejoicing and from this moment was the avowed hero of the entire nation. There was not a dry eye and those of the many mothers especially shone with pride and happiness. For them it was the greatest day in their lives. The troops marched past below fluttering banners, each regiment with its music corps at the head. It was an unforgettable spectacle.

There were also many touching incidents, evincing a proud patriotism, as when a little four-year-old, who had been lifted up on his mother's arm so that he could see, howled with despair and shouted, "I want to go, too. I want to go, too!" while his mother tried to hush him, explaining that he was too small. "Small am I, eh?" he exclaimed, punching her face so that her nose bled. The evening papers were full of such episodes showing the mood of the people and of the troops who were so sure of victory. The big march past was broadcast and the C.-in-C.'s speech which had been recorded, was broadcast every evening during the days that followed, at 7:15 P.M.

Military operations had already begun, however, and reports of victory began to come in at once from the front. The children had quickly taken the offensive and on one sector of the front had inflicted a heavy defeat on the enemy, seven hundred dead and wounded and over twelve hundred prisoners, while their own losses amounted to only a hundred or so fallen. The victory was celebrated at home with indescribable rejoicing and with thanksgiving services in the churches. The newspapers were filled with accounts of individual instances of valour and pictures several columns wide of the high command, of which the leading personalities, later so well-known, began to appear now for the first time. In their joy, mothers and aunts sent so much chocolate and other sweets to the army that headquarters had to issue a strict order that all such parcels were, for the time being at any rate, forbidden, since they had made whole regiments unfit for battle and these in their turn had nearly been surrounded by the enemy.

For the child army was already far inside enemy territory and still managed to keep the initiative. The advance sector did retreat slightly in order to establish contact with its wings, but only improved its positions by so doing. A stalemate ensued in the theatre of war for some time after this.

During July, however, troops were concentrated for a big attack along the whole line and huge reserves — the child army's in comparison with those of its opponent, were almost inexhaustible — were mustered to the front. The new offensive, which lasted for several weeks, resulted, too, in an almost decisive victory for the whole army, even though casualties were high. The children defeated the enemy all along the line but did not manage to pursue him and thereby exploit their success to the full, because he was greatly favoured by the fact that his legs were so much longer, an advantage of which he made good use. By dint of forced marches, however, the children finally succeeded in cutting the enemy's right flank to pieces. They were now in the very heart of the country and their outposts were only a few days' march from the capital.

It was a pitched battle on a big scale and the newspapers had enormous headlines every day which depicted the dramatic course of events. At set hours the radio broadcast the gunfire and a résumé of the position. The war correspondents described in rapturous words and vivid colors the state of affairs at the front — the children's incredible feats, their indomitable courage and self-sacrifice, the whole morale of the army. It was no exaggeration. The youngsters showed the greatest bravery; they really behaved like heroes. One only had to see their discipline and contempt of death during an attack, as though they had been grown-up men at least.

It was an unforgettable sight to see them storm ahead under murderous machine-gun fire and the small medical orderlies dart nimbly forward and pick them up as they fell. Or the wounded and dying who were moved behind the front, those who had had a leg shot away or their bellies ripped open by a bayonet so that their entrails hung out — but without one sound of complaint crossing their small lips. The hand-to-hand fighting had been very fierce and a great number of children fell in this, while they were superior in the actual firing. Losses were estimated at 4000 on the enemy side and 7000 among the children, according to the secret reports. The victory had been hard won but all the more complete.

The battle became very famous and was also of far greater importance than any previously. It was now clear beyond all doubt that the children were incomparably superior in tactics, discipline and individual courage. At the same time, however, it was admitted by experts that the enemy's head-long retreat was very skillfully carried out, that his strength was evidently in defense and that he should not be underrated too much. Toward the end, also, he had unexpectedly made a stubborn resistance which had prevented any further penetration.

This observation was not without truth. In actual fact the enemy was anything but a warlike nation, and indeed his forces found it very difficult to hold their own. Nevertheless, they improved with practice during the fighting and became more efficient as time went on. This meant that they caused the children a good deal of trouble in each succeeding battle. They also had certain advantages on their side. As their opponents were so small, for instance, it was possible after a little practice to spit several of them on the bayonet at once, and often a kick was enough to fell them to the ground.

But against this, the children were so much more numerous and also braver. They were everywhere. They swarmed over one and in between one's legs and the unwarlike people were nearly demented by all these small monsters who fought like fiends. Little fiends was also what they were generally called — not without reason — and this name was even adopted in the children's homeland, but there it was a mark of honour and a pet name. The enemy troops had all their work cut out merely defending themselves. At last, however, they were able to check the others' advance and even venture on one or two counter-attacks. Everything then came to a standstill for a while and there was a breathing-space.

The children were now in possession of a large part of the country. But this was not always so easy. The population did not particularly like them and proved not to be very fond of children. It was alleged that snipers fired on the boys from houses and that they were ambushed when they moved in small detachments. Children had even been found impaled on stakes or with their eyes gouged out, so it was said. And in many cases these stories were no doubt true. The population had quite lost their heads, were obviously goaded into a frenzy, and as they were of little use as a warlike nation and their cruelty could therefore find no natural outlet, they tried to revenge themselves by atrocities. They felt overrun by all the foreign children as by troublesome vermin and, being at their wits' end, they simply killed whenever they had the chance. In order to put an end to these outrages the children burned one village after the other and shot hundreds of people daily, but this did not improve matters. The despicable deeds of these craven guerrillas caused them endless trouble.

At home, the accounts of all this naturally aroused the most bitter resentment. People's blood boiled to think that their small soldiers were treated in this way by those who had nothing to do with the war, by barbarous civilians who had no notion of established and judicial forms. Even greater indignation was caused, however, by an incident that occurred inside the occupied area some time after the big summer battle just mentioned.

A lieutenant who was out walking in the countryside came to a stream where a large, fat woman knelt washing clothes. He asked her the way to a village close by. The woman, who probably suspected him of evil intent, retorted, "What are you doing here? You ought to be at home with your mother." Whereupon the lieutenant drew his sabre to kill her, but the woman grabbed hold of him and, putting him over her knee, thwacked him black and blue with her washboard so that he was unable to sit down for several days afterward. He was so taken aback that he did nothing, armed though he was to the teeth. Luckily no one saw the incident, but there were orders that all outrages on the part of the population were to be reported to headquarters. The lieutenant therefore duly reported what had happened to him. True, it gave him little satisfaction, but as he had to obey orders he had no choice. And so it all came out.

The incident aroused a storm of rage, particularly among those at home. The infamous deed was a humiliation for the country, an insult which nothing could wipe out. It implied a deliberate violation by this militarily ignorant people of the simplest rules of warfare. Everywhere, in the press, in propaganda speeches, in ordinary conversation, the deepest contempt and disgust for the deed was expressed. The lieutenant who had so flagrantly shamed the army had his officer's epaulettes ripped off in front of the assembled troops and was declared unworthy to serve any longer in the field. He was instantly sent home to his parents, who belonged to one of the most noted families but who now had to retire into obscurity in a remote part of the country.

The woman, on the other hand, became a heroic figure among her people and the object of their rapturous admiration. During the whole of the war she and her deed were a rallying national symbol which people looked up to and which spurred them on to further efforts. She subsequently became a favourite motif in the profuse literature about their desperate struggle for freedom; a vastly popular figure, brought to life again and again as time passed, now in a rugged, everyday way which appealed to the man in the street, now in heroic female form on a grandiose scale, to become gradually more and more legendary, wreathed in saga and myth. In some versions she was shot by the enemy; in others she lived to a ripe old age, loved and revered by her people.

This incident, more than anything else, helped to increase the bad feelings between the two countries and to make them wage the war with ever greater ruthlessness. In the late summer, before the autumn rains began, both armies, ignorant of each other's plans, simultaneously launched a violent offensive, which devastated both sides. On large sectors of the front the troops completely annihilated each other so that there was not a single survivor left. Any peaceful inhabitants thereabouts who were still alive and ventured out of their cellars thought that the war was over, because all were slain.

But soon new detachments came up and began fighting again. Great confusion arose in other quarters from the fact that in the heat of attack men ran past each other and had to turn around in order to go on fighting; and that some parts of the line rushed ahead while others came behind, so that the troops were both in front of and behind where they should have been and time and again attacked each other in the rear. The battle raged in this way with extreme violence and shots were fired from all directions at once.

When at last the fighting ceased and stock was taken of the situation, it appeared that no one had won. On both sides there was an equal number of fallen, 12,924, and after all attacks and retreats the position of the armies was exactly the same as at the start of the battle. It was agreed that both should claim the victory. Thereafter the rain set in and the armies went to earth in trenches and put up barbed-wire entanglements.

The children were the first to finish their trenches, since they had had more to do with that kind of thing, and settled down in them as best they could. They soon felt at home. Filthy and lousy, they lived there in the darkness as though they had never done anything else. With the adaptability of children, they quickly got into the way of it. The enemy found this more difficult; he felt miserable and home-sick for the life above ground to which he was accustomed. Not so the children. When one saw them in their small grey uniforms, which were caked thick with mud, and their small gas masks, one could easily think they had been born to this existence. They crept in and out of the holes down into the earth and scampered about the passages like mice. When their burrows were attacked they were instantly up on the parapet and snapped back in blind fury. As the months passed, this hopeless, harrowing life put endurance to an increasingly severe test. But they never lost courage or the will to fight.

For the enemy the strain was often too much; the glaring pointlessness of it all made many completely apathetic. But the little ones did not react like this. Children are really more fitted for war and take more pleasure in it, while grown-ups tire of it after a while and think it is boring. The boys continued to find the whole thing exciting and they wanted to go on living as they were now. They also had a more natural herd instinct; their unity and camaraderie helped them a great deal, made it easier to hold out.

But, of course, even they suffered great hardship. Especially when winter set in with its incessant rain, a cold sleet which made everything sodden and filled the trenches with mud. It was enough to unman anyone. But it would never have entered their heads to complain. However bad things were, nothing could have made them admit it. At home everyone was proud of them. All the cinemas showed parades behind the front and the little C.-in-C. and his generals pinning medals for bravery on their soldiers' breasts. People thought of them a great deal out there, of their little fiends, realizing that they must be having a hard time.

At Christmas, in particular, thoughts went out to them, to the lighted Christmas trees and all the sparkling childish eyes out in the trenches; in every home people sat wondering how they were faring. But the children did not think of home. They were soldiers out and out, absorbed by their duty and their new life. They attacked in several places on the morning of Christmas Eve, inflicting fairly big losses on the enemy in killed and wounded, and did not stop until it was time to open their parcels. They had the real fighting spirit which might have been a lesson even to adults.

There was nothing sentimental about them. The war had hardened and developed them, made them men. It did happen that one poor little chap burst into tears when the Christmas tree was lighted, but he was made the laughing-stock of them all. "Are you homesick for your mummy, you bastard?" they said, and kept on jeering at him all evening. He was the object of their scorn all through Christmas; he behaved suspiciously and tried to keep to himself. Once he walked a hundred yards away from the post and, because he might well have been thinking of flight, he was seized and court-martialled. He could give no reason for having absented himself, and since he had obviously intended to desert he was shot.

If those at home had been fully aware of the morale out there, they need not have worried. As it was, they wondered if the children could really hold their ground and half-regretted having entrusted them with the campaign, now that it was dragging on so long because of this nerve-racking stationary warfare. After the New Year help was even offered in secret, but it was rejected with proud indignation.

The morale of the enemy, on the other hand, was not so high. They did intend to fight to the last man, but the certainty of a complete victory was not so general as it should have been. They could not help thinking, either, how hopeless their fight really was; that in the long run they could not hold their own against these people who were armed to the very milk teeth, and this often dampened their courage.

Hardly had nature begun to come to life and seethe with the newly awakened forces of spring before the children started with incredible intensity to prepare for the decisive battle. Heavy mechanized artillery was brought up and placed in strong positions; huge troop movements went on night and day; all available fighting forces were concentrated in the very front lines. After murderous gunfire which lasted for six days, an attack was launched with great force and extreme skill. Individual bravery was, if possible, more dazzling than ever. The whole army was also a year older, and that means much at that age. But their opponents, too, were determined to do their utmost. They had assembled all their reserves, and their spirits, now that the rain had stopped and the weather was fine, were full of hope.

It was a terrible battle. The hospital trains immediately started going back from both sides packed with wounded and dying. Machine guns, tanks and gas played fearful havoc. For several days the outcome was impossible to foresee, since both armies appeared equally strong and the tide of battle constantly changed. The position gradually cleared, however. The enemy had expected the main attack in the centre, but the child army turned out to be weakest there. Use was made of this, especially because they themselves were best prepared at this very point, and this part of the children's front was soon made to waver and was forced farther and farther back by repeated attack. Advantage was also taken of an ideal evening breeze from just the right quarter to gas the children in thousands. Encouraged by their victory, the troops pursued the offensive with all their might and with equal success.

The child army's retreat, however, turned out to be a stratagem, brilliantly conceived and carried out. Its centre gave more and more and the enemy, giving all his attention to this, forgot that at the same time he himself was wavering on both wings. In this way he ran his head into a noose. When the children considered that they had retreated far enough they halted, while the troops on the outermost wings, already far ahead, advanced swiftly until they met behind the enemy's back. The latter's entire army was thereby surrounded and in the grip of an iron hand. All the children's army had to do now was to draw the noose tighter. At last the gallant defenders had to surrender and let themselves be taken prisoner, which in fact they already were. It was the most disastrous defeat in history; not a single one escaped other than by death.

This victory became much more famous than any of the others and was eagerly studied at all military academies on account of its brilliantly executed, doubly effective encircling movement. The great general

Sludelsnorp borrowed its tactics outright seventy years later at his victory over the Slivokvarks in the year 2048.

The war could not go on any longer now, because there was nothing left to fight, and the children marched to the capital with the imprisoned army between them to dictate the peace terms. These were handed over by the little commander-in-chief in the hall of mirrors in the stately old palace at a historic scene which was to be immortalized time and again in art and even now was reproduced everywhere in the weekly press. The film cameras whirred, the flashlights hissed and the radio broadcast the great moment to the world. The commander-in-chief, with austere and haughty mien and one foot slightly in front of the other, delivered the historic document with his right hand. The first and most important condition was the complete cession of the country, besides which the expenses of its capture were to be borne by the enemy, who thus had to pay the cost of the war on both sides, the last clause on account of the fact that he had been the challenging party and, according to his own admission, the cause of the war. The document was signed in dead silence, the only sound was the scratching of the fountain pen, which according to the commentator's whisper, was solid gold and undoubtedly a future museum piece.

With this, everything was settled and the children's army returned to its own country, where it was received with indescribable rapture. Everywhere along the roads the troops were greeted with wild rejoicing; their homecoming was one long victory parade. The march into the capital and the dismissal there of the troops, which took place before vast crowds, were especially impressive. People waved and shouted in the streets as they passed, were beside themselves with enthusiasm, bands played, eyes were filled with tears of joy. Some of the loudest cheering was for the small invalids at the rear of the procession, blind and with limbs amputated, who had sacrificed themselves for their country. Many of them had already got small artificial arms and legs so that they looked just the same as before. The victory salute thundered, bayonets flashed in the sun. It was an unforgettable spectacle.

A strange, new leaf was written in the great book of history which would be read with admiration in time to come. The nation had seen many illustrious deeds performed, but never anything as proud as this. What these children had done in their devotion and fervent patriotism could never be forgotten.

Nor was it. Each spring, on the day of victory, school children marched out with flags in their hands to the cemeteries with all the small graves where the heroes rested under their small white crosses. The mounds were strewn with flowers and passionate speeches were made, reminding everyone of the glorious past, their imperishable honor and youthful, heroic spirit of self-sacrifice. The flags floated in the sun and the voices rang out clear as they sang their rousing songs, radiant childish eyes looking ahead to new deeds of glory.

★

Part IV

Death

The confrontation of and ultimate reconciliation with death is the theme of the first three stories in this section. Tayama Katai's "One Soldier" is a powerful story set in Manchuria during the Russo-Japanese War. In this story, a deathly ill soldier becomes separated from his company and wanders further and further away from human society and closer and closer to death. The title emphasizes the isolation of the dying soldier. The stream-of-consciousness narrative shows the soldier's self-awareness as he sees himself becoming more and more detached from the war and from the magnificent scenes of nature that he observes as he walks despairingly through the countryside.

As in "One Soldier," the man in Knuts Lesins's "The Dove" senses his imminent death and becomes keenly aware of himself and the world around him. Objects from nature catch the protagonist's attention as he wanders further and further from human companionship, which he has shunned all his life. He has spent his life as a loner, but as he gradually realizes he cannot escape death in the war that rages all around him, he discovers a longing for a sense of place and purpose. The farmhouse where he seeks refuge for the night becomes his first home, and as he recognizes the importance of having roots in life, his need for community also increases. In the end, he first risks his life to protect what he thinks is another human being, and then he sacrifices his life while defiantly standing up in symbolic defense of his country.

Jean-Paul Sartre's "The Wall" takes readers inside a cold prison cell in which three men are awaiting execution during the Spanish Civil War. As daylight and death approach, the first-person narrator becomes increasingly accepting of his imminent death, gradually becoming detached from his own body, his past, and the world around him.

The foreboding emptiness and silence of death are artfully rendered in "One Certain Night" by Ting Ling. The story opens with the sounds of boots sloshing through snow. The boots belong to a group of twenty-five Chinese Communist prisoners of war who are about to be executed. The men are described as "shadows," and, accordingly, the reader hears them rather than sees them: "There was the clanking of chains, the rattling of bayonets" and the "sound of their feet in the night was like the disordered beating of victorious drums on every side." They do not speak, however, and the narrator draws attention to their silence. Then, as they are facing execution and their hearts have grown tense "like drawn bowstrings," the sound imagery culminates with the twenty-five men bursting into song to spite their executioners. The story closes with the whistle of bullets rapidly and systematically flying through the air and gradually silencing the men's voices until they are all "dumb," silent in death.

In "The People Who Walked On," Tadeusz Borowski describes the responses of individuals who are forced to watch and cooperate in the mass killings at a Nazi concentration camp. Some seem indifferent; others are steeled against their own emotional responses in order to survive. The power of this story derives from the contrast between the first-person narrator's reporting of mundane, everyday events in the camp and the daily spectacle of thousands of people being marched to the death chambers. In one section of the camp, some of the healthier and stronger male prisoners are kept alive to do day labor. They are even given the task of "planting flowers under the barracks windows and decorating the blocks with intricate zigzag designs made of crushed red brick." The lives of these stand in stark contrast to the images of three thousand people walking to their deaths: the narrator plays a few minutes of soccer while terrible human screams emanate from the ovens. The matter-of-fact tone used to describe sickening scenes of inhumanity only serves to underscore the story's theme.

Although it is rarely depicted in conventional war fiction, one of the most common thoughts that a soldier in war has is of desertion. Two major modern war novels, *Catch-22* and *Going After Cacciato*, focus on this subject. In Imre Sarkadi's "The Deserter," a young Hungarian soldier, marching close to his home, succumbs to the temptation to sneak away for a night and visit his wife and parents. After a night of home and hearth, he is found by a group of non-regulars and is shot. It is a seemingly simple story but one that gives poignant meaning to the war-weariness and homesickness of the common soldier. The young soldier tells of his own execution. As in Randall Jarrell's famous poem "The Death of the Ball Turret Gunner," the loss of human life in war acquires a special meaning as we see death through the eyes of the dead.

Desertion is also Arturo Uslar Pietri's subject in "The Drum Dance." The narrator conveys with great urgency a young conscript's desperate fear of being caught and his knowledge that arrest and flogging are inevitable. As he awaits the two hundred lashes that he knows will kill him, his senses become so heightened that he feels the "weight" of the nearby houses and "the sleepy, dark water of the river Tuy." The intensification of his senses culminates when the only sound that he can hear is the footsteps of the provost marshal coming to take him to his "skinning." The drum dance of the story's title symbolizes pulsating life; the protagonist only ceases to hear it as death nears.

"Acquiring a Graveyard" is an almost absurd tale of a small Jewish village in rural Russia. The townsfolk, never having had to face death, and therefore never having had a communal graveyard, are forced to confront reality. Avrom Reyzen's story reads like a whimsical fable and draws the reader unsuspectingly to its startling last sentence.

"Cannonfodder," by George Bernard Shaw, is set at the time of the Second Boer War. The importance of this story lies in its portrayal of common men as "cannonfodder" — their lives and deaths are meaningless except when spent to ensure the welfare of the elite. Are wars pursued for the "good" of those who must make the supreme sacrifice or for the "good" of those who rule?

★

★ ★ ★ ★

AUTHOR: *Tayama Katai (1871–1930) was one of the first authors in Japan to combine the style and techniques of European literature with the reality of Japanese life. He is best known for his novel* The Quilt, *published in 1908, which tells the story of a love affair between a married writer and a young woman. Katai served with the Japanese army in the Russo-Japanese War of 1904–1905. That experience may help explain the strongly anti-militaristic slant of his work.*

SETTING: *In 1903 the Japanese government, angered over insulting treatment by the Russians, sank two Russian warships and torpedoed the main Russian force in Port Arthur. It then sent thousands of troops into Korea and Manchuria. These were clearly the actions of an expansionist, militaristic state demanding international recognition. In the treaty signed at Port Arthur on September 5, 1905, Russia capitulated, recognizing Japanese political, military, and economic interests in Korea; transferring to Japan territory in Liaotung; paying the Japanese costs of maintaining Russian prisoners; and granting fishing rights off the coast of Siberia. Most importantly, Japan's stunning and unexpected victory led to its recognition as a world power.*

One Soldier

Tayama Katai

He started walking again.

The rifle was heavy, the pack was heavy, his legs were heavy. His aluminum canteen clanked noisily against his bayonet. The sound jarred horribly on his strained nerves, and he tried first one, and then another and another way of silencing it; but the clanking went on and on. He gave up.

The sickness had not really gone, and he breathed with difficulty. Shivering fits, spasms of heat and icy cold, passed incessantly through his frame. His head burned like fire, and his temples throbbed. What had made him leave the hospital, he wondered? Why — when the army doctor had asked him to stay — why had he left the hospital? He asked

---

Translated by G. W. Sargent. "One Soldier" is reprinted from *Modern Japanese Literature: An Anthology,* edited by Donald Keene (New York: Grove Press, 1956).

the question, but he felt no regrets over his decision. There had been fifteen of them there, sick and wounded, lying on bare boards in a small room, part of a dilapidated house which the retreating enemy had abandoned. For twenty days he had endured the decay and the dirt, the moaning, the oppressive closeness, and the swarms of frightening flies. For food they had had rice-bran porridge with the merest pinch of salt, and he had often known the pangs of hunger. He felt sick even now as he recalled the latrine at the rear of the hospital. The pits were shallow, dug in haste, and the stench struck forcibly at your eyes and nostrils. Flies zoomed around you. Dirty, and black as coal.

Anything was better than that. It was better to be here on this broad open plain. You could not imagine how much better. The plains of Manchuria were vast and deserted, endless fields of tall, ripening cane. But the air was fresh and clean. There was sunshine, there were clouds, there were mountains — he became suddenly aware of a dreadful clamor, and he stopped and turned in its direction. It was the same train that he had seen before, still over there on the track. Hundreds of Chinese coolies swarmed about the long, boiler-less, funnel-less monster, pushing frantically, like ants returning home with some gigantic prey.

The rays of the evening sun slanted across the scene, giving it the unreal clarity of a painting.

The noncommissioned officer he had noticed before was still riding on the train. There he was, the one standing aloft on the freight car with the tallest load of rice bales. He shouted to him.

"I'm sick. I can't walk. Can you give me a lift as far as Anshan?"

The fellow was laughing at him. "This train's not for soldiers. I don't know any regulation which says the infantry should ride on trains."

"I'm sick. Can't you see I'm sick? It's beriberi. If I can get to Anshan my unit will be there, I'm certain. Soldiers should help each other, you know. Give me a lift, please!"

He was imploring him, but the fellow would not listen. He only mocked. "Still a private, eh? Time you got yourself some stripes!"

The battles at Chin Chou and Têli-ssu had been won by common soldiers, hadn't they? Blockhead! Brute!

Suddenly a different train — the train in which he had set out for the war from the barracks at Toyohashi — passed before his mind's eye. The station was a mass of flags. Cheers resounded — banzai! banzai! Then, without warning, he was gazing into his wife's face. It was not the tear-stained face which had bade him good-bye at the gate, but a beautiful, smiling face from some moment — he could not remember the time or

place exactly — when he had wondered at its loveliness with all his heart.
His mother was shaking him by the shoulder now. It was time to get up,
she was saying. He would be late for school. Somehow his mind had
slipped back to his school-days. And now the evening sun was glistening on
the bald pate of a ship's captain, in the bay at the back of the house. The
captain was scolding a group of children, and one of those children was
himself.

These shadows from the past and the painful, unpleasant realities of
the present were clearly differentiated in his mind, but only a hairsbreadth
separated them. The rifle was heavy, the pack was heavy, his legs were
heavy. From the waist down he might have been another man, and he
hardly knew whether it was he or someone else walking. The brown road —
its parched mud surface deeply pocked and rutted by the boots, straw
sandals, and gun-carriage wheels which had once sunk into it — stretched
on and on before him. He had little love left for these Manchurian roads.
How far must he go before the road came to an end? How far before he
need walk no farther along it? The pebbled roads of his home district, the
sandy roads along the seashore, wet after rain . . . how he longed for those
smooth pleasant surfaces. This was a big broad highway, but there was not
a smooth level patch to be seen. After a day's rain it would be as sticky as
wet wall-plaster, and your boots, perhaps even the calves of your legs,
would sink halfway into the mud. On the night before the battle at
Ta-shih-ch'iao he had trudged in darkness through ten miles of oozy mire.
Flecks of it had caked the back of his blouse and even the hair at the back
of his head. That was the time when they were detailed to convoy the
gun-carriage. The carriages had sunk into the mud and wouldn't budge an
inch, and they had shoved and shoved to get them moving again. If the
Third Regiment's artillery failed to move on ahead and take up their
positions there could be no attack. And after working the night through
there was that battle the next day. Endless streams of shells, theirs and the
enemy's, passing overhead with a nasty, whining rush. The hot midday sun
scorching down from directly above. Past four o'clock they came to close
quarters with the enemy infantry. There was the sharp crackle of rifle fire,
like beans popping in a frying pan. Now and again a shot had zipped close
by his ear. Someone nearby in the line had gasped. He had looked around
startled, and seen the soldier topple forward, blood oozing slowly from a
bullet wound in his stomach, glistening red in the warm evening sun. That
soldier had been a good sort: cheerful, a nondrinker, at home in any
company. After the landing they had gone out together on foraging duties,
and they had rounded up pigs together. But that man was gone from the

world of the living. It was somehow impossible to think it, but impossible to deny it.

Overtaking him, along the brown road, came a line of wagons loaded with army provisions. Some were drawn by donkeys, some by mules and he listened to the strident shouts of their Chinese drivers — whoa, whoa, whee! — and to the cracking of the long whips, as they flashed in the evening sun. The road was so deeply pitted that the carts moved forward in a series of uneasy lurches, like ships crashing into waves. He felt weak. His breathing was as difficult as ever. He could go no farther like this. He started running after the wagons to ask for a lift.

The canteen went clank-clank. It jarred horribly. The odds and ends in his pack and the rounds in his ammunition pouches clattered noisily up and down. At times the butt of his rifle struck against his thigh, and he almost leapt in agony.

"Hi! Hi!"

They could not hear him.

"Hi! Hi!"

He put his body's whole strength behind his shouts. They had heard, of course, but not one of them turned to look. They must have guessed that there was no money in it. Momentarily he slackened his pace, but he ran forward again, and this time managed to draw level with the last wagon in the line.

The load of rice bales towered above him like a mountain. He saw the Chinaman glance behind. It was a plump, unpleasant face — but he gave the man no chance to say yes or no. He jumped on, and, gasping painfully for breath, settled himself among the bales. The Chinaman urged on his mules, seemingly resigned to suffer the intrusion. The wagon bumped and lurched on its way.

His head reeled, and heaven and earth seemed to revolve about him. His chest was aching, his forehead throbbing. He was going to be sick. A sense of uneasiness and foreboding invaded every corner of his being with fearful insistence. And at the same time, while the dreadful lurching started again, all kinds of voices whispered inside his head and close around his ears. He had experienced similar bouts before, but none of them had been as bad as this.

They must have left the open plain and entered a village. A greenness of thick shady willows waved above him. The rays of the evening sun, piercing the greenness, clearly revealed each tiny leaf. He saw low shapeless roofs, and as he passed they seemed to be quivering as though

shaken by a violent earthquake. Suddenly he realized that the cart had
stopped.

They were on a stretch of road shaded by willows. He counted five
carts, drawn up close one behind the other.

Someone grasped him by the shoulder.

It was a Japanese, a corporal.

"You there, what are you up to?"

He raised his aching body.

"What are you doing, riding on this cart?"

It was too much trouble to explain things. He had even lost the will to
speak.

"You can't ride up there. Even if it was allowed, the load's already too
heavy. You're from the Eighteenth Regiment, aren't you?"

He nodded in agreement.

"What's the matter?"

"I was in the hospital until yesterday."

"Are you better now?"

He nodded again, but without any particular meaning.

"It's hard luck your being sick, but you've got to get off this cart. We're
in a hurry. The fighting's started at Liaoyang."

"Liaoyang!" The single word was enough to set his nerves on edge
again. "Has it started already?"

"Can't you hear those guns?"

Some time back he had imagined that a kind of rumbling noise had
begun over beyond the horizon, but he had told himself it could hardly be
Liaoyang yet.

"Has Anshan fallen?"

"We took it the day before yesterday. Looks as if they'll put up some
resistance this side of Liaoyang. It started at six this evening they say."

Yes, there was a faint, distant rumbling and if you listened carefully
there could be no mistake. They were guns. The old disagreeable noises
moved through the air above his head. The infantry was attacking, weaving
through the thick of it. Blood was flowing. As the thoughts flashed through
his mind he experienced a strange mixture of panic and attraction. His
comrades were in that battle. They were shedding their blood for the
Japanese Empire.

He pictured the horrors of the battlefield and the scenes of triumph.
But here, twenty miles away, here on the Manchurian plain all was at
peace, only a sad autumn breeze blowing beneath the evening sun. The

tide of great armies had swept over these villages and their peace was as if it had never been disturbed.

"It'll be a big battle, I suppose?"

"Certainly will."

"Not over in a day?"

"Of course not."

The corporal was speaking eagerly to him now, as one soldier to another, while the distant booming of the guns sounded in their ears. The drivers of the five heavily loaded wagons and the foremen of the Chinese coolies were squatting in a circle, jabbering noisily among themselves. The rays of the evening sun shone aslant the donkeys' long ears, and at times the air was rent with piercing brays. Over among the willows stood a row of five or six white-walled Chinese country houses, and in their gardens he could see tall pagoda trees. There were wells, too, and sheds. An old woman with bound feet hobbled by laboriously. Behind, visible through the leaves of the willows, was the vast empty plain. The corporal was pointing to a chain of brown hills. Beyond them rose a purple-tinged mountain. That was where the guns were firing.

The five wagons moved off.

He was left behind, alone again. He had been told that the next army supply depot was at Hsin-t'ai-tzu. That was another three miles, but there was nowhere to stay the night unless he reached there.

He made up his mind to go on, and he started walking again.

He moved with the utmost difficulty, he was so dog-tired, but somehow even walking was a relief after that wagon. The pain in his stomach was no better, but there was no sense in worrying about that now.

Again the same brown road ahead, the same fields of cane on either side, the same evening sunshine. The same train, even, was passing by on the track. This time it was returning, on the downgrade, and traveling at considerable speed. A train with a locomotive could not have traveled faster, and it made him giddy to watch the cars flashing in and out of the cuttings. The Japanese flag was fluttering on the last car, and he watched it appear and disappear a hundred times amid the cane fields. When it disappeared for a last time, only the noise of the train was left, and mingled with it, the insistent rumble of distant gunfire.

On the road itself there was not a village in sight, but to the west, discernible among gloomy clusters of willow trees, were the occasional brown or white shapes of cottages. There was no sign of inhabitants, but from the cottages rose thin threads of bluish smoke, lonely and cheerless.

The evening shadows had grown to great lengths. Those of the tall canes were darkening the whole breadth of the road, and had already begun to climb the canes opposite. Even the shadows of small weeds by the roadside were stretching enormous distances. In contrast, the hills to the east were now so sharply illuminated that they seemed to float in the air. With its indescribable strength of shadows the loneliness of evening came pressing in upon him.

He came to a break in the canes. Suddenly he saw his own shadow before him, amazingly long. The rifle on his shoulder was moving across the grass far out in the fields. He was stricken with a sense of his isolation.

Insects were singing in the grass. Their cries were strangely unlike those to which he had listened in the fields around his home. This foreignness, coupled with the immensity of the plain, sent a stab of pain through him. The flow of recollections, checked for more than an hour, came suddenly flooding in again.

The face of his mother, his wife, his brother, the faces of women he had known, passed before him in rapid succession as though they were pictures on a revolving paper lantern. The old house in the village, the warm security of his life at home, a fleeting image of himself — so very young he looked — setting out for Tokyo to earn his living. Tokyo. He saw the busy streets at night, the flower-shops, the magazine booths, the rows of newly published books, and — around the corner — the crowded vaudeville theatres and the reception houses: he heard the strumming of samisens, and the forced laughter of the women. Those were good times. The girl he liked best was in a house in Naka-cho, and he had gone there often. She had a round, winsome face, and even now he remembered her with affection. As the eldest son of a prosperous country household he had never known the lack of money, and life had been a series of pleasant experiences. His friends of those days had all gone out into the world now. Only a little while back he had run across one of them, an army captain of the Sixth Division. The fellow had a very high opinion of himself now.

Nothing was more cruel, he thought, than the narrow discipline of army life. But today, oddly enough, the thought roused in him none of the usual spirit of rebellion, not even a sense of martyrdom. He was gripped with fear. When he set out for the war he had dedicated himself body and soul to the service of his country and the Emperor. He had made a fine speech on the theme at his old school in the village. "I have no wish to return alive," he had said. He was in the prime of spirits and health, at that time. He had made that speech, but, of course, he had never expected to die. Beneath it all had been nothing but dreams of victory and glory.

Now, for the first time, he was experiencing an uneasiness on the score of death. He really felt that it was possible that he might not, after all, return alive, and the thought filled him with terror. There was this sickness, this beriberi — and even if he recovered, the war itself was nothing but a vast prison from which, no matter how he struggled and craved for freedom, there was no escape. He recalled some words which his comrade who had been killed had once used to him.

"There's no way out of this hole. We have to be ready to die, and we have to put a good face on it."

And how on earth could he — a prey to fatigue, sickness, and fear — expect to escape from this dreadful inferno? Desertion? He would try even that if it were any good. The undying disgrace to his name would be bad enough, of course, but on top of that, on the dawn after his recapture, there was still the firing squad. The end was death again. But what were his prospects if he pressed on? He must become a man of the battlefields. A man of the battlefields must be resigned to annihilation. For the first time he marveled at his stupidity in leaving the hospital. It would have been so easy to have had himself invalided to the rear. . . .

It was too late now, he was trapped, there was no road of escape. Negative despair invaded his whole being, pressing upon him with irresistible strength. The will to walk was gone. Tears flowed uncontrollably. If there are any gods in this life, help me, help me! Show me a way out! I shall bear every trial with patience after this! I shall do any amount of fine deeds! If I promise you anything I shall never go back on it!

He raised his voice, shouting and sobbing.

His breast heaved. He cried like a baby, the tears streaming down his cheeks. The thought that his body might perish was agonizing. In his breast, until this moment, passions of patriotism had often blazed. On the deck of the transport ship, joining with the others in the military songs, his imagination had been fired by notions of heroic death. If an enemy warship were to appear, he had thought, and sink their ship with a shot . . . if he were destined to be a corpse drifting among the weeds on the sea bottom, he would be proud to die in such a way. At the battle of Chin Chou, crouching low amid the death-dealing rattle of machine guns, he had gone bravely forward. Though there were times when he had been horrified at the bloodshed, the suffering of his comrades, he had felt that it was all for the motherland, all for honor. But the blood of his comrades was not his blood. Face to face with his own death the bravest soldier panicked.

His legs were heavy and weary. He felt sick. The thirty-mile journey — two days on the road, and a bitterly cold night in the open — had certainly played havoc with his already disordered system. The dysentery was gone, but the mild beriberi had become acute. He knew what that might mean . . . paralysis of the heart. He shuddered at the thought. Was there no way of escape at all? He wept aloud as he walked, his nerves on edge, his body shaking, his legs racked with cramp.

The plain was at peace. Now that the huge red sun was about to sink beneath the horizon one half of the sky was gold, the other a dark, deep blue. A speck of cloud, like a bird whose wings were tipped with gold, drifted across the sky. The shadows of the cane merged with the general shadow, and across the vast plain blew the autumn wind. Only a few minutes ago the guns from Liaoyang had been rumbling steadily and distinctly, but now they too had dwindled imperceptibly to silence.

Two privates were running up behind him.

They continued past for a dozen yards or so. Then one turned and started back.

He pulled himself together. He was ashamed to be seen like this, weeping aloud.

"Hi! What's the trouble?"

"Beriberi."

"That's hard luck. Is it bad?"

"It's pretty painful."

"You *are* in a mess. If beriberi affects your heart it's no joke. How far are you going?"

"My unit's over beyond Anshan, I think."

"You can't get that far today."

"I suppose not."

"Come along with us as far as Hsin-t'ai-tzu. We'll get a doctor to look at you."

"Is it a long way?"

"Just over there. You see that hill? This side of it there's the railroad. Where you see the flag flying, that's the Hsin-t'ai-tzu depot."

His spirits revived. He walked along behind the two of them. They were sorry for him, and they carried his rifle and pack. As they walked in front they talked of the day's fighting at Liaoyang.

"Plenty of reserves moving up, aren't there?"

"We're too few to attack. The enemy positions are pretty strong, I'm told."

"Do you think we'll win?"

"We're in for it if we lose."

"If only we could cut behind them for once."

"We'll do it properly this time. You'll see."

He listened intently to what they said. The guns opened up again in the distance.

The supply depot at Hsin-t'ai-tzu was a scene of tremendous activity and confusion. A regiment of the reserve had arrived, and in the shadow of the buildings above the railroad, alongside the stacks of provisions, were rows and rows of soldiers' caps, rifles, and swords. Five barrack buildings, formerly occupied by the enemy railway guard, flanked the rails. A flag fluttered above the building which now served as the supply depot headquarters, and there the confusion was at its worst. Soldiers were gathered outside it in a dense throng, and in and out, in endless succession, hurried officers with long swords hanging at their sides. Fires were lit beneath the depot's three large rice caldrons, and clouds of smoke curled upwards into the evening sky. In one the rice was already cooked, and the mess sergeant, bellowing commands at his subordinates, was supervising a hasty distribution of rations to the assembled soldiers. But since these three caldrons were obviously insufficient to meet the requirements of a whole regiment, the majority had been issued with a ration of hulled rice in their mess kits and were scattering to various parts of the field to prepare their suppers for themselves. The neighborhood was soon dotted with the flames of hundreds of cane fires.

Near one of the barrack buildings men were settling down to the nightlong labor of loading ammunition boxes on to freight trains bound for the front. Infantrymen and railway troops moved to and fro among the freight cars in feverish, ceaseless activity. A single noncommissioned officer directed their movements, issuing rapid words of command from a perch high on the load of a car.

The day was over, but the war went on. From beyond the dark saddle-shaped mountain of Anshan the sound of guns persisted.

Now that he had arrived he made inquiries about a doctor. But there was something incongruous about asking for a doctor here. This was no time or place for people to stop and concern themselves over the life or death of a single soldier. He managed, thanks to the efforts of his two friends, to get himself a small portion of boiled rice. That was all. We can't do much more now. Just wait a little longer. As soon as this regiment moves on we'll find the doctor and bring him to you. Take things easy and get a rest. If you go straight along the road from here, three or four hundred yards at most, you'll see a big house. You'll recognize it without any trouble — there's a sake stall in the entrance. Go right inside and get some sleep . . . that was all they could suggest.

He was sick to death of walking. He took back his rifle and pack, but when he placed them across his shoulders he almost collapsed beneath the weight. But it was impossible to give up here. If he were going to die, he must die in privacy. Yes, privacy . . . anywhere would do. He longed to enter some quiet place and sleep, and rest.

The dark road went on and on. Here and there he passed groups of soldiers. His mind returned suddenly to the barracks at Toyohashi. He had slipped away to a quiet bar and had drunk solidly. In his drunkenness he had struck a sergeant. They gave him a spell in detention. This really was a long road. There was no sign of anything resembling the house they had described. Three or four hundred yards, they had said. He must have come a thousand yards already. Perhaps he'd missed it. He turned and looked back — in the supply depot he could see the gleam of lamps and watchfires, and dark groups of soldiers moving uncertainly, as though they had lost their way. The shouts of the men at work on the ammunition trains reached him through the night air with startling clarity.

It was secluded here. Not a soul around. Suddenly he felt horribly sick. Even if there was no house to hide himself in, he thought, this was a good place to die; and he sank to the ground in exhaustion. Strangely enough he no longer felt as dejected and miserable as before. No memories came back from the past. The shimmering light of the stars shone into his eyes. He raised his head and glanced casually around.

He was surprised to see that a little way before him, somehow unnoticed till now, was a solitary Western-style house. Inside a lamp was burning, and he could see a round, red paper lantern hanging in the doorway. He heard voices.

Sure enough, in the entrance was something which might well be a sake stall. It was difficult to be certain in the dark, but in one corner of the entrance there appeared to be an object like a stove, with embers glowing red beneath it. A straggle of smoke curled up, lightly enfolding the lantern. He could read the writing on the lantern: "Sweet Bean Soup. 5Sen."

He moved forward to see better. In the darkness at one side of the entrance he could make out a low stone step. This is the place, he thought. His first reaction, on realizing that now he might rest, was a feeling of unutterable content. Silently and stealthily he mounted the stone step. It was dark inside. He could not be sure, but he seemed to have entered a corridor. He pushed at what he thought was the first door, but it would not open. Two or three steps farther on was another door. He pushed, but again it would not open.

He went farther inside.

The corridor came to an end. There was no turning. Not knowing what to do next he pressed against the wall on his right, and suddenly the darkness was broken. A door swung back. He could see nothing inside the room, but stars were shining at him, and he knew that in front was a glass window.

He set down his rifle, unhitched his pack, and dropped, suddenly, full length to the floor. He drew a deep, laborious breath. He had reached his haven of peace.

Beneath the feeling of satisfaction a new uneasiness was advancing and taking possession of him. Something akin to fatigue, mental exhaustion, and despair pressed heavily upon his whole being like a weight of lead. Recollections came in disjointed fragments, sometimes flashing at lightning speed, sometimes growing slowly upon his consciousness with the ponderous insistence of a bullock's breathing.

There were throbbing pains in his calves like those of cramp. He writhed on the floor. His body was nearing the limit of its endurance. He tossed and turned, without knowing what he did.

The pain advanced on him like the tide. It raged with the ferocity of a great wind. He raised his legs and banged them on the hard wooden boards. He rolled his body to this side and to that. "This pain . . . !" Not thinking or knowing what he said he cried aloud.

In reality the pain did not yet seem unbearable. It was severe, but he told himself constantly that he must reserve his strength for the next great pain, and that helped, if only a little, to lessen the suffering of the moment.

He did not think so much how sad it was to die, but rather how best to conquer this pain. The weak, tearful, spiritless despair which gripped him was more than matched by this positive will to resist, which stemmed from his conviction, as a human being, that he had a right to live.

He was beyond knowing how much time had passed. He wished the doctor would come, but he had little leisure to dwell on the thought. New pains gripped him.

Nearby, beneath the floor boards, a cricket was singing. Even as he struggled in agony he said to himself that a cricket was singing. The insect's monotonous note of melancholy sank deep into him.

The cramp was returning. He writhed on the boards.

"This pain, this pain, this pain!"

He screamed the words at the top of his voice.

"This pain! Somebody . . . is there no one here?"

The powerful instinct to resist, to live, had fast dwindled, and he was not consciously calling for assistance. He was almost in a stupor. His outbursts were the rustling of leaves disturbed by forces of nature, the voices of waves, the cries of tragic humanity.

"This pain, this pain!"

His voice echoed startlingly in the silence of the room. In this room, until a month ago, officers of the Russian railway guard had lived and slept. When Japanese soldiers first entered it they had found a soot-stained image of Christ nailed to the wall. Last winter those officers had looked out through this window at the incessant snowstorms sweeping across the Manchurian plain, and they had drunk vodka. Outside had stood sentries, muffled in furs. They had joked among themselves about the shortcomings of the Japanese army, and they had bragged. In this room, now, sounded the agonized cries of a dying soldier.

He lay still a moment. The cricket was singing the same melancholy, pleasing song. A late moon had risen over the broad Manchurian plain, the surroundings had grown clearer, and the moonlight already illuminated the ground outside the window.

He cried again. Moaning, despairing, he writhed on the floor. The buttons of his blouse were torn away, the flesh on his neck and chest was scratched and bloody, his army cap was crushed, the strap still about his chin, and one side of his face was smeared with vomit.

Suddenly a light shone into the room. In the doorway, like some statue in its niche, he saw a man, a candle in one hand. The man came silently into the room and held the candle above the sick soldier, where he lay twisting and turning on the floor. The soldier's face was colorless, like that of a dead man.

"What's the matter?"

"This pain, this pain!"

The man hesitated to touch the soldier. He stood by his side a while, looking down; then he placed the candle on the table, fixing it firmly in drops of molten wax, and hurried out of the room. Every object in the room stood clearly revealed in the candlelight. He saw that the untidy bundle in the corner of which he had been dimly aware was his own rifle and pack.

The flame on the candle flickered. The wax rolled down like tears.

After a while the man returned, bringing a soldier with him. He had roused one of a unit lodged for the night in a house across the way. The soldier looked at the sick man's face, and glanced around the room. Then he peered closely at the regimental markings on his shoulder.

The sick man could hear everything they said.

"He's from the Eighteenth Regiment."

"Is that so?"

"When did he come in here?"

"I've no idea. I woke about ten to hear someone screaming in pain. I couldn't make it out — there shouldn't have been anyone in the rest of the house. After I'd listened for a while I heard the cries again, getting louder, and I came here to see what was wrong. It's beriberi . . . a heart attack, too. There's nothing anyone can do about it."

"I suppose there's a doctor at the depot?"

"There is, but I doubt whether he'd come so late as this."

The two stood in silence.

The pain came flooding back again. He groaned. Cry followed cry, in unbearable crescendo.

"He's suffering terribly. Where's he from, I wonder?"

He felt the soldier searching in his breast pocket, removing his regimental paybook. He saw the man's dark, strong features, and he watched him walk close to the candle on the table to examine what he had found, his form dark against the light.

He heard the soldier read, every word reaching him distinctly . . . Private Kato Heisuke, Fukue Village, Atsumi District, Province of Mikawa. Again images of home floated before his eyes. His mother's face, his wife's face, the great house standing amid camphor trees, the slippery rocks on the beach, the blue sea, the faces of the fishermen he had known so well.

The two watchers stood in silence. Their faces were white. From time to time they muttered words of sympathy. He knew now that he was going to die, but the knowledge did not carry with it any particular terror or sadness. He felt that the object which those two were regarding with such anxiety was not himself, but some inanimate thing in which he had no part. If only he could escape from this pain, this intolerable pain!

The candle flickered. The cricket sang on.

At dawn, when the doctor arrived from the depot, the soldier had been dead an hour. He died at about the time that loud cheering from the depot workers announced the departure of the first ammunition train for Anshan, while the morning moon, pale and wan, hung in the sky.

Soon the steady rumble of the guns was heard again. It was the morning of the first of September, and the attack on Liaoyang had begun.

★

★ ★ ★ ★

AUTHOR: *Knuts Lesins (1909--) was born to a talented family in Riga, Latvia. He is known as a musician, journalist, literary and art critic, and author. His first volume of short stories,* Omens in the Dark, *was published in 1938. It was followed by* Faces and Problems in Latvian Music *in 1939 and his first novel,* The Seal of Love, *in 1943. He left Latvia in 1944 when Russia invaded, first going to Germany and then settling in the United States. As a Latvian refugee, who was also an author, he continued to give Latvia a voice in such works as:* Reflections *(1946),* Things That Arrange Themselves *(1948),* The Wine of Eternity *(1949), and* The Proud Hearts *(1952).*

SETTING: *Latvia won its independence from Russia after the First World War and claimed sovereignty between 1918 and 1940. As part of the Molotov-Ribbentrop understanding, the Soviet Union demanded military bases in Latvia and eventually made it a puppet state. This resulted in summary arrests, massive executions, and the deportation of more than thirty-five thousand people. The Germans were welcomed as liberators in 1941. Only later did the harshness of Nazi rule become apparent; again there were arrests and executions. As many as one hundred thousand individuals were taken to Germany as laborers. The German armies were eventually defeated by the Allies and Latvia returned to Soviet control.*

The Dove

Knuts Lesins

It was a clear, chilly morning in August 1944, steeped in the calm radiance peculiar to days that turn towards autumn.

Supervised by Germans of the Todt Organization, the group of men in the wood had begun to fell trees along the wide gravel road to obstruct the passage of tanks. Suddenly the rumbling of caterpillar tracks could be heard, and several men nearest the road raised their heads and listened.

"Tanks," one of them said.

A pale man with a bandaged foot smiled as he sat down under an alder bush. "Retreat! How will they advance again if we set up such grand obstacles all over the place?"

Translated by H. Kundjins and R. Spiers. "The Dove" is reprinted from Ruth Speirs, *The Wine of Eternity* (Minneapolis, Minn.: Univ. Press of Minnesota, 1957) by permission of the publisher.

"Oh well, what does advance or retreat mean these days, anyway? You can only tell by your trousers what's front or back," another man retorted.

Grey shapes could now be seen through the gaps between the trees; they loomed up where the road climbed a hillock, and rapidly bore down upon the wood. The rumbling of their tracks grew louder.

A man dashed excitedly across the road, shouted something, and ran into the wood. He had flung his coat over his shoulder, and his knapsack, dangling from his hand, knocked against his legs and hampered his progress. "Tanks, tanks!" he screamed as he ran past the foremost group of men.

"All right — tanks! So what?" one of them remarked peacefully.

"Russian tanks, with a star!" shouted the man. He stopped, as though the men's presence made this part of the wood safer than any other, and put on his coat and re-arranged his knapsack. At that moment the boom of two explosions reverberated above the wood, and there was a quick rattle of machine-gun fire. A small German defense post had been set up in the gravel pit by the little bridge; they were equipped with anti-tank rockets and had evidently tried to carry out their duties. Several men came running from that direction. Abandoning their saws, axes, and spades, the working party — including the German supervisors — picked up their coats and knapsacks and took to their heels.

"*Die Organisation Todt ist doch tot,*" remarked the man with the bandaged foot, but there was no one left to hear him.

Applying the same tactics the Germans had used at the beginning of the war, the Russians now sent tanks forward wherever they sensed a weak spot in the crumbling body of the front line, not bothering about their rear and putting their new slogan into practice: "The Germans taught us to fight, but we'll give them a refresher course."

Daugavpils had fallen. Demoralized detachments of the German army dragged themselves along various roads towards Riga, their fighting capacity weakened by contingents of the older generation of reservists who were already doubtful about the outcome of the war. Civilians were rounded up, formed into working parties and set to work on entrenchments of which nobody knew for whom, or exactly at what place, they were required. Lines of newly dug trenches often fell undefended into the enemy's hands. But bridges were blown up, crops and houses were burned to the ground, and the roads were crowded with bewildered civilians in full flight.

Paying no attention to the men who had been erecting obstacles, the Russian tanks passed them by and continued on their way, and it was only then that panic broke out in earnest, aroused by the sudden shock and the din of the firing. The wood filled with fugitives, each concerned about his own safety, looking for shelter and hoping to make his way to Riga later on to rejoin his relatives. This working party consisted entirely of citizens of Riga; there were a few manual laborers among them, but mostly they were civil servants and employees of various firms.

Very soon the wood became empty along the road. The only person still remaining was the man with the bandaged foot. The unaccustomed jackboots had bruised his feet, the little toe on the left had begun to fester, and he could not get his foot back into the boot. This alone was sufficient reason for not keeping up with the others, but he did not even try to. He lay down on his stomach behind an alder bush and scanned the countryside around him. He saw several German soldiers from the gravel pit bolting for shelter into an unmown field of rye, and then everything was as quiet and empty as if nothing had happened. The tanks were not interested in individual people, he reasoned; in any case, they had gone, and probably there were no others to follow. "Never go where others go," he repeated to himself; it was a maxim life had taught him, though he could not remember where or when. He was not afraid, and he felt safest when he was alone. The presence of others only depressed him and deprived him of his independence. "Keep away from crowds, something always goes wrong there," he said to himself and calmly stepped out into the road which was gutted by the tanks; he eyed the sun, his knapsack slung over his back, a jackboot in his hand.

His thin, ash-blond hair was tousled; he had calm, regular features, except for his slightly wide mouth which habitually wore a faint smile and gave him a rather boyish look. On closer scrutiny, though, his face revealed a network of fine lines wrought by some secret suffering; he was not young any more. "What can happen to me? Bah! Forward, always forward— that's the safest method of running away," he said to himself; he pushed the jackboot behind the straps of his knapsack and struggled across the ditch.

Limping a little, he made his way southward along its soft, grassy verge, but his apparently carefree air concealed a good deal of defiant despair. Walking in the sun, he soon felt hot, his foot hurt him, and he realized that he would not get very far. After this break-through of the tanks there was no chance of meeting anyone on the road who might give him a lift, no matter in which direction; but he was drawn on by the feeling that there was a farmstead somewhere close at hand. After a while he lay down in the shade to rest. Everything around was silent, warm, and peaceful. Above his head, a sunbeam penetrated through the branches of a pine tree, alighting on its needles with the sharp brilliance of a diamond and breaking up into many little rainbows. He suddenly felt faint with the beauty of this tranquil scene and with some inner yearning which overcame him whenever he was alone and let his mind wander.

"I'll go on my way and pass this branch, and perhaps I'll never see it again," he mused. "I may see other branches, but this particular one — no, never, never again." The thought gave him pain though it was not new to him; it had often crossed his mind when he found himself in places he had not seen before. The same thought had struck him at the sight of a little railway station, or cattle by the roadside, or a girl's kerchief; and every time he had felt inextricably bound, with no power on earth to release him — as water cannot be released from the compulsion to flow downhill.

"Have I grown old?" he asked himself. "Why should this make me sad? No matter where one goes, there'll always be something one sees for the last time. What an unpleasant thought . . ."

In the past he had coveted everything he saw for the first time. And when he groped among his memories his mind lingered over things he had carelessly passed by. He was restless, with a roving mind, capricious and fickle, a man who chased after sunbeams but whose hand remained empty. Somehow, the Goddess of Fortune had granted him too much or too little of her bounty. He had achieved nothing, gained nothing. Yet he had no regrets; rather, there was a certain impudence in his attitude toward things which others clung to and valued highly — they did not seem worth his while.

In the last few years he had seen perish everything that people had attached themselves to. Apparently he had been right all along. But somehow there was a great deal of bitterness in having been so right, and it recoiled upon himself. He had nothing to lose in this thing called war — this whirlpool of feelings, earthly possessions, life, death — as a leaf driven by the wind has nothing to lose. He wanted least of all to stop anywhere, to get entangled with anything; he pursued something vague and intangible, something destined for him alone; but now he had begun to get attached to any trifle, even to the branch of a pine tree. The sunbeam had already moved on; the irritating pain in his foot brought him back to realities.

"Well," he argued, "millions of Chinese have had a hard life for thousands of years. Why be surprised if I don't get on too well either!"

Neither a believer nor an unbeliever, he was one of those who at times come to a sudden halt and wonder for an instant: Can this really be all that fate has in store for me? He had the impression that the whole world was holding its breath at this moment; close to death, everyone feels he is the one person on this earth who commands universal solicitude. But he was not prepared to die. His defiant mood returned, and he reviewed his position with all the stoicism he could muster. "There are sure to be farm buildings here. I'll walk in and wash my foot, and I'll drink milk and lie down to sleep, even if it has to be above the stables, and I'll be better off than all those cowards who scurried into the wood."

Limping, he continued on his way. He stopped by the edge of the wood and surveyed the sun-drenched countryside and the wrecked little bridge which seemed to have been the only victim in the short battle. He had not been mistaken; there was a farmstead; there even were two of them. The one on the hillock had been burned down, and smoke was still rising from its ruins, but the one in the valley had escaped destruction, probably because it was tucked away behind trees which screened it from the road. There were two faded, warped little wooden notice boards by the road leading to the farms, and he read: New Veveri — 0.5 km; Old Veveri — 0.8 km. It was Old Veveri, then, to which the inscrutable course of this day's wanderings was to lead him. He increased his pace as though he were a guest expected at the farm.

It was a beautiful old farmstead; the yard lay in the shade of three lime trees, and there was an orchard lower down the slope. None of the buildings showed any signs of damage; they seemed to regard him with welcoming, kindly faces. There were marigolds, sweetpeas, and pansies blossoming in flowerbeds all along the front of the main building, and the pretty sand-strewn path was clean and newly raked. He stopped for a moment at the sight of this miracle, this complete unawareness of war or human anguish. The windows sparkled in the sun like pure silver, some hens strutted about in the yard, and a cat which had been sitting on the bench bristled up when it saw him and slid away round the corner of the house. But no dogs barked, and the doors of the cowshed, stable, and cart house stood ajar; he looked inside and saw that there were neither horses, cattle, nor carts; the only things left were old sledges and pieces of harness.

Without hope of finding anyone, he hammered with his fist on the closed kitchen door, but nobody answered. He rattled at the windows, but they gave him an empty stare. He thought for a moment, and then he carefully groped under the stones beneath the porch and — he was right — he found a key there, buried in the earth. Perhaps the owners of the farm had left it there out of long-established habit, or perhaps with the forlorn hope that they might come back again.

As though reluctant to give him access, the old door creaked in its hinges as it slowly opened and revealed a dark kitchen. There were bacon rinds in the frying pan on the hearth, and the remains of porridge in the saucepan. He walked through the rooms and found them in greater disorder than had appeared when he looked in through the windows. Chests of drawers, cupboards, and table drawers had been carelessly, hurriedly shut, but had not been completely emptied. In great haste, probably frightened by the fire on the neighboring farm, the people had obviously snatched up the most useful things — linen, clothes, food — and had taken as much as they could load onto a few carts. A clock was still calmly ticking on the parlor wall. There were crumpled sheets and pillows on the beds, but no blankets, and an old sheepskin coat hung in the corner by the wardrobe. In the larder he discovered half a loaf of bread, buttermilk, gooseberry jam, a little dish full of melted fat, a jar of pickled cucumbers, vinegar in a fluted bottle, and coarse grey salt on a saucer.

He walked through the rooms, ill at ease, feeling he ought to knock at each door before entering, though he knew it would serve no purpose since he was the only person here. Suddenly he began to enjoy being in sole possession. True, he was sorry for these people who had been forced to abandon in a few hours what had taken a lifetime to build up. Every trifling object left behind was part of a ruined life; it was sad to look at them. They reminded him of water plants cast out on the shore and withering into greyness, though a short time ago, in the depth of the lake, they had been of fantastic beauty, full of life and color.

But he did not wish for human company. He settled down comfortably in the kitchen and ate whatever came to hand, supplementing his meal with things out of his knapsack, and he grew calm and peaceful — though with that little touch of peevishness that comes to people who have dined well. Then he cleaned himself and bathed his foot; the sore was developing into an abscess, and he wrapped a warm woolen cloth round his foot, closed the shutters of the back room, locked the door, and went to bed, covering himself with the old sheepskin coat. Smiling, he thought that this bed and coat very likely belonged to the master of the farm himself, and he fell asleep.

*   *   *

He woke at the sound of distant firing, refreshed by sleep, alert, but slightly puzzled. His brain and his instinct of self-preservation sprang into action, sharp and quick. For a moment he sat on the edge of the bed, trying to grasp the situation and remember where he was. A series of vivid images flitted through his mind, showing him the progress of his wanderings that had ultimately led him right into the farmer's bed, and he sprang to his feet and pushed the window and the shutters wide open. The sky was clear, and the firing far off. The garden unfolded before him in the golden light of the afternoon: in the foreground, a tall tree with some rosy apples still on its topmost branches and, beyond the currant bushes, uniform rows of low trees with boughs drooping under the weight of large green and yellow apples.

"But where is the battle?" he asked himself. Had the front line moved on past the farm while he was asleep, and had it been consolidated? Tanks were usually followed by mechanized infantry units, and if that happened he would be in a tight spot. Suddenly he realized how easily he was moving about the room: his foot gave him no trouble at all. When he unwound the wrappings he saw that the abscess had burst, "Just at the right moment," he thought. "A bit of salve and some muslin, and I'll be able to march back." He needed warm water, but it was risky to light a fire: they might begin to shell the farmhouse. He tended the abscess as well as he could, praising himself for his foresight which had prompted him to put iodized salve and strips of muslin into his knapsack.

"There isn't really much difference between a man's body and his mind," he said to himself. "In fact, the mind is worse: some idea takes root in you, and no amount of medicine can rid you of it." With great difficulty he forced his neatly bandaged foot into the boot, but it hurt when he tried to walk; he obviously would not be able to march. "Nature, like fate, does everything at the right moment," he thought, and hunted up a pair of old wooden clogs in the kitchen, slipped his feet comfortably into them and began to consider the idea of marching in them.

"Principles are like wooden clogs," he remembered Bismarck's saying, "useful when wading though mud, but no good if one has to run." Well, he was not going to run; he would wait until the battle was over and then try to slip away in the evening dusk. But the battle had already ceased; there was no sound of firing when some airplanes roared into view and disappeared again.

He spent some time going from window to window, expecting to catch sight of the unknown victors and thinking it might be a bad thing if he were found here on the farm. But the road and the surrounding countryside remained quiet, and the orchard was suffused with the tints of sunset. Waiting for darkness to fall, he packed his knapsack and had a meal; finally he went out and stood on the threshold. Pink clouds of dust suddenly rose from the road leading up to the farm, and there was the rattle of cart wheels. What victors were these who rode in carts? He stepped into the yard to have a better look; recognizing German uniforms, he went back to the house and stood in the door.

They were probably the office staff of some disorganized German company of reservists. They drove into the yard in three carts, wagoners, rear-line men, with complete lack of military bearing, dusty, tired, and altogether peaceable. He pushed his knapsack under the bench and waited.

"Well, at last a human being," said the stout sergeant, extricating himself from amid sacks and boxes of various sizes. "Anything to eat?"

The man shrugged his shoulders. "I'm alone and ill."

"Never mind, we'll find something."

"You're welcome to it," he retorted and seated himself on the bench where the cat had been sitting when he entered the yard; like the cat, he bristled slightly, but he did not run away.

At first his presence seemed to embarrass the Germans, but gradually they became more free and easy: there was a thumping and clattering in the house, and from the hen coop came a swiftly stifled cackling.

A thin corporal came up to have a chat with him; it was obvious that he wanted to distract the attention of the master of the farm from what was going on inside the house. But the man on the bench was not talkative.

There was only one thing that interested him: "What has become of the Russian tanks?"

"Oh — smashed up, finished, our Rudel did for them!" They smoked the corporal's cigarettes. Yes, Rudel's dive bombers had destroyed the Russian tanks, as usual. The front was holding firm; it had been nothing to speak of, merely an unsuccessful break-through. And the corporal began to fidget, afraid that he had been talking too long; by not keeping an eye on his dispersed comrades he might have missed the chance of getting something good for himself.

The Germans, it seemed, were doing well for themselves. They discussed whether they should spend the night on the farm, but the sergeant said sharply No; and they all dispersed once more. At the backs of the carts they found room for a few hens with scraggy necks, and then went off to look for something else, striding through the farm buildings and the yard with the curiosity and animation characteristic of people unrestrained by respect for another's property. They dragged out a few armfuls of towels and strips of carpet. The carts grew fuller. They were loaded with all sorts of trash: boxes, saucepans, chairs. But the latter were old and broken, and a solder carried two new wicker chairs from the parlor into the yard; when he noticed the man on the bench watching him he nodded understandingly and took the battered chairs from the cart: "Here's something to replace the others; they aren't really bad at all, but you must understand — war — we've no time to repair them," and he carried them back into the house. Thus they strode about, backwards and forwards, and at times it seemed as though they carried more into the house than out of it. They were newcomers to the front and had only just begun to taste the sweetness of looting; they were not experienced enough to distinguish between the useful and the useless.

At last silence descended on the farm buildings. All activity was transferred to the orchard, trees were being shaken, and then there was the sound of breaking branches. The loads on the carts grew bigger. The last rays of the sun streaked the sky with a calm, clear yellow. Loud voices and laughter rang out behind the apple trees in the garden, and the noise continued for some time. Several bees flew confusedly about the yard. The man on the bench raised his head and gazed thoughtfully in the direction of the garden; then he hid his knapsack among the firewood in the kitchen and went to see what was going on. The soldiers had discovered half a dozen beehives. Two men had put on gas masks and, their hands protected by leather gloves, busied themselves about the hives with knives and plates while the others stood laughing at a safe distance. It had long become clear to these soldiers that gas, regarded as the most dangerous weapon in the previous war, would not be a decisive factor this time; part of the army had been issued gas masks, but they signified just as little as the words *Gott mit uns* on the German soldiers' belts, also dating back to the previous war.

The man stopped about ten paces from the soldiers; a bitter taste rose to his mouth as he said: "At last you need gas masks."

"Perhaps you need one, too" one of the bystanders called out, throwing him a gas mask. He trod on it contemptuously and went straight towards the bee hives. The soldiers collected the honeycombs they had taken from the hives, and stepped back. They were only rear-line men. "What a hellish day," the man thought, "what do I care about this farm and these hives."

But an inner voice said: There comes a time when you must go. And he went. He felt three, four stings on his neck and cheeks, but he went. He put his head into the open hive; there was a dark, quiet throng of bees, and as he had no idea what to do he arranged the remaining honeycombs in equal distances from each other. The bees crawled over his hands, and he hurt none of them and none stung him. Some kind of friendship had sprung up between him and the bees, and it was stronger than any he had ever felt before. He replaced the roof on the first hive and then busied himself about the second one in the same manner, fully aware that this was not a beekeeper's way of doing things but an action absolutely essential to himself. The soldiers stood about in silence, and then they began to drift back to the yard.

"Yes, yes," the corporal said, "bees know their master," and he slapped the man on the shoulder. "But it's war now, and who can tell when I'll get home again." They all assembled in the yard, and the sergeant, climbing into one of the carts, pressed five Reichsmarks into the man's hand and said "Goodnight." Then the soldiers made ready to leave, convinced that Europe had never seen an army as honest as theirs.

"Perhaps you'd like to come with us?" suggested the thin corporal, but he stopped short when he saw the sergeant's forbidding look. For the sergeant had a secret that was not to be divulged to anyone: the German army was in retreat. This was obvious to everybody, but no one was allowed to mention it. Even in retreat this army was marching forward.

The man tersely said: "No!" And while he said it he felt that he was doing violence to his own good sense, that he ought to leave with the soldiers, that he would not get anywhere by himself with his sore foot, that he ought to scramble out of the invisible stream which was sweeping him along. But the bee stings hurt him, and he felt as though he had received a slap in the face — aimed at himself and, through him, at the farmer with whose fur coat he had covered himself in the night.

He sat down on the bench and said to himself: "There are countries whose people could live happily if it weren't for droughts or floods, earthquakes, locusts, snakes, and crocodiles, oil or gold; but we have none of these, we only have the sunset and sunrise and the fruits of our labor; this land of ours is so bright and clean that nothing impure wells up from it, only the sap of the birch trees in the spring, and it intoxicates none but those who have gazed deeply into the sun. . . . But all this is outweighed by the fact that we are situated between two gigantic nations who always imagine that they are too small to be happy; and this is worse than droughts and floods, earthquakes, snakes, crocodiles, mosquitoes, and all the rest of it. It is so much worse that even I, who have never troubled myself about doing anything particular for this country, have to take to the road tonight."

But everything is equally safe and equally endangered in this world where, who knows for what reason, the swallow under the eaves and the ant on the path feel safer than the best-equipped soldier; where at times everything is decided by the momentary conjunction of a few events — a conjunction which seems accidental but flows from a will that is free precisely because it cannot foresee the consequences of the actions it has engendered.

The man with the knapsack could have slammed the door and walked away toward the north; but instead he invented reasons for staying yet a while. He closed the shutters, lit the oil lamp in the farmer's room, rummaged about until he found a dusty mirror, and extracted the bees' stings from his face. It had begun to swell, and for an instant his jocular mood returned. "A few more stings," he thought, "and this mirror would be too small to reflect my face." Well, never mind, at least he had saved the rest of the beehives.

Yet, hadn't he, too, come to this farm like a thief, to warm himself by the cold embers? And then something inexplicable had turned him into its protector.

Once more he walked through all the rooms and, compelled by a suddenly awakened love, began to put them in order. He carefully arranged the chairs in the corners, closed the drawers, picked up some books that had tumbled from the shelf and put them back in their places in a neat row; indeed, he was overcome by such an urge for tidiness that he went to look for a broom and swept the floors, which had been dirtied by the soldiers' boots. Now and then he glanced at the framed photographs on the walls: bearded men, women in blouses buttoned up to the throat and with hair swept upwards and tightly curled, a young girl in her long white confirmation dress, a hymnbook in her hands. Yet her eyes were full of the usual alluring promise of bliss — virtuous and wedded — and he gazed at her with pleasure. "Look," he thought, "these people have lived, and they still live, and I never knew of their existence, but now I am thinking of them!" He felt they were watching him at his work.

He went out again, stood on the threshold, and smoked and watched the darkness thicken. "Shall I go or shall I stay?" he wondered. There was coolness and peace in the dark shadows, but also some secret terror, mysterious like life or death. In his heart the vagabond struggled with the fugitive who had warmed himself under a stranger's roof and did not want to leave a shelter he had sought so long. He had attached importance to so many things in the course of his life but, after all, nothing had really been important. He had cast aside the women who loved him; they had either been too good to him or had wished him to be different from what he was, and he never wanted to stop anywhere, to make the least sacrifice. The others, the women for whose sake he had thought he might alter his ways, had not loved him. Or perhaps he was wrong, perhaps he could not think clearly, his face was so sore and swollen with the bee stings. . . .

He had always craved something unusual. But there was nothing unusual here: a forsaken farmstead, the same as a hundred others these days, and a fugitive who happened to have walked in. It was only in his mind that the unusual existed.

"I've never had a farm," he meditated, "and I'll never have one either — except tonight. I have entered perfectly free, and I shall leave perfectly free; but for one more night I'll cover myself with the farmer's fur coat. I am the protector of this farm, and to the best of my abilities I am its master. Only this one night! Then I'll go away, and I'll never get entangled with anything; I'll care for nothing, and nothing will make me stop and linger — neither the branch of a pine tree nor other people's misfortunes. . . .

Perhaps, if I had known nothing but this farm and this girl in her confirmation dress, I might always have been as calm and peaceful as I am today. I might just as well have given up my life to her as to my doubts and my restlessness, my unsatisfied ambitions; my life would have completed the same circle, and at least I'd know why I am here at this place to which I have now come with no volition on my part. As things are, it seems as though this farm were the purpose of my existence."

Perhaps he was one of the last to feel that thoughts had no boundaries and that God had not yet chained Himself to two alternatives. He covered himself with the farmer's old fur coat, thinking that all things preserve the best that has been granted them: the fur coat — warmth, the human being — sleep.

*　*　*

They came at daybreak, a patrol of five men, half-frozen, their uniforms saturated with dew; they must have been lying for an hour or so in the bushes, watching the farmhouse before venturing to enter it.

When the knock came on the shutters the man woke with a start and knew at once what it meant. The knock was like the sound of a bell he had been expecting all his life. Why had he closed the shutters? It had been childish — stupid to do so! He had wanted to sit in this house for a while by the light of the lamp. If the shutters had been left open they would never have thought of knocking.

No, that wouldn't have been much use either. He ought to have slept somewhere above the cowshed. But who could tell whether that would have made any difference. He ought to have left the farm yesterday. Why had he not gone? Because he had nowhere in the world to go.

For a moment he was overcome by the purely animal fear of the hunted man, and he even thought of fleeing. But his panic subsided; he passed his hand over his face, collected his thoughts, threw his coat over his shoulders, and went to open the door — slowly, deliberately, trying to regain his self-control.

The eyes of five men and the barrels of two automatics turned sharply upon him, and a voice shouted: "Hands up!" He did not raise his hands; he had never done so in all his life; the command insulted him. But the Russians were not so rigidly formalistic as the Germans. After one of them had hurriedly gone through the man's pockets and found nothing there, the command lost its force. They forgot having given it.

"You — the farmer?" one of them asked, but before the man had time to reply another soldier exclaimed: "Look, he's a proper fat-face!" His face was so swollen with the bee stings that it had become perfectly round.

Two men went off to search the rest of the house while the other three remained with him in the farmer's room. "Have you seen any Germans?" asked the lieutenant.

"Yes, I have."

"Many?"

"Six."

"What's become of them?"

"They left yesterday."

"Where did they go?"

"They followed the road."

He had left his watch lying on the table, and now he saw it disappear into a man's pocket while he was being interrogated.

They searched the place; questioned him, taking him with them wherever they went; climbed to the attics, the lofts above the stable, and the cowshed. They had been brought up to trust nobody.

"Where are the others? Why didn't you run away?"

"That's none of your business," he retorted.

The Russian raised his head: "Listen, you — kulak! You've stayed behind in order to spy, haven't you?"

But at that moment they had reached the granary, and it attracted their attention because the door was locked.

"Why is it locked? Where's the key?" they asked.

"I don't know, I haven't got it."

"Of course you know! Get it at once!"

He realized that the moment had come to end this play acting, to tell them that he was not the owner of this farm but only a man who had been set to work digging entrenchments, that he had got here by chance, that he was sick and had been stung by bees; but his mouth stayed obstinately shut.

One of the men put his ear to the door of the granary and smiled cunningly.

"Where's the mistress of the farm?" he asked.

"She's not here."

"She's hidden herself, hasn't she?" With a crafty grin he hammered on the door.

"Open up!" the lieutenant called out.

"Listen, there's someone in there!" The soldier took hold of the man's collar and pulled his head down to the keyhole.

He was puzzled: there were strange sounds behind the door — a kind of rustling, a tripping about — and he could not make out what they meant. But it was clear that there was someone in the granary.

Was somebody really hiding there? One of the household, or perhaps a fugitive? That was a bad thing to do, just as stupid as his not leaving the farm.

"I don't hear anything," he said.

"So that's it, eh? You don't hear anything. Perhaps you'll hear better now!" The pistol butt struck his temple, lightly, it seemed, just a little knock, but he found himself sitting on the grass which seemed strangely green — never in his life had he seen such brilliantly green grass. He was violently sick; he saw them break the door in, and saw a blue pigeon suddenly fly out of the granary.

"Oh, the devils," said one of the soldiers, and he gave the man on the grass a look in which there was almost a hint of compassion. But that was exactly what the man did not need.

He raised his head and smiled. The five men understood nothing.

A pigeon, an ordinary pigeon, had found its way into the granary; perhaps it had entered by the hatch on the roof and scrambled through a gap between the planks of the ceiling, and then it had come upon some scattered grains of corn. This man was an eccentric who staked his life against the pigeon's.

He was happy; this moment set the crown on his useless existence. Holding his head high, he said: "What did you come here for, you scum? To capture doves?" The defiance of a race that had been beaten, humiliated, flogged, rose in him; it had furnished the vagabond with a sound contempt for his enemies. Contempt is harder to bear than hatred; at once the pistol was pointed at him, but at the same moment the lieutenant shouted, "Don't shoot!" He interfered not out of mercy but because they were reconnaissance men, ordered not to give themselves away unnecessarily.

The pistol was turned round, and the butt struck the man another blow, heavier than the first. "Even while we die we are happier than you are while you live," he sighed and surrendered to the dark stream that washed away his consciousness.

The sun rose slowly above the wood.

★

★ ★ ★ ★

AUTHOR: *Jean-Paul Sartre (1905–1980) is best known as one of France's leading existentialists. He received an early formal education at the Lycée de la Rochelle and during World War I attended the Lycée Henri IV. Between the wars he received his* Agrégation de Philosophie *and then taught and wrote, mainly on theories of the imagination and the emotions. He was drafted into the French army as a private in 1939 and sent to the Maginot Line. He was taken prisoner by the Germans and held for nine months. After returning to France, he took a writer's role in the French Resistance, writing for* Combat *(edited by Albert Camus) while teaching at the Lycée Pasteur. His writings are extensive.* The Age of Reason, The Reprieve, Being and Nothingness, *and* Troubled Sleep *are well known. The following story was first published in 1936.*

SETTING: *The Spanish Civil War of 1936–1939 was the culmination of years of political and social strife. The Spanish Republic, established in 1931, fell when the leftist "Popular Front" won the 1936 elections and instituted a program of secular reforms. In reaction, a military coup was staged later in that year by the extreme right of the Falange (Fascist) party, headed by General Francisco Franco. The ensuing civil conflict became a testing ground for World War II. Volunteers from Britain, France, and the United States fought the Falange alongside Loyalists (Republicans) and Communists. The eventual Fascist victory was used by Germany and Italy to support their own incipient nationalist movements. At the conclusion of the war, men and women from virtually every major country were tried, convicted, and executed. This is the story of one such trial.*

The Wall

Jean-Paul Sartre

They pushed us into a large white room and my eyes began to blink because the light hurt them. Then I saw a table and four fellows seated at the table, civilians, looking at some papers. The other prisoners were herded together at one end and we were obliged to cross the entire room to join them. There were several I knew, and others who must have been foreigners. The two in front of me were blond with round heads. They looked alike. I imagine they were French. The smaller one kept pulling at his trousers, out of nervousness.

Translated by Marie Jolas. "The Wall" is reprinted from *The Bedside Book of Famous French Stories* (New York: Random House, 1945).

This lasted about three hours. I was dogtired and my head was empty. But the room was well-heated, which struck me as rather agreeable; we had not stopped shivering for twenty-four hours. The guards led the prisoners in one after the other in front of the table. Then the four fellows asked them their names and what they did. Most of the time that was all — or perhaps from time to time they would ask such questions as "Did you help sabotage the munitions?" or, "Where were you on the morning of the ninth and what were you doing?" They didn't even listen to the replies, or at least they didn't seem to. They just remained silent for a moment and looked straight ahead, then they began to write. They asked Tom if it was true he had served in the International Brigade. Tom couldn't say he hadn't because of the papers they had found in his jacket. They didn't ask Juan anything, but after he told them his name, they wrote for a long time.

"It's my brother José who's the anarchist," Juan said. "You know perfectly well he's not here now. I don't belong to any party. I never did take part in politics." They didn't answer.

Then Juan said, "I didn't do anything. And I'm not going to pay for what the others did."

His lips were trembling. A guard told him to stop talking and led him away. It was my turn.

"Your name is Pablo Ibbieta?"

I said yes.

The fellow looked at his papers and said, "Where is Ramon Gris?"

"I don't know."

"You hid him in your house from the sixth to the nineteenth."

"I did not."

They continued to write for a moment and the guards led me away. In the hall, Tom and Juan were waiting between two guards. We started walking. Tom asked one of the guards, "What's the idea?" "How do you mean?" the guard said. "Was that just the preliminary questioning, or was that the trial?" "That was the trial," the guard said. "So now what? What are they going to do with us?" The guard answered drily, "The verdict will be told you in your cell."

In reality, our cell was one of the cellars of the hospital. It was terribly cold there because it was very drafty. We had been shivering all night long and it had hardly been any better during the day. I had spent the preceding five days in a cellar in the archbishop's palace, a sort of dungeon that must have dated back to the Middle Ages. There were lots of prisoners and not much room, so they housed them just anywhere. But I was not homesick for my dungeon. I hadn't been cold there, but I had been alone, and that gets to be irritating. In the cellar I had company. Juan didn't say a word: he was afraid, and besides, he was too young to have anything to say. But Tom was a good talker and knew Spanish well.

In the cellar there was a bench and four straw mattresses. When they led us back we sat down and waited in silence. After a while Tom said, "Our goose is cooked."

"I think so too," I said. "But I don't believe they'll do anything to the kid."

Tom said, "They haven't got anything on him. He's the brother of a fellow who's fighting, and that's all."

I looked at Juan. He didn't seem to have heard.

Tom continued, "You know what they do in Saragossa? They lay the guys across the road and then they drive over them with trucks. It was a Moroccan deserter who told us that. They say it's just to save ammunition."

I said, "Well, it doesn't save gasoline."

I was irritated with Tom; he shouldn't have said that.

He went on, "There are officers walking up and down the roads with their hands in their pockets, smoking, and they see that it's done right. Do you think they'd put 'em out of their misery? Like hell they do. They just let 'em holler. Sometimes as long as an hour. The Moroccan said the first time he almost puked."

"I don't believe they do that here," I said, "unless they really are short of ammunition."

The daylight came in through four air vents and a round opening that had been cut in the ceiling, to the left, and which opened directly onto the sky. It was through this hole, which was ordinarily closed by means of a trapdoor, that they unloaded coal into the cellar. Directly under the hole, there was a big pile of coal dust; it had been intended for heating the hospital, but at the beginning of the war they had evacuated the patients and the coal had stayed there unused; it even got rained on from time to time, when they forgot to close the trapdoor.

Tom started to shiver. "God damn it," he said, "I'm shivering. There, it is starting again."

He rose and began to do gymnastic exercises. At each movement, his shirt opened and showed his white, hairy chest. He lay down on his back, lifted his legs in the air and began to do the scissors movement. I watched his big buttocks tremble. Tom was tough, but he had too much fat on him. I kept thinking that soon bullets and bayonet points would sink into that mass of tender flesh as though it were a pat of butter.

I wasn't exactly cold, but I couldn't feel my shoulders or my arms. From time to time, I had the impression that something was missing and I began to look around for my jacket. Then I would suddenly remember they hadn't given me a jacket. It was rather awkward. They had taken our clothes to give them to their own soldiers and had left us only our shirts and these cotton trousers the hospital patients wore in midsummer. After a moment, Tom got up and sat down beside me, breathless.

"Did you get warmed up?"

"Damn it, no. But I'm all out of breath."

Around eight o'clock in the evening, a Major came in with two Falangists.

"What are the names of those three over there?" he asked the guard.

"Steinbock, Ibbieta and Mirbal," said the guard.

The Major put on his glasses and examined his list.

"Steinbock — Steinbock . . . Here it is. You are condemned to death. You'll be shot tomorrow morning."

He looked at his list again.

"The other two, also," he said.

"That's not possible," said Juan. "Not me."

The Major looked at him with surprise. "What's your name?"

"Juan Mirbal."

"Well, your name is here," said the Major, "and you're condemned to death."

"I didn't do anything," said Juan.

The Major shrugged his shoulders and turned toward Tom and me.

"You are both Basque?"

"No, nobody's Basque."

He appeared exasperated.

"I was told there were three Basques. I'm not going to waste my time running after them. I suppose you don't want a priest?"

We didn't even answer.

Then he said, "A Belgian doctor will be around in a little while. He has permission to stay with you all night."

He gave a military salute and left.

"What did I tell you?" Tom said, "We're in for something swell."

"Yes," I said. "It's a damned shame for the kid."

I said that to be fair, but I really didn't like the kid. His face was too refined and it was disfigured by fear and suffering which had twisted all his features. Three days ago, he was just a kid with a kind of affected manner some people like. But now he looked like an aging fairy, and I thought to myself he would never be young again, even if they let him go. It wouldn't have been a bad thing to show him a little pity, but pity makes me sick, and besides, I couldn't stand him. He hadn't said anything more, but he had turned gray. His face and hands were gray. He sat down again and stared, round-eyed, at the ground. Tom was good-hearted and tried to take him by the arm, but the kid drew himself away violently and made an ugly face. "Leave him alone," I said quietly. "Can't you see he's going to start to bawl?" Tom obeyed regretfully. He would have liked to console the kid; that would have kept him occupied and he wouldn't have been tempted to think about himself. But it got on my nerves. I had never thought about death, for the reason that the question had never come up. But now it had come up, and there was nothing else to do but think about it.

Tom started talking. "Say, did you ever bump anybody off?" he asked me. I didn't answer. He started to explain to me that he had bumped off six fellows since August. He hadn't yet realized what we were in for, and I saw clearly he didn't *want* to realize it. I myself hadn't quite taken it in. I wondered if it hurt very much. I thought about the bullets; I imagined their fiery hail going through my body. All that was beside the real question; but I was calm, we had all night in which to realize it. After a while Tom stopped talking and I looked at him out of the corner of my eye. I saw that he, too, had turned gray and that he looked pretty miserable. I said to myself, "It's starting." It was almost dark, a dull light filtered through the air vents across the coal pile and made a big spot under the sky. Through the hole in the ceiling I could already see a star. The night was going to be clear and cold.

The door opened and two guards entered. They were followed by a blond man in a tan uniform. He greeted us.

"I'm the doctor," he said. "I've been authorized to give you any assistance you may require in these painful circumstances."

He had an agreeable, cultivated voice.

I said to him, "What are you going to do here?"

"Whatever you want me to do. I shall do everything in my power to lighten these few hours."

"Why did you come to us? There are lots of others: the hospital's full of them."

"I was sent here," he answered vaguely. "You'd probably like to smoke, wouldn't you?" he added suddenly. "I've got some cigarettes and even some cigars."

He passed around some English cigarettes and some *puros*, but we refused them. I looked him straight in the eye and he appeared uncomfortable.

"You didn't come here out of compassion," I said to him. "In fact, I know who you are. I saw you with some fascists in the barracks yard the day I was arrested."

I was about to continue, when all at once something happened to me which surprised me: the presence of this doctor had suddenly ceased to interest me. Usually, when I've got hold of a man I don't let go. But somehow the desire to speak had left me. I shrugged my shoulders and turned away. A little later, I looked up and saw he was watching me with an air of curiosity. The guards had sat down on one of the mattresses. Pedro, the tall thin one, was twiddling his thumbs, while the other one shook his head occasionally to keep from falling asleep.

"Do you want some light?" Pedro suddenly asked the doctor. The other fellow nodded, "Yes." I think he was not over-intelligent, but doubtless he was not malicious. As I looked at his big, cold blue eyes, it seemed to me the worst thing about him was his lack of imagination. Pedro went out and came back with an oil lamp which he set on the corner of the bench. It gave a poor light, but it was better than nothing; the night before we had been left in the dark. For a long while I stared at the circle of light the lamp threw on the ceiling. I was fascinated. Then, suddenly, I came to, the light circle paled, and I felt as if I were being crushed under an enormous weight. It wasn't the thought of death, and it wasn't fear; it was something anonymous. My cheeks were burning hot and my head ached.

I roused myself and looked at my two companions. Tom had his head in his hands and only the fat, white nape of his neck was visible. Juan was by far the worst off; his mouth was wide open and his nostrils were trembling. The doctor came over to him and touched him on the shoulder, as though to comfort him; but his eyes remained cold. Then I saw the Belgian slide his hand furtively down Juan's arm to his wrist. Indifferent, Juan let himself be handled. Then, as though absentmindedly, the Belgian laid three fingers over his wrist; at the same time, he drew away somewhat and managed to turn his back to me. But I leaned over backward and saw him take out his watch and look at it a moment before relinquishing the boy's wrist. After a moment, he let the inert hand fall and went and leaned against the wall. Then, as if he had suddenly remembered something very important that had to be noted down immediately, he took a notebook from his pocket and wrote a few lines in it. "The son-of-a-bitch," I thought angrily. "He better not come and feel my pulse; I'll give him a punch in his dirty jaw."

He didn't come near me, but I felt he was looking at me. I raised my head and looked back at him. In an impersonal voice, he said, "Don't you think it's frightfully cold here?"

He looked purple with cold.

"I'm not cold," I answered him.

He kept looking at me with a hard expression. Suddenly I understood, and I lifted my hands to my face. I was covered with sweat. Here, in this cellar, in midwinter, right in a draft, I was sweating. I ran my fingers through my hair, which was stiff with sweat; at the same time, I realized my shirt was damp and sticking to my skin. I had been streaming with perspiration for an hour, at least, and had felt nothing. But this face hadn't escaped that Belgian swine. He had seen the drops rolling down my face and had said to himself that it showed an almost pathological terror; and he himself had felt normal and proud of it because he was cold. I wanted to get up and go punch his face in, but I had hardly started to make a move before my shame and anger had disappeared. I dropped back onto the bench with indifference.

I was content to rub my neck with my handkerchief because now I felt the sweat dripping from my hair onto the nape of my neck and that was disagreeable. I soon gave up rubbing myself however, for it didn't do any good; my handkerchief was already wringing wet and I was still sweating. My buttocks, too, were sweating, and my damp trousers stuck to the bench.

Suddenly, Juan said, "You're a doctor, aren't you?"

"Yes," said the Belgian.

"Do people suffer — very long?"

"Oh! When . . . ? No, no," said the Belgian, in a paternal voice, "it's quickly over."

His manner was as reassuring as if he had been answering a paying patient.

"But I . . . somebody told me — they often have to fire two volleys."

"Sometimes," said the Belgian, raising his head, "it just happens that the first volley doesn't hit any of the vital organs."

"So they have to reload their guns and aim all over again?" Juan thought for a moment, then added hoarsely, "But that takes time!"

He was terribly afraid of suffering. He couldn't think about anything else, but that went with his age. As for me, I hardly thought about it any more and it certainly was not fear of suffering that made me perspire.

I rose and walked toward the pile of coal dust. Tom gave a start and looked at me with a look of hate. I irritated him because my shoes squeaked. I wondered if my face was as putty-colored as his. Then I noticed that he, too, was sweating. The sky was magnificent; no light at all came into our dark corner and I had only to lift my head to see the Big Bear. But it didn't look the way it had looked before. Two days ago, from my cell in the archbishop's palace, I could see a big patch of sky and each time of day brought back a different memory. In the morning, when the sky was a deep blue, and light, I thought of beaches along the Atlantic; at noon, I could see the sun, and I remembered a bar in Seville where I used to drink manzanilla and eat anchovies and olives; in the afternoon, I was in the shade, and I thought of the deep shadow which covers half of the arena while the other half gleams in the sunlight: it really gave me a pang to see the whole earth reflected in the sky like that. Now, however, no matter how much I looked up in the air, the sky no longer recalled anything. I liked it better that way. I came back and sat down next to Tom. There was a long silence.

Then Tom began to talk in a low voice. He had to keep talking, otherwise he lost his way in his own thoughts. I believe he was talking to me, but he didn't look at me. No doubt he was afraid to look at me, because I was gray and sweating. We were both alike and worse than mirrors for each other. He looked at the Belgian, the only one who was alive.

"Say, do you understand? I don't."

Then I, too, began to talk in a low voice. I was watching the Belgian.

"Understand what? What's the matter?"

"Something's going to happen to us that I don't understand."

There was a strange odor about Tom. It seemed to me that I was more sensitive to odors than ordinarily. With a sneer, I said, "You'll understand, later."

"That's not so sure," he said stubbornly. "I'm willing to be courageous, but at least we ought to know . . . Listen, they're going to take us out into the courtyard. All right. The fellows will be standing in line in front of us. How many of them will there be?"

"Oh, I don't know. Five, or eight. Not more."

"That's enough. Let's say there'll be eight of them. Somebody will shout 'Shoulder arms!' and I'll see all eight rifles aimed at me. I'm sure I'm going to feel like going through the wall. I'll push against the wall as hard as I can with my back, and the wall won't give in. The way it is in a e . . . I can imagine all that. Ah, if you only knew how well I can imagine it!"

"Skip it!" I said. "I can imagine it too."

"It must hurt like the devil. You know they aim at your eyes and mouth so as to disfigure you," he added maliciously. "I can feel the wounds already. For the last hour I've been having pains in my head and neck. Not real pains — it's worse still. They're the pains I'll feel tomorrow morning. And after that, then what?"

I understood perfectly well what he meant, but I didn't want to seem to understand. As for the pains, I, too, felt them all through my body, like a lot of little gashes. I couldn't get used to them, but I was like him. I didn't think they were very important.

"After that," I said roughly, "you'll be eating daisies."

He started talking to himself, not taking his eyes off the Belgian, who didn't seem to be listening to him. I knew what he had come for, and that what we were thinking didn't interest him. He had come to look at our bodies, our bodies which were dying alive.

"It's like in a nightmare," said Tom. "You want to think of something, you keep having the impression you've got it, that you're going to understand, and then it slips away from you, it eludes you and it's gone again. I say to myself, afterward, there won't be anything. But I don't really understand what that means. There were moments when I almost do — and then it's gone again. I start to think of the pains, the bullets, the noise of the shooting. I am a materialist, I swear it; and I'm not going crazy, either. But there's something wrong. I see my own corpse. That's not hard, but it's *I* who see it, with *my* eyes. I'll have to get to the point where I think — where I think I won't see anything more. I won't hear anything more, and the world will go on for the others. We're not made to think that way, Pablo. Believe me, I've already stayed awake all night waiting for something. But this is not the same thing. This will grab us from behind, Pablo, and we won't be ready for it."

"Shut up," I said. "Do you want me to call a father confessor?"

He didn't answer. I had already noticed that he had a tendency to prophesy and call me "Pablo" in a kind of pale voice. I didn't like that very much, but it seems all the Irish are like that. I had a vague impression that he smelled of urine. Actually, I didn't like Tom very much, and I didn't see why, just because we were going to die together, I should like him any better. There are certain fellows with whom it would be different — with Ramon Gris, for instance. But between Tom and Juan, I felt alone.

In fact, I liked it better that way. With Ramon I might have grown soft. But I felt terribly hard at that moment, and I wanted to stay hard.

Tom kept on muttering in a kind of absent-minded way. He was certainly talking to keep from thinking. Naturally, I agreed with him, and I could have said everything he was saying. It's not *natural* to die. And since I was going to die, nothing seemed natural any more: neither the coal pile, nor the bench, nor Pedro's dirty old face. Only it was disagreeable for me to think the same things Tom thought. And I knew perfectly well that all night long, within five minutes of each other, we would keep on thinking things at the same time, sweating or shivering at the same time. I looked at him sideways and, for the first time, he seemed strange to me. He had death written on his face. My pride was wounded. For twenty-four hours I had lived side by side with Tom, I had listened to him, I had talked to him, and I knew we had nothing in common. And now we were as alike as twin brothers, simply because we were going to die together. Tom took my hand without looking at me.

"Pablo, I wonder . . . I wonder if it's true that we just cease to exist."

I drew my hand away.

"Look between your feet, you dirty dog."

There was a puddle between his feet and water was dripping from his trousers.

"What's the matter?" he said, frightened.

"You're wetting your pants," I said to him.

"It's not true," he said furiously. "I can't be . . . I don't feel anything."

The Belgian had come closer to him. With an air of false concern, he asked, "Aren't you feeling well?"

Tom didn't answer. The Belgian looked at the puddle without comment. "I don't know what that is," Tom said savagely, "but I'm not afraid. I swear to you, I'm not afraid."

The Belgian made no answer. Tom rose and went to the corner. He came back, buttoning his fly, and sat down, without a word. The Belgian was taking notes.

We were watching the doctor. Juan was watching him too. All three of us were watching him because he was alive. He had the gestures of a living person, the interests of a living person; he was shivering in this cellar the way living people shiver; he had an obedient, well-fed body. We, on the other hand, didn't feel our bodies any more — not the same way, in any case. I felt like touching my trousers, but I didn't dare to. I looked at the Belgian, well-planted on his two legs, master of his muscles — and able to plan for tomorrow. We were like three shadows deprived of blood; we were watching him and sucking his life like vampires.

Finally, he came over to Juan. Was he going to lay his hand on the nape of Juan's neck for some professional reason, or had he obeyed a charitable impulse? If he had acted out of charity, it was the one and only time during the whole night. He fondled Juan's head and the nape of his neck. The kid let him do it, without taking his eyes off him. Then, suddenly, he took hold of the doctor's hand and looked at it in a funny way. He held the Belgian's hand between his own two hands and there was nothing pleasing about them, those two gray paws squeezing that fat red hand. I sensed what was going to happen and Tom must have sensed it too. But all the Belgian saw was emotion, and he smiled paternally. After a moment, the kid lifted the big red paw to his mouth and started to bite it. The Belgian drew back quickly and stumbled toward the wall. For a second, he looked at us with horror. He must have understood that we were not men like himself. I began to laugh, and one of the guards started up. The other had fallen asleep with his eyes wide open, showing only the whites.

I felt tired and over-excited at the same time. I didn't want to think any more about what was going to happen at dawn — about death. It didn't make sense, and I never got beyond just words, or emptiness. But whenever I tried to think about something else I saw the barrels of rifles aimed at me. I must have lived through my execution twenty times in succession; one time I thought it was the real thing; I must have dozed off for a moment. They were dragging me toward the wall and I was resisting; I was imploring their pardon. I woke with a start and looked at the Belgian. I was afraid I had cried out in my sleep. But he was smoothing his mustache; he hadn't noticed anything. If I had wanted to, I believe I could have slept for a while. I had been awake for the last forty-eight hours, and I was worn out. But I didn't want to lose two hours of life. They would have had to come and wake me at dawn. I would have followed them, drunk with sleep, and I would have gone off without so much as "Gosh!" I didn't want it that way, I didn't want to die like an animal. I wanted to understand. Besides, I was afraid of having nightmares. I got up and began to walk up and down and, so as to think about something else, I began to think about my past life. Memories crowded in on me, helter-skelter. Some were good and some were bad — at least that was how I had thought of them *before*. There were faces and happenings. I saw the face of a little *nivolero* who had gotten himself horned during the *Feria*, in Valencia. I saw the face of one of my uncles, of Ramon Gris. I remembered all kinds of things that had happened: how I had been on strike for three months in 1926, and had almost died of hunger. I recalled a night I had spent on a bench in Granada; I hadn't eaten for three days. I was nearly wild, I didn't want to give up the sponge. I had to smile. With what eagerness I had run after happiness, and women, and liberty! And to what end? I had wanted to liberate Spain, I admired Py Margall, I had belonged to the anarchist movement, I had spoken at public meetings. I took everything as seriously as if I had been immortal.

At that time I had the impression that I had my whole life before me, and I thought to myself, "It's all a god-damned lie." Now it wasn't worth anything because it was finished. I wondered how I had ever been able to go out and have a good time with girls. I wouldn't have lifted my little finger if I had ever imagined that I would die like this. I saw my life before me, finished, closed, like a bag, and yet what was inside was not finished. For a moment, I tried to appraise it. I would have liked to say to myself, "It's been a good life." But it couldn't be appraised, it was only an outline. I had spent my life writing checks on eternity, and had understood nothing. Now, I didn't miss anything. There were a lot of things I might have missed: the taste of manzanilla, for instance, or the swims I used to take in summer in a little creek near Cadiz. But death had taken the charm out of everything.

Suddenly, the Belgian had a wonderful idea.

"My friends," he said to us, "if you want me to — and providing the military authorities give their consent — I could undertake to deliver a word or some token from you to your loved ones . . ."

Tom growled, "I haven't got anybody."

I didn't answer. Tom waited for a moment, and then he looked at me with curiosity. "Aren't you going to send any message to Concha?"

"No."

I hated that sort of sentimental conspiracy. Of course, it was my fault, since I had mentioned Concha the night before, and I should have kept my mouth shut. I had been with her for a year. Even as late as last night, I would have cut my arm off with a hatchet just to see her again for five minutes. That was why I had mentioned her. I couldn't help it. Now I didn't care any more about seeing her. I hadn't anything more to say to her. I didn't even want to hold her in my arms. I loathed my body because it had turned gray and was sweating — and I wasn't even sure that I didn't loathe hers too. Concha would cry when she heard about my death; for months she would have no more interest in life. But still it was I who was going to die. I thought of her beautiful, loving eyes. When she looked at me something went from her to me. But I thought to myself that it was all over; if she looked at me *now* her gaze would not leave her eyes, it would not reach out to me. I was alone.

Tom, too, was alone, but not the same way. He was seated astride his chair and had begun to look at the bench with a sort of smile, with surprise, even. He reached out his hand and touched the wood cautiously, as though he were afraid of breaking something, then he drew his hand back hurriedly, and shivered. I wouldn't have amused myself touching that bench, if I had been Tom, that was just some more Irish play-acting. But somehow it seemed to me too that the different objects had something funny about them. They seemed to have grown paler, less massive than before. I had only to look at the bench, the lamp or the pile of coal dust to feel I was going to die. Naturally, I couldn't think clearly about my death, but I saw it everywhere, even on the different objects, the way they had withdrawn and kept their distance tactfully, like people talking at the bedside of a dying person. It was *his own death* Tom had just touched on the bench.

In the state I was in, if they had come and told me I could go home quietly, that my life would be saved, it would have left me cold. A few hours, or a few years of waiting are all the same, when you've lost the illusion of being eternal. Nothing mattered to me any more. In a way, I was calm. But it was a horrible kind of calm — because of my body. My body — I saw with its eyes and I heard with its ears, but it was no longer I. It sweat and trembled independently, and I didn't recognize it any longer. I was obliged to touch it and look at it to know what was happening to it, just as if it had been someone else's body. At times I still felt it, I felt a slipping, a sort of headlong plunging, as in a falling airplane, or else I heard my heart beating. But this didn't give me confidence. In fact, everything that came from my body had something damned dubious about it. Most of the time it was silent, it stayed put and I didn't feel anything other than a sort of heaviness, a loathsome presence against me. I had the impression of being bound to an enormous vermin.

The Belgian took out his watch and looked at it.

"It's half past three," he said.

The son-of-a-bitch! He must have done it on purpose. Tom jumped up. We hadn't yet realized the time was passing. The night surrounded us like a formless, dark mass; I didn't even remember it had started.

Juan started to shout. Wringing his hands, he implored, "I don't want to die! I don't want to die!"

He ran the whole length of the cellar with his arms in the air, then he dropped down onto one of the mattresses, sobbing. Tom looked at him with dismal eyes and didn't even try to console him any more. The fact was, it was no use: the kid made more noise than we did, but he was less affected, really. He was like a sick person who defends himself against his malady with a high fever. When there's not even any fever left, it's much more serious.

He was crying. I could tell he felt sorry for himself; he was thinking about death. For one second, one single second, I too felt like crying, crying out of pity for myself. But just the contrary happened. I took one look at the kid, saw his thin sobbing shoulders, and I felt I was inhuman. I couldn't feel pity either for these others or for myself. I said to myself, "I want to die decently."

Tom had gotten up and was standing just under the round opening looking out for the first signs of daylight. I was determined, I wanted to die decently, and I only thought about that. But underneath, ever since the doctor had told us the time, I felt time slipping, flowing by, one drop at a time.

It was still dark when I heard Tom's voice.

"Do you hear them?"

"Yes."

People were walking in the courtyard.

"What the hell are they doing? After all, they can't shoot in the dark."

After a moment, we didn't hear anything more. I said to Tom, "There's the daylight."

Pedro got up yawning, and came and blew out the lamp. He turned to the man beside him. "It's hellish cold."

The cellar had grown gray. We could hear shots at a distance.

"It's about to start," I said to Tom. "That must be in the back courtyard."

Tom asked the doctor to give him a cigarette. I didn't want any; I didn't want either cigarettes or alcohol. From that moment on, the shooting didn't stop.

"Can you take it in?" Tom said.

He started to add something, then he stopped and began to watch the door. The door opened and a lieutenant came in with four soldiers. Tom dropped his cigarette.

"Steinbock?"

Tom didn't answer. Pedro pointed him out.

"Juan Mirbal?"

"He's the one on the mattress."

"Stand up," said the Lieutenant.

Juan didn't move. Two soldiers took hold of him by the armpits and stood him up on his feet. But as soon as they let go of him he fell down.

The soldiers hesitated a moment.

"He's not the first one to get sick," said the Lieutenant. "You'll have to carry him, the two of you. We'll arrange things when we get there." He turned to Tom. "All right, come along."

Tom left between two soldiers. Two other soldiers followed, carrying the kid by his arms and legs. He was not unconscious; his eyes were wide open and tears were rolling down his cheeks. When I started to go out, the Lieutenant stopped me.

"Are you Ibbieta?"

"Yes."

"You wait here. They'll come and get you later on."

They left. The Belgian and the two jailers left too, and I was alone. I didn't understand what had happened to me, but I would have liked it better if they had ended it all right away. I heard the volleys at almost regular intervals; at each one, I shuddered. I felt like howling and tearing my hair. But instead, I gritted my teeth and pushed my hands deep into my pockets, because I wanted to stay decent.

An hour later, they came to fetch me and took me up to the first floor in a little room which smelt of cigar smoke and was so hot it seemed to me suffocating. Here there were two officers sitting in comfortable chairs, smoking, with papers spread out on their knees.

"Your name is Ibbieta?"

"Yes."

"Where is Ramon Gris?"

"I don't know."

The man who questioned me was small and stocky. He had hard eyes behind his glasses.

"Come nearer," he said to me.

I went nearer. He rose and took me by the arms, looking at me in a way calculated to make me go through the floor. At the same time he pinched my arms with all his might. He didn't mean to hurt me: it was quite a game; he wanted to dominate me. He also seemed to think it was necessary to blow his fetid breath right into my face. We stood like that for a moment, only I felt more like laughing than anything else. It takes a lot more than that to intimidate a man who's about to die: it didn't work. He pushed me away violently and sat down again.

"It's your life or his," he said. "You'll be allowed to go free if you tell us where he is."

After all, these two bedizened fellows with their riding crops and boots were just men who were going to die one day. A little later than I, perhaps, but not a great deal. And there they were, looking for names among their papers, running after other men in order to put them in prison or do away with them entirely. They had their opinions on the future of Spain and on other subjects. Their petty activities seemed to me to be offensive and ludicrous. I could no longer put myself in their place. I had the impression they were crazy.

The little fat fellow kept looking at me, tapping his boots with his riding crop. All his gestures were calculated to make him appear like a spirited, ferocious animal.

"Well? Do you understand?"

"I don't know where Gris is," I said. "I thought he was in Madrid."

The other officer lifted his pale hand indolently. This indolence was also calculated. I saw through all their little tricks, and I was dumbfounded that men should still exist who took pleasure in that kind of thing.

"You have fifteen minutes to think it over," he said slowly. "Take him to the linen-room, and bring him back here in fifteen minutes. If he continues to refuse, he'll be executed at once."

They knew what they were doing. I had spent the night waiting. After that, they had made me wait another hour in the cellar, while they shot Tom and Juan, and now they locked me in the linen-room. They must have arranged the whole thing the night before. They figured that sooner or later people's nerves wear out and they hoped to get me that way.

They made a big mistake. In the linen-room I sat down on a ladder because I felt very weak, and I began to think things over. Not their proposition, however. Naturally I knew where Gris was. He was hiding in his cousins' house, about two miles outside of the city. I knew, too, that I would not reveal his hiding place, unless they tortured me (but they didn't seem to be considering that). All that was definitely settled and didn't interest me in the least. Only I would have liked to understand the reasons for my own conduct. I would rather die than betray Gris. Why? I no longer liked Ramon Gris. My friendship for him had died shortly before dawn along with my love for Concha, along with my own desire to live. Of course I still admired him — he was hard. But it was not for that reason that I was willing to die in his place; his life was no more valuable than mine. No life was of any value. A man was going to be stood up against a wall and fired at till he dropped dead. It didn't make any difference whether it was I or Gris or somebody else. I knew perfectly well he was more useful to the Spanish cause than I was, but I didn't give a God damn about Spain or anarchy, either; nothing had any importance now. And yet, there I was. I could save my skin by betraying Gris and I refused to do it. It seemed more ludicrous to me than anything else; it was stubbornness.

I thought to myself, "Am I hard headed!" And I was seized with a strange sort of cheerfulness.

They came to fetch me and took me back to the two officers. A rat darted out under our feet and that amused me. I turned to one of the Falangists and said to him, "Did you see that rat?"

He made no reply. He was gloomy, and took himself very seriously. As for me, I felt like laughing, but I restrained myself because I was afraid that if I started, I wouldn't be able to stop. The Falangists wore mustaches. I kept after him, "You ought to cut off those mustaches, you fool."

I was amused by the fact that he let his hair grow all over his face while he was still alive. He gave me a kind of half-hearted kick, and I shut up.

"Well," said the fat officer, "have you thought things over?"

I looked at them with curiosity, like insects of a very rare species.

"I know where he is," I said. "He's hiding in the cemetery. Either in one of the vaults, or in the gravediggers' shack."

I said that just to make fools of them. I wanted to see them get up and fasten their belts and bustle about giving orders.

They jumped to their feet.

"Fine. Moles, go ask Lieutenant Lopez for fifteen men. And as for you," the little fat fellow said to me, "if you've told the truth, I don't go back on my word. But you'll pay for this, if you're pulling our leg."

They left noisily and I waited in peace, still guarded by the Falangists. From time to time I smiled at the thought of the face they were going to make. I felt dull and malicious. I could see them lifting up the grave stones, or opening the doors of the vaults one by one. I saw the whole situation as though I were another person: the prisoner determined to play the hero, the solemn Falangists with their mustaches and the men in uniform running around among the graves. It was irresistibly funny.

After half an hour, the little fat fellow came back alone. I thought he had come to give the order to execute me. The others must have stayed in the cemetery.

The officer looked at me. He didn't look at all foolish.

"Take him out in the big courtyard with the others," he said. "When military operations are over, a regular tribunal will decide his case."

I thought I must have misunderstood.

"So they're not — they're not going to shoot me?" I asked.

"Not now, in any case. Afterward, that doesn't concern me."

I still didn't understand.

"But why?" I said to him.

He shrugged his shoulders without replying, and the soldiers led me away. In the big courtyard there was a hundred or so prisoners, women, children and a few old men. I started to walk around the grass plot in the middle. I felt absolutely idiotic. At noon we were fed in the dining hall. Two or three fellows spoke to me. I must have known them, but I didn't answer. I didn't even know where I was.

Toward evening, about ten new prisoners were pushed into the courtyard. I recognized Garcia, the baker.

He said to me, "Lucky dog! I didn't expect to find you alive."

"They condemned me to death," I said, "and then they changed their minds. I don't know why."

"I was arrested at two o'clock," Garcia said.

"What for?"

Garcia took no part in politics.

"I don't know," he said. "They arrest everybody who doesn't think the way they do."

He lowered his voice.

"They got Gris."

I began to tremble.

"When?"

"This morning. He acted like a damned fool. He left his cousins' house Tuesday because of a disagreement. There were any number of fellows who would have hidden him, but he didn't want to be indebted to anybody any more." He said, "I would have hidden at Ibbieta's, but since they've got him, I'll go hide in the cemetery."

"In the cemetery?"

"Yes. It was the god-damnedest thing. Naturally they passed by there this morning; that had to happen. They found him in the gravediggers' shack. They opened fire at him and they finished him off."

"In the cemetery!"

Everything went around in circles, and when I came to I was sitting on the ground. I laughed so hard the tears came to my eyes.

★

★ ★ ★ ★

AUTHOR: *Ting Ling (Ding Ling, 1904–) is one of the most beloved and revered of Chinese authors. She belongs to a group of Chinese writers who were persecuted by the Blue Jackets in the early part of the 1930s. The Blue Jackets was Chiang Kai-shek's semiprivate, anti-Communist paramilitary organization, which adopted some of the Nazis' methods: intimidation, beatings, kidnappings, torture, and murder. Their special target was anything or anyone connected with writing, including authors, books, and publishing houses. Ting Ling eventually had to endure twelve years of exile and labor reform in the Great Northern Wilderness. With a profound belief in literature's importance to a society, she continued to write with the support of her family and friends, producing a large number of essays and stories. Most, unfortunately, are not available in English. Ting Ling was finally rehabilitated by the Chinese Communist party in 1979.*

SETTING: *The author writes from experience: she was kidnapped by the Blue Jackets on May 4, 1933. Her husband, the father of her new baby, was executed with five other writers and nineteen other persons. This story is Ting Ling's literary account of their deaths. The account is unique in that it combines the experiences of the individual and the group in the face of death.*

One Certain Night

Ting Ling

Slish-slosh-slish, slish-slosh, slosh. . . .

From out of the greenish lamplight of the hall an indistinguishable mass of human shadows was moving in the direction of the open field on the outside. Boots and shoes stamped heavily through the deep snow that covered the ground. The furious blasts of a winter night met them full in the face, assaulting them with the fine sleet and heavy snowflakes that had been falling for half a month. The sudden attack of the icy wind drew involuntary shivers, but the shadows proceeded — slish-slosh, slish-slosh.

Translated by George A. Kennedy. "One Certain Night" was first published in 1931. Reprinted from Harold Robert Isaacs, *Straw Sandals Chinese Short Stories* (Cambridge, Mass.: The MIT Press, 1974) by permission of the publisher.

393

A second gust, roaring mightily, swept pitilessly over them, cruelly
lashing their faces and their bodies. In the middle of the group,
surroundedhelped, driven forward by the momentum of the others, a
delicate youth, handsome in spite of his haggard look, seemed to awake
with a sudden start. The past — all that had happened — seemed to appear
somewhat distantly, yet clearly, before him. He saw a crafty face, filled
with malice and greed, a full round face, embellished with the hated,
foreign-style moustaches. There was repressed glee in the evil, arrogant
voice as the man had spoken, looking impudently at them from his high
platform. "Have you anything further to say? Sentence has been passed
upon you and the sentence will be carried out immediately."

Remembering all this the youth felt consumed by fires that blazed up
in his soul. He wanted to tear that face to pieces! He would extinguish that
voice! For one mad moment he thought of forcing his way out of the crowd
and he quickened his step. A short while ago, when he had been
condemned to death without a trial, he had been unable to preserve his
composure as the rest of his comrades had done, but had lost
consciousness in a powerful wave of rage and anguish.

He was a poet, ardent, sincere, energetic.

Bang! A rifle butt crashed heavily on his chest. Thin-chested to begin
with, he had grown more emaciated from twenty days of malnourishment
in the dark and sunless prison. His thoughts were interrupted by the curses
of the soldier who struck viciously at him.

"Rape of your mother, what's your hurry! The King of Hell can't wait
to get you!"

Clank, clank. The rattle of iron shackles rattled on his hands and feet,
and on the hands and feet of the others. There was a confusion of sounds
all around him — hobnailed boots crunching more heavily in the thick
snow. Slish, slosh! Slish, slish!

Something else became clear. He realized that he was walking
somewhere. A strange thought came into his head. He seemed to see
another pair of eyes above his own, a pair of lovely, unforgettable eyes that
gazed eternally into his soul. He was distinctly conscious of something in
the recesses of his heart that was stabbing him there and painfully tearing
away his flesh and blood, inch by inch.

The sky was black — illimitable blackness! Out of the blackness the
sleet and the snow sifted down and out of it hissed the roaring north wind.
The world was all gray and foggy, and the snow threw a dead ashen hue on
the night. The black shadows of the men — the escort and the victims —
moved silently over the snow. There was the clanking of chains, the rattling

of bayonets, but no word spoken. No one moaned. No one sighed or wept. Steadily they moved toward the hidden corner of the field which was being used temporarily as a place of execution.

"Damnation!" some were saying to themselves. "How far do they have to take us to slice off our heads. . . ."

In the second line a girl comrade threw back her head from time to time with an impatient gesture. The wind kept blowing her bobbed hair over her forehead and eyes.

The youth made a great effort to suppress the screams that seemed to be driving him mad with their insistence. He bit hard on his lips and shuddered with the rage he could not express. With staring eyes that were scorched with anger he looked about him devouringly as though in search of something, peering first at this one, then at that.

The faintly reflected light from the snow illuminated the faces of those near him. A soldier — beetling brows, fierce eyes! A soldier — the face of an idiot, spreading nostrils, thick lips! Another. . . . Suddenly his glance lighted on a dear and familiar face. The face turned on him with a look of tenderness and quiet, a look that transcended all the power of words, a look such as only one comrade can give to another in the time of a martyr's death, to comfort and hearten. Then a great part of his anger and anxiety slipped formlessly away. Love and something else which could only be described as *life* took possession of his tortured breast. He yearned to enfold that face and to shower kisses upon it. He returned the look with a nod full of courage and determination. . . .

Slish, slosh. . . . The sound of their feet in the night was like the disordered beating of victorious drums on every side as the twenty-five marched forward. Above their heads the whistling of the wind was like a giant red banner flapping over them.

"Halt! This is the place!" shouted the uniformed executioner fiercely, tightly clutching his Mauser pistol. "Where are you walking to, you sons of bitches?"

"This is it!" came the dull echo in all hearts.

"Line up the condemned! Tie them up!" The officer spat out the order. The soldiers in their quilted overcoats began to push them recklessly and roughly about, clubbing them with rifle butts and putting ropes around their chests to bind them securely to the stakes behind them. Boots and shoes clumped around in increased confusion over the snow-covered ground.

Not a word was said. An angry silence reigned. It was impossible now to find anything that would express the hatred they felt for their enemies.

Hands and feet were shackled already and in addition they were being tightly bound to stakes which had been set up a few days previously. They were not far now from the border of death.

Darkness stretched away before their eyes. The wind and the rain and the snow came down incessantly. The marrow-penetrating cold relentlessly lashed the bodies of the twenty-five, whose overcoats and gowns had been taken from them in the hall. But they had already lost all consciousness of cold.

They stood close together in a row.

"Over here, get over a bit! Dress up that line!"

In the gloom of the night a group of human forms could be dimly perceived, tugging and pushing at some heavy instrument.

"All right! Put it here! Count the criminals!"

"One . . . two . . . three . . . !" A soldier walked past and counted.

The officer in charge of the execution, coarse of face, passed in front of the line following the soldier and pointed at each one. In that brutal face there seemed to be concentrated all the ferocity of the rulers toward the oppressed. Angry passions flamed up once more in their breasts and burned their eyes and bodies with a fever of pain. They would have lunged out and beaten this devil to death, but their hands were bound fast behind them. They gnashed their teeth in anger and shivered in the icy wind, not from cold but from rage.

"Comrade, be brave," said the one on his right.

He turned his head to look. It was the dear friend with whom he had talked so much at supper time.

"Don't worry, I'm all right."

" . . . Twenty-three . . . twenty-four . . . twenty-five! Correct! Good!" The man who had been counting bellowed out the last figure as he stalked heavily across the snow to the heavy black object set there on the ground.

Illimitable emptiness! Incessant wind and snow! Grayness without end, darkness without end. . . !

Gigantic shadows were reflected in that deathlike grayness.

"Good, get ready! Wait for the whistle!" bellowed the officer again.

All hearts grew tenser, like drawn bowstrings. The heavy object before their eyes was death. Several soldiers were busily working over it. The sky was crushing down upon them — darkness would crush down upon them — on the bodies of the twenty-five.

"Comrades!" shouted someone in a ringing voice. "Don't forget! They tell us we are to die, but somewhere else today there is a great convention of our representatives. Our government takes form today. Let us wish our government well. Long live our government . . . !"

At this they all commenced to shout wildly. All the things that had been stored up in their hearts and that they had forgotten to express came back with sudden clarity, so that each one shouted his own feelings.

Darkness disappeared and a light glowed before their eyes — the birth of a new nation.

The shrill whistle blew. Twenty-five strong heroic voices took up the song:

"Arise, ye prisoners of starvation. . . ."

Pit! Pat! Pit! Pat!

The heavy object swept the line horizontally, spitting out a score of bullets.

The singing grew a little weaker although a few voices seemed to swell in volume.

"'Tis the last fight we face. . . ."

Again the wail of the whistle.

Pit! Pat! Pit! Pat!

A second sweeping across and another score of bullets struck.

The singing began to die more rapidly. Only a few voices remained.

"The Interna. . . ."

A third whistle. A third sweeping patter. The song was silenced.

"Rape of their mothers! The bastards! Now go ahead and sing!" The execution officer swore and turned back in the direction from which he had come.

"Take up the gun," he ordered. "Return to your posts immediately. We'll bury the bodies tomorrow. You don't suppose the corpses will walk off?"

He went back to the hall and the soldiers stamped back homeward over the same snow. Slish, slosh!

The night was ugly and forbidding. The huge snowflakes and the fine sleet drifted through. The wild wind of winter roared by only to come roaring back again. The snow piled up on the hanging heads, to be blown off again by the gale. They were all dumb and motionless, fastened there. In some spots — in one, in two, in three spots — the blood trickled down and mottled the snow in the darkness.

Will the sky ever grow light?

★

★ ★ ★ ★

AUTHOR: *Tadeusz Borowski (1922–1951) survived Auschwitz and Dachau only to die by his own hand — by opening a gas valve. Acclaimed as a master of Polish literature, his works include:* Farewell to Maria, A World of Stone, *and* Wherever the Earth. *He was an apostle, inquisitor, and eventual victim of communism in Poland. His concentration camp stories will certainly survive as masterpieces of Polish literature.*

SETTING: *During World War II more than ten million men and women were driven from German-occupied countries into concentration camps for two ostensible purposes: annihilation and/or forced labor. Using prisoners for forced labor meant that those unable to work were deemed "useless" and were destroyed. Women, children, the crippled, and the elderly were first to be killed. The camps at Dachau, Buchenwald, Auschwitz, and Birkenau were the most notorious. The killing became almost desperate near the end of the war. As the Soviet army approached from the east and the Allied forces from the west, the Nazis attempted to move the camps. Inmates incapable of walking were hurriedly destroyed. The paths taken by the "death marches" were lined with corpses. When the British army liberated Bergen-Belsen on April 13, 1945, ten thousand corpses lay on the ground; of the thirty-eight thousand prisoners remaining alive, barely one-third could be saved. The total number of deaths directly attributable to the concentration camps is between seven and eleven million people.*

The People Who Walked On

Tadeusz Borowski

It was early spring when we began building a soccer field on the broad clearing behind the hospital barracks. The location was excellent: the gypsies to the left, with their roaming children, their lovely, trim nurses, and their women sitting by the hour in the latrines; to the rear — a barbed-wire fence, and behind it the loading ramp with the wide railway tracks and the endless coming and going of trains; and beyond the ramp, the women's camp — *Frauen Konzentration Lager*. No

---

one, of course, ever called it by its full name. We simply said F.K.L. — that was enough. To the right of the field were the crematoria, some of them at the back of the ramp, next to the F.K.L., others even closer, right by the fence. Sturdy buildings that sat solidly on the ground. And in front of the crematoria, a small wood which had to be crossed on the way to the gas.

We worked on the soccer field throughout the spring, and before it was finished we started planting flowers under the barracks windows and decorating the blocks with intricate zigzag designs made of crushed red brick. We planted spinach and lettuce, sunflowers and garlic. We laid little green lawns with grass transplanted from the edges of the soccer field, and sprinkled them daily with water brought in barrels from the lavatories.

Just when the flowers were about to bloom, we finished the soccer field.

From then on, the flowers were abandoned, the sick lay by themselves in the hospital beds, and we played soccer. Every day, as soon as the evening meal was over, anybody who felt like it came to the field and kicked the ball around. Others stood in clusters by the fence and talked across the entire length of the camp with the girls from the F.K.L.

One day I was goalkeeper. As always on Sundays, a sizeable crowd of hospital orderlies and convalescent patients had gathered to watch the game. Keeping goal, I had my back to the ramp. The ball went out and rolled all the way to the fence. I ran after it, and as I reached to pick it up, I happened to glance at the ramp.

A train had just arrived. People were emerging from the cattle cars and walking in the direction of the little wood. All I could see from where I stood were bright splashes of colour. The women, it seemed, were already wearing summer dresses; it was the first time that season. The men had taken off their coats, and their white shirts stood out sharply against the green of the trees. The procession moved along slowly, growing in size as more and more people poured from the freight cars. And then it stopped. The people sat down on the grass and gazed in our direction. I returned with the ball and kicked it back inside the field. It travelled from one foot to another and, in a wide arc, returned to the goal. I kicked it towards a corner. Again it rolled out into the grass. Once more I ran to retrieve it. But as I reached down, I stopped in amazement — the ramp was empty. Out of the whole colourful summer procession, not one person remained. The train too was gone. Again the F.K.L. blocks were in unobstructed view, and again the orderlies and the patients stood along the barbed-wire fence calling to the girls, and the girls answered them across the ramp.

Between two throw-ins in a soccer game, right behind my back, three thousand people had been put to death.

In the following months, the processions to the little wood moved along two roads: one leading straight from the ramp, the other past the hospital wall. Both led to the crematoria, but some of the people had the good fortune to walk beyond them, all the way to the Zauna, and this meant more than just a bath and a delousing, a barber's shop and a new prison suit. It meant staying alive. In a concentration camp, true, but — alive.

Each day, as I got up in the morning to scrub the hospital floors, the people were walking — along both roads. Women, men, children. They carried their bundles.

When I sat down to dinner — and not a bad one, either — the people were walking. Our block was bathed in sunlight; we threw the doors and the windows wide open and sprinkled the floors with water to keep the dust down. In the afternoons I delivered packages which had been brought that morning from the Auschwitz post office. The clerk distributed mail. The doctors dressed wounds and gave injections. There was, as a matter of fact, only one hypodermic needle for the entire block. On warm evenings I sat at the barracks door reading *Mon frère Yves* by Pierre Loti — while the procession continued on and on, along both roads.

Often, in the middle of the night, I walked outside; the lamps glowed in the darkness above the barbed-wire fences. The roads were completely black, but I could distinctly hear the far-away hum of a thousand voices — the procession moved on and on. And then the entire sky would light up; there would be a burst of flame above the wood . . . and terrible human screams.

I stared into the night, numb, speechless, frozen with horror. My entire body trembled and rebelled, somehow even without my participation. I no longer controlled my body, although I could feel its every tremor. My mind was completely calm, only the body seemed to revolt.

Soon afterwards, I left the hospital. The days were filled with important events. The Allied Armies had landed on the shores of France. The Russian front, we heard, had started to move west towards Warsaw.

But in Birkenau, day and night long lines of trains loaded with people waited at the station. The doors were unsealed, the people started walking — along both roads.

Located next to the camp's labour sector was the deserted, unfinished Sector C. Here, only the barracks and the high voltage fence around them had been completed. The roofs, however, were not yet covered with tar sheets, and some of the blocks still had no bunks. An average Birkenau block, furnished with three tiers of bunks, could hold up to five hundred people. But every block in Sector C was now being packed with a thousand or more young women picked from among the people on the ramp . . . Twenty-eight blocks — over thirty thousand women. Their heads were shaved and they were issued little sleeveless summer dresses. But they were not given underwear. Nor spoons, nor bowls, nor even a rag to clean themselves with. Birkenau was situated on marshes, at the foot of a mountain range. During the day, the air was warm and so transparent that the mountains were in clear view, but in the morning they lay shrouded in a thick, icy mist. The mornings were cold and penetrating. For us, this meant merely a refreshing pause before a hot summer day, but the women, who only twenty yards to our right had been standing at roll-call since five in the morning, turned blue from the cold and huddled together like a flock of partridges.

We named the camp — Persian Market. On sunny, warm days the women would emerge from the barracks and mill around in the wide aisles between the blocks. Their bright summer dresses and the gay kerchiefs on their shaved heads created the atmosphere of a busy colourful market — a Persian Market because of its exotic character.

From afar, the women were faceless and ageless. Nothing more than white blotches and pastel figures.

The Persian Market was not yet completed. The Wagner Kommando began building a road through the sector, packing it down with a heavy roller. Others fiddled around with the plumbing and worked on the washrooms that were to be installed throughout all the sectors of Birkenau. Still others were busy stocking up the Persian Market with the camp's basic equipment — supplies of blankets, metal cups and spoons — which they arranged carefully in the warehouses under the direction of the chief supervisor, the assigned S.S. officer. Naturally, much of the stuff evaporated immediately, expertly "organized" by the men working on the job.

My comrades and I laid a roof over the shack of every Block Elder in the Persian Market. It was not done on official order, nor did we work out of charity. Neither did we do it out of a feeling of solidarity with the old serial numbers, the F.K.L. women who had been placed there in all the responsible posts. In fact, we used "organized" tar-boards and melted "organized" tar, and for every roll of tar-board, every bucket of tar, an Elder had to pay. She had to pay the Kapo, the Kommandoführer, the

Kommando "bigwigs." She could pay in various ways: with gold, food, the women of her block, or with her own body. It depended.

On a similar basis, the electricians installed electricity, the carpenters built and furnished the shacks, using "organized" lumber, the masons provided metal stoves and cemented them in place.

It was at that time that I came to know the anatomy of this strange camp. We would arrive there in the morning, pushing a cart loaded with tar-sheets and tar. At the gate stood the S.S. women-guards, hippy blondes in black leather boots. They searched us and let us in. Then they themselves went to inspect the blocks. Not infrequently they had lovers among the masons and carpenters. They slept with them in the unfinished washrooms or the Block Elders' shacks.

We would push our cart into the camp, between the barracks, and there, on some little square, would light a fire and melt the tar. A crowd of women would immediately surround us. They begged us to give them anything, a pen-knife, a handkerchief, a spoon, a pencil, a piece of paper, a shoe string, or bread.

"Listen, you can always manage somehow," they would say. "You've been in the camp a long time and you've survived. Surely you have all you need. Why won't you share it with us?"

At first we gave them everything we happened to have with us, and then turned our pockets inside out to show we had nothing more. We took off our shirts and handed them over. But gradually we began coming with empty pockets and gave them nothing.

These women were not so much alike as it had seemed when we looked at them from another sector, from a distance of twenty metres.

Among them were small girls, whose hair had not been shaved, stray little cherubs from a painting of the Last Judgment. There were young girls who gazed with surprise at the women crowding around us, and who looked at us, coarse, brutal men, with contempt. Then there were married women, who desperately begged for news of their lost husbands, and mothers trying to find a trace of their children.

"We are so miserable, so cold, so hungry," they cried. "Tell us, are they at least a little bit better off?"

"They are, if God is just," we would answer solemnly, without the usual mocking and teasing.

"Surely they're not dead?" the women asked, looking searchingly into our faces.

We would walk away without a word, eager to get back to work.

The majority of the Block Elders at the Persian Market were Slovak girls who managed to communicate in the language of the new inmates. Every one of these girls had behind her several years of concentration camp. Every one of them remembered the early days of the F.K.L., when female corpses piled up along the barracks walls and rotted, unremoved, in hospital beds — and when human excrement grew into monstrous heaps inside the blocks.

Despite their rough manner, they had retained their femininity and human kindness. Probably they too had their lovers, and probably they too stole margarine and tins of food in order to pay for blankets and dresses, but . . .

. . . but I remember Mirka, a short, stocky "pink" girl. Her shack was all done up in pink too, with pink ruffled curtains across the window that faced the block. The pink light inside the shack set a pink glow over the girl's face, making her look as if she were wrapped in a delicate misty veil. There was a Jew in our Kommando with very bad teeth who was in love with Mirka. He was always running around the camp trying to buy fresh eggs for her, and then throwing them, protected in soft wrapping, over the barbed-wire fence. He would spend many long hours with her, paying little attention to the S.S. women inspecting the barracks or to our chief who made his rounds with a tremendous revolver hanging from his white summer uniform.

One day Mirka came running over to where several of us were laying a roof. She signalled frantically to the Jew and called, turning to me:

"Please come down! Maybe you can help too!"

We slid off the roof and down the barracks door. Mirka grabbed us by the hands and pulled us in the direction of her shack. There she led us between the cots and pointing to a mass of colourful quilts and blankets on top of which lay a child, she said breathlessly:

"Look, it's dying! Tell me, what can I do? What could have made it so sick so suddenly?"

The child was asleep, but very restless. It looked like a rose in a golden frame — its burning cheeks were surrounded by a halo of blonde hair.

"What a pretty child," I whispered.

"Pretty!" cried Mirka. "All you know is that it's pretty! But it can die any moment! I've had to hide it so they wouldn't take it to the gas! What if an S.S. woman finds it? Help me!"

The Jew put his arm around her shoulders. She pushed him away and suddenly burst into sobs. I shrugged, turned around, and left the barracks.

In the distance, I could see trains moving along the ramp. They were bringing new people who would walk in the direction of the little wood. One Canada group was just returning from the ramp, and along the wide camp road passed another Canada group going to take its place. Smoke was rising above the treetops. I seated myself next to the boiling bucket of tar and, stirring it slowly, sat thinking for a long time. At one point a wild thought suddenly shot across my mind: I too would like to have a child with rose-coloured cheeks and light blonde hair. I laughed aloud at such a ridiculous notion and climbed up on the road to lay the hot tar.

And I remember another Block Elder, a big redhead with broad feet and chapped hands. She did not have a separate shack, only a few blankets spread over the bed and instead of walls a few other blankets thrown across a piece of rope.

"I mustn't make them feel," she would say, pointing to the women packed tightly in the bunks, "that I want to cut myself off from them. Maybe I can't give them anything, but I won't take anything away from them either."

"Do you believe in life after death?" she asked me once in the middle of some lighthearted conversation.

"Sometimes," I answered cautiously. "Once I believed in it when I was in jail, and again once when I came close to dying here in the camp."

"But if a man does evil, he'll be punished, won't he?"

"I suppose so, unless there are some criteria of justice other than the man-made criteria. You know . . . the kind that explain causes and motivations, and erase guilt by making it appear insignificant in the light of the overall harmony of the universe. Can a crime committed on one level be punishable on a different one?"

"But I mean in a normal, human sense!" she exclaimed.

"It ought to be punished. No question about it."

"And you, would you do good if you were able to?"

"I seek no rewards. I build roofs and want to survive the concentration camp."

"But do you think that they," she pointed with her chin in an indefinite direction, "can go unpunished?"

"I think that for those who have suffered unjustly, justice alone is not enough. They want the guilty to suffer unjustly too. Only this will they understand as justice."

"You're a pretty smart fellow! But you wouldn't have the slightest idea how to divide bread justly, without giving more to your own mistress!" she said bitterly and walked into the block. The women were lying in the rows of bunks, head to head. Their faces were still, only the eyes seemed alive, large and shining. Hunger had already started in this part of the camp. The redheaded Elder moved from bunk to bunk, talking to the women to distract them from their thoughts. She pulled out the singers and told them to sing, the dancers — and told them to dance, the poets — and made them recite poetry.

"All the time, endlessly, they ask me about their mothers, their fathers. They beg me to write to them."

"They've asked me too. It's just too bad."

"Ah you! You come and then you go, but me? I plead with them, I beg them — if anyone is pregnant, don't report to the doctor, if anyone is sick, stay in the barracks! But do you think they believe me? It's no good, no matter how hard you try to protect them. What can you do if they fall all over themselves to get to the gas?"

One of the girls was standing on top of a table singing a popular tune. When she finished, the women in the bunks began to applaud. The girl bowed, smiling. The redheaded Elder covered her face with her rough hands.

"I can't stand it any longer! It's too disgusting!" she whispered. And suddenly she jumped up and rushed over to the table. "Get down!" she screamed at the singer.

The women fell silent. She raised her arm.

"Quiet!" she shouted, though nobody spoke a word. "You've been asking me about your parents and your children. I haven't told you, I felt sorry for you. But now I'll tell you, so that you know, because they'll do the same with you if you get sick! Your children, your husbands and your parents are not in another camp at all. They've been stuffed into a room and gassed! Gassed, do you understand? Like millions of others, like my own mother and father. They're burning in deep pits and in ovens . . . The smoke which you see above the rooftops doesn't come from the brick plant at all, as you're being told. It's smoke from your children! Now go on and sing," she finished calmly, pointing her finger at the terrified singer. Then she turned around and walked out of the barracks.

It was undeniable that the conditions in both Auschwitz and Birkenau were steadily improving. At the beginning, beating and killing were the rule, but later this became only sporadic. At first, you had to sleep on the floor lying on your side because of the lack of space, and could turn over only on command; later you slept in bunks, or wherever you wished, sometimes even in bed. Originally, you had to stand at roll-call for as long as two days at a time, later — only until the second gong, until nine o'clock.

In the early years, packages were forbidden, later you could receive 500 grams, and finally as much as you wanted. Pockets of any kind were at first strictly taboo, but eventually even civilian clothes could sometimes be seen around Birkenau. Life in the camp became "better and better" all the time — after the first three or four years. We felt certain that the horrors could never again be repeated, and we were proud that we had survived. The worse the Germans fared at the battle front, the better off we were. And since they fared worse and worse . . .

At the Persian Market, time seemed to move in reverse. Again we saw the Auschwitz of 1940. The women greedily gulped down the soup which nobody in our blocks would even think of touching. They stank of sweat and female blood. They stood at roll-call from five in the morning. When they were at last counted, it was almost nine. Then they were given cold coffee. At three in the afternoon the evening roll-call began and they were given dinner: bread with some spread. Since they did not work, they did not rate the *Zulage*, the extra work ration.

Sometimes they were driven out of the barracks in the middle of the day for an additional roll-call. They would line up in tight rows and march along the road, one behind the other. The big, blonde S.S. women in leather boots plucked from among them all the skinny ones, the ugly ones, the big-bellied ones — and threw them inside the Eye. The so-called Eye was a closed circle formed by the joined hands of the barracks guards. Filled out with women, the circle moved like a macabre dance to the camp gate, there to become absorbed by the great, camp-wide Eye. Five hundred, six hundred, a thousand selected women. Then all of them started on their walk — along the two roads.

Sometimes an S.S. woman dropped in at one of the barracks. She cased the bunks, a woman looking at other women. She asked if anyone cared to see a doctor, if anyone was pregnant. At the hospital, she said, they would get milk and white bread.

They scrambled out of the bunks and, swept up into the Eye, walked to the gate — towards the little wood.

Just to pass the time of day — for there was little for us to do at the camp — we used to spend long hours at the Persian Market, either with the Block Elders, or sitting under the barracks walls, or in the latrines. At the Elders' shacks you drank tea or dozed off for an hour or two in their beds. Sitting under the barracks wall you chatted with the carpenters and the bricklayers. A few women were usually hanging around, dressed in pretty little pullovers and wearing sheer stockings. Any one of them could be had for a piece of bright silk or a shiny trinket. Since time began, never has there been such an easy market for female flesh!

The latrines were built for the men and the women jointly, and were separated only by wooden boards. On the women's side, it was crowded and noisy, on ours, quiet and pleasantly cool inside the concrete enclosure. You sat there by the hour conducting love dialogues with Katia, the pretty little latrine girl. No one felt any embarrassment or thought the set-up uncomfortable. After all, one had already seen so much . . .

That was June. Day and night the people walked — along the two roads. From dawn until late at night the entire Persian Market stood at roll-call. The days were warm and sunny and the tar melted on the roofs. Then came the rains, and with them icy winds. The mornings would dawn cold and penetrating. Then the fair weather returned once again. Without interruption, the trains pulled up to the ramp and the people walked on . . . Often we had to stand and wait, unable to leave for work, because they were blocking the roads. They walked slowly, in loose groups, sometimes hand in hand. Women, old men, children. As they passed just outside the barbed-wire fence they would turn their silent faces in our direction. Their eyes would fill with tears of pity and they threw bread over the fence for us to eat.

The women took the watches off their wrists and flung them at our feet, gesturing to us to take them.

At the gate, a band was playing foxtrot and tangos. The camp gazed at the passing procession. A man has only a limited number of ways in which he can express strong emotions or violent passions. He uses the same gestures as when what he feels is only petty and unimportant. He utters the same ordinary words.

"How many have gone by so far? It's been almost two months since mid-May. Counting twenty thousand per day . . . around one million!"

"Eh, they couldn't have gassed that many every day. Though . . . who the hell knows, with four ovens and scores of deep pits . . ."

"Then count it this way: from Koszyce and Munkacz, almost 600,000. They got 'em all, no doubt about it. And from Budapest? 300,000 easily."

"What's the difference?"

"*Ja*, but anyway, it's got to be over soon. They'll have slaughtered every single one of them."

"There's more, don't worry."

You shrug your shoulders and look at the road. Slowly, behind the crowd of people, walk the S.S. men, urging them with kindly smiles to move along. They explain that it is not much farther and they pat on the back a little old man who runs over to a ditch, rapidly pulls down his trousers, and wobbling in a funny way squats down. An S.S. man calls to him and points to the people disappearing round the bend. The little old man nods quickly, pulls up his trousers and, wobbling in a funny way, runs at a trot to catch up.

You snicker, amused at the sight of a man in such a big hurry to get to the gas chamber.

Later, we started working at the warehouses, spreading tar over their dripping roofs. The warehouses contained mountains of clothing, junk, and not-yet-disembowelled bundles. The treasures taken from the gassed people were piled up at random, exposed to the sun and the rain.

Every day, after lighting a fire under the bucket of tar, we went to "organize" a snack. One of us would bring a pail of water, another a sack of dry cherries or prunes, a third some sugar. We stewed the fruit and then carried it up on the roof for those who took care of the work itself. Others fried bacon and onions and ate it with corn bread. We stole anything we could get our hands on and took it to the camp.

From the warehouse roofs you could see very clearly the flaming pits and the crematoria operating at full speed. You could see the people walk inside, undress. Then the S.S. men would quickly shut the windows and firmly tighten the screws. After a few minutes, in which we did not even have time to tar a piece of roofing board properly, they opened the windows and the side doors and aired the place out. Then came the *Sonderkommando*[1] to drag the corpses to the burning pits. And so it went on, from morning till night — every single day.

Sometimes, after a transport had already been gassed, some late-arriving cars drove around filled with the sick. It was wasteful to gas them. They were undressed and Oberscharführer Moll either shot them with his rifle or pushed them live into a flaming trench.

Once, a car brought a young woman who had refused to part from her mother. Both were forced to undress, the mother led the way. The man who was to guide the daughter stopped, struck by the perfect beauty of her body, and in his awe and admiration he scratched his head. The woman, noticing this coarse, human gesture, relaxed. Blushing, she clutched the man's arm.

"Tell me, what will they do to me?"

"Be brave," said the man, not withdrawing his arm.

"I am brave! Can't you see, I'm not even ashamed of you! Tell me!"

"Remember, be brave, come. I shall lead you. Just don't look."

He took her by the hand and led her on, his other hand covering her eyes. The sizzling and the stench of the burning fat and the heat gushing out of the pit terrified her. She jerked back. But he gently bent her head forward, uncovering her back. At that moment the Oberscharführer fired, almost without aiming. The man pushed the woman into the flaming pit, and as she fell he heard her terrible, broken scream.

When the Persian Market, the gypsy camp and the F.K.L. became completely filled with the women selected from among the people from the ramp, a new camp was opened up across from the Persian Market. We called it Mexico. It, too, was not yet completed, and there also they began to install shacks for the Block Elders, electricity, and windows.

Each day was just like another. People emerged from the freight cars and walked on — along both roads.

The camp inmates had problems of their own: they waited for packages and letters from home, they "organized" for their friends and mistresses, they speculated, they schemed. Nights followed days, rains came after the dry spells.

Towards the end of the summer, the trains stopped coming. Fewer and fewer people went to the crematoria. At first, the camp seemed somehow empty and incomplete. Then everybody got used to it. Anyway, other important events were taking place: the Russian offensive, the uprising and burning of Warsaw, the transports leaving the camp every day, going West towards the unknown, towards new sickness and death; the revolt at the crematoria and the escape of a *Sonderkommando* that ended with the execution of all the escapees.

And afterwards, you were shoved from camp to camp, without a spoon, or a plate, or a piece of rag to clean yourself with.

Your memory retains only images. Today, as I think back on that last summer in Auschwitz, I can still see the endless, colourful procession of people solemnly walking — along both roads; the woman, her head bent forward, standing over the flaming pit; the big redheaded girl in the dark interior of the barracks, shouting impatiently:

"Will evil be punished? I mean in human, normal terms!"

And I can still see the Jew with bad teeth, standing beneath my high bunk every evening, lifting his face to me, asking insistently:

"Any packages today? Couldn't you sell me some eggs for Mirka? I'll pay in marks. She is so fond of eggs . . ."

★

Note

1. The *Sonderkommando*, a labour gang composed mostly of Jews and assigned specifically to crematorium duties.

★ ★ ★ ★

AUTHOR: *Imre Sarkadi (1921–1961), prose writer and dramatist, was one of the most talented writers to appear after the liberation of Hungary in 1945. He wrote some of the finest short stories in Hungarian literature, combining the rich Hungarian prose heritage and his own originality.*

SETTING: *Hungary fought all the major protagonists of the Second World War. Initially aligned with Germany as a member of the Anti-Comintern Pact, it later joined in the aggression against Yugoslavia and declared war on the Soviet Union and the Allies. The underground Hungarian Anti-Fascist Independence Front, formed under the leadership of the Party of Hungarian Communists, rallied the working class to fight against fascism and the war. In March 1944, with the consent of Miklós Horthy, Hitler's troops invaded the country only to be defeated by Soviet troops in October.*

The Deserter

Imre Sarkadi

It was on Tuesday evening that we passed through Újhely, so close to our farmstead that if the sergeant-major had given me an hour's leave of absence I'd have been able to pop home. Should I ask him? Or shouldn't I . . . ? It would have been a good idea because I had lice all over me. But I didn't dare ask him, we were not allowed a rest, and there's no leaving the column when it's on the move.

The others prodded me on, they told me not to mind, to go home, I'd catch up with them somewhere, we surely wouldn't march all night. It must have been about ten when we came to the bend in the road nearest the farm — three fields away. But we took the turn, and now it would be even further off. "Well, I'd go home if I were you," said Dani Pap. "You bet I would." He didn't say any more, but I had a feeling that he really would go home. And as we went on, silently, with the rifle and kit-bag growing heavier on our shoulders, I felt that Dani Pap was thinking just what I was.

Translated by József Hatvany. "The Deserter" is reprinted from József Bognár, *Landmark: Hungarian Writers on Thirty Years of History* (Budapest: Corvina Press, 1965) by permission of the publisher and the author's heir.

If I was to pop home, I could sleep in a bed that night.

"And with the wife," Pap was thinking beside me. I knew he was, he even smoked his cigarette differently.

We had neither of us had leave for eighteen months. And the soles of my boots leaked, the December slush squelched about inside them. "Well," I said to Dani, "I'll try. At the next rest." And we looked anxiously ahead, to see where the next rest would be. What if it was a long way off . . . ? It takes less courage to walk back one mile than three. I fell out and went down to the ditch to adjust my boots, and they slowly passed by me. Everyone slithered and squelched in the mud, and the lance-corporal at the end of the file yelled down at me: "Hey, don't get left behind, there . . ." And when he had gone another ten or fifteen paces: "Are you coming, you man there? There'll be a rest in a moment, you can adjust your boots when we get there."

I adjusted them for a good long time, and when they were a fair distance off I stepped across the ditch, ran back a little to put some more distance between us, and cut across the ploughland. It hadn't actually been ploughed, it was just stubble. Last year, I remembered, there had been maize on it. I couldn't make out in the dark and the mud what there had been this year. I soon reached the road, and our house too. Of course they were all asleep by now.

I rattled away and the old folk woke first. I heard Mother's voice as she looked for some matches and said: "Who's there?" She just asked the darkness outside, because when she had lit the lamp she asked again from the doorway who it was. "It's me." I said, "me," but of course she didn't recognize my voice straight away. Who would have thought it? Even Margit could hardly believe her eyes when I went in. They busied themselves straight away round the fire, asking me what I'd like to eat. And Father wanted to know how I'd got home.

I told them I wouldn't mind some food, but I'd like some warm water for my feet first. I took off my boots and tried to warm my feet by the side of the oven. They were sore and had got frostbitten the previous day, and the one before. The dry warmth felt fine, but soaking them would be even better. They put on the water and the food. Father asked if I had any cigarettes. I told him I hadn't, he'd better give me some tobacco instead. All I had was a bit of dust in my pocket. "Are you that badly off?" he asked. "Yes," I said, "and worse. The only cigarettes we have are what we can scrounge."

"And they tell us we don't get them because they're needed for the soldiers."

They kept asking how long I'd stay. I didn't want to say anything, you never know ahead, and you can never tell how much the others'll blab. I told them to stop asking, I'd tell them the next day.

I let my feet soak and all of a sudden I had become so sleepy, I almost dropped off as I sat. It was certainly better than to be sitting with Dani and the lads, by the ditch-side.

I don't really know which I wanted more: the wife or some sleep. As I leaned my head against the wall for a bit and my feet tingled in the warm water it was sleep. And once we got to bed I had quite a job not to go to sleep before the old folk put out the light. I didn't really sleep well — I woke up during the night because I was sweating all over, and later because I didn't know where I was. Towards dawn I heard Father talking outside.

The sun was shining by the time I got up. There was no one in the room, I heard the fire crackling in the kitchen and a horse being led across the yard. Margit was cooking — she had killed some chickens, several as far as I could make out. I asked her what for, for breakfast. "Not for us," she said. "Some guests came at dawn; they brought them." I didn't like it — why the devil kill chickens for guests who come at dawn? When they'd written they hardly had any chickens. "Had to," she said. "They're soldiers. They've quartered themselves here and bought them."

Mother also came in, and I asked her what kind of soldiers they were. I didn't like them having come to us of all places. "They're sort of half civilians," she said. "About ten of them. They came by lorry."

"The hell," I said. "And when are they going? Didn't they say?"

"No, they didn't."

"I wouldn't mind if they did go. And if they come in here to eat in the kitchen, where can I go? What with them in the yard and the stable I can't even go out."

"Why?" asked Mother. "Surely you're not afraid of them, are you? You're a soldier yourself."

"Yes, but I'd prefer not to met this lot. You said yourself they were kind of half civilian."

"Something of that sort, but they're soldiers for all that. They're armed . . ."

I went back to the room and Mother came after me. She obviously wanted to say something, but didn't dare. And she kept peering at my face to see if it wouldn't get more friendly. I began to get dressed, because if they did happen to come in I didn't want them to go pulling me out of bed in my pants and vest.

"What's wrong?" I asked Mother finally, as she was putting the things away round me. She didn't really say anything, but just began muttering that surely nothing bad could come of it, and them having put up here, and anyway they hadn't done much asking whether we'd let them or not.

Of course they hadn't, I knew that myself, you don't do much asking when you put up somewhere. Especially if you come with a lorry. But mother wanted to know why it would be bad if I was to meet them.

"It would," I said. "Never mind why, but it would. And don't ask too many questions. I don't want you to go mentioning that I'm here, and you'd be as well to bring my kit in from the kitchen."

"Oh they've seen that," she said. "In fact they asked whose it was, so I had to tell them. But they didn't seem to mind. They asked me how many of my sons were soldiers and they even praised me when I told them that the older one had died at the front last year."

"Well," I said, "then we're in a fine stew." And I went back to the kitchen, so that if they'd seen me anyway, I should at least be where it's warm. Margit just looked at me anxiously, and asked whether it was very bad that they'd come. I said it might be. I waited for them to come in at last, and I didn't know whether I'd do better to stay there, or to go into the room and hope they'd forget about me, or to pack up and set out as though I had just been about to go.

Father came in too, and one of the soldiers came with him. Only his submachine-gun and his cap showed that he was a soldier. He didn't say good-day, just looked round and started sniffing round the fireplace. I got up when he came in, and as I didn't have my cap on I just stood to attention. He didn't have any markings. You can never tell these days what a man's rank is. And since he didn't take any notice, I just went on standing to attention because I didn't want him to find me sitting by the table when he first looked at me.

He came nearer, sat down; the door opened, another two came in, then one more. I tossed my head to salute each of them, though only one wore a military tunic and that didn't have markings either. None of them returned my salute; they sat down by the table, and I stood beside them because there were no more chairs left for me to sit on. Mother and Margit fussed around the fire, while Father sat on the stool by the door. "Wait a minute," said Mother, "I'll bring another chair, and if you move up closer on the bench there'll be room for another there too." Margit told them to bring in their mess-tins if they had any, because she couldn't give that many plates. "Why, there's some outside as well," she said.

The man in the uniform said they'd be all right as they were, first the four of them would eat and the rest would come in later. This was when he first looked at me — he didn't say anything, just looked. Mother also felt that he was looking, for she turned round at the fireplace, while Father got up from the stool and opened the door to let the cat out, then stood smoking his pipe and didn't sit down again.

"And you," said the man in uniform. As though he was asking what he was to do with me.

There was nothing I could answer him, so I said "Sir." He lit a cigarette and put his elbows on the table, deep in thought, and it almost seemed he had forgotten about me because he called over impatiently to ask whether the food was ready. "How long are we to wait?" he said.

They began eating and I searched my pockets for tobacco, but as I wasn't wearing my tunic but only my trousers and a knitted jacket, I wanted to go in for the tobacco. The man in the tunic looked at me as I opened the door, and called after me to ask where I was going.

"Beg to report sir, I'd like to fetch something from my tunic pocket."

They went on eating and didn't answer, so I went in and took out the tobacco, but I didn't dare stay there if they were all that keen to know where I was, so I went back to the kitchen. There I rolled a cigarette and lit it. "Well, did you fetch it?" asked the man in the tunic. "Yes sir," and I was sorry I had lit up — I didn't know where to put the cigarette when he spoke to me. He didn't say anything for a while, but I felt pretty bad as they sat by the table and ate. The four of us just stood around them, Father by the door, Margit and Mother by the fire, and now that they had finished dishing out the food they didn't know what to do.

Of all the times to choose to come!

When they had eaten they became a bit gayer. The one in the tunic took some brandy from his pocket and offered it to the others as well. Mother was about to rush and get them some glasses, but they waved to her and said they'd do without. Then she asked whether she could serve the rest and began taking the plates to wash them. But again they said they'd do as they were, she needn't waste time with them. It was just that they didn't want to get up and go out. The one with the cap, who had been the first to come in and had not taken off his cap even while he ate, now looked at me. He also just looked for a while like the other, the way that you look at a horse at the market, then asked:

"Are you a soldier?"

"Yes sir," I said.

"Ah. So you're a soldier."

"Fine soldiers we have," said the one in the tunic.

"No wonder we're always retreating."

I saw now that there'd be trouble. They hadn't asked for my papers yet — what would they do when they found out I didn't even have a ticket of leave.

"Where's your unit?" asked the man with the cap.

"Beg to report sir," I began, but I could not go on. I didn't know where my unit had got since yesterday, and I couldn't very well say that yesterday it was still here.

"Where was it last?" the tunic-owner grated at me.

"At Újhely, beg to report sir."

"And you're looking for it, are you?"

They gave a mocking laugh, all four of them. And they began saying contemptuously that the country was full of soldiers who were all looking for their units, but they were careful not to find them, because that would mean the end of their fine lives, of loitering about and dodging the front. There's some that go straight home to look for their units, to stuff their faces and play about a bit. "That right?" the man in the tunic kept asking me at the end of every sentence, but I didn't know what to answer him.

"Tell me, you hero, how long have you been looking for your unit?"

I should have said something. A week. Or a month. But I couldn't think of anything suddenly, so I said since yesterday.

They didn't understand this of course, so they looked at me stupidly for a while, then the man in the tunic waved to me.

"Fetch me your papers."

I fetched them. I saw from the door how scared Margit was as she looked after me, and how she was twisting the corner of her apron in her hand.

I searched my pockets so that time would pass, though I could have taken them out straight away. I glanced at the window, thinking I might jump out. But what was the use when there were more of them outside?

I was sweating by the time I went back with the book. I handed it to the man in the tunic, hoping he might not open it. But he did open it straight away, glanced through it, looked up at me once, then thumbed back again through the book. He ran over the pages with his fingers a couple of times and didn't say anything. Then he looked at me again and tossed the book on the table.

Mother nodded her head a little, I saw that her mouth was moving, and she spread her hands out encouragingly. She was asking whether it was all right, and there was nothing wrong?

I didn't nod back to her, I looked away. He must have known by now that I wasn't looking for my unit, that I had neither leave nor leave ticket. He must have noticed, and I was sure he had, but he said nothing. He lit another cigarette and said to the one with the cap:

"Tell the others they can come and eat."

And he got up from the table and paced up and down a couple of times, to the door and back.

"Why, he only came home last night," said mother to put him in a better mood. I was annoyed that she said that, because though the man in the tunic knew what he knew, why should we talk about it. As long as these things are not talked about, the situation's not so bad.

"Last night," he said with satisfaction, and he even nodded. As though this was what he had been waiting for. And he looked at me from the corner of his eye, but only the way you look at an object in a room. As though he didn't care about me any longer. In fact that was just how he behaved, so I thought perhaps nothing would come of it. I ought to take my book back. And I moved as though to reach for it on the table.

"Leave it," he said.

In the meanwhile the one in the cap came back with the others. They sat down, this lot got up, and I saw Mother beginning to dish out food on their plates. Margit helped her. The room became cramped all of a sudden, and Father stood by the door so as not to get in anyone's way.

"Come on then," the one in the tunic waved to me.

He went ahead, I followed, and the others came after me. I stopped outside the door to wait for them all to come out and shut the door behind them. "Keep moving," said the man in the cap who came behind me. I saw that Father was looking after me through the glass. The dog was scampering around my feet.

"Beat it," I said to him, to get him out of the way, before these men kicked him.

As we crossed the yard the one in the tunic stopped a bit to look round, and we also stopped behind him. Then we set off towards the stacks, walked past one of them, and at the other end the man in the tunic stopped and lit another cigarette.

"Just come and stand here," he said.

I stood where he showed me. They went further off, but as the one in the tunic looked round at me, he called back: "Face the stack. About turn."

I turned round and looked at the stack in front of me. They took about three or four paces behind my back. I heard the damp straw creak under their boots. There they stopped, shuffled about, in the meantime unslinging their submachine-guns from their shoulders I suppose. They were going to shoot me there and then, from a distance of three or four paces.

They were going to do it without even hearing me. They had asked no questions, just looked at my paybook . . . it occurred to me that I might possibly have had a leave pass, and if I had, and it had accidentally dropped out of the book, then it now would be unjust . . . And suddenly I felt as though I really had had one, only it had slipped out somehow, and I turned round to explain this misunderstanding. They were standing side by side now, all four of them, and the one in the cap was messing about with his submachine-gun. The other three were waiting for him, that's why they hadn't fired before. They didn't even glance at me though I'd turned round. I waited a second, because I didn't know how to start, then I began good and loud, saying I begged to report.

"Beg to report sir, the leave pass slipped out of my paybook," and at this I took half a pace toward them, "and that was why you didn't notice it, Captain, but please sir, I'll find it straight away . . ." — I'd have liked to get them back to the house, what if my leave pass really was there . . . and anyway, Mother was there, and Father, Margit, the dog . . . I'd even sent him away . . . and if I'd known, I wouldn't have come out with them so meekly . . . I just thought they wanted something . . . "Beg to report sir, I'll bring it immediately . . ." I said quickly again. And I wiped my brow with my shirt-sleeve.

They wouldn't listen to me, I took another half pace forward, they wouldn't listen to me, maybe I didn't really say anything but only tried to say it, gesticulating for all I was worth. The straw was damp under their boots and the one in the cap now looked up from his submachine-gun, and all four fired. I thought of the dog and the soaking water and Margit's hip on which I had kept my hand as I went to sleep last night.

★

★ ★ ★ ★

AUTHOR: *Arturo Uslar Pietri (1906-) is a writer, lawyer, professor of political and social science at the University of Venezuela, and a member of both the Academy of Language and the Academy of History. He is best known for two collections of short stories,* Red *and* Treinta hombres y sus sombras, *and a novel,* Las lanzas coloradas.

SETTING: *This story is about a young conscript who deserts his unit at a remote outpost in Venezuela. In many areas of Latin America in the 1960s, poor young men, usually of minority African or Amerindian heritage, were conscripted to serve in military units regardless of their suitability or willingness. The Venezuelan army, according to some estimates, had eighteen thousand such conscripts out of a total of eighty thousand soldiers at one time. Needless to say, these young men were seldom eager to "serve": they often were given the dirtiest and most dangerous of jobs. Deserters were flogged or "skinned." In this story, Hilario, an unwilling recruit who has fled into the jungle, envisions his skinning to the beat of drums.*

The Drum Dance

Arturo Uslar Pietri

They threw him down on the brick floor of the cell and shut the door. Everything was dark. The bricks were cool and it felt good to be lying on them. To be calm and quiet. To let himself slide down into sleep without being suddenly surprised.

The heavy footsteps of the provost marshal were going away. They were Ño Gaspar's steps, who was bowlegged and square-shouldered as a sack of cocoa beans, with his white sandals, his shirt unbuttoned at the throat, his chest crossed by the shoulder belt of yellow silk for the rooster's-tale saber.

The sound of the drums came into the cell, a harsh, infinite, unchanging rhythm — the tenor drum clear and the bass husky — and you could imagine in the darkness the sound of the Negroes' feet, beating up the dust in the square.

Translated by G. Alfred Mayer. "The Drum Dance" is reprinted from Barbara Howes, ed. *The Eye of the Heart: Short Stories from Latin America* (Indianapolis, Ind.: Bobbs Merrill, 1973) by permission of the author.

419

A few smoking lamps that streaked rays of light across the sweaty faces of the Negroes in the darkness hung from the leafy *saman* trees.

That's where Ño Gaspar had found him. He had kept coming closer and closer, slowly, timidly, sticking to the side of a wall, hiding behind a tree, away from the lights. But his feet shuffled to the rhythm and he chewed the vibrant tune between his teeth. He started to dance by himself. And then, without knowing how, he was dancing with the colored girl, her eyes, laughter, fragrance, on fire in the dark.

"Wow, Soledad, we're dancing together."

"Wow, Hilario, you're back."

But just then or a little later or much later Ño Gaspar got there. He didn't have to see him to know it was he. He knew his voice, knew his steps, could feel him coming. He knew that he had come.

"So, Hilario, I knew you were going to come back of your own accord. That you were going to be caught easy. When the search parties went to look for you, I sent them for the hell of it. I know my men. And there it is. You came all by yourself."

They tied his hands behind his back quickly with a piece of rope. The drum dance did not stop but many of those present got wind of what was happening and began to come over to them.

"It's Hilario."

"Yeah. The peon from El Manteco."

"He deserted from the camp in Caucagua."

"They're going to skin him for sure."

He let them lead him away without putting up a fight. From the darkness the eyes of the Negroes converged on him. As he passed under the lamps you could see how emaciated he was; his skin had become discolored and leathery, his lips cracked, his eyes sunken, dull.

The provost marshal himself was led to observe: "You're a sack of bones, Hilario. There's not enough meat on you for a meatball. Ah, the black boy was so solid."

But he said nothing. He hardly seemed to see. He only heard in snatches, confusedly. The voices of some of the women:

"Poor thing. Letting himself get caught that way!"

"He's all bones. He won't be able to stand the whip."

He wasn't sure if he was hearing all that or just imagining it, as he went from the square that was full of the drumbeat, into the dark entry hall of Headquarters, and, too weak to resist the push they gave him, fell onto the bricks of the cell.

Strangled by the rope, his wrists were pounding like the drum, almost with the same beat. He was thirsty. He pressed his dry lips against a damp brick.

He had known that all this was going to happen. He had thought about it an infinite number of times. He had constantly imagined it while he hid, starving, in the forest and came down at night to drink at the river or steal from the farms. He had known it since the day he had run away from camp.

He would have to come back to town and Ño Gaspar would come to get him and tie his hands behind his back, as he had them now, as he had had them when Ño Gaspar tied them on recruiting day.

"So that you'll know what's good for you and become a man."

But he felt like sleeping. To make up for all those days and nights in the bush. He felt peaceful there on the bricks.

He pressed his face to the floor and couldn't feel his own weight.

"I feel sort of light."

He could no longer hear the drum. It must be very late at night. But he could sort of feel the weight of the houses resting on the ground. There weren't many. The six on their lots around the square. There were more corrals than farmhouses. But he felt how they weighed down the ground. And he could feel the sleepy, dark water of the River Tuy sliding near or far off. And the wind passing over the roofs, and the trees and the water, and he stroked the dirt on the ground. The wind sped faster than the Tuy toward the sea.

He also seemed to be sliding along and floating.

But suddenly he felt as if he had fallen and he opened his eyes in the darkness.

"And now all that's left is Corporal Cirguelo's whip," he said between his teeth, and he felt a chill.

While he had been in camp he had seen a deserter flogged.

"Taiiiiin . . . shun!" the officer roared. The company came to attention.

It was time for the punishment. Long before daybreak, Corporal Cirguelo and an assistant prepared the whips. They had placed the deserter in front of the company. They had pulled down his pants. It was as cold then as now. They had tied his hands and, put into a crouching position, they had stuck guns down through his arms and his hams, as a brace.

The corporal shoved him with his foot until he came to rest on his side, and before he swung his whip the band started right off playing the "turkey trot" so that they wouldn't hear the cries of the man they were "skinning."

One lash, two lashes, three lashes. The soldiers in the company groaned at each stroke, but the screams of the one being punished could not be heard because the band was playing the trot without stopping and as loud as possible. The black boy, Hilario, was humming it.

"Tara rara rarah, the turkey."

"Tara rara rarah, the gobbler."

Before turning him on his other side to continue, they threw a bucket of salt water on the flayed cheek.

Corporal Cirguelo swung his whip. Now you could hardly hear the groans of the punished soldier.

"Tara rara rarah, the turkey."

Now he couldn't get the catchy tune of the "turkey trot" out of his head. Corporal Cirguelo wore long sideburns and had a gold-capped tooth. He must still be there at the barracks in Caucagua.

Next morning the search party would come to take him. They would put him on a boat on the river. Without untying his hands. They would land him ashore again. When they passed by the houses the people would come out to see him.

"It's a deserter they're taking in."

They would enter Caucagua. Late in the afternoon. Through the back street. They would go by the Islander's general store. And there, around the corner, was the camp. And there, at the door or outside, Corporal Cirguelo would no doubt be waiting.

There was a lot of walking to do. Before they got there. They had to take him out of here. Go down the river to the coast. Spend the morning. Time to sleep in the boat. To see, from the bottom where he would be lying, the treetops turning over in the sky. Tie up again. People would come to the riverbank. It would be very late afternoon. And the questions would begin again.

"How did they catch him?"

"Where was he hiding?"

"Did the search party find him?"

And that word that they were going to repeat, were repeating just as he had been repeating it so many times: The skinning. They're going to skin him. He can't get out of skinning. One hundred lashes. Ah, good skinning. Two hundred lashes on each cheek. A skinning for a complete man. Corporal Cirguelo's gold-capped tooth. Tara, rara, rarah, the turkey.

He couldn't get that out of his head from the time he ran away from camp. From the time he had seen that other deserter flogged. From the time he had seen them pick him up sagging and wobbly as a rag-doll effigy of Judas.

And now, lying on the floor of the cell, he felt so helpless, without any strength. He wouldn't be able to resist the blows. He wouldn't even be able to resist half of them. One, sang the corporal. Two. Three. The first ones burned like a live coal. Then the bleeding would begin. And then it was as if they were tearing off strips of flesh little by little. Then it began to hurt inside. Thirty. Thirty-one. Along his guts. His spleen. His lungs. Sixty-six. Sixty-seven. And that's where the groaning started. Where they stayed on. Where they went away. Where they began to feel numb.

The brick on which his cheek rested was hot now. He dragged himself farther along the ground until he lay on a cool piece of floor. Everything was still dark and quiet. He started to listen. Not even the wind was going by now. But somewhere in the distance a dog had barked.

Far beyond the guardhouse, the building, the square. The barking came from somewhere outside the village. Somewhere near the river. The forest. The night. The solitude.

"Oh damn."

The barking was coming from the forest. Who could ever catch him now if he were there again. He used to hear the dogs barking far away like that whenever he peered out of the bushes on a slope and saw a farm in a clearing on a little hill. Hunger brought him out of the forest at night. He had learned to walk noiselessly and stop to listen like the deer. To cock his ear into the wind. Sometimes he heard something, would hide in a cluster of corn, and see the men in the search party going by with machetes, guns, and blankets slung diagonally across chest and shoulder.

When a dog scented him and barked, he had to stop. He would lose sight of the farm again and go back into the forest. He ate guavas and roots. Sometimes he got dizzy from hunger. Sometimes he managed to approach a farm without a dog's barking, grabbed everything there was to eat on the stove, and scampered away.

He had never actually gone far from the village. If he appeared somewhere else, where he was a stranger, they could discover him. He kept on foraging through the woods near the waterfalls. He would look at the river from a distance. The Tuy rolled along quietly. Sometimes a canoe passed and he recognized some of the peons from where he was.

"Oh damn."

Sometimes, after drinking on his stomach at the river's edge, he released a dry leaf to see it go down the current and remained watching it in a sort of daze until the cry of a *guacharaca* in the forest or the babble of a flock of parrots crossing the sky shook him out of it.

He could see the village from certain points. The *saman* trees in the square, the church, Headquarters, the long street. People at the door of the general store. If he were there where his eyes were, where that man was, leaning against the door. Wouldn't that cause a stir!

"Wow. Here's Hilario."

"The deserter."

"Grab him!"

But he was far off among those trees where the wind made noise. At night all you could see were the lights flickering in the darkness. The village seemed farther away and smaller.

He hadn't kept track of how long he had been in the forest. He was becoming thinner. His skin was getting lighter. He was changing from black to a greenish color, like the alligator's tail. He was less nimble as he walked. He got tired faster when he climbed. He lost his breath and had to rest a while. Doubled over, breathing hard, he would sit there looking at his feet and hands. They were bonier and more skinny. The palms of his hands were purplish and his nails yellow. There were nights when he didn't have the strength to go near the farms. He would stay under a tree, chattering with the cold. All that was left of his trousers were rags. But it was very cold. If he heard a sound, he was too weak to get up. It could be an animal. It could be a search party. If it was the search party they would capture him. He didn't have the will to resist or even listen. He would remain there for a while, worried, waiting, but the sound was not repeated and he sighed, at ease.

Instead of going farther away, the more ill and weaker he felt, he kept coming closer to town. Every once in a while he would think: "If they catch me now, I won't be able to resist the whip. I won't survive the whip."

But something inside him made him feel that distant, inevitable thing that kept coming dangerously closer.

On two or three occasions, he had gone so far as to follow the riverbank up to the first houses in town. He had even dared sneak into a yard to steal a piece of beef hanging out to dry in the sun.

Some day they would catch him. If it pleased God.

"Oh damn!"

He neither sleeps nor stays awake. He feels the floor turning warm under his body. His whole body throbbing without stopping, on the bricks.

A cold tickling sensation in his hands, strangled by the rope behind his back. His bones aching with the sweet pain of a fever. He closes his eyes hard in order to sleep. Vague sparks pass through them. Red spots, rushing through. His pulse keeps on knocking and shaking him without relief.

Prrrm. Prrrrrm. Prrrrmpumpum. Prrrrmpumpum. Pum. Pumpum. Like the drum. Sometimes clear like the tenor, sometimes thick and husky like the bass. Like the drum.

Even from the river he could already hear it like that. From the time he started to sneak nearer, in the shadow of the first houses. He hadn't heard the drum for a long time. All he had heard was the sound of the branches, dogs barking, the songs of birds. But not the hot beat of the drum. As he crouched low, hiding, he beat on the ground with his foot and his hand. Dum dum, dum dum, dum dum. It was like a hot wave of water going around his body.

He was near the lights in the square now and he heard the heavy rhythm of the steps. The shadow of the Negroes moved as one solid mass. The lights seemed to go up and down under the branches of the *saman* trees.

Under the protection of a wall, he has drawn near the square. Something like a feverish tremor carries him along with the drum. Everything sounds inside and outside his head like the drumskin pounded by the black fists. He is all worked up. Everything comes and goes with the drum. Women. Lights. The names of things. His own name which calls and calls him without stopping.

Hilario, it says. Hilario, it repeats. Hilario, the drum. Hilario the shadows. Hilario, Hilarito, Hilarion. Larito, larion. Larito, ito, ito, ito. The rhythm resounds. Everything makes him shake. Sounds and resounds. Booms in the darkness. Booms.

Everything staggers. Tum tum. Tum tum. Hilario staggers. So much darkness. So much night. So much drumming. The drum keeps time in the darkness. Hilario trembles. Hilario shuffles. So many women are shaking in the darkness. Hilario, Hilarito, Hilarion.

Leaping shadows moved past him. They and the drum and the square and the lights. He was in their midst. The rhythm beat in his bones and his eyes. Panting mouths and clouded eyes went by.

And that woman in front of him, brought, carried by the drumbeat. Shaking together with him. Bound to him. Beat together with him.

"Yeah! Yeah! Yeah!"

"Wow, Soledad, we're dancing together!"

"Wow, Hilario, you're back!"

And that's where he felt him coming. Felt his footstep without seeing him. He could distinguish his footsteps between the drumbeats. Ño Gaspar's steps. The heavy, solid, sure step. He recognized his step without turning his head.

He could count them. One. A moment went by. Two. He was coming closer. All you could hear was the footstep of Ño Gaspar, the provost marshal. You couldn't hear the drum or the dance. All you could hear was that footstep.

The door squeaked. His eyes were open. From the brick floor he noticed the cell filled with the ashes of dawn and, in the doorway, tall and broad, Ño Gaspar, and behind Ño Gaspar the faces, the blankets, the guns and the machetes of the men in the search party.

★

★ ★ ★ ★

AUTHOR: *Avrom Reyzen (1875-1953) was born in Minsk. He was a pioneer of Yiddish language development in Russia and edited a weekly journal devoted to Yiddish translations from European languages. His short stories show rare compassion and sensitivity and are intensely personal sketches.*

SETTING: *This story could have taken place in any of the many shtetls in Eastern Europe during the past several hundred years. Shtetls, often considered the symbol of Ashkenazi civilization, were small, self-contained Jewish communities. Although each was unique, they all had several things in common: life centered around family, religion, and making a living, and all had a graveyard. In this story, soldiers from the emperor's army, searching for spies, invade the sanctity of the shtetl. The community in this story is unique: it does not have a graveyard.*

Acquiring a Graveyard

Avrom Reyzen

The tiny Jewish town was isolated from the rest of the world. Only rare echoes came straying here from the cities or even the large towns. No one needed the little shtetl, and it needed no one. It got along all on its own. With potatoes from its own fields, flour from its own windmill, and meat from its own sheep. As for clothing, Leybe the Tailor was a genius at his trade, and he sewed for both women and men. True, the material was brought in from the city, but this was done by Yankel, who was practically the only storekeeper in town; once a year, he would travel to the state capital to buy various goods. But Yankel was a quiet man. You didn't have to hawk your wares in the shtetl. And he was so quiet about his trip that it almost seemed like a secret: Every year, he would vanish for two days with no sign of life, and when he came back, only a few people, not all, would find out where he'd been. The curious ones would pounce upon him:

"Yankel, what's happening out in the world?"

Translated by Joachim Neugroschel. "Acquiring a Graveyard" is reprinted from Joachim Neugroschel, ed. *The Shtetl* (New York: G. P. Putnam's Sons, 1979) by permission of Joachim Neugroschel.

But Yankel had nothing to say. To his way of thinking, there was nothing to tell — everything was trivial! Once though, when they really cornered him and he felt he had to tell them something, he smirked, stroked his black beard, and replied:

"It's like, well, say — a hundred shtetls rolled into one. Altogether, it's a hundred times bigger than our little town, so how can you be surprised at the hubbub!"

And that was the only news that the townsfolk, Jews of course, ever received from the big world, once in a blue moon.

But while they never knew about real life (though they imagined they were having a fine time!), they also never knew about real death. Because of the tiny number of people, the "mortality rate" (as the statisticians phrase it) was generally very low, close to zero, and so the town had no graveyard of its own. The few old people there were diehards, they kept on living, on and on. The townsfolk even bore a grudge against Hendel the Bagel-baker, who was so old that no one could remember his age. People would count and count, always getting mixed up. And there was nothing you could do but start all over again! . . . Now one old man did finally get around to dying. But after thinking it over, he slipped off to Palestine. Once there, he actually died six months later, but it took the town any number of years to find out. Old Hendel was the one who told them. He broke the news with a smile, one weekday evening in synagogue:

"Didya hear about old Henekh? . . . He up and died!"

And the men simply couldn't understand, and decided this miracle was somehow connected with Palestine. . . . They were sure that if he hadn't left town, he would even have outlived old Hendel. On the other hand, they were jealous, for if you're buried in the Diaspora, the Angel of Death comes to your grave and pounds your corpse into dust and ashes, and Henekh, by coming to rest in the Holy Land, was spared this fate.

What with the old people so stubbornly refusing to die, it is quite understandable why a corpse was such a rarity in town! Now the middle-aged people were less stubborn, and every now and then, one of them, a man or a woman, would fall dangerously ill. But with no doctor around, the patient would be taken to the next town, which was slightly bigger, and there he would usually die, and be buried in the local cemetery.

And thus, the little shtetl had no graveyard of its own.

Strolling around on a Sabbath or a holiday, some of the philosophically inclined burghers would talk about the town's lack of a graveyard. And even on a weekday, someone or other would come out with:

"And what about a graveyard?"

Only the elderly people kept tactfully silent about this defect, but those who were in their middle years or even quite young harped on it, insisting it was a matter of life and death. . . .

The community bigwigs even called a town meeting, and this important issue was hotly debated. Old Hendel himself showed up at one session. He did most of the talking and pointed out that for now a graveyard was still unnecessary. There was no hurry. . . .

The younger people, who fully believed that there is such a thing as death in the world, and that a human being has to die sooner or later, were resolutely in favor of a graveyard. One of them, Chaim the Carpenter, even drew up a plan of the site and the layout. But, since nobody died for a long while after the meeting, people forgot about the graveyard issue.

And that was how things stood for years and years.

Till the war broke out.

Before the war was even officially declared, soldiers appeared in town, from our own emperor's army. Our own countrymen. Yankel the Storekeeper was certain he'd do good business: Soldiers, he had once heard, do a lot of buying. But these soldiers were of a different kidney. They did walk off with a lot of stuff, but they wouldn't pay, and you could argue with them till doomsday. So Yankel hit upon the idea of shutting down his store: Let them think it was a holiday! Whereupon they opened it up themselves and took the few left-over wares they needed. Then they went to Yankel:

"Who do you think you are closing your store to military men!"

And one of them stuck his rifle up against Yankel's chest.

Yankel was sure the soldier was joking, the man wouldn't actually go and shoot someone for such stuff and nonsense.

And Yankel's face lit up with a good-natured smile, as if to say:

"C'mon now! Would you shoot one of your own countrymen? Wait till the enemy comes! You'll have enough work on your hands then!"

But the soldier took the smile as an insult, and soon Yankel was lying stretched out in front of his store, wide-eyed and gaping, as if bowled over by the whole business! . . .

And so the little town found itself face to face with death.

Even Old Hendel now realized that a graveyard is an important matter, and that there is indeed such a thing as death.

A few days after that, the soldiers began searching for spies. Mottl the Butcher, who was bringing two oxen from a nearby village, was thought to be a provider for the enemy army. Forty-eight hours later, he was publicly hanged.

Next, the enemy army arrived. The battle took place behind the shtetl.

The shrapnel and the bullets flew over the shtetl like hail. The Jews took cover wherever they could.

But their hiding places were of little use. After three days of battle, the Jews had twelve casualties.

They could never have imagined so many corpses. Being new to such matters, they tried to awaken the bodies as though they were asleep. But none of them got up — they were dead.

Now the graveyard had at last become an urgent matter.

Even Old Hendel, who once again had managed to slip away from death, freely admitted:

"Yes, now we've got to have a graveyard! . . . This is just the right time! . . ."

But one of the younger men waved him off:

"The whole town's become a graveyard! . . ."

★

★ ★ ★ ★

AUTHOR: *George Bernard Shaw (1856–1950), dramatist, essayist, and critic, was born of Irish Protestant parents in Dublin. Leaving Ireland for London in 1876, he became a leading writer of socialist tracts, editor of* Fabian Essays, *and a noted political speaker and personage. An underlying theme throughout much of his life — one reflected in his writing — was a quest for ethics in public life. He wrote with honesty, satire, and a clean, astringent style. Some of his better-known works are:* The Intelligent Woman's Guide to Socialism and Capitalism, Pygmalion, Saint Joan, Androcles and the Lion, *and* The Apple Cart.

SETTING: *This story is set during the Second, or Great, Boer War (1899–1902). The First Boer War (1880–1881), between the Boers (Dutch) and the British, had resulted in a new South African Republic, which had a measure of independence in internal affairs but which maintained ambiguous British "suzerainty." The Second Boer War erupted after the discovery of large, rich deposits of gold, which brought a rush of foreigners (mainly British) to the area and exacerbated British-Boer tensions. The ensuing war was again won by the British. Although it was fought in Africa over ostensibly colonial issues, the war had a unique bearing on future wars, especially World War I. Among other things, it brought the British face to face with the consequences of having a class-based military structure.*

The narrator writes from the perspective of a cool observer of all situations where common citizens are asked to fight a distant war in which they have little interest. In this story, working-class conscripts, referred to as "tommies" or "Tommy Atkins," are going to Natal, the Union of South Africa, to fight the Boers. The title is taken from the German word Kanonenfutter, *translated as "cannonfodder" — an apt description of the cheapness and expendability of the king's common soldiers.*

Cannonfodder

George Bernard Shaw

One very fine day in the late unlucky and infamous nineteenth century, I found myself on the Lake of Como, with my body basking in the Italian sun and the Italian color, and my mind uneasily busy on the human drawbacks to all that loveliness.

"Cannonfodder" was first published in 1902.

431

There it was, at its best, the Italian beauty which makes men of all nations homesick for it, whether Italy be their home or not. Worth millions, this beauty, yet displaying itself for nothing to the just and the unjust, the rich and the poor. So undervaluing itself, in fact, that Italian labor, waiting on the pier at Cadenabbia to catch our hawser as we graze the piles, will not look at it, not being quite so cheap itself though very nearly: to be precise, a penny an hour, one London dock laborer being thus worth six Italians on the stricken field of industry.

On the pier, ready to embark, is a pretty lady in one of those fairy frocks which women never seem to produce until they go abroad, when the gravest tourist may, on any evening, see his respectable wife appear at *table d'hôte* with a dazzling air of having come straight from Vienna, and left her character behind. But as this young lady carries her frock like one born to such luxuries, we surmise that she is American, and speculate as to whether she is coming aboard.

She is; but, not to deceive you, she has nothing whatever to do with my story. I remember nothing of her, except that the gangway through which the fairy frock brushed was held by labor at a penny an hour, and that the friends who sent off the lady in a cloud of kissings and wavings, and messages and invitations, were chiefly, Mr and Mrs Henry Labouchere and party.

The Laboucheres, I may remark, have no more to do with this story than their friend in the fairy frock. But Mr Labouchere increased the trouble of my mind; for he stood there for Republican Radicalism, just as Mrs Labouchere, born Henrietta Hodson, stood, very gracefully, for Dramatic Art, the penny-an-hour basis being none the better for either.

Presently Cadenabbia fades in our wake, Mr Labouchere becoming indistinguishable five minutes before Mrs Labouchere, who still waves her and so artistically that the young lady in the fairy frock seems quite awkward in comparison.

I am standing on the brink of a sort of hurricane deck, looking down upon the impecunious or frugal mob on the main-deck. Among them are the men who travel third-class because there is no fourth. *I* travel first class because there is no double first. Beside me, watching the lake for artistic effects (as I guess; but perhaps he guesses the same about me) is Cosmo Monkhouse, who is soon after to have his obituary notices as a Civil Servant by necessity, and by choice a loving student of the arts, and even a bit of a poet. I like Monkhouse very well: he is, for the matter of that, a more agreeable person than I look. Rather elderly is Cosmo: sufficiently so, at any rate, for his way of life to have stamped its mark on him. I wander into mental arithmetic, and finally come out with a rough calculation that he works six hours a day, and gets ten shillings an hour or thereabouts, allowing for Sundays and holidays. He is, therefore, worth 120 Italian laborers. He represents high-class criticism, my own game at that time. I study his face as he looks straight ahead at the horizon, where the cloud effects are. I find in his flesh an appearance I have noticed in all the elderly men of my acquaintance who have been in love with Art all their lives; who, proud and happy to write about what great artists have done, make the masterpieces of Art the touchstone to try all life by; and who have even achieved some little piece of art work themselves (usually a little poem or tale) which they would never have produced if they had never known the work of their favorite masters. It is a curious sunken look, as if the outermost inch of the man had lost its vitality and would have mummied completely if the evaporation from the submerged reality were not keeping it a little sodden. But as I mark this aspect in Monkhouse, I see also that he is smoking a cigar. All the other dilettanti of my acquaintance smoke too; and the problem that now rises to bother me is whether it is the habit of smoking, or the habit of substituting Art for Life as the diet of the mind, that causes men to die at the surface in this odd fashion. I begin to muse on my own beginnings, and on my early determination not to let myself become a literary man, but to make the pen my instrument, and not my idol. I speedily become very arrogant over this, and am positively thanking Providence for the saving grace that has prevented me from becoming one of the Art-voluptuaries of the literary clubs, when a strange outburst of song comes up from below, uproarious, rowdy, and yet with a note in it as of joy frozen at its source.

I look over the rail. There, just below me, stand three young men, just too big to be called lads, each with a document like an Income Tax return in his hatband, and each with his arm affectionately round his neighbor's neck, singing with all his might. They are a little drunk, but not so drunk as Englishmen would be in like circumstances on English liquor. They are determined to be in the highest spirits; and ribbons in the hat of one of them proclaim a joyful occasion. I try to catch the words of their song, and just manage to make out the general sense of it, which, after the manner of songs, is not sense at all, but nonsense. They sing the joys of a soldier's life, its adventures, its immoralities, its light loves, its drinkings and roysterings, and its indifference to all consequences. Suddenly the poor devil in the middle, who has led the song, and shouted the loudest, stops, and begins to cry. The man on his right breaks down too, from sympathy; but he on the left, the quietest, rallies them; and they sing more defiantly than ever.

A stave or two, and the song goes to pieces again for ever. Its last moanings are dispelled by a fresh start made by the man on the right, who begins a most melting air about parting from home and mother, and so forth. This they rather enjoy: indeed, they finish it quite successfully. With soothed nerves, they talk a little, drink a little, then begin to joke a little and swagger a little; finally bursting into a most martial and devil-may-care song of the conquests that await them when the sword and the bowl and the admiration of women shall be their only occupations. They got through two verses without crying; and then the man in the middle falls on the neck of his comrade, and howls openly and pitifully.

Then I understand the papers in their hatbands. They are conscripts, newly drawn, and on their way to their service. They get off at the next pier. And I remember no more of that evening on Lake Como than if my own embarkation and landing had never taken place.

*   *   *

My memory comes to the surface again years later, on a threatening evening at Malta, where I am being rushed by an Orient liner between the lines of the British Mediterranean squadron. Ahead is darkness and a dirty sea. I do not want to get there; but the Captain does, being a better sailor than I, and on business besides. The fleet drops behind; and the harbor lights are shut off as we turn to the right (starboard, we landsmen call it). As the open sea catches us, we reel almost off our sea-legs, and shake in our pipeclayed shoes, which we wear as piously on the ship as we wear blackened shoes on the land. The pipeclay gives somebody a lot of trouble, and is bad for his lungs; but he would not respect us as gentlemen if we did not insist on it. After all, I am able to appear at the half-deserted dinner that evening; and though the fiddles are on the tables, and the two ladies to windward are twice bowled at me as at a wicket, I eat, drink, and am merry with less misgiving than I had expected. But the weather retains its dirty look; and I am not sorry when we reach Gibraltar, where two persons come on board. The first puts up printed notices that any person daring to take photographs of the rock or harbor will incur the doom of Dreyfus. The other unrolls a peddlar's bag, and publicly offers for sale a large assortment of photographs and models of the said rock and harbor.

I go ashore, and join a party of British pilgrims to visit the fortifications. We are shewn a few obsolete guns, and a few squads of soldiers (we call them Tommies) at drill; and we go away firmly persuaded that we have really seen the business part of the fortress. In that persuasion we liberally tip the military impostor who has pretended to shew us round; and we tell one another, roguishly, that the place is pretty safe for a while yet, eh? One man says that Gibraltar is all rot; that it could be shelled from Ceuta by modern guns; and that nothing but popular sentiment prevents us from dropping it like a hot potato. So indignant do the other Britons become at this, that I have to divert their wrath by suggesting that it is an excellent thing for the Spaniards to have their coast fortified at England's expense, and that we might do worse than offer Portsmouth to the Germans on the same terms. This is received as paradoxical madness; and the talk which ensues shews that we are unusually excited on the subject of England's military greatness.

There is a reason for this. At Malta the news reached us — or, rather, we reached the news — that the Boers have invaded Natal, and that England is at war.

In the afternoon the weather looks dirtier than ever. The sun hides behind slaty clouds; and the sea is restless and irritable, caring nothing for England and her troopships. I wander round the coast. On my return, I come round a corner, and find myself before a big barrack. On the long flagged platform before that barrack sit those who have been spoken of all the morning as "our Tommies." Every man has his sea kit with him; and every man is contemplating the comfortless sea and the leaden sky with an expression which the illustrated papers will not reproduce, and could not if they tried. Many of them are, I suspect, young men who have had their first scare of seasickness on their way to Gibraltar, and have not got over it yet. I doubt if any of them think much of the Mausers waiting beyond the waves. They impress me unspeakably; for I have never seen a whole regiment of men intensely unhappy. They do not speak; they do not move. If one of my fellow-sightseers of that morning were to come and talk to them about how irresistible they are when it comes to the bayonet, I doubt whether they would even get up and kill him. They brood and wait. I wait, too, spellbound; but my boat is on the shore, and my bark is on the sea; so I soon have to leave them.

A lady says something about the matter-of-fact quietness of Englishmen in the presence of a call to duty. She means, as I take it, that Englishmen do not behave as the conscripts did on the Lake of Como.

In due time we wallow through the Bay with fearful rollings, and trudge through the Channel head down, overcoat buttoned, and umbrella up. Then the episode sinks again into the sea of oblivion.

*   *   *

Recollection rises again on the Ripley Road, where I am lighting a bicycle lamp an hour after sunset. I am bound for Haslemere. I am also tired; and it occurs to me that if I ride hard, I may just catch the Portsmouth train at Guildford, and go to Haslemere in it. The next thing I remember is being told at Guildford that I am in the wrong half of the train. I make a precipitous dash, race along the platform like the wild ass of the desert, jump at a moving footboard, and am pushed and pulled and hustled into pandemonium.

Out of nine men in a third-class compartment, eight are roaring "God bless you, Tommy Atkins," at the top of their voices. One of them is distinctly sober; but he is cynically egging on the others by pretending to be as wild as they. The one who is not singing is an innocent-looking young sailor. Room is gradually made for me; and the man who makes it puts his arms affectionately round my neck the moment I sit down. They hail me by the honorable title of Governor, and convey to me that they are all going to the front, except the sailor, who is going to rejoin his ship at Portsmouth. I perceive at once that the sober man is going to do nothing of the sort, though he allows it to be assumed that he is. A racecourse possibly; certainly not a battlefield.

We now sing "Soldiers of the Queen" with tremendous enthusiasm. I sing *fortissimo* to keep out the noise of the others; and this clears me of all suspicion of offensive gentility. My new comrade next propounds the question "What will Buller do to Kruger?" The question goes round the company; and each strives to exceed his fellow-catechumen in the obscenity of the answer. By the time four have exercised their wit, the possibilities of foul language are exhausted. To my great relief — for I feared they would presently put the question to me — the man whose arm is round my neck releases me, and breaks frantically into "God bless you, Tommy Atkins," again. When it flags, the soberest of the reservists (they are all reservists) starts an obscene song on his own account. It is a solo, and my neighbor, not knowing the chorus, is silenced. Now this friendly man who had made room for me, and embraced me, has made himself drunk, and has been roaring songs, and clinging to the subject of Buller and Kruger for two reasons: to wit (1) he wants to forget about his wife, from whom he has parted at Waterloo Station without a notion of how she is going to live until his return (should he ever return); and (2) he wants to prevent himself from crying. The stupid, ribald nonsense the other man is bawling cannot hold his attention for a moment. "*I* dunno what she's to do," he says to me, even his drunkenness failing him completely. "I had a bit of drink at the station, you know. I left her there. I dunno whats to become of her." And he cries feelingly, and cannot for the life of him start the roaring again, though he makes an effort or two.

Then the sailor, perhaps to distract attention from this unsoldierly weakness, pulls out a copy of The Westminster Gazette, on which he has spent a penny, thinks that it is right, on a great political occasion, to buy something that he vaguely understands to be a great political paper. Over The Westminster a debate begins as to the Government. They have all heard that Chamberlain is "a good man"; and the young sailor has heard reassuring accounts of Lord Rosebery, who will see to it that things are done right. They have never heard of any other statesman, except Lord Salisbury; and we were falling back on Buller again when one of the reservists suddenly conceives that the sailor is claiming to ride to Portsmouth at Service fare, which works out cheaper than the reservists' fare. This piece of favoritism is taken in bad part; and were not the sailor obviously the most powerful man in the carriage, as well as the youngest and decentest, we should quarrel with him over it. As it is, all that happens is an absurd discussion, which shews that, eager as we are to wreak political justice on President Kruger in the most unmentionable ways, we are as ignorant of the nature of a railway ticket as of the relations between the Government and Lord Rosebery. My neighbor has by this time cried himself asleep. He is lulled into deeper slumber by the happy thought of two reservists, who strike up "Auld Lang Syne." But they get it so horribly mixed up with "Home, sweet home" that the sleeper wakes with a yell of "God bless you, Tommy Atkins"; and all three tunes are raging in an infernal counterpoint when the train stops at Haslemere, and I get out with judicious suddenness; for by that time they are all persuaded that I too am going to the front; and my disappearance probably seems to them a strange combination of a cowardly and unpatriotic desertion with an audacious and successful dash for liberty.

They were very like the Italian conscripts after all, only a good deal drunker, and, being unrestrained by the presence of signorinas in fairy frocks, much more blackguardly. English and Italians alike were being helplessly shovelled into the ranks as *Kanonenfutter:* cannonfodder, as the German generals candidly put it. I am no more sentimental over their homesickness than over their seasickness: both affections soon pass, and leave no bones broken. Nor am I under any illusions as to the possibility of carrying on the arts of war, any more than the arts of peace, by men who understand what they are doing. Had I been in good time for my train, and made my journey in a first class carriage with Lord Lansdowne, Mr Brodrick, Lord Methuen, Sir Redvers Buller, and Lord Roberts, the conversation would have come to the same point: namely, the point of the bayonet. So don't suppose that this tale has any moral. I simply tell what I have seen, and what I have heard.

★ ★ ★